觀光英語 Let's Go!

三版

作者:
Kiwi Cheng
Cosmos Language Workshop
審訂者:
Jim Knudsen
Helen Yeh

HAVE A NICE TRIP: TRAVEL ENGLISH

前言

本書上一版出版至今已四個年頭，接獲不少讀者來信來電，不僅提供寶貴的建議，更分享了實際運用本書的經驗。故此次改版歸功於多年累積的意見，並經過專業編輯的再三校對，外籍老師的專業審訂，重新設計版面，錄製英語MP3等過程，期許本書能夠帶給讀者更加全面完善的學習體驗。

改版後的《觀光英語Let's Go!》，專為不希望因語言隔閡，而錯失旅行機會的旅遊者所量身訂作，精心設計了**十大情境主題**，更依情境主題詳細分類規畫了**40單元**，從出國前的準備到身處異鄉的各種情況，本書皆為讀者考慮到了。

每個單元的結構分為三大部分：**情境式對話、旅遊小句和旅遊資訊補充包**，讀者可循序漸進，從中找到適切的英語表達加以活用，吸收真實並且實用的旅遊資訊，全面提升旅遊的英語戰鬥力。

情境式對話的主題分類清楚，精心設計配合主題的實用對話，讓讀者彷彿身歷其境於該情境中；**旅遊小句**按中文句意編排，例句豐富，讀者不僅充分了解各語句適用的時機與場合，更可以在最短的時間找到最需要的例句；**旅遊資訊補充包**則提供實用的旅遊經驗及資訊，希望藉此幫助愛旅遊的讀者，省掉許多摸索及找尋資料的時間。除此之外，貼心的各種**圖解說明**，進一步針對英語和旅遊常識，提供最有效率的學習與認識途徑。

出國旅遊是食衣住行育樂樣樣不可少，本書將各類情況中常見實用的詞彙例句，以配合實境彩圖的方式呈現。中英對照的內容、變化多樣的語句、深度解說的旅遊知識、精美的彩圖佐文字說明、口音道地的發音範例，只此一本，讓旅遊再無後顧之憂！

使用導覽

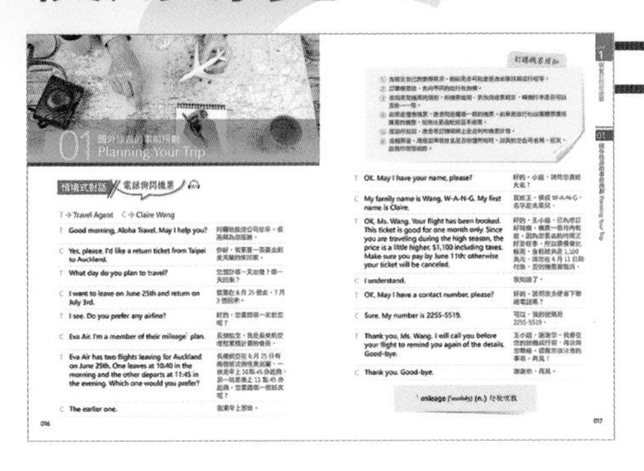

情境式對話

每一單元由情境式對話開始，幫助讀者先對該情境有基本的了解。在情境式對話中，讀者會學習到最常用的情境用語，迅速掌握必要的專業溝通訣竅。

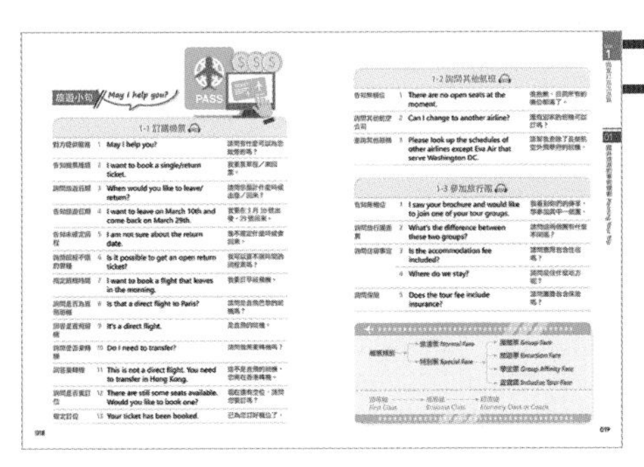

旅遊小句

旅遊小句為每一單元的重點，彙整旅遊時最常使用的語句，並以中文句意主題為主要編排方式，使方便尋找所需的英語説法。將此英文語句靈活應用，出門在外更是駕輕就熟。

旅遊資訊補充包

旅遊資訊的補充，讓讀者使用本書時，不僅可以加強英語能力，也可以了解不同文化風情及語言使用習慣。身處國外時，能迅速融入當地，玩得盡興又得體。

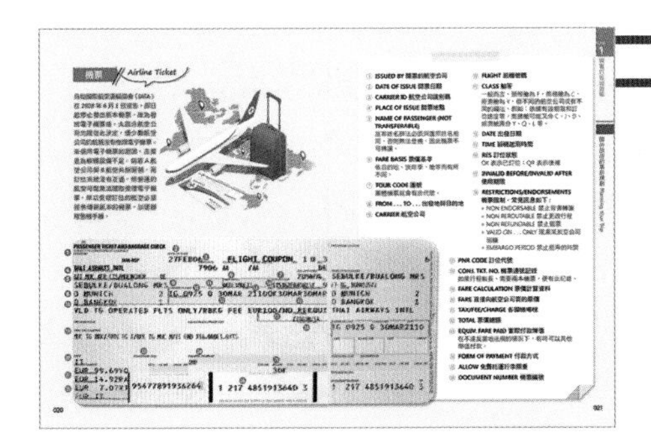

清晰圖解

從主題延伸出來的彩圖與圖解，讓讀者用視覺輔助情境聯想，不僅一看就懂，更能輕鬆記憶各種實用語彙。搭配旅遊資訊補充包相輔相成，觀光旅遊so easy！

Contents

Unit 1 興奮打包出境篇 Departure

Unit 2 翱翔天際飛航篇 Flight

Unit 3 愉悅心情入境篇 Arrival

養精蓄銳住宿篇 Accommodation

四通八達交通篇 Transport

垂涎三尺餐廳篇 Restaurants

動靜皆宜娛樂篇 Entertainment

Unit 8 血拼高手購物篇 Shopping

Unit 9 無遠弗屆通訊篇 Communication

Unit 10 疑難雜症緊急篇 Problem Solving

Unit 1

Departure
興奮打包出境篇

Chapter

01 國外旅遊的事前規劃 Planning Your Trip

情境式對話 電話詢問機票 001

T → Travel Agent　C → Claire Wang

T	Good morning, Aloha Travel. May I help you?	阿囉哈旅遊公司您早。很高興為您服務。
C	Yes, please. I'd like a round-trip ticket from Taipei to Auckland.	你好，我要買一張臺北到奧克蘭的來回票。
T	Which day do you plan to travel?	您預計哪一天出發？哪一天回來？
C	I want to leave on June 25th and return on July 3rd.	我要在 6 月 25 號去，7 月 3 號回來。
T	I see. Do you prefer any airline?	好的。您要搭哪一家航空呢？
C	Eva Air. I'm a member of their mileage[1] plan.	長榮航空。我是長榮航空哩程累積計畫的會員。
T	Eva Air has two flights leaving for Auckland on June 25th. One leaves at 10:40 in the morning and the other departs at 11:45 in the evening. Which one would you prefer?	長榮航空在 6 月 25 日有兩個班次飛往奧克蘭，一班是早上 10 點 40 分起飛，另一班是晚上 11 點 45 分起飛。您要選哪一個班次呢？
C	The earlier one.	我要早上那班。

訂購機票須知

① 先確定自己的實際需求，例如是否可能會更改出發日期或行程等。
② 訂購機票前，先向不同的旅行社詢價。
③ 查詢清楚機票的限制，如機票效期、更改與退票規定，轉機行李是否可以直掛……等。
④ 如果是優惠機票，應查問是屬哪一類的機票。如果是旅行社以團體票價所購買的機票，則無法更改航班且不退票。
⑤ 確認付款前，應查看訂購明細上是否列有機票詳情。
⑥ 出機票後，應確認乘客姓名是否與護照相符，以及航空公司名稱、班次、起飛時間等細節。

T	OK. May I have your name, please?	好的。小姐，請問您貴姓大名？
C	My family name is Wang, W-A-N-G. My first name is Claire.	我姓王，拼成 W-A-N-G，名字是克萊兒。
T	OK, Ms. Wang. Your flight has been booked. This ticket is good for one month only. Since you are traveling during the high season, the price is a little higher, $1,100 including taxes. Make sure you pay by June 11th; otherwise your ticket will be canceled.	好的，王小姐，已為您訂好班機，機票一個月內有效。因為您要去的時間正好是旺季，所以票價會比較高，含稅總共是 1,100 美元。請您在 6 月 11 日前付款，否則機票會取消。
C	I understand.	我知道了。
T	OK. May I have a contact number, please?	好的。請問您方便留下聯絡電話嗎？
C	Sure. My number is 2255-5519.	可以，我的號碼是 2255-5519。
T	Thank you, Ms. Wang. I will call you before your flight to remind you again of the details. Good-bye.	王小姐，謝謝您。我會在您的班機成行前，再次與您聯絡，提醒您該注意的事項。再見！
C	Thank you. Good-bye.	謝謝你，再見。

[1] mileage [ˋmaɪlɪdʒ] (n.) 哩程數

旅遊小句 May I help you?

1-1 訂購機票 002

對方提供服務	1	May I help you?	請問有什麼可以為您效勞的嗎？
告知機票種類	2	I want to book a single/round-tip ticket.	我要買單程／來回票。
詢問旅遊日期	3	When would you like to leave/return?	請問您預計什麼時候出發／回來？
告知旅遊日期	4	I want to leave on March 10th and come back on March 29th.	我要在 3 月 10 號出發，29 號回來。
告知未確定回程	5	I am not sure about the return date.	我不確定什麼時候會回來。
詢問回程不限的票種	6	Is it possible to get an open return ticket?	我可以買不限時間的回程票嗎？
指定班機時間	7	I want to book a flight that leaves in the morning.	我要訂早上起飛的班機。
詢問是否為直飛班機	8	Is that a direct flight to Paris?	請問是直飛巴黎的班機嗎？
回答是直飛班機	9	It's a direct flight.	是直飛的班機。
詢問是否要轉機	10	Do I need to transfer?	請問我需要轉機嗎？
回答要轉機	11	This is not a direct flight. You need to transfer in Hong Kong.	這不是直飛的班機，您需在香港轉機。
詢問是否要訂位	12	There are still some seats available. Would you like to book one?	現在還有空位，請問您要訂嗎？
確定訂位	13	Your ticket has been booked.	已為您訂好機位了。

1-2 詢問其他航班 003

告知無機位	1	There are no open seats at the moment.	很抱歉，目前所有的機位都滿了。
詢問其他航空公司	2	Can I change to another airline?	還有別家的班機可以訂嗎？
查詢其他班機	3	Please look up the schedules of other airlines except Eva Air that serve Washington DC.	除了長榮航空飛華府的班機不要之外，請幫我查其他班機。

1-3 參加旅行團 004

告知無機位	1	I saw your brochure and would like to join one of your tour groups.	我看到你們的簡章，想參加其中一個團。
詢問旅行團差異	2	What's the difference between these two groups?	請問這兩個團有什麼不同嗎？
詢問住宿事宜	3	Is the accommodation fee included?	請問費用包含住宿嗎？
	4	Where do we stay?	請問是住什麼地方呢？
詢問保險	5	Does the tour fee include insurance?	請問團費包含保險嗎？

機票 Airline Ticket

自從國際航空運輸協會（IATA）在 2008 年 6 月 1 日宣告，即日起停止發出紙本機票，改為發出電子機票後，大部分航空公司均跟從此決定，僅少數航空公司的航班沒有使用電子機票。未使用電子機票的原因，主要是為軟體設備不足，倘若 A 航空公司與 B 航空共掛班號，而訂位系統沒有互通，則營運的航空可能無法讀取受理電子機票，所以受理訂位的航空必須提供傳統紙本的機票，以便辦理登機手續。

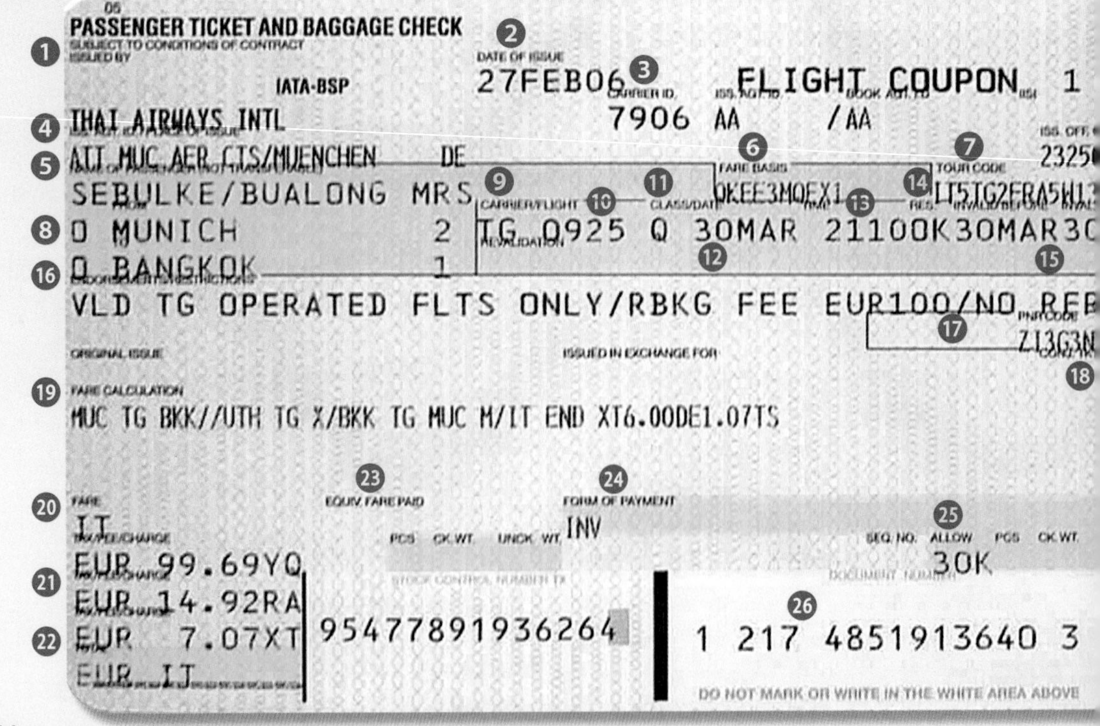

PASSENGER TICKET AND BAGGAGE CHECK
SUBJECT TO CONDITIONS OF CONTRACT
① ISSUED BY
IATA-BSP
THAI AIRWAYS INTL
② DATE OF ISSUE
27FEB06
③ CARRIER ID.
7906 AA /AA
FLIGHT COUPON 1
④ ATT MUC AER CTS/MUENCHEN DE
ISS. OFF. 2325
⑤ SEBULKE/BUALONG MRS
⑥ FARE BASIS QKEE3MQEX1
⑦ TOUR CODE IT5TG2FRA5H1
⑧ FROM O MUNICH 2
⑨ CARRIER/FLIGHT TG 0925
⑪ CLASS/DATE Q 30MAR
⑬ TIME 2110
⑭ RES. OK
NOT VALID BEFORE 30MAR
⑮ 30
⑯ TO O BANGKOK 1
ENDORSEMENTS/RESTRICTIONS
VLD TG OPERATED FLTS ONLY/RBKG FEE EUR100/NO REF
⑰ PNR CODE Z13G3N
⑱ CONJ. TKT.
ORIGINAL ISSUE
ISSUED IN EXCHANGE FOR
⑲ FARE CALCULATION
MUC TG BKK//UTH TG X/BKK TG MUC M/IT END XT6.00DE1.07TS
⑳ FARE IT
㉓ EQUIV. FARE PAID
㉔ FORM OF PAYMENT INV
PCS CK.WT. UNCK. WT.
㉕ SEQ. NO. ALLOW PCS CK.WT.
30K
㉑ TAX/FEE/CHARGE EUR 99.69YQ
EUR 14.92RA
㉒ EUR 7.07XT
TOTAL EUR IT
STOCK CONTROL NUMBER
95477891936264
DOCUMENT NUMBER
㉖ 1 217 4851913640 3
DO NOT MARK OR WRITE IN THE WHITE AREA ABOVE

① **ISSUED BY 開票的航空公司**

② **DATE OF ISSUE 開票日期**

③ **CARRIER ID 航空公司識別碼**

④ **PLACE OF ISSUE 開票地點**

⑤ **NAME OF PASSENGER (NOT TRANSFERABLE)**
旅客姓名拼法必須與護照姓名相同，否則無法登機，因此機票不可轉讓。

⑥ **FARE BASIS 票價基準**
依目的地、淡旺季、艙等而有所不同。

⑦ **TOUR CODE 團號**
團體機票就會有此代號。

⑧ **FROM . . . TO . . . 出發地與目的地**

⑨ **CARRIER 航空公司**

⑩ **FLIGHT 班機號碼**

⑪ **CLASS 艙等**
一般而言，頭等艙為 F，商務艙為 C，經濟艙為 Y，但不同的航空公司或有不同的編法，例如：依據有效期限和訂位速度等，商務艙可能又分 C、J、D、經濟艙再分 Y、Q、L 等。

⑫ **DATE 出發日期**

⑬ **TIME 班機起飛時間**

⑭ **RES 訂位狀態**
OK 表示已訂位；QR 表示後補。

⑮ **INVALID BEFORE/INVALID AFTER 使用期限**

⑯ **RESTRICTIONS/ENDORSEMENTS 機票限制，常見訊息如下：**
- NON ENDORSABLE 禁止背書轉讓
- NON REROUTABLE 禁止更改行程
- NON REFUNDABLE 禁止退票
- VALID ON . . . ONLY 限乘某航空公司班機
- EMBARGO PERIOD 禁止搭乘的時間

⑰ **PNR CODE 訂位代號**

⑱ **CONJ. TKT. NO. 機票連號記錄**
如果行程較長，需要兩本機票，便有此紀錄。

⑲ **FARE CALCULATION 票價計算資料**

⑳ **FARE 直接向航空公司買的票價**

㉑ **TAX/FEE/CHARGE 各國機場稅**

㉒ **TOTAL 票價總額**

㉓ **EQUIV. FARE PAID 實際付款幣值**
在不違反當地法規的情況下，有時可以其他幣值付款。

㉔ **FORM OF PAYMENT 付款方式**

㉕ **ALLOW 免費托運行李限重**

㉖ **DOCUMENT NUMBER 機票號碼**

1-4 預定住房 005

詢問空房	1	Do you have a vacant double room from February 5th to February 8th?	請問你 2 月 5 號到 8 號有空的雙人房嗎？
回覆詢問	2	There's still a room available.	我們還有一間空房。
	3	I'm afraid there are no vacancies.	很抱歉，我們目前沒有空房。
詢問價錢	4	How much do you charge per night?	請問住一晚多少錢？
	5	It's €50 per night.	住一晚是 50 歐元。
詢問更低價的房間	6	Do you have anything cheaper?	有便宜一點的嗎？
詢問是否含早餐	7	Is breakfast included?	請問房價包含早餐嗎？
	8	Yes, breakfast is included.	是的，包含早餐。
	9	The breakfast charges €10 per person.	早餐每人是 10 歐元。
詢問房間細節	10	Is that an en-suite room?	請問那間是套房嗎？

客房種類 Room Types

一般說來，旅館的房間約分為以下幾種：

單人房（single room）

房間內僅有一張單人床。有些旅館的單人床較大，可以容納兩位體型較嬌小的女生一起睡，是自助旅行者省錢的方式之一。但若是會提供早餐的飯店，則只會提供一份，且有些時候被飯店查到，會要求補上差額，需注意。

雙人單床房（double room）

房間有一張雙人床，適合家人、夫妻出遊時住宿。

半雙人房（semi-double room）

日本飯店特有的房型。房間內有一張床，床型尺寸介於通常單人床和雙人床之間。可以讓兩個人入住，但因房型比雙人房更小，預訂前請三思。

雙人雙床房（twin room）

房間有兩張分開的單人或雙人床鋪，對於不習慣與他人同床共眠的旅行者來說，較為合適。

三人房（triple room）

房間內有一張雙人床及一張單人床，此類房間多提供給家庭使用。但若是三人旅遊時住此種房間，可比一間雙人房加一間單人房划算。有些旅館並無所謂三人房，而只是在雙人房內多加一張小床供使用。

家庭房（family room）

顧名思義是供全家人一起旅遊時使用，房間大小則依旅館不同而有差異，一般說來是給四人以上的家庭使用。

套房（suite room）

房間除了床與基本設施外，尚包括臥室和客廳，有時甚至會有廚房、會議室、另外一至兩間臥室與浴室，就像一個家一樣。適合一家人入住，也適合商務旅行時，招待客戶之用。

旅遊資訊補充包

住宿種類 Accommodation Types

飯店／旅館（hotel）

最為普遍，規模較大且大多是連鎖集團經營，依照服務、設施、裝潢不同等級分有星級，提供客房服務（room service），也會有人幫忙清理房間（house keeping）。

青年旅館（hostel）

通常以床位最為銷售單位，為背包客首選的下榻方式。旅客一般需與其他陌生旅客共用房間、衛浴與大廳等設施。對於經費有限並喜歡結交各國朋友的旅客來說，是非常有吸引力的選擇。

膠囊旅館（capsule hotel）

與青年旅館一樣以床位（膠囊）為銷售單位，空間卻更為有限，適合不需要傳統旅館服務、僅一個晚上有地方過夜的旅客。最大的優點在於價格便宜，且通常膠囊旅館位於交通方便的市中心。

B&B（bed and breakfast）

顧名思義，B&B 為提供床位過夜和早餐的住房種類，也可譯作民宿，通常由普通住家的房間作為旅客住宿之用。

度假村（resort hotel）

坐落於度假勝地提供休閒與娛樂之用的建築群，通常佔地較廣且設施完善，用以吸引旅客瀏覽停留旅遊景點的住宿選擇。

汽車旅館（motel）

與一般旅館最大的不同，在於提供的停車位與房間相連。汽車旅館多位在高速公路交流道附近，或是離城鎮較偏遠處的公路上，但亦也有位於市區者，便於以汽車或機車作為旅行工具的旅客投宿。

民宿（guesthouse）

大多由私人或家族經營的家庭旅館，提供數間客房，與 B&B 的差別僅在不一定提供早餐。

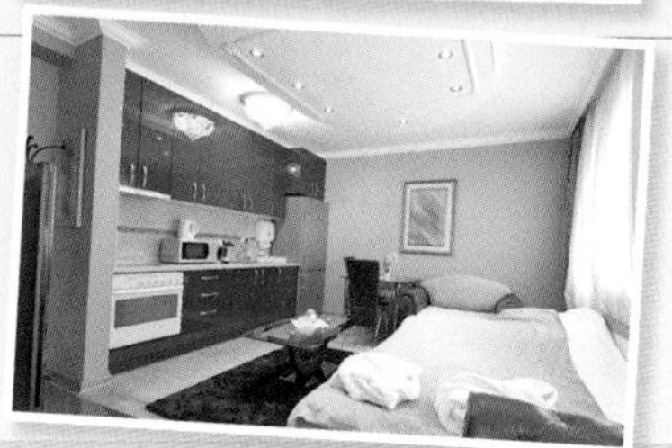

公寓式飯店（apartment hotel）

提供旅客一處既有飯店便利性又有個人公寓感覺的住宿場所，因此來到這裡，就好像回到自己的家一樣，只是比起單純的家，飯店所應當提供的各式服務均不能少。

新型態的住宿選擇

Airbnb

原稱為 Airbed and Breakfast，原因在於希望完全實現「B&B」的概念，即在家裡放個氣墊床並且準備一份早餐，就可以把房子變成民宿了。對於 Airbnb 上的房東而言，既可以將家裡多出來的房間的利用率提高，也可以因此多一份不錯的收入；對於房客來說，他們不再只是遊客，而是向當地人一樣居住並且生活，真正體驗景致與當地風情。

Couchsurfing

與 Airbnb 一樣，此平台讓全世界各地的人都可以提供自己的房間、客廳、甚至只是一張沙發來接待旅行者（通稱沙發客），然差異在於，Couchsurfing 沒有強制收取任何費用，且沙發客通常會與房東生活在共同的空間。這種與當地人免費借宿的方式，不但可以交到許多不同文化背景的朋友、真正感受當地的生活方式，也可以省下一大筆住宿費。

去信訂房 Reserving a Hotel Room

To Holiday Inn

Subject Reserve a family room from 10/10 to 10/15

To whom it may concern,

We are a family of four who will pay a visit to America next month. I would like to reserve a family room at your hotel from 10/10 to 10/15. Do you have a vacancy?

Could you please tell me your room rates and payment method? Also, do I need to pay a deposit? Any other information you could provide would be highly appreciated.

Thank you for your attention. I am looking forward to hearing from you soon.

Yours sincerely,

Mr. Chia-hao Chang

收件者 貴飯店

主　旨 訂 10/10 到 10/15 的家庭房一間

貴飯店您好：

我們有四名臺灣人將於下個月去美國旅遊，共兩位大人與兩位小孩。我們想在貴飯店訂 10 月 10 日至 15 日的家庭房一間，不知貴飯店是否仍有空房？

煩請貴飯店告知房價及付款方式，另外，是否要先付訂金呢？若有其他相關資訊也煩請提供，十分感謝。

謝謝貴飯店人員抽空看信，希望很快能有消息。

張家豪敬上

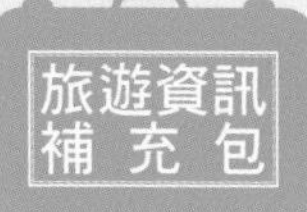

對方覆信 Receiving a Reply from the Hotel

To Mr. Chia-hao Chang

Subject Re: Reserve a family room from 10/10 to 10/15

Dear Mr. Chang,

Thank you very much for your inquiry. In answer to your question, yes, we have a family room available from 10/10 to 10/15. The rate is $80 per night. To reserve the room, we require a deposit of one night's room charge. You can send us a personal or traveler's check in US dollars, or you can pay online by VISA or MasterCard.

If you would like to go ahead and book the room, or if you have any further inquiries, please do not hesitate to contact me. I am happy to assist you.

Looking forward to meeting you and your family soon.

All the best,

Jack Watts, Customer Care Manager

收件者 張家豪先生

主　旨 回覆：訂 10/10 到 10/15 的家庭房一間

張先生您好：

非常感謝您的來信，很榮幸能為您服務解惑。本飯店在 10 月 10 日至 10 月 15 日間，可提供您一間家庭房，費用是一晚 80 美元。若您欲訂此房，須預繳一晚的訂金。您可將個人或旅行支票（幣別為美元）寄至敝飯店，亦可於網路上以信用卡付款。本飯店接受威士卡或萬事達卡。

若您確定要訂房，或是還有其他疑慮，請隨時與我聯絡，本人將非常樂意為您服務。

期待您與您家人儘快蒞臨本飯店。

敬祝

一切安好

客戶服務部主任 傑克華特 敬上

簽證介紹 Visa

旅遊地點不同，需要申請的簽證也不同，常見的簽證種類可分為以下幾項：

簽證種類	說明
❶ 單一國家簽證 individual visa	只要是在期限內，就可單次或多次進入該國。可用此類簽證的地區，包括澳洲、土耳其、俄羅斯、巴西等國。
❷ 申根簽證 Schengen visa	申根簽證起緣於《申根公約》，這是歐盟國家之間的條約協定，其目的是取消相互的邊境檢查點，並協調對申根區之外的邊境控制。持有任一成員國有效身分證或簽證的人，可以在所有成員國境內自由流動。根據該協定，旅遊者如果持有其中一國的旅遊簽證，即可合法地到所有其他申根國家。 申根簽證分「單次入境」（single entry）及「多次入境」（multiple entry）。申請單次入境者，一旦自申根國家出境後，其簽證即無效、不可再使用。 國人向申根國家駐台單位申請簽證時，依首先入境國家或停留時間最長國家提出申請，以防止遭拒絕入境的麻煩。

- **持有我國護照的旅客，自 2011 年起前往申根區國家，在 90 天以內不需要申請簽證。**

簽證種類	說明
❸ 落地簽證 visa granted upon arrival/landing visa	泰國、柬埔寨等國，為落地簽證的國家，手續很簡便，到了當地機場即可辦理。
❹ 免簽證 visa free/exempt entry visa	鄰近國家新加坡、南韓、馬來西亞和日本等，都是屬於免簽證的國家。一般說來，免簽證之國家都會有一個約 30-90 天不等的最長停留期限。

- **持有我國晶片護照之旅客，前往美國雖不需簽證，卻須先透過旅行授權電子系統（ESTA）取得授權許可，取得 ESTA 的旅客可於美國停留 90 天**

簽證種類	說明
❺ 過境免簽證 transit without visa	方便過境旅客在轉機時，欲停留該國而提供之簽證，如馬來西亞提供 72 小時過境免簽證，旅客只要備妥前往第三國之機票，在機場即可取得過境免簽，相當方便。
❻ 電子旅遊簽證 electronic travel authority (簡稱 ETA)	澳洲政府於 1998 年首創隱藏式電子憑證，旅客申請核發後，可領到一張「機器可判讀簽證」（machine readable visa，簡稱 MRV），並憑此入境。除了澳洲外，現在前往土耳其、菲律賓等地也可申請電子簽證。這種方式將可在一至兩天內快速取得簽證，費用也較為低廉，為許多旅客的最佳選擇。

美國簽證 United States Visa

① **ISSUING POST NAME** 簽證核發地

② **CONTROL NUMBER** 簽證編號

③ **SURNAME** 姓

④ **GIVEN NAME** 名

⑤ **VISA TYPE** 簽證種類

⑥ **CLASS** 等級 B1 代表商務；B2 代表觀光，通常會一起核發。

⑦ **PASSPORT NUMBER** 護照號碼

⑧ **SEX** 性別 M 為男性；F 為女性。

⑨ **BIRTH DATE** 生日

⑩ **NATIONALITY** 國籍

⑪ **ENTRIES** 入境次數 M 為多次入境；S 為單次入境。

⑫ **ISSUE DATE** 簽證核發日

⑬ **EXPIRATION DATE** 簽證到期日

⑭ **ANNOTATION** 註解

申根簽證 Schengen Visa

① **VALID FOR** 此證件適用於（申根國家）

② **FROM . . . UNTIL . . .** 簽證有效期限

③ **TYPE OF VISA** 簽證種類 C 為短期簽證；D 為長期簽證。

④ **NUMBER OF ENTRIES** 入境次數 MULTI 為多次入境；01 為單次入境。

⑤ **DURATION OF STAY** 可停留時間

⑥ **ISSUED IN** 簽證辦理處

⑦ **ON** 簽證辦理時間

⑧ **PASSPORT NUMBER** 護照號碼

⑨ **SURNAME, NAME** 申辦人姓名

⑩ **REMARKS** 備註

1-5 辦理觀光簽證 (006)

詢問是否需要辦理簽證	1	Do I need a visa to enter Switzerland?	請問去瑞士要辦簽證嗎？
準備資料	2	What do I need in order to apply for a visitor's visa?	請問辦觀光簽證要什麼資料？
是否需面談	3	Do I need to have an interview to apply for the visa?	請問辦這個簽證要經過面談嗎？

Chapter

02 準備出發 Getting Ready to Depart

情境式對話 電話更改機票航班 007

V → Vanessa Lee　G → Ground Staff

	On the telephone	電話中
G	China Airlines. How may I help you?	中華航空您好。很高興為您服務。
V	I would like to change my return flight to Taipei.	我想改回程飛臺北的班機。
G	I see. May I have your name, please?	好的。請問貴姓大名？
V	Sure. My family name is Lee. My first name is Vanessa.	我姓李，名字是凡妮莎。
G	Thanks, Ms. Lee. What change would you like to make?	李小姐，謝謝您。您想怎麼改呢？
V	My reservation is on flight CI 627 to Taipei on January 9th. I want to change it to the 10th. Is that possible?	我是訂 1 月 9 號到臺北的 CI 627 班機，我想改成 1 月 10 號。可以改嗎？
G	Just let me check your reservation, Ms. Lee. OK, no, there doesn't seem to be any problem with changing your flight to January 10th. Which flight would you like to take instead?	李小姐，我查查您的訂位記錄。要改成 1 月 10 號的班機，應該沒問題。請問您想改搭哪個班次呢？

V	Is there a flight departing in the afternoon?	有下午起飛的嗎？
G	We have two available[1] flights leaving in the afternoon. One is at 3 p.m., the other at 5:30 p.m.	我們有兩個下午出發的班次，一個是下午三點，另一個是下午五點半。
V	Do you have any later flights?	有更晚的嗎？
G	I am afraid that all our other flights are fully booked.	很抱歉，其他班次都訂滿了。
V	Then I want the 5:30 flight.	那我搭五點半的。
G	OK, Ms. Lee. Your flight has been confirmed[2]. Check-in time is 3:30.	好的。李小姐，您的機位已確認，報到時間為三點半。
V	Which terminal[3] are you in?	你們是在第幾航廈？
G	We are in the third terminal. If you have any questions, please contact us at any time.	我們在第三航廈。如果您遇到任何問題，請隨時與我們聯絡。
V	Thanks a lot.	謝謝你。

[1] available [ə`veləbḷ] (adj.) 有空位的
[2] confirm [kən`fɝm] (v.) 確認
[3] terminal [`tɝmənḷ] (n.) 航廈

旅遊小句 // Please put me on the list

2-1 班機確認 008

確認航班	1	I want to reconfirm my flight.	我想再次確認我的班機。
告知班機號碼	2	What's your flight number?	請問您的班機編號是什麼？
	3	The flight number is BA 518 leaving for Taipei at 5:30 p.m.	BA 518，下午五點半飛往臺北。
詢問報到時間	4	When do you start check-in?	請問什麼時候開始報到呢？
	5	You should check in two hours before departure.	您要在班機起飛前兩小時來報到。
機位已確認	6	Your return flight has been confirmed.	您的回程機位已確認了。

2-2 變更原飛行航班 009

更改班機	1	I want to change my flight.	我想改班機。
	2	Which flight would you like to change to?	您想改搭哪一個班次呢？
改變時間	3	I would like to change to the same flight tomorrow.	我想改搭明天同一個班次的飛機。
班機客滿	4	I would like to change to an afternoon flight.	我想改搭下午的班機。
	5	All the afternoon flights are fully booked.	下午所有的班機都客滿了。
詢問空位	6	Which flight has seats available?	哪一架班機還有空位呢？

要求候補	7	Please put me on standby.	我要候補。
	8	Please put me on the waiting list.	請把我排到候補名單裡。
	9	Do you want me to put you on the waiting list?	請問您要排入候補名單嗎？

2-3 原航班取消 010

因天候不佳班機取消	1	All the flights have been canceled due to weather conditions.	因為天候關係，全部的班機都已取消。
告知班機取消	2	Your flight has been canceled.	您要搭乘的班機已取消。
詢問解決方案	3	What can I do?	那怎麼辦？
	4	Is there another flight I can take?	還有別的班機可以搭嗎？
搭別班機	5	We will arrange another flight for you.	我們會安排您搭乘其他班機。
詢問是否要搭早班飛機	6	There are some seats available on the earlier flight. Do you want to take it?	前一個班次還有空位，請問您要搭乘嗎？

2-4 前往機場 011

前往機場	1	How do I get to the airport?	請問機場怎麼去？
	2	You can take the shuttle bus in front of the hotel.	您可以在飯店前搭乘接駁巴士。
詢問車程	3	How long does it take to get to the airport?	請問多久可以到機場？
	4	It's about one hour's drive.	大約一個小時的車程可以到。
詢問航廈	5	Which terminal should I go to for United Airlines?	請問聯合航空是在第幾航廈？
前往另一航廈的方式	6	How do I get to the second terminal from the first one?	請問怎麼從第一航廈去第二航廈？
	7	You can take the airport subway to get from terminal to terminal.	您可以搭乘機場地鐵往返航廈。

班機出發時間表 Airport Departure Board

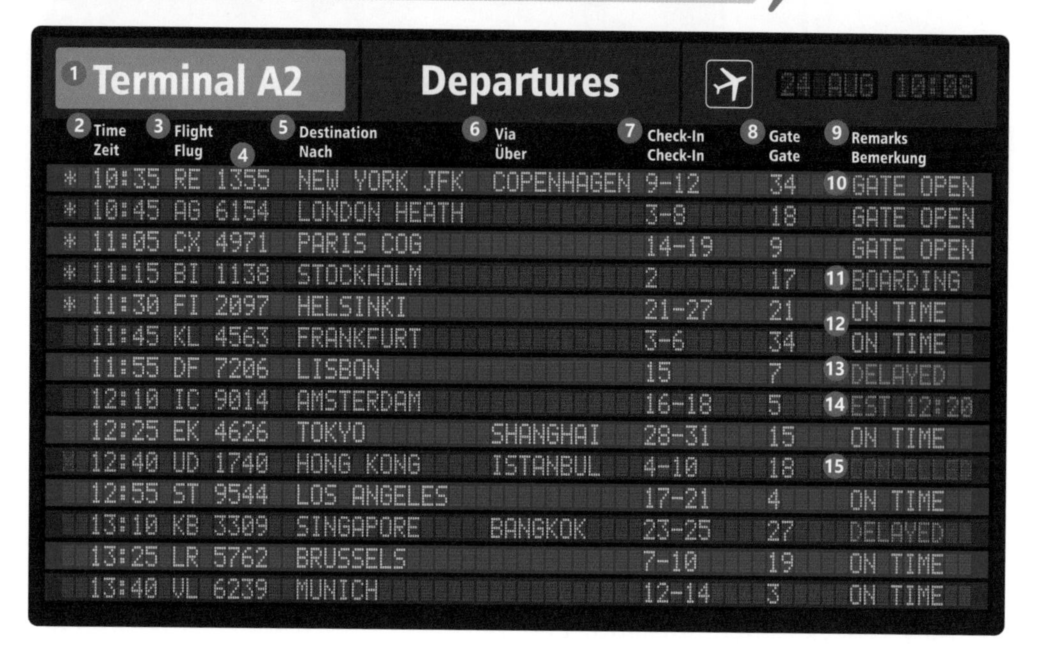

① **TERMINAL** 航廈

② **TIME** 起飛時間

③ **AIRLINE** 航空公司

④ **FLIGHT NUMBER** 班機號碼

⑤ **DESTINATION** 目的地

⑥ **VIA** 轉機點

⑦ **CHECK-IN** 報到時間

⑧ **GATE** 登機門

⑨ **REMARKS** 備註

⑩ **GATE OPEN** 登機門開啟

⑪ **BOARDING** 登機中

⑫ **ON TIME** 準時起飛

⑬ **DELAYED** 誤點

⑭ **EST-TIME (ESTABLISHED TIME)** 實際起飛時間

⑮ **CANCELED** 取消

備註欄的班機狀態還有可能出現下列訊息：

- **FINAL CALL** 最後登機廣播
- **CHECK-IN NOW** 辦理登機手續中
- **DEPARTED** 已起飛
- **TIME CHANGE** 時間更改

Chapter 03 辦理出境手續 Departure Procedures

情境式對話 // 登機前的報到手續 012

A → Alivin Wang　G → Ground Staff

A	May I check in here for flight CI 612 to Amsterdam?	我要搭飛往阿姆斯特丹的 CI 612 班機，是在這裡報到嗎？
G	Yes. May I have your passport and ticket, please?	是。請給我您的護照和機票。
A	Here you are. Can I have a seat by the window?	給你。我可以選靠窗的座位嗎？
G	I'm sorry, Mr. Wang. All the window seats are fully taken. How about an aisle[1] seat?	王先生，很抱歉，靠窗的座位都滿了。請問您介意坐靠走道的座位嗎？
A	Well, OK, if that's all that's left.	只剩那種座位的話，那就好吧。
G	Do you have any baggage to check in?	請問您有行李要託運嗎？
A	Yes, just one suitcase.	有，一個行李箱。
G	All right. Just put it on the scale[2], please.	好的。請您放在磅秤上就可以了。

A	OK. I think it weighs about 25 kilograms. Is it overweight?	好。我想是重 25 公斤，超重了嗎？
G	Don't worry. The allowance[3] is 30 kilograms.	請別擔心，限重是 30 公斤。
A	Oh! By the way, I have already earned more than 30,000 air miles. Can I upgrade to business class?	對了，我已經累積超過 3 萬哩的哩程，可以升級到商務艙嗎？
G	Sorry, our business-class seats are all taken today. If you'd like, I will put you on the list for the return trip, though.	很抱歉。商務艙今天已經客滿了。如果您要，我可以將您列入回程的候補名單中。
A	That will be great!	那太好了！
G	OK. Here is your ticket, baggage claim tag[4], boarding pass, and your passport. You will be boarding from Terminal 2, Gate Number 21. The boarding time starts at 11:40.	好的，這是您的機票、行李牌、登機證和護照。您的登機門在第二航廈 21 號登機門，11 點 40 分開始登機。
A	Thank you very much.	非常謝謝你。

1 aisle [aɪl] (n.) 走道
2 scale [skel] (n.) 磅秤
3 allowance [əˋlaυəns] (n.) 限制重量
4 tag [tæg] (n.) 牌子

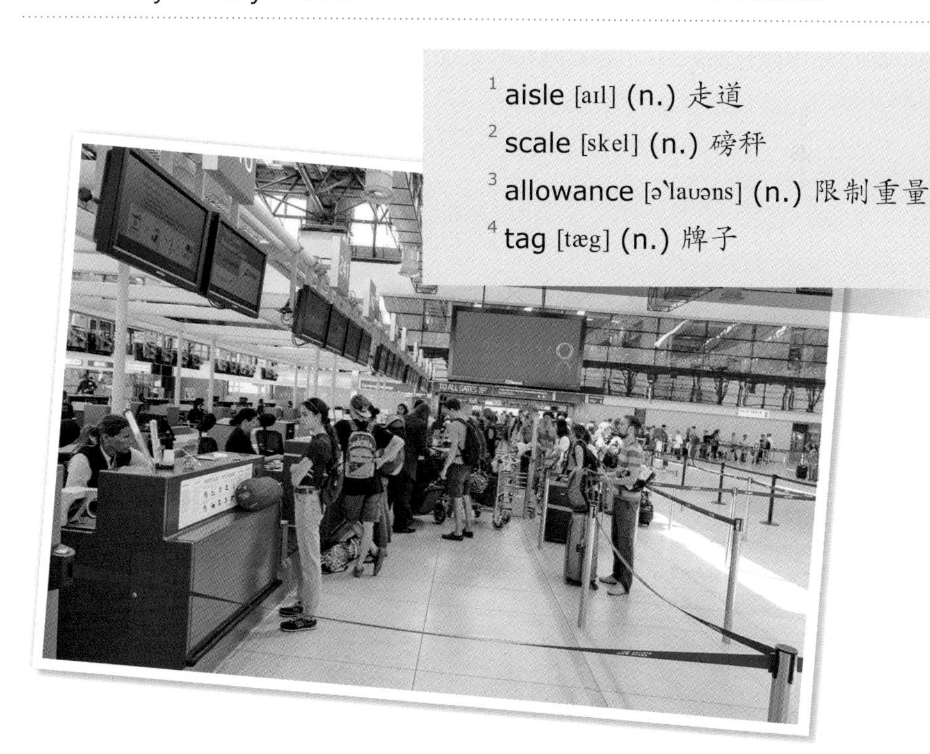

出境流程 Departure Procedures

A Check-in Counter 到航空公司的劃位櫃檯辦理報到手續

❶ 機場有兩個不同的大廳，分別是出境大廳（Departure Hall）及入境大廳（Arrival Hall）。出國時一定要前往出境大廳，到了那裡找到要搭乘的航空公司劃位櫃檯（check-in counter）或前往自助登機櫃檯（self check-in kiosk）辦理手續。

❷ 一般說來，出國旅遊須在飛機起飛前兩個小時到達機場，所辦理之手續如下：

- 核對證件：機票（ticket）、護照（passport）、簽證（visa）。
- 託運行李：過磅（weigh）、檢查、發行李牌。
- 行李若超重（overweight），則須支付行李超重費（overweight charge/excess baggage charge）。若無太多手提行李（hand carry luggage/carry-on luggage/hand baggage），則可隨身攜帶部分行李。
- 選座位：各種座位的說法如下：
  ① 靠窗座位 window seat ② 走道座位 aisle seat ③ 中間座位 middle seat。
- 領取登機證（boarding pass）及行李認領牌（claim tag）。登機證上會記載你的：① 飛機班次：Flight No. ② 登機門：Gate No.
  ③ 座位號碼：Seat No. ④登機時間：boarding time。
- 依各機場的規定付機場稅（airport/departure tax）。有些國家的機場稅不包在機票內含，所以需要另付機場稅，請於出發前確認。

B Passport Inspection Area / Passport Counter 護照查驗

將護照及登機證交付查驗，護照也會蓋上一個註明日期的出境章（departure stamp），表示已經出國。有時會問一兩個簡單的問題，如為何停留該國、接下來要去哪國等等。

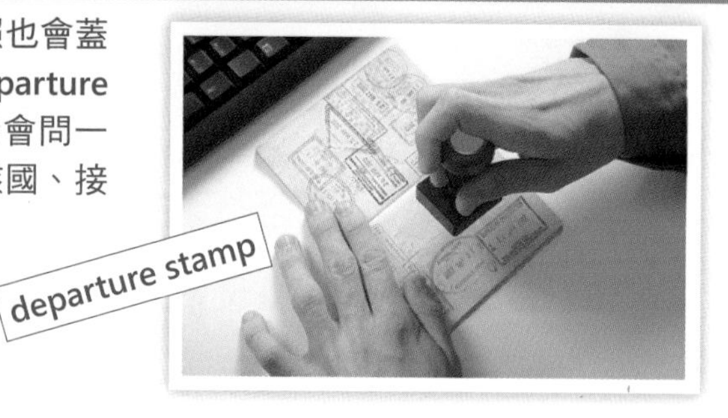
departure stamp

C Passenger and Baggage Inspection 旅客及隨身行李檢查

分為人走的「金屬探測器」（metal detector）， 及隨身行李及物品走的「行李 X 光」（baggage x-ray）的兩項檢查裝置。

baggage x-ray

metal detector

D Boarding Gate 進入登機門

進入所屬的登機門號碼（登機證上會註明登機門號碼），到候機室（lounge）。此時可利用時間到美食部與免稅商品店（duty free shop，簡稱 DFS）逛逛。切記！如果在免稅店買東西，一定要出示護照跟登機證才能購買。

duty free shop

lounge

boarding gate

E Boarding 登機

聽到登機廣播後，拿出登機證以供服務人員查驗並登機。

旅遊小句 *I would like to check in.*

3-1 訂購機票 013

尋找櫃檯	1	Where is the check-in counter for British Airways?	請問搭乘英航要到哪裡報到？
確認劃位櫃檯	2	May I check in here for flight CI 321 to Barcelona?	請問飛巴塞隆納的 CI 321 班機，是在這裡報到嗎？
旅行團報到櫃檯	3	I am sorry, but this is the check-in counter for tour groups.	很抱歉，這裡是受理旅行團報到的櫃檯。
沒有航空公司專屬櫃檯	4	We don't have a counter for Emirates.	這裡沒有阿聯酋航空的櫃檯。
前往櫃檯	5	I would like to check in.	我要辦理報到。
	6	Passport and flight ticket, please.	請給我您的護照及機票。
是否需付機場稅	7	Do I need to pay the airport tax?	請問要付機場稅嗎？
	8	No, it's included in your ticket.	不用，已內含在機票裡了。
需另付機場稅	9	You can't leave the country unless you pay the airport tax on the second floor.	您必須去二樓櫃檯付機場，憑單據才可出境。

登機證 Boarding Pass

① **NAME OF PASSENGER** 乘客姓名

② **FROM . . . TO . . .** 出發地與目的地

③ **FLIGHT NUMBER** 航班號碼

④ **DATE** 搭乘日期

⑤ **SEAT** 座位號碼

⑥ **GATE** 登機門

⑦ **BOARDING TIME** 登機時間

3-2 劃位 014

已事先劃位	1	I have already checked in online.	我在網路上劃過位了。
確認所劃位置	2	Did you book seat 34D?	請問您是劃 34D 嗎？
要求座位	3	Is there any particular seat you'd like?	請問您有特別的座位要求嗎？
	4	Where do you want to sit, window or aisle?	請問您想坐靠窗還是靠走道的座位？
	5	A window seat, please.	請給我靠窗的座位。
要求的座位已滿	6	There are no more aisle seats.	很抱歉，已沒有靠走道的空位了。
要求相連的座位	7	Do you have any other seats open where we could sit together?	請問還有相連的空位嗎？
	8	The only two seats together are in the middle.	只剩中間一排的兩個相連空位了。
	9	Do you mind sitting between two other people in the middle row? They are the only seats together.	只剩下兩名乘客中間的兩個相連空位， 您要嗎？
團體要求分組坐	10	If all four of us can't sit together, we would like two two-seat locations, if possible.	如果我們四人沒辦法坐在一起，我們希望可以兩個兩個坐。

飛機上的位子 In-Flight Seats

長途飛行也是旅行中的一部分，若能選個舒服的位置坐，也能減輕旅遊的勞累。要選到好位置的方法，除了儘早到機場劃位，有些航空公司提供預先劃位的服務（是否可以預先選位除依不同的航空有不同的規定之外，也一票種有所區別，有時較便宜的特惠票可能無法預先選位）。若是參加旅行團，由於位置已事先以團體票的方式劃好區位，比較沒辦法要求（座位數、寬度，座位號碼的安排依各家航空公司而有所差異）。

以波音 **747-400** 機型為例：

｜★★★ 最佳的位子｜★★ 各有利弊的位子｜★ 較差的位子｜

■ **靠近出入口的位子 ★★★**

離引擎遠，是經濟艙較安靜的座位，既可伸腳，出入又方便。

■ **靠二樓階梯的位子 ★★★**

大多為商務艙，也有開放的經濟艙。為安靜舒服的整潔空間，還可使用窗戶兩旁的置物櫃。

■ **逃生門前方的位子 ★★★**

就在空服人員座位前方，有空間可伸腳，離出入口也很近。

■ **螢幕前方的位子 ★★**

有人會因為螢幕太亮而無法入睡，但伸腳與進出方便，適合不怕螢幕太亮依然可入睡或短程旅行的旅客。

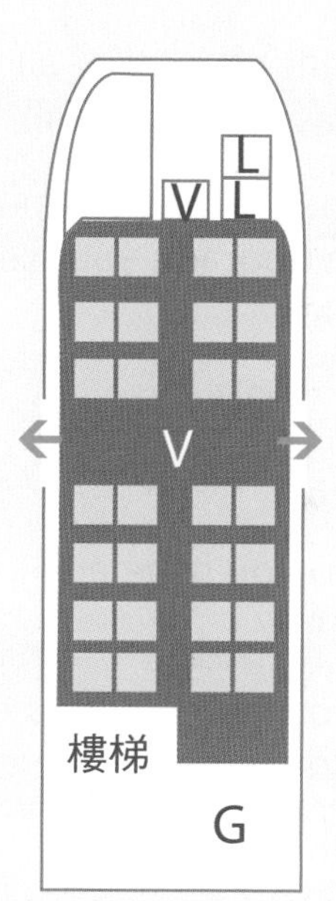

■ **機尾的雙人席 ★★**

座位離窗戶還有些空間，即使靠窗也不覺得擠。離引擎近，所以不是很安靜，而且離出口最遠，最後才能出去。

■ **四個座位中間的兩個位子 ★**

兩側皆有人坐，被夾在中間會很難受，上化妝室也比較不方便。

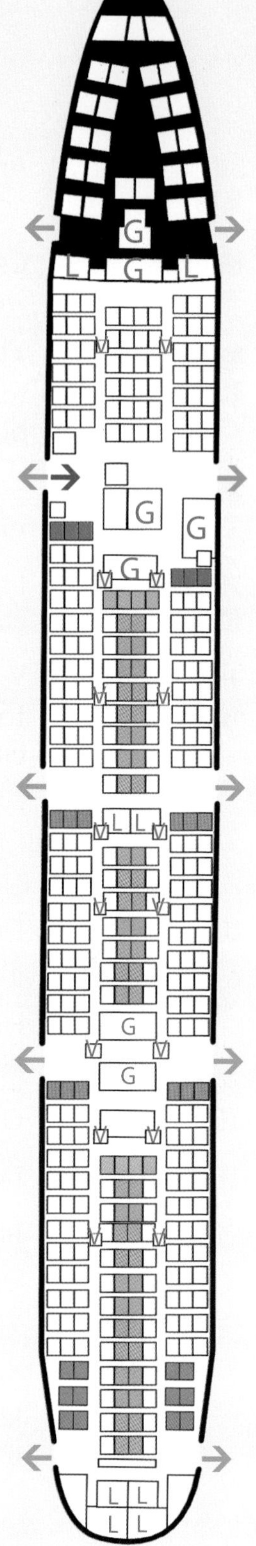

｜G 走道｜L 化妝室｜V 螢幕監視器｜➔ 入口｜➔ 逃生門｜

3-3 機位升等 015

詢問哩程是否累積	1	Are the miles being credited to my account?	請問我的哩程累積了嗎？
機位升等	2	Can I upgrade to business class with my present air miles?	我現有的哩程，可以升等至商務艙嗎？
艙等已滿將自動升等	3	All the economy seats are full today, but we can upgrade you to business class.	經濟艙今天已客滿了，我們會為您升等至商務艙。
累積哩程不夠	4	Sorry, you don't have enough air miles yet.	很抱歉，您目前的哩程還不夠。
升等艙等無空位	5	I am afraid that all the business class seats are full.	很抱歉，商務艙已客滿。
升等艙等須另付費	6	You will need to pay $500 extra to upgrade your seat to business class.	您要升等至商務艙，必須另外付 500 美元。

3-4 行李託運 016

詢問是否託運行李	1	Do you have any luggage to check in?	請問您有行李要託運嗎？
	2	How many pieces of baggage would you like to check in?	您有幾件行李要託運？
託運一件行李	3	One suitcase.	一件行李要託運。
託運全部行李	4	I want to check in all these bags.	這些行李都要託運。
行李秤重	5	Please put it on the scale.	請您將行李放在秤上。
行李重量限制	6	What is the baggage allowance?	請問行李限重多少？
	7	30 kilos for business class and 20 kilos for economy.	商務艙可帶 30 公斤，經濟艙可帶 20 公斤。

詢問行李是否超重	8	Is it overweight?	請問行李有沒有超重？
超重付款	9	What is the cost for excess baggage?	請問行李超重要付多少錢？
	10	You have to pay $20 per extra kilogram.	每多一公斤要付 20 美元。
轉機行李	11	Can my bags be sent directly on to London?	請問行李能直掛到倫敦嗎？
	12	We will send your bags directly to your final destination.	您的行李會直接運到目的地。

3-5 申請成為航空公司會員 017

詢問辦法	1	How do I become a member?	請問要怎麼成為你們的會員？
	2	To apply for membership, you can either fill out this form or register on our website.	請您填這張表格或上我們的網站註冊，就可成為會員了。
詢問舊有哩程	3	Can I get credit for my previous miles?	我之前的哩程可以累計嗎？
	4	You need to have your boarding pass and it must be within six months of the flight.	如果您有半年內的登機證，就可以。
詢問會員福利	5	What benefits will I get by joining?	請問成為你們的會員有什麼好處？
	6	You could earn air miles whenever you travel with us.	您每次旅行的哩程都可以累計。
其他會員福利	7	Once you have earned enough air miles, you can upgrade to business class or get a free ticket.	如果您累積了一定的哩程，就可升等至商務艙，或是獲得免費機票。

Chapter 04 出境與海關 Immigration & Customs

情境式對話 // 辦理退稅 (018)

J → Jeff Zhang　C → Customs Officer

J	Excuse me, I would like to apply for the tax exemption[1]. Is this the right window?	不好意思，我想辦理退稅。請問是在這個窗口辦嗎？
C	Yes, it is. Do you have your tax refund forms with you, and your passport and flight ticket, too?	是。請問您有退稅單嗎，也請給我您的護照與機票？
J	Right here.	在這裡。
C	Let me see. Mr. Zhang, the forms show that you purchased two platinum[2] necklaces, two gold rings, three pairs of shoes, and several handbags. Can I see the goods you bought?	我看看。張先生，單子上列出您買了兩條白金項鍊、兩枚金戒指、三雙鞋，還有幾個手提包。請出示您買的商品。
J	No problem. But do you need to see them all? I put some of them in my checked baggage since they were too heavy to carry on the plane.	沒問題。但全部都要看嗎？有些我放在檢查過的行李裡，那些東西太重了，帶不上飛機。

C	I understand. Just let me see all the merchandise you have with you. That will be fine.	我知道了。只要出示您隨身攜帶的所有商品就可以了。
J	OK. Here you are.	好，都在這裡了。
C	OK. Mr. Zhang, since I have no further questions, I'll stamp your forms for you. Here you go. Just put them into the mail box over there and send them back to the shops where you purchased the goods.	是。張先生，我沒有其他的問題了，您的退稅單會蓋上章。單子還給您。只要把單子投到那裡的郵筒，寄回您當初購物所在的店家，就可以了。
J	How long will it take to get my money back?	請問多久會收到退還的錢呢？
C	I am afraid I can't tell you exactly. It usually takes a couple of weeks or so. But I would say you should definitely get your refund within three weeks.	很抱歉，我沒辦法確切告知，通常會花上幾週左右的時間。不過我可以告訴您，您在三週內一定會收到退稅。
J	I see. Thanks for your help.	明白了。謝謝你的協助。
C	It's my pleasure.	我的榮幸。

[1] exemption [ɪgˋzɛmpʃən] (n.) 免稅
[2] platinum [ˋplætṇəm] (n.) 鉑；白金

旅遊小句 Excuse me, sir, but I need to search you.

4-1 安全檢查 019

要求通關	1	Please (set down your belongings and) walk through the security gate.	請（您拿出隨身物品後）通過安檢門。
	2	Please put your carry-on luggage on the X-ray machine.	請您將隨身行李放在 X 光檢查儀上。
詢問通關物品	3	Is the X-ray safe for film?	請問底片可以通過 X 光檢查嗎？
要求搜身	4	Excuse me, sir, but I need to search/frisk you.	先生很抱歉，我必須搜一下身。
由女海關人員檢查	5	The female customs officer will do the body search.	女性海關人員會為您做搜身檢查。
帶了手機	6	I have my mobile phone with me.	我帶了手機。
帶了零錢	7	I am sorry. I still have some coins on me.	抱歉，我還有些零錢。
檢查行李	8	For security reasons, we have to check your bag.	為了安全起見，我們必須檢查您的行李。
	9	Please open your luggage. We'd like to have a look.	請打開您的行李，我們要檢查一下。
	10	No problem. Anything to cooperate.	沒問題，很樂意配合。
帶了藥粉	11	What is the white powder in this bottle?	這瓶白色粉末是什麼？
	12	It's my stomach medicine.	這是我的胃藥。

4-2 辦理退稅 020

找尋退稅櫃檯	1	Is this the counter for tax refunds?	請問是在這裡辦退稅嗎？
告知辦理退稅	2	I would like to apply for/claim a tax refund.	我要辦理退稅。
要求出示文件	3	Could you please show me the document?	可以請出示您的文件嗎？
	4	Here is the tax refund form, and my passport and boarding pass.	這是我的退稅單、護照和登機證。
要求出示商品	5	Can I see the merchandise?	可以請出示您買的商品嗎？
詢問可退費用	6	How much of a refund can I get?	請問可以退多少錢？
文件無問題	7	Your document seems to be in order. Here's your form.	您的文件應該沒問題。退稅單還您。
詢問後續動作	8	What do I do now?	請問我現在該怎麼做？
將表格寄回店家	9	You have to send this form back to the company. There's a mailbox there.	您必須將這份表格寄回該公司。那裡就有郵筒。
詢問等候時間	10	How long does it take to get the tax refund?	請問要多久才會收到退款呢？

在臺灣之外籍旅客購物退稅須知

申請購物退稅之條件	① 持有「非中華民國國籍之護照、無戶籍之中華民國護照及入出境證」者。 ② 至臺灣向經核准貼有核准銷售特定貨物退稅標誌（TRS）之商店，當日同一家購買可退稅貨品達新臺幣 3,000 元以上，並在 30 天內將隨行貨物攜帶出境者。
申請退稅地點	設置於機場或港口之海關「外籍旅客退稅服務台」。
申請退稅程序	① 出示退稅明細申請表、護照、攜帶出境之退稅範圍內貨物及統一發票收執聯正本，供海關人員查核。 ② 海關審核後，核發「外籍旅客購買特定貨物退稅明細核定單」。 ③ 持憑海關核發之「外籍旅客購買特定貨物退稅明細核定單」，向設置於出境機場或港口之指定銀行申領退稅款。

4-3 逛免稅商店 021

詢問價錢	1	How much is this bottle of wine?	請問這瓶酒多少錢？
詢問顏色	2	Do you have this lipstick in another color?	請問這種口紅還有別的顏色嗎？
告知喜好	3	I prefer the lighter scent.	我比較喜歡淡香水。
詢問特惠商品	4	Is there any discount on cosmetics at the moment?	現在買化妝品有什麼優惠嗎？
告知買煙優惠	5	If you buy three cartons of cigarettes, you can receive a small suitcase for free.	如果您一次買三條煙，將獲贈一個小行李箱。
要求出示登機證	6	Please show me your boarding pass.	請出示你的登機證。
詢問每人可攜帶的量	7	How many bottles of wine can I take with me?	請問我可以帶幾瓶酒？
包裝禮品	8	Could you please wrap this box of chocolates as a gift?	可以請你幫我包裝這盒巧克力嗎？

Chapter 05 準備登機 Getting Ready to Board the Plane

情境式對話 // 登機門改變 (022)

A → Amy Chen　G → Ground Staff

A	Hi. Is this the boarding gate for flight LH 212 to Frankfurt?	你好。請問這是飛法蘭克福的 LH 212 班機登機門嗎？
G	It was, but the gate has been changed. Didn't you hear the announcement?	這個班的登機門改了。您沒有聽到廣播嗎？
A	No, I didn't. What happened? Where should I go now?	沒有。有什麼狀況嗎？那我現在要怎麼走？
G	Don't worry. Flight LH 212 has been canceled due to a maintenance[1] problem, so passengers are being re-directed to flight LH 202. The new boarding gate is Gate 70.	請別擔心。LH 212 班機因維修問題已經取消，旅客要改搭 LH 202 班機，由 70 號門登機。
A	Gate 70? This is Gate 10. How do I get there?	70 號門？這是 10 號門，70 號門怎麼走呢？
G	Gate 70 is upstairs. Take the escalator[2] over there to the upper floor. You will see a sign for Gate 70. Just follow the sign.	70 號門請往樓上走。請搭乘那裡的電扶梯上樓。您上樓後會看到 70 號門的指示牌，照指示牌走就可以了。

A	Thanks. By the way, could you tell me the boarding time? Is it still the same?	謝謝。可以請你順便告訴我登機時間嗎？還是一樣的時間嗎？
G	I'm afraid not. You're going to have to wait another two hours.	很抱歉，時間改了，您必須要多等兩小時。
A	That's OK. Then I can do some more shopping at the duty free shops.	沒關係。那我可以在免稅商店多逛一會兒。
G	Take your time! And have a wonderful journey!	請慢慢逛。也祝您旅途愉快！

[1] maintenance [ˋmentənəs] (n.) 維修
[2] escalator [ˋɛskəˏletɚ] (n.) 電扶梯

旅遊小句 What is the boarding time?

5-1 詢問登機時間與地點 023

詢問登機時間	1	What is the boarding time?	請問什麼時候登機？
起飛時間	2	When is the plane scheduled to depart?	請問班機什麼時候起飛？
詢問登機門	3	Where should I go to board the plane?	請問要在哪裡登機？
	4	The flight departs from Gate 11.	班機在 11 號門起飛。

5-2 前往登機門 024

確認登機門	1	Is this the boarding gate for flight CI 325 to Taipei?	這是飛臺北的 CI 325 班機登機門嗎？
詢問何時登機	2	How much longer do I have to wait before boarding?	請問要多久才可以登機？
告知更換登機門	3	The boarding gate for your flight has been changed to Gate 8.	您的班機已改在 A8 門登機了。
詢問如何前往	4	How do I get to the new boarding gate?	請問新的登機門怎麼走？
	5	Go straight along here, and it will be on your right.	請往前直走，在右手邊。

5-3 班機延誤起飛 025

班機延後廣播 1 Ladies and gentlemen. Due to weather conditions, all flights to Hong Kong will be delayed. We truly regret the inconvenience. We will inform you of the new departure times as soon as possible. Thank you for your cooperation and patience.

各位旅客請注意，由於天候不佳，所有飛往香港的班機將延後起飛。造成各位旅客的不便，我們深表歉意。我們會儘速通知新的起飛時間，感謝各位旅客的配合及耐心等候。

轉搭其它班機廣播	2	May I have your attention, please. British Airways flight BA 123 to London is now canceled. All passengers will be transferred to flight BA 128 leaving at 9:25 p.m. All passengers please go to our main counter to have your seats reassigned and then proceed to gate A63 for boarding. Thank you. 各位旅客請注意，英國航空飛往倫敦的 BA 123 班機已取消，所有要搭乘此班機的乘客，將改搭晚間 9 點 25 分起飛的 BA 128 班機。各位旅客請至本公司櫃檯重新劃位，並前往 A63 門登機。謝謝各位旅客。

5-4 開始登機 026

告知開始登機的廣播	1	Attention, please. Passengers to Tokyo, Honolulu, and Los Angeles on Delta Airlines flight DL 166, please board through Gate 50. 請注意，要搭乘達美航空 DL 166 班機前往東京、檀香及洛杉磯的旅客，請前往 50 號門登機。
請頭等艙優先登機的廣播	2	Attention, please. Delta Airlines flight DL 166 to Tokyo, Honolulu, and Los Angeles is now boarding. Passengers in first class, please proceed to the boarding gate. 請注意，飛東京、檀香山及洛杉磯的達美航空 DL 166 班機， 已開始登機，請頭等艙的旅客前往登機門登機。
請老弱殘障旅客優先登機的廣播	3	May I have your attention, please. Delta Airlines flight DL 166 to Tokyo, Honolulu, and Los Angeles is now boarding. Passengers with small children, and those who require special assistance, please proceed to the boarding gate now. 請注意，飛東京、檀香山及洛杉磯的達美航空 DL 166 班機，已開始登機，請有幼童同行和需要特殊協助的旅客現在前往登機門登機。

Unit 2

Flight
翱翔天際飛航篇

Chapter 06 起飛前 Before Takeoff

情境式對話 確認座位 027

S → Stewardess J → Jared Meng B → Bill Chen

J	Excuse me, but can you help me? I think there's a problem with my seat.	不好意思，我想我的座位有問題，可以請你幫忙嗎？
S	Yes, of course. What's the problem?	當然可以。有什麼問題嗎？
J	Well, my boarding pass says seat 25C. I went back there, but I am afraid there is somebody sitting in the seat. Could you check it out for me?	是這樣的，我登機證上的座位是寫 25C，但我去那裡時好像已經有人坐。你能幫我確認一下嗎？
S	No problem.	沒問題。
	The stewardess goes to seat 25C and talks to the other passenger, Bill Chen.	空服員走到 25C 座位，對另一位乘客比爾·陳説話。
S	Excuse me, sir. May I see your boarding pass, please?	先生，不好意思，請您出示登機證。
B	Is anything wrong?	哪裡不對嗎？
S	This is seat 25C. I think it belongs to this gentleman.	這是 25C 座位。我想是這位男士的座位。

B	Let me see. Oh, I'm sorry. My mistake. My seat is 26C. I'll move now.	我看看。噢，抱歉，我看錯了，我是坐 26C 才對。我現在就移。
J	(To the stewardess) Thank you for your help. By the way, could you help me with my carry-on[1] luggage? All the overhead compartments[2] seem to be full. Is there anywhere else I can put it?	（對空服員說話）謝謝你幫忙。可以順便請你幫忙另一件事嗎？我要把行李放在上面的置物箱裡，但好像沒有地方可以放了。還有別的地方嗎？
S	I am really sorry about this. I will check to see if there are any empty overhead compartments anywhere. If you'd like, you can also place your bag under the seat in front of you.	真的很抱歉，我會查查看還有沒有地方可以放。如果您願意的話，也可以把您的行李放在您前面座位的下方。
J	Could you please see if there's an overhead cabinet for me first?	可以先請你幫我看上面有沒有空的置物櫃嗎？
S	Sure. Please wait here. I will be right back.	沒問題。請您在此等候，我馬上回來。

1 carry-on [ˋkærɪˏɑn] (adj.) 隨身攜帶的
2 compartment [kəmˋpɑrtmənt] (n.) 置物櫃

旅遊小句 Where is my seat located?

6-1 登機入座 028

找座位	1	Where is my seat located?	請問我的座位在哪裡？
詢問明確座位	2	Where is seat 30E?	請問30E座位在哪裡？
空服員帶位	3	Please follow me.	麻煩請跟我來。
確認座位	4	Is this seat 40D?	請問這是40D座位嗎？
別人坐錯時	5	Sorry, sir. I think this is my seat.	先生，不好意思，我想您坐了我的位子。
交換座位	6	May I change seats with you?	請問可以和您換位子嗎？

6-2 置放行李 029

要求幫忙放行李	1	Could you please help me put my baggage up there?	請問你可以幫我把行李放到上面嗎？
要求幫忙拿行李	2	Could you please get my baggage for me up there?	請問你可以幫我把行李拿下來嗎？
詢問置放處	3	Can I put my bag here?	請問可以把行李放在這裡嗎？
	4	Where can I leave my bag?	請問可以把行李放在哪裡？
置物櫃已滿	5	The overhead compartments are all full. Where can I leave my bag?	上面的置物櫃都滿了，我可以把行李放在哪裡？
放在地上	6	You can place your luggage under the seat in front of you.	您可以把行李放在前面的座位下方。

6-3 起飛前機上廣播 030

歡迎登機

1 This is flight attendant Jessica Lin speaking. On behalf of Sky Airlines, we welcome you aboard flight SK 412 from Tokyo to New York City. The flight time today is 12 hours and 10 minutes. Our expected time of arrival is 10:40 a.m. local time, March 4th.

我是空服員潔西卡．林，謹代表天空航空公司，歡迎各位搭乘從東京飛紐約市的 SK 412 班機。飛行時間是 12 小時 10 分鐘，我們預計會於紐約當地時間 3 月 4 日早上 10 時 40 分抵達。

禁止使用電器用品

2 Radios, CD players, mobile phones and radio-controlled toys and devices must remain switched off during take-off and landing.

收音機、CD 隨身聽、行動電話及無線電遙控玩具和儀器，在起飛與下降過程中，全面禁止使用。

電子產品的使用

3 Laptop computers and other electronic devices cannot be used until 15 minutes after take-off, or after the seat belt sign has been turned on for landing.

在飛機起飛 15 分鐘前，或是飛機準備降落前，繫上安全帶指示燈亮後，手提電腦等電子用品皆禁止使用。

準備起飛

4 For safety reasons, the use of personal electronic devices is prohibited during take-off and landing. Since this is a non-smoking flight, you are kindly requested to refrain from smoking anywhere aboard the aircraft. Thank you for your cooperation. We will take off immediately. Please be seated, fasten your seat belt, and make sure your seat back is upright, your tray table is closed, and your carry-on items are securely stowed in the overhead bin or under the seat in front of you. We hope you enjoy the flight! Thank you!

為了安全起見，起飛和降落時，嚴禁使用個人電子用品。由於本班機全面禁煙，所以請勿在機艙內吸煙，謝謝各位旅客的配合。飛機很快就要起飛了，請您坐好、並繫好安全帶，豎直椅背和收好小桌板。請您確認您的手提物品是否妥善安放在頭頂上方的行李櫃內或座椅下方。祝您有趟愉快舒適的旅程，謝謝！

6-4 機上設備的使用與索取 031

找會中文的空服員	1	Does anyone of you speak Chinese?	請問有沒有會說中文的空服員？
如何使用安全帶	2	Please tell me how to fasten/ unfasten the seat belt.	請問你可以告訴我怎麼繫上／鬆開安全帶嗎？
詢問開關燈	3	How do I turn on/off the light?	請問這燈是怎麼開／關？
放下椅背	4	How do I recline my seat?	請問椅背要怎麼放下來？
索取毛毯／枕頭	5	An extra blanket/pillow, please.	麻煩多給一條毛毯／一個枕頭。
索取耳機	6	May I have a headset, please?	請問可以給我一副耳機嗎？

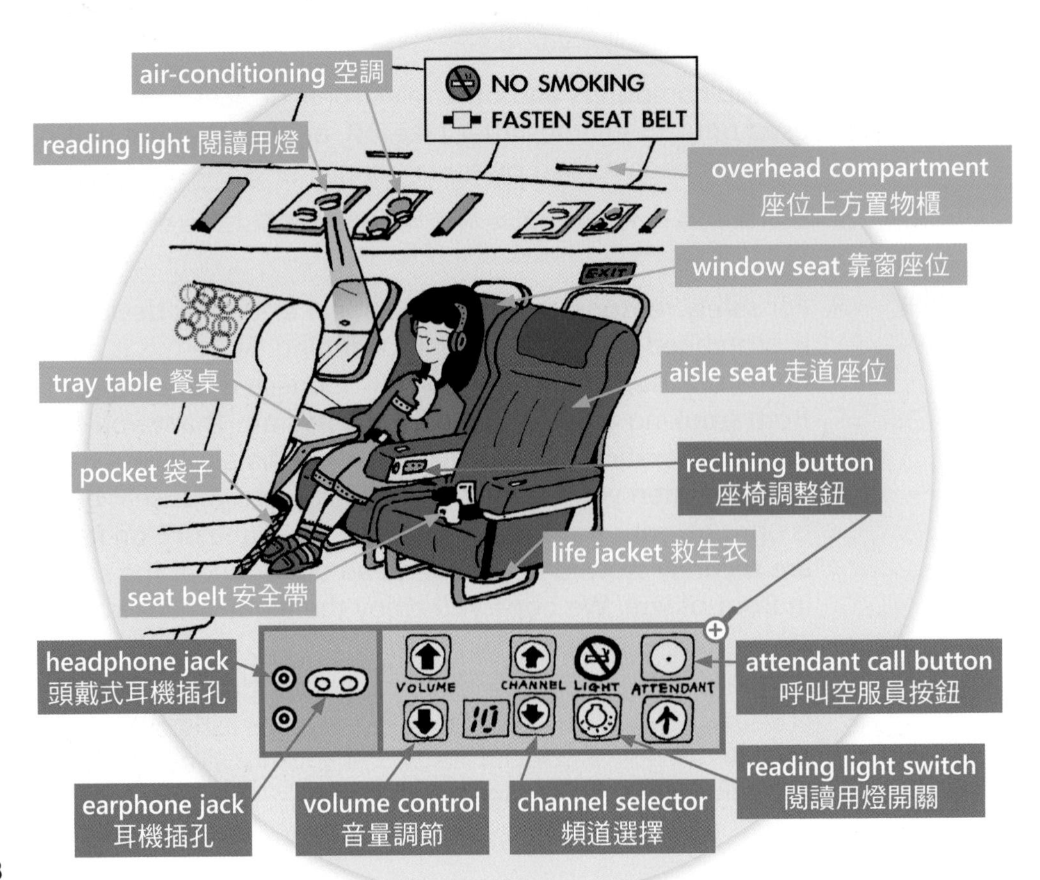

機艙內設施 In-Flight facilities

display screen 機上電視

life jacket 救生衣

airsickness bag 嘔吐袋

reading light
閱讀用燈

seat belt 安全帶

overhead compartment
座位上方置物櫃

window 窗戶

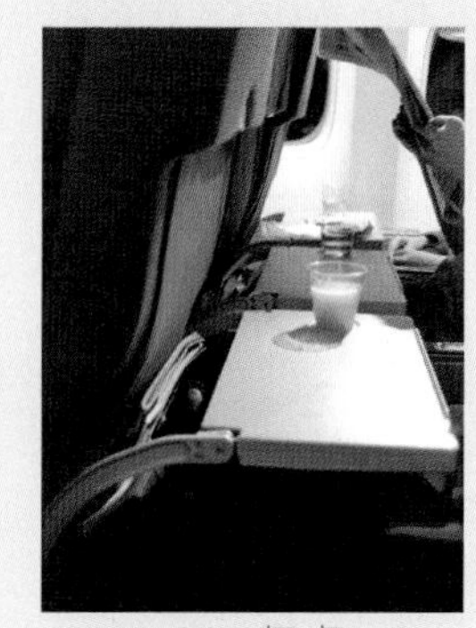
tray table 餐桌

no-smoking sign
禁止吸煙警示燈

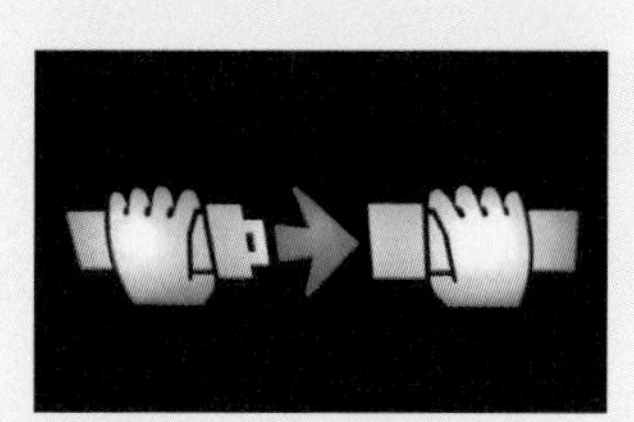
fasten-seat-belt sign
繫緊安全帶警示燈

pocket 收納袋

reclining button
座椅調整鈕

duty-free goods magazine

6-5 詢問事項與服務 032

找洗手間	1	Can you tell me where the nearest lavatory is?	請問洗手間怎麼走？
使用洗手間	2	Can I use the lavatory now?	請問現在可以用洗手間嗎？
詢問使用電子用品時機	3	When can I use my electronic devices?	請問什麼時候可以用電子用品？
空中娛樂服務時間	4	When does the audio/video program begin?	請問音樂節目／電影是什麼時候播放？
詢問免稅商品	5	Do you sell duty-free items on this flight?	請問這個班機會販售免稅商品嗎？
詢問免稅商品販賣時間	6	When can I buy duty-free goods?	請問什麼時候開始賣免稅商品？
索取免稅商品明細	7	Do you have a duty-free goods magazine?	請問有免稅商品的目錄嗎？
東西壞了	8	My headset doesn't seem to be working.	我的耳機好像不能用。

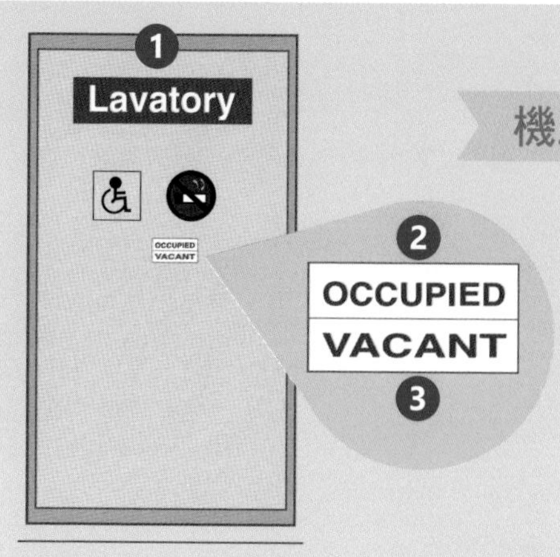

① TOILET/LAVATORY 洗手間

② OCCUPIED 使用中

③ VACANT 無人使用

④ PAPER TOWEL 紙巾

⑤ WASTE DISPOSAL 垃圾桶

⑥ AIRSICKNESS BAG 嘔吐袋

⑦ TOILET SEAT 馬桶座

⑧ EMERGENCY BUTTON 緊急按鈕

⑨ COSMETICS 化妝品

⑩ RETURN-TO-YOUR-SEAT SIGN 請回到座位警示燈

⑪ FAUCET 水龍頭

⑫ TOILET PAPER 衛生紙

⑬ SANITARY NAPKIN 衛生棉

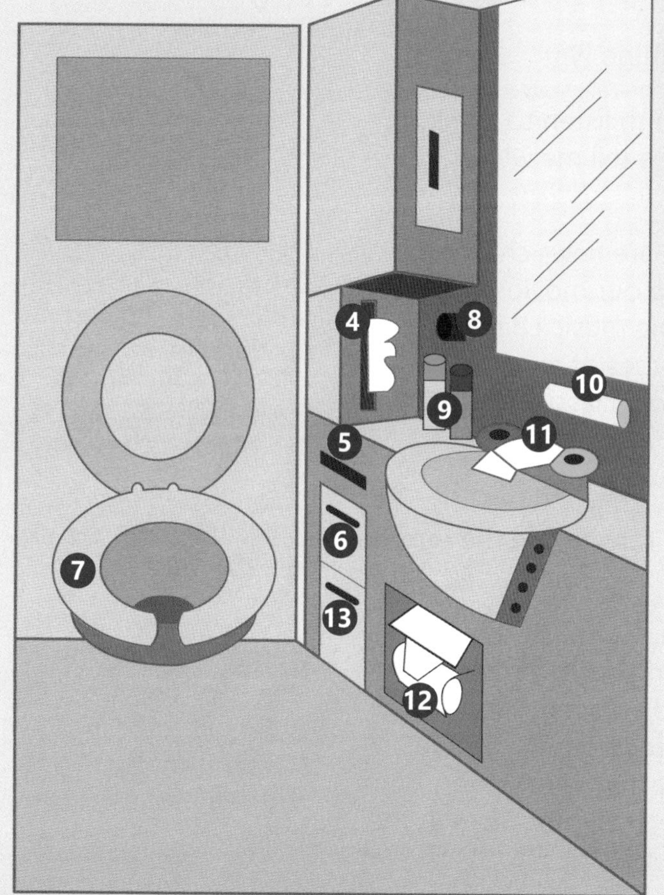

Chapter

07 飛行中 During the Flight

情境式對話 使用娛樂頻道 033

S → Steward J → Josephine Niu

J	Excuse me. I would like to listen to some music. Could you please tell me which channel I should use?	請問一下，我想聽點音樂，音樂頻道是哪一個？
S	Well, channels 1 and 2 are news channels, and channels 3 to 5 are our movie channels. Channels 6 to 18 are the music channels. You have lots of different types of music to choose from, including jazz, pop, classical, country, and so on.	好的，第一和第二頻道是新聞臺，第三到第五頻道是電影臺，第六到第十八頻道都是音樂臺。有許多不同的音樂類型可以選擇，包括爵士樂、流行音樂、古典樂、鄉村音樂等等。
J	I see. But I don't know how to use the remote control.	了解。但是我不知道遙控器怎麼用。
S	Here, let me show you. Just push the "up" and "down" buttons on your remote control to switch channels and adjust the volume. If you want to know more about the various programs, you can get that information from our in-flight magazine. It is right there in the seat pocket in front of you.	我為您示範一遍。只要按遙控器的「上」與「下」按鈕，就可以選臺和調整音量。如果您想進一步了解各項節目資訊，可以參考您面前椅袋中的機上專刊。

J	Thank you! By the way, I don't think my headphones are working. Can you please get me a new one? Or could you check if there's something wrong with it?	謝謝你。另外，我的耳機好像壞了。可以請你換一副嗎？或是你可以看一下哪裡有問題嗎？
S	I'll just go and get you a new pair. Sorry about that.	我馬上為您換副新的。很抱歉發生此事。
J	That's all right.	沒關係。
S	I'll be right back with your headset[1].	我會立刻拿耳機來。
J	Thanks a lot.	非常謝謝你。

[1] **headset** [ˋhɛdˏsɛt] **(n.)**（尤指帶有話筒的）耳機

旅遊小句 May I help you?

7-1 餐點與娛樂廣播 034

供應機上餐點

1 Ladies and gentlemen, the captain has turned off the fasten seat belt sign, so you may now move around the cabin. However, we recommend that you keep your seat belt fastened while you're seated. In a few moments, we will be serving you your meal and drinks. Please put down the table in front of you. For the convenience of the passenger behind you, please return your seat back to the upright position during the meal service. Thank you!

各位貴賓您好，機長已經熄滅繫緊安全帶指示燈，現在您可以離開座位，然而我們依然建議您留在座位的同時繫上安全帶。在幾分鐘後，空服員將會提供餐飲服務。需要用餐的旅客，請您將小桌板放下。為了方便其他旅客，在供餐期間，請您豎直椅背。謝謝！

2 We will be serving drinks and a light snack soon. Please return to your seats. Thank you.

本班機即將供應飲料及點心，請各位旅客回到座位上，謝謝。

參閱機上指南

3 For your inflight entertainment, it is our pleasure to present the latest motion pictures and other programs. Please refer to our entertainment brochure for detailed information.

本班機在旅途中，提供最新的電影及其他節目，詳情請參考飛機上的娛樂手冊。

7-2 販賣免稅商品的廣播 035

販售免稅商品 1 We will start selling duty-free goods now. Please refer to the in-flight magazine in the pocket in front of your seats for a list of duty-free items available. We accept VISA, MasterCard, US dollars and euros. Please tell the flight attendant which items you are interested in. Thank you.

本班機將開始販售免稅商品，請參考座位前方袋中的免稅商品專刊。本班機接受威士卡、萬事達卡、美金及歐元。如果對任何商品有興趣，請洽詢機上服務人員，謝謝。

告知販賣內容 2 As a special service, we have cigarettes, liquor, perfumes, cosmetics, and toys for sale in flight. Please contact your cabin attendant if you wish to purchase any of these items. Thank you.

本班機於旅途中販售菸品、各式酒類、香水、化妝品和玩具。如果想要購買，請洽詢機上服務人員，謝謝。

7-3 經過亂流的廣播 036

有亂流請回座並繫好安全帶 1 We are approaching an area of turbulence. For your own safety and comfort, please go back to your seats, and fasten your seat belts. Please keep your belts fastened until the "fasten-seat-belt" sign goes off. Thank you.

本班機正接近亂流區，為讓各位旅客能安全、舒適地度過，請各位旅客回到座位，繫上安全帶，直到「繫上安全帶」的燈號熄滅為止，謝謝。

7-4 詢問視聽娛樂與索取報紙 037

要求換耳機	1	This headset is not working. May I have another one?	請問，這副耳機沒辦法用，可以換一副新的？
詢問如何聽音樂	2	Could you please show me how to listen to the music channels?	請問你可以教我要怎麼聽音樂頻道？
找電影頻道	3	Which is the movie channel?	請問電影頻道是那一個？
索取中文報紙	4	Do you have any Chinese newspapers?	請問有中文報紙嗎？

7-5 身體不適 038

不舒服	1	I feel a little sick.	我覺得不太舒服。
暈機	2	I am feeling airsick.	我好像暈機了。
耳鳴	3	My ears are ringing.	我耳鳴了。
想吐	4	I feel like vomiting. vomite	我想吐。
要求給藥	5	May I have some airsickness medicine?	請問有暈機藥嗎？
需要嘔吐袋	6	I need an airsickness bag.	我需要嘔吐袋。
需要找醫生	7	Is there a doctor onboard?	飛機上有醫生嗎？
告知他人不舒服	8	This lady doesn't feel well.	這位小姐好像不太舒服。
別人暈機	9	She seems to be airsick.	她好像暈機了。
請求幫助	10	Would you mind checking on her?	可以請你看看她怎麼了嗎？

7-6 餐飲服務 039

告知不要點心	1	No snack for me, please, but thanks anyway.	我不要點心，但還謝謝你。
詢問用餐時間	2	When will you start to serve lunch?	請問午餐何時供應？
	3	How long before the meal service begins?	請問還要多久才開始供餐？
	4	We will start to serve lunch in twenty minutes.	午餐在20分鐘後供應。
詢問餐點選擇	5	What are my choices for lunch?	請問午餐有什麼選擇？
	6	We have chicken with noodles and pork with rice. Which would you like?	我們有雞肉麵和豬肉飯。您想要哪一種呢？
多要一個麵包	7	May I have some more bread, please?	請問可以再給我一些麵包嗎？
詢問飲品選擇	8	Would you care for something to drink?	請問您要什麼飲料？
	9	What kind of drinks do you have?	有什麼飲料？
飲料不加冰	10	One orange juice without ice, please.	請給我一杯柳橙汁不加冰塊。
飲品要加冰	11	One coke with ice, please.	請給我一杯可樂加冰塊。
詢問飲用咖啡或茶	12	Would you like some coffee or tea?	請問您要咖啡或是茶？
再要一杯	13	Some more coffee, please.	請再給我一杯／些咖啡。
要求稍後再用餐	14	I want to eat lunch later.	我想晚點吃午餐。
要求換素食	15	May I have a vegetarian meal instead?	請問可以換素食嗎？

詢問用餐進度	16	Are you finished?	請問您用完餐了嗎？
	17	Yes, I've finished. Please take the tray away.	用完了，請把餐盤取走。
還沒用完餐	18	I haven't finished yet.	我還沒用完餐。
肚子餓的請求	19	I am a little hungry. Is there anything I could eat?	我有點餓，請問有什麼可以吃嗎？
想吃泡麵	20	Do you have any instant noodles?	請問有泡麵嗎？
想吃冰淇淋	21	I would like to have some ice cream.	我想要一些冰淇淋。

旅遊資訊補充包

飛機上的菜單 In-flight Menu

短程只供應一餐的班機，並不會印製菜單，而是在用餐前，由空服人員告知；若是長途且會供應兩餐以上的班機，則大多會印出每餐的菜單並放在座位前，讓旅客清楚了解有什麼餐點。另外，如果是選擇特別餐的旅客，請記得在訂機票時向航空公司提出要求，以免餐點不夠餓肚子囉！

特殊餐種類（特殊餐食的供應項目依航空公司有所區別，需求前可向航空公司確認）：

東方素食餐（又稱中式素食餐，不含五辛）
Vegetarian Oriental Meal

奶蛋素食餐 **Vegetarian Lacto-Ovo Meal**

兒童餐 **Child Meal**

嬰兒餐 **Baby Meal**

水果餐 **Fruit Platter Meal**

糖尿病飲食餐 **Diabetic Meal**

印度教餐（不含牛肉、豬肉及其副產品）
Hindu Meal

伊斯蘭教餐（不含豬肉及其副產品與酒精成分）
Moslem Meal

7-7 購買免稅商品 040

告知要買品牌	1	I would like to buy one YSL K21 mascara.	我要買一支聖羅蘭K21 型號的睫毛膏。
詢問產品其它顏色	2	Do you have other colors?	請問有別的顏色嗎？
	3	Sorry, we only have this color on this flight.	很抱歉，目前機上只有這種顏色。
其他可買到商品的方法	4	You may be able to find the color you like in the duty-free shop.	您可以至免稅商店購買您想要的顏色。
告知價錢	5	The total comes to $80.	一共是 80 美元。
能否刷卡	6	Do you take credit cards?	請問可以刷卡嗎？
	7	We accept most major credit cards.	我們接受主要的幾家信用卡。
使用幣別	8	Which currencies do you accept, euros, US dollars, or British pounds?	請問你們收歐元、美金還是英鎊？
	9	We accept only US dollars and euros.	我們只接受美金和歐元。

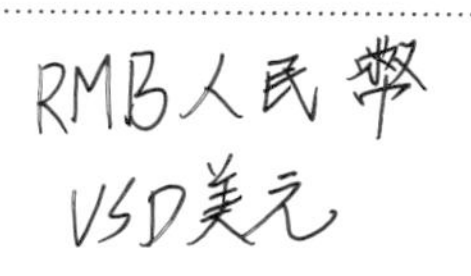

Chapter

08 降落前 Before Landing

情境式對話 // 轉機與相關文件

S → Stewardess　H → Henry Kuo

S	Excuse me, sir. Do you need a Disembarkation[1] Card and Customs Declaration Form?	先生，不好意思。請問您需要入境登記表與海關申報表嗎？
H	I'm not sure. What are they for?	我不清楚，那些是要做什麼用的。
S	Well, if you're staying in Germany, you'll need to fill out the forms to enter the country. If you are a transit[2] passenger, you don't need them.	是這樣的，如果您要在德國停留，就必須填寫這些文件才能入境。如果您要轉機，就不需填寫。
H	I'm getting on a connecting flight to Berlin at Frankfurt Airport.	我是要在法蘭克福機場轉機到柏林。
S	Then you'll need to go through immigration and customs in Frankfurt. Here are your forms.	那麼您就必須獲得法蘭克福移民及海關官員批准才能入境。這些是您的表格。
H	Thank you. Sorry, but could you please tell me how to fill these forms out?	謝謝你。不好意思，但可以請你告訴我怎麼填嗎？

S	The instructions are on the back. It's pretty simple. Make sure you write your information in capital letters.	表格背後有說明，很簡單的。只是請注意，資料都是要以大寫字母填寫的。
H	What should I do when I'm finished? Should I return them to you afterwards?	我寫完以後要怎麼做？要交給你嗎？
S	No. You have to hand the Disembarkation Card to the immigration officer along with your passport, and give the Customs Declaration Form to the customs officers.	不是。您必須把入境紀錄卡連同護照交給移民官員，並把海關申報表交給海關官員。
H	I see. Thanks for your help.	我了解了。謝謝你幫忙。
S	No problem. It's my pleasure.	不客氣，我的榮幸。

[1] disembarkation [ˌdɪsɛmbɑrˋkeʃən] (n.) 入境
[2] transit [ˋtrænsɪt] (n.) 中途過境

入境登記表 Disembarkation Card

每位旅客入境前，都將被要求填寫兩種表：	
入境登記表 • Disembarkation Card • Immigration Form • Arrival Card • E/D Card • I-94 Form（美國）	海關申報表 (有些國家不用） • Customs Declaration Form

一般說來，空服員會在飛機落地前提供這些表格，若不明白可直接詢問服務人員。
填表格時，應盡量提供詳細資料，許多國家甚至要求要以大寫 (block capitals) 方式書寫，以方便判讀。

① **This form must be completed by all persons except US citizens, returning resident aliens, aliens with immigrant visas, and Canadian Citizens visiting or in transit.** 除了美國公民、美國海外僑民、新移民外籍人士和加拿大公民外，所有旅遊或過境的人士都必須填寫此表。

② **Type or print legibly with pen in ALL CAPITAL LETTERS. Use English. Do not write on the back of this form.** 請以大寫字母打字或用筆填寫清楚。請用英文填寫，不要在此表背面謄寫。

③ **This form is in two parts. Please complete both the Arrival Record (Items 1 through 13) and the Departure Record (Items 14 through 17).** 此表包括兩部分。請填寫入境記錄（第 1 項至第 13 項）和離境記錄（第 14 項至第 17 項）兩部分。

④ **When all items are completed, present this form to the CBP Officer.** 填寫完畢後，請將此表交給美國海關及邊境保衛局人員。

⑤ **Item 7—If you are entering the United States by land, enter LAND in this space. If you are entering the United States by ship, enter SEA in this space.** 第 7 項內容說明——如果您是從陸地進入美國，請在空格內填寫 LAND。如果您是乘船進入美國，請在空格內填寫 SEA。

⑥ Family Name 姓

⑦ First (Given) Name 名

⑧ Birth Date 生日
Day (D) 日
Mo (M) 月
Yr (Y) 年

⑨ Country of Citizenship
國籍

⑩ Sex 性別
Male (M) / Female (F)
男／女

⑪ Passport Number
護照號碼

⑫ Airline and Flight Number
航空公司及航班號碼

⑬ Country Where You Live
居住國家

⑭ City Where You Boarded
登機地點

⑮ City Where Visa Was Issued
簽證核發地點

⑯ Date Issued 簽證核發時間

⑰ Address While in the United States (Number and Street) 在美國的地址（門牌號碼與街名）

⑱ City and State 城市及州名

DEPARTMENT OF HOMELAND SECURITY
U.S. Customs and Border Protection — OMB No. 1651-0111

Admission Number — *Welcome to the United States*

392923282 18

I-94 Arrival/Departure Record - Instructions

1. This form must be completed by all persons except U.S. Citizens, returning resident aliens, aliens with immigrant visas, and Canadian Citizens visiting or in transit.
2. Type or print legibly with pen in ALL CAPITAL LETTERS. Use English. Do not write on the back of this form.
3. This form is in two parts. Please complete both the Arrival Record (Items 1 through 13) and the Departure Record (Items 14 through 17).
4. When all items are completed, present this form to the CBP Officer.
5. Item 7 - If you are entering the United States by land, enter **LAND** in this space. If you are entering the United States by ship, enter **SEA** in this space.

CBP Form I-94 (10/04)

Admission Number — OMB No. 1651-0111

392923282 18

Arrival Record

⑥ 1. Family Name
⑦ 2. First (Given) Name — ⑧ 3. Birth Date (Day/Mo/Yr)
⑨ 4. Country of Citizenship — ⑩ 5. Sex (Male or Female)
⑪ 6. Passport Number — ⑫ 7. Airline and Flight Number
⑬ 8. Country Where You Live — ⑭ 9. City Where You Boarded
⑮ 10. City Where Visa was Issued — ⑯ 11. Date Issued (Day/Mo/Yr)
⑰ 12. Address While in the United States (Number and Street)
⑱ 13. City and State

CBP Form I-94 (10/04)

Departure Number — OMB No. 1651-0111

392923282 18

I-94
Departure Record

14. Family Name
15. First (Given) Name — 16. Birth Date (Day/Mo/Yr)
17. Country of Citizenship

CBP Form I-94 (10/04)

See Other Side — **STAPLE HERE**

海關申報表 Customs Declaration Form

① Each arriving traveler or responsible family member must provide the following information (only ONE written declaration per family is required)
每位入境旅客或家庭代表均須填妥下列資料（每個家庭只需填寫一張）

② Family Name 姓

③ First (Given) Name 名

④ Birth Date 生日

⑤ Day 日

⑥ Month 月

⑦ Year 年

⑧ Number of Family members traveling with you 同行家屬人數

⑨ U.S. Street Address (hotel name/destination) 美國居住地址（飯店名稱／目的地）

⑩ City 城市名

⑪ State 州名

⑫ Passport Issued by (country)
護照簽發國家

⑬ Passport number 護照號碼

⑭ Country of Residence 居住國家

⑮ Countries visited on this trip prior to U.S. arrival
此趟行程抵美前，曾去過的國家

⑯ Airline/Flight Number or Vessel Name
航空公司／班機號碼或船艦名稱

⑰ The primary purpose of this trip is business. 此行主要目的為洽公。

⑱ I am (We are) bringing
我（我們）攜帶了

ⓐ fruits, vegetables, plants, food, insects 蔬果、植物、食物、昆蟲

ⓑ meats, animals, animal/wildlife products 肉品、動物、動物／野生動物製品

ⓒ disease agents, cell cultures, or snails 病原體、細胞培養、蝸牛

ⓓ soil or have you visited a farm/ranch/pasture 土壤，或你曾到農場／牧場／牧草地參觀

⑲ I have (We have) been in close proximity of (such as touching or handling) livestock 我（我們）曾經近距離接觸家畜（例如觸摸或處理）

⑳ I am (We are) carrying currency or monetary instrument over $10,000 U.S. or foreign equivalent 我（我們）攜帶了 1 萬美元以上或等值的外國貨幣

㉑ I have (We have) commercial merchandise (articles for sale, samples used for soliciting orders, or goods that are not considered personal effects.) 我（我們）攜帶了商品（待售之物品、用以招徠訂單之樣品，或是任何非屬私人之物品）

㉒ Residents —（美國居民填寫）
攜帶商品總值

㉓ Visitors —（旅客填寫）
攜帶商品總值

㉔ 填妥表格後，在此處簽名

U.S. Customs and
Border Protection

Customs Declaration

1 Each arriving traveler or responsible family member must provide the following information (only ONE written declaration per family is required)

1. Family Name 2
3 First (Given) Middle
4 2. Birth date Day 5 Month 6 Year 7
8 3. Number of family members traveling with you
9 4. (a) U.S. Street Address (hotel name/destination)
(b) City 10 (c) State 11
12 5. Passport issued by (country)
13 6. Passport number
14 7. Country of residence
15 8. Countries visited on this trip prior to U.S. arrival
16 9. Airline/Flight Number or Vessel Name
17 10. The primary purpose of this trip is business. Yes No
18 11. I am (We are) bringing
(a) fruits, vegetables, plants, food, insects Yes No
(b) meats, animals, animal/wildlife products Yes No
(c) disease agents, cell cultures, or snails Yes No
(d) soil or have you visited a farm/ranch/pasture Yes No
19 12. I have (We have) been in close proximity of (such as touching or handling) livestock Yes No
20 13. I am (We are) carrying currency or monetary instrument over $10,000 U.S. or foreign equivalent Yes No
(see definition of monetary instrument on reverse)
21 14. I have (We have) commercial merchandise Yes No
(articles for sale, samples used for soliciting orders, or goods that are not considered personal effects.)
22 15. Residents — the total value of all goods, including commercial merchandise I/we have purchased or acquired abroad. (including gifts for someone else, but not items mailed to the U.S.) and am/are bringing to the U.S. is $
23 Visitors — the total value of all articles that will remain in the U.S. including commercial merchandise is: $

Read the instruction on the back of this form. Space is provided to list all the items you might declare.

I HAVE READ THE IMPORTANT INFORMATION ON THE REVERSE SIDE OF THIS FORM AND HAVE MADE A TRUTHFUL DECLARATION.

24 X
(Signature) Date (day/month/year)

For Official Use Only

CBP Form 00540 (0104)

旅遊小句 // We will be landing at . . .

8-1 降落前的廣播 042

收回耳機	1	We will be landing very soon. We have to discontinue our in-flight entertainment programs at this time. Your flight attendant will come around and collect your headsets. We hope that you have enjoyed our program today. 本班機即將降落，現在會停止播映娛樂節目，機上服務員會向各位旅客收回耳機。希望各位還滿意今天的節目。
準備降落，要求乘客回座	2	In a short while, we will be landing at London Heathrow Airport. Please return to your seats and put your seatbacks in the upright position. If your table is down, please return it to the locked position. Now, please fasten your seat belt. Thank you. 本班機即將降落於倫敦希斯羅機場。請各位旅客回到座位豎直椅背。如果桌子是放下來的，請回歸到原位置並扣上，並繫好安全帶。謝謝。
預報當地時間及氣溫	3	We are now approaching Tokyo Narita International Airport. The local time is 2:25 p.m. and the ground temperature is 25 degrees Celsius, or 77 degrees Fahrenheit. 本班機正接近東京成田國際機場，當地時間為下午 2 點 25 分， 地面溫度是攝氏 25 度，華氏 77 度。

感謝乘客搭乘

4 Captain David Chang and all the members of his crew thank you for flying with us today. We hope you enjoyed your flight and that we will have the chance to serve you again.

機長大衛・張與所有的服務員，感謝各位旅客搭乘本班機。希望各位旅客還滿意本次的空中之旅，期待能有機會再次為各位服務。

需在空中停留

5 We are now in a holding pattern over New York City. It will be another 15 minutes or so before we can land due to heavy air traffic. Thanks for your patience.

本班機目前在紐約市上空盤旋等候降落。因空中交通繁忙的緣故，本班機需再等候 15 分鐘左右才能降落，謝謝各位旅客耐心等候。

需轉降其他機場

6 We are sorry to inform you that due to the weather conditions in Singapore, it is necessary for us to divert our flight to Bangkok International Airport. We regret the inconvenience, and we will do our best to help you reach your final destination as quickly as possible.

敬向各位旅客致歉，因新加坡天候狀況的關係，本班機必須轉降曼谷國際機場，對於造成各位旅客的不便，深表歉意。我們將盡力協助各位旅客盡快抵達預定的目的地。

需緊急降落

7 We will be landing in five minutes. Please listen very carefully to the following instructions.

本班機將於五分鐘後降落，請仔細聽好接下來的指示。

8-2 轉機旅客須知廣播 043

轉機的候機地點	1	We will be on the ground at Amsterdam Schiphol Airport for about 50 minutes. Due to government regulations, transit passengers are required to disembark and to proceed to the transit lounge. Thank you. 本班機將停留阿姆斯特丹史基浦機場 50 分鐘。按當地政府規定，要轉機的旅客必須辦理過境手續，並前往轉機候機室等候。謝謝。
由服務人員安排轉機事宜	2	Transit passengers going through the United States with "Transfer-without-visa" status are requested to kindly identify themselves to our ground staff at the cabin door. They will escort you to your connecting flight. Thank you. 要在美國轉機且「免過境簽證」的旅客，請於下機後向門口的地勤人員表明身分，他們會陪同您前往轉機地點。謝謝。
告知因加油需停在第三地	3	We are approaching Anchorage International Airport. We will be making a brief refueling stopover here. It will take about 30 minutes. The aircraft will be continuing on to New York City. All continuing passengers please stay onboard. 本班機將暫停於安克拉治國際機場加油，時間約為 30 分鐘，過後將繼續前往紐約市。請要前往紐約市的旅客繼續留在機上。
轉機乘客的登機時間	4	This aircraft will be continuing on to Rome in one hour and 20 minutes. The reboarding time is 7:40 p.m. The local time now is 6:20 p.m. Please board the plane on time. 本班機將於 1 小時 20 分鐘後繼續前往羅馬，我們將於 7 點 40 分再次登機，現在本地時間為晚上 6 點 20 分，請各位旅客準時登機。

8-3 降落後廣播 044

要求乘客留在座位

1 We have landed at Sydney International Airport. Please remain seated until the aircraft has come to a complete stop. Thank you.

本班機已抵達雪梨國際機場。在飛機完全停穩前，請各位旅客留在座位上，謝謝。

提醒勿忘隨身行李

2 We have landed at Singapore Changi Airport. Please do not forget to take all your personal belongings. Thank you.

本班機已抵達新加坡樟宜機場，各位旅客請別忘了隨身行李，謝謝。

檢疫及隔離需注意事項

3 Passengers who are bringing in animals or plants, please proceed to the quarantine counter before entering the customs inspection area.

攜帶動植物的旅客，請於進入海關檢查區前，先至動植物檢疫櫃檯受檢。

每人均須填寫一份表格

4 The Australia Customs, Health and Immigration Authorities are very strict with their clearance. So would you please be sure to complete a separate immigration form for each passenger, including one for each baby or child. Thank you.

澳洲海關和健康及移民當局的入境標準非常嚴格，請各位旅客務必一人填一張入境表，包括嬰兒和孩童，謝謝。

填寫表格需知

5 According to US Immigration regulations, all passengers, except US citizens, are required to complete the I-94 form in duplicate. The form must be filled out properly and clearly in capital letters. All blanks in the form should be filled in. Please be sure that the carbon copy is as clear as the original. Thank you.

按美國海關規定，非美國公民的旅客都必須填 I-94 表，此表一式二份。表上所有的格位，都必須以大寫字母填寫，內容必須正確無誤。表上的所有欄位均需填寫，也請確認複寫的部分如同正本一般清晰可讀，謝謝。

Unit 3

Arrival
愉悅心情入境篇

Chapter

09 辦理入境手續 Immigration Procedures

情境式對話 入境海關對話 045

C → Customs Officer　J → Jeremy Fang

J	Excuse me. Is this the window for non-citizens?	請問一下，這是非公民的窗口嗎？
C	Yes. Your passport, boarding pass and disembarkation card, please.	是，請出示您的護照、登機證及入境登記表。
J	Here you are.	在這裡。
C	And what is your purpose for visiting Australia?	請問您來澳洲的目的是什麼？
J	Sightseeing. I am a tourist.	我是來觀光的。
C	Are you traveling alone?	您是一個人來嗎？
J	I am with a friend. We plan to stay here for one week.	我和一位朋友來，我們打算要待一個星期。
C	Where do you intend to visit?	您打算要去哪些地方？

J	We will stay in Sydney for three days, and then fly to Cairns. We're going to visit the Great Barrier Reef and do some snorkeling[1] there for three days. After that we will fly back to Sydney and it'll be the time to go home.	我們會在雪梨待個三天，然後飛去凱恩斯。我們會去大堡礁浮潛玩個三天。之後我們會飛回雪梨，然後就要回家了。
C	That sounds like a lot of fun.	聽起來很有趣。
J	Unfortunately, we only have enough time to visit these two places.	可惜我們的時間只夠玩這兩個地方而已。
C	Yes, there is a lot to see in Australia, that's for sure. One week is not enough. Where are you going to stay in Sydney and Cairns?	的確，澳洲有很多地方可以看，一個星期是不夠的。您們在雪梨和凱恩斯要住哪裡？
J	We've booked a hotel in Sydney and a B&B near the Great Barrier Reef. Here are the confirmation letters.	我們在雪梨的一間飯店訂了房，在大堡礁附近訂了一間民宿。這些是住宿處的確認回函。
C	OK. I have no more questions for you. Here's your passport. Enjoy your stay.	好了，我沒有別的問題了。您的護照還給您。祝您玩得愉快。
J	I will! Thank you!	我會的！謝謝！

[1] snorkeling [ˋsnɔrkəlɪŋ] (n.) 浮潛

9-1 轉機 046

詢問是否需換機	1	Do I need to transfer?	請問我需要轉機嗎？
	2	You don't have to change planes or check in again.	您不需轉機，也不需再次報到。
發轉機卡	3	Transit passengers to Seattle, please remember to pick up a transit card.	要轉機到西雅圖的旅客，請領取轉機卡。
找尋轉機櫃檯	4	Where is the transfer counter?	請問轉機櫃檯怎麼走?
	5	Follow the signs. You can't miss it.	請跟著那個指標走就可以了，你不會錯過的。
	6	It's on the second floor, near the exit.	請到二樓靠近出口的地方。
告知在某地轉機	7	I am transferring in Kuala Lumpur.	我要在吉隆坡轉機。
告知欲轉機到某地	8	I will transit to New Delhi.	我要轉機到新德里。
詢問登機時間	9	When should I reboard the plane?	請問什麼時候要回到機上？
詢問轉機班機的起飛時間	10	When will the transit flight take off?	請問轉機班機是什麼時候起飛？
	11	You can find the flight information on the monitor.	您可以在班機資訊佈告欄找到航班資訊。
詢問等候時間	12	How long do I have to wait here?	請問在這裡要等多久?
	13	You have to wait for about five hours.	您必須等大約五個小時。
遺失轉機卡	14	I lost my transit card. What should I do now?	我的轉機卡掉了，我現在要怎麼辦？
	15	Please go to the transfer counter. They will give you a new one.	請到轉機櫃檯，他們會再發一張新的給你。

機場標示 Airport Signs

初次抵達旅遊地時，可能會對入境大廳感到陌生，尤其是國際型的機場，入境大廳充滿了遊客，很容易迷路，而機場外的交通服務亦是多樣。以下介紹機場常見的機場標示，看懂了就不怕迷路。

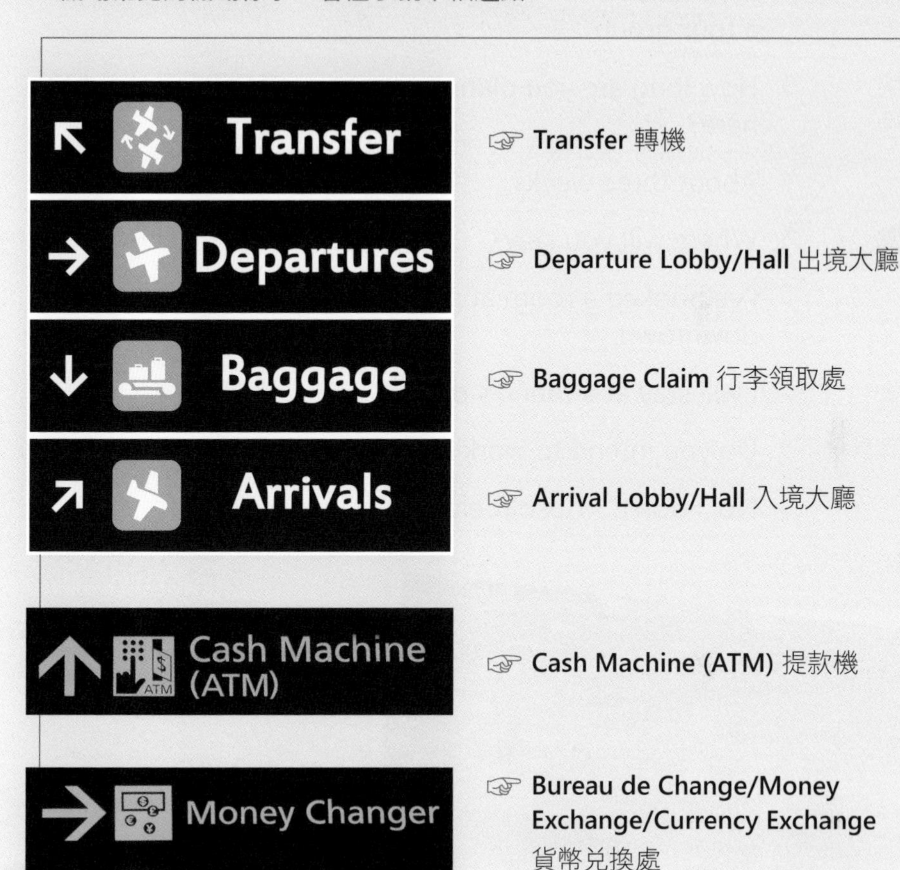

☞ Transfer 轉機

☞ Departure Lobby/Hall 出境大廳

☞ Baggage Claim 行李領取處

☞ Arrival Lobby/Hall 入境大廳

☞ Cash Machine (ATM) 提款機

☞ Bureau de Change/Money Exchange/Currency Exchange 貨幣兌換處

☞ Toilets 廁所

☞ Post Box 郵筒

☞ Information Center 旅客服務中心

9-2 護照查驗 047

旅行目的	1	What's the purpose of your visit?	請問您此行的目的是什麼？
跟團旅行	2	My friends and I are traveling with a tour group.	我和一些朋友跟團旅行。
停留時間	3	How long are you planning to be here?	請問您預計要在本地待多久？
	4	About three weeks.	大約三個星期。
停留地點	5	Where will you stay?	請問您會住在哪裡？
住飯店	6	I've booked a room at a hotel downtown.	我住在市區的飯店。
住朋友家	7	I will stay at a friend's place.	我住朋友家。
有無工作計畫	8	Do you intend to work here?	請問您會留下來工作嗎？
	9	No, I don't. / Absolutely not.	不會。

immigration counter

baggage carousel

9-3 提領行李 048

找尋行李提領區	1	Which baggage carousel is for flight VS 254?	請問維珍航空 254 班機的行李轉盤在哪裡？
找尋手推車	2	Do you know where I can find a baggage cart?	請問哪裡有行李手推車？
詢問行李是否已出來	3	Is this all the baggage for this flight?	請問這是此班機所有的行李嗎？
請求借過拿行李	4	Excuse me. That is my bag.	不好意思借過一下，那是我的行李。
確認外型相似	5	Your suitcase looks similar to mine. Would you mind if I check it?	您的行李和我的很像，我可以看一下嗎？
行李未到	6	My baggage is not here yet.	我的行李還沒到。

9-4 報失行李與尋回 049

找不到行李	1	I can't find my bags.	我找不到我的行李。
只找到一件	2	I checked in two pieces of baggage, but only this one came out.	我托運兩件行李，但我只找到這一件。
行李少一件	3	One of my bags is missing.	我有一件行李不見了。
找櫃檯	4	Where is the lost baggage counter?	請問申報行李遺失的櫃檯怎麼走？
描述行李外觀	5	What does your bag look like?	請問您的行李是什麼樣子？
	6	It's a red suitcase with wheels.	是一個有輪子的紅色行李箱。

行李抵達時間	7	What time can I expect the baggage to arrive?	請問我能知道我的行李什麼時候會到嗎？
	8	Around midday tomorrow. / Sometime tomorrow afternoon.	您的行李預計明天中午左右／大約下午會到。
是否需親自領取	9	Do I need to come back here for my bag?	請問我需要回來領行李嗎？
要求快速送達	10	Please send my bags to my hotel as soon as possible.	請儘快把我的行李送到旅館。
行李受損	11	My suitcase is broken.	我的行李箱壞了。
要求賠償	12	I expected to be compensated for this damage.	我希望能為這此損失得到賠償。
詢問是否賠償	13	Is the airline going to compensate me for this?	請問航空公司會賠償我嗎?

baggage cart

9-5 入境 050

出示證件	1	Your passport and customs declaration form, please.	請您出示護照和海關申報表。
不申報櫃檯	2	Anything in particular to declare?	請問您有東西要申報嗎?
	3	I have nothing to declare.	沒有。
申報現金	4	I am carrying more than US$10,000 in cash.	我有超過一萬美元的現鈔。
要求打開行李	5	Please open your suitcase.	請打開您的行李箱。
告知內容物	6	These are some souvenirs for my friends.	這些是一些要送朋友的紀念品。
是否攜帶菸酒	7	Any alcohol or cigarettes?	請問您有沒有帶酒或菸?
	8	Yes. One bottle of wine and a carton of cigarettes.	有一瓶酒和一條菸。
超過規定的數量	9	I have three cartons of cigarettes.	我帶了三條菸。
	10	I am sorry, but you're only allowed one carton.	很抱歉，依規定您只能帶一條菸。
詢問是否需額外付稅	11	Do I need to pay for it?	要繳稅嗎?
	12	The first carton is duty-free. You'll have to pay tax on the others.	第一條菸免稅，從第二條起要繳稅。
詢問需支付稅金	13	How much is the tax?	要付多少稅?
	14	You need to pay US$20 for each extra carton.	每多一條菸要 20 美元的稅。
不付稅的情況	15	If you don't want to pay the tax, we will have to confiscate this carton.	如果您不願繳稅，我們海關將會沒收這條菸。
允許通過	16	You may leave now.	您可以通關了。

旅遊資訊補充包

入境流程 Entry Procedures

坐了好幾個小時的飛機，終於抵達夢想的國度，心裡一定既緊張又興奮。
看懂以下通關的流程，通關將易如反掌！

1 Immigration Counter 入境審查

通過此關前，請先選擇正確的櫃檯。外國人辦理的櫃檯不外乎以下幾種：

- **Foreigner** 外國人專門櫃檯
- **Non-Citizen** 非公民專門櫃檯
- **Non-Resident** 非當地居民專門櫃檯

要準備好護照、入出境登記表和回程機票（**return ticket**），以便通關。
如果有旅館訂房證明（**hotel booking form**）或是朋友邀請信（**invitation letter**），通關會更順利。

2 Passport Inspection 查驗護照

查驗人員會查看簽證和護照有效期限（**passport expiration**），並詢問一些如旅行目的（**purpose**）、停留時間（**duration**）以及住宿（**accommodation**）等相關問題。

3 Bag/Baggage Claim 提領行李

到達提領行李區，依照螢幕上顯示的航班號碼，到指定的行李轉盤（carousel）找尋自己的行李。如果行李遺失或是破損，則須至行李遺失暨招領處（Lost-and-Found Office）或是行李服務處（Baggage Service），請航空公司處理。

4 Quarantine 動植物檢疫

如果攜帶動植物入境，須填妥動植物檢疫表（quarantine form），到檢疫處辦理手續。

報關單 CUSTOMS DECLARATION CN 22
(本件得由海關開拆 May be opened officially) Pos 401G (3/05)
Postal administration
香港郵政 HONGKONG POST
重要 Important!
請參閱背頁說明
See instructions on the back

☑ 禮物 Gift ☐ 商用樣本 Commercial sample
☐ 文件 Documents ☐ 其他 Other
(在適當方格內剔上"✓"號) (Tick as appropriate)

(1) 內載物品詳情及數量 Quantity and detailed description of contents	(2) 重量 Weight (公斤 kg)	(3) 價值 Value
Gift		N/A
只適用於商品 For commercial items only (4) 協制編號及 (5) 物品原產地 (如有) If known, HS tariff number (4) and country of origin of goods (5)	(6) 總重量 Total weight (公斤 kg)	(7) 總共價值 Total value

在下面簽署，以證明此報關單上列資料全屬正確，及此郵件並不載有任何法例或郵政規例或海關條例所禁寄的危險物品。本人的姓名及地址已載於郵件上。
I, the undersigned, whose name and address are given on the item, certify that the particulars given in this declaration are correct and that this item does not contain any dangerous article or articles prohibited by legislation or by postal or customs regulations.
(8) 日期及寄件人簽署
Date and sender's signature

5 Customs Declaration 海關申報

如果有東西需要申報，須至「申報」（declare）的櫃檯；若不需申報，則至「不申報」（nothing to declare）的櫃檯。這時須出示海關申報表與護照，有時須打開行李供海關人員檢查。

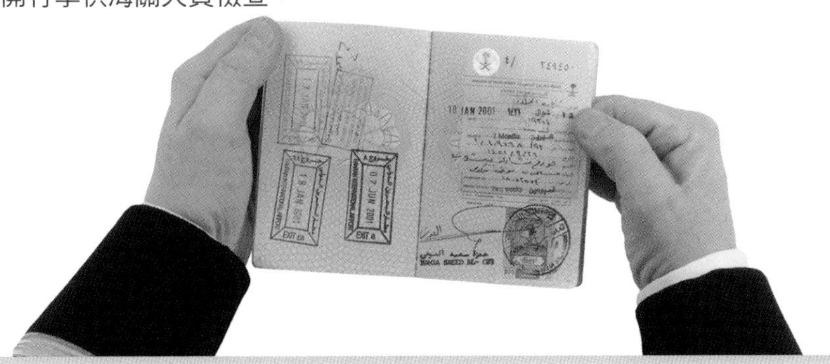

Chapter 10

機場服務 Airport Services

情境式對話 在機場訂旅館 051

S → Stella Black　C → Charles Hardy

S	Good morning. How may I help you?	早安，有什麼可以為您服務的嗎？
C	My wife and I would like to find a hotel in downtown Sydney.	我和我太太想在雪梨市區找間旅館住。
S	May I have your name, please?	請問您貴姓大名？
C	Charles Hardy. H-A-R-D-Y.	查理斯・哈迪，拼法是 H-A-R-D-Y。
S	How many days do you intend to stay, Mr. Hardy?	哈迪先生，你們預計要停留多少天呢？
C	Four nights.	四個晚上。
S	Let me see what I can do for you. Here is a nice hotel, only a five-minute walk from Central Park Station. The price is AU$120 for one night for a double room. The price also includes continental breakfast.	我看看可以怎麼幫你們。有一間不錯的旅館，從中央公園車站走只要五分鐘就到了。雙人房一晚是 120 澳元，包括歐式早餐。

C	Sounds good. We'll take it.	聽起來不錯，我們就住那間吧。
S	We charge an additional AU$10 for commission[1], which brings the total to AU$490 for the four nights.	我們會收您 10 澳元的手續費，四晚總共是 490 澳元。
C	OK. Here's my credit card.	好。這是我的信用卡。
S	Thank you. Here is your receipt[2]. To get to your hotel, take the metro and get off at Central Park Station. When you come out of the station, you will be on Queensway Road. Your hotel is located a short walk to the right. You can't miss it.	謝謝您，這是收據。要到旅館，請搭地鐵到中央公園站下車，出站後就是昆士威路。往右走一小段路，就是您要住的旅館了，很容易找的。
C	Thank you very much. You've been very helpful.	非常感謝妳，妳幫了很多忙。
S	You are welcome. Enjoy your stay in Sydney.	不客氣。祝您的雪梨行愉快。

[1] commission [kəˈmɪʃən] (n.) 手續費；佣金

[2] receipt [rɪˈsit] (n.) 收據

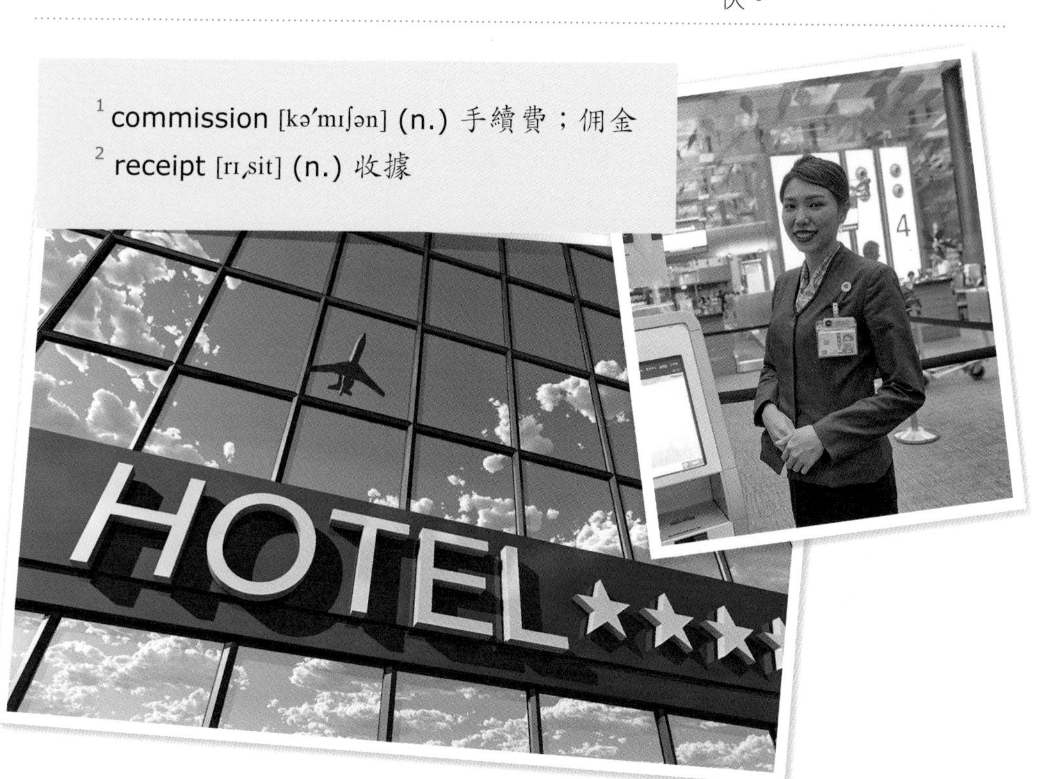

旅遊小句 Where can I exchange some money?

10-1 幣值兌換 052

尋找兌換處	1	Where is the Currency Exchange?	請問兌幣處在哪裡？
	2	Where can I exchange some money?	請問哪裡可以換錢？
詢問當日匯率	3	What is the exchange rate between the US dollar and the euro today?	請問今天美元對歐元的匯率是多少？
告知欲兌換金額	4	I would like to buy US$1,000, please.	我想換一千美元。
	5	I want to exchange New Taiwan dollars for US$1,000.	我想把新臺幣換成一千美元。
詢問手續費	6	Do I need to pay a handling charge?	請問要付手續費嗎？
	7	We charge a $1 commission on each deal.	每筆交易我們會收一美元的手續費。
兌換面額	8	How would you like your money to be changed?	請問您的錢要怎麼換？
	9	May I have eight 100s, three 50s, and some coins, please?	可以請幫我換成八張100，三張50元，剩下的換成零錢嗎？
要求換零	10	May I have this in coins, please?	可以請幫我換成零錢嗎？
	11	Can I have this in smaller bills, please?	請問可以幫我換成小鈔嗎？
要求開收據	12	May I have the receipt?	可以請幫我開收據嗎？

旅遊資訊補充包　英美幣制 UK and US Currencies

美國貨幣 The US Dollars

美國貨幣單位有 dollar（元）與 cent（分）
1 美元等於 100 分（1 美元通常使用紙幣）

1 cent = penny　　5 cents = nickel　　10 cents = dime
25 cents = quarter　　50 cents = half dollar　　100 cents = dollar

1 分　5 分　10 分　25 分　50 分

美英貨幣 US and UK Coins

美國	英國
1 cent（分）	1 penny（便士）
5 cents	5 pence
10 cents	10 pence
25 cents	20 pence
50 cents	50 pence
1 dollar（口語說法為 buck）	1 pound（口語說法為 quid）

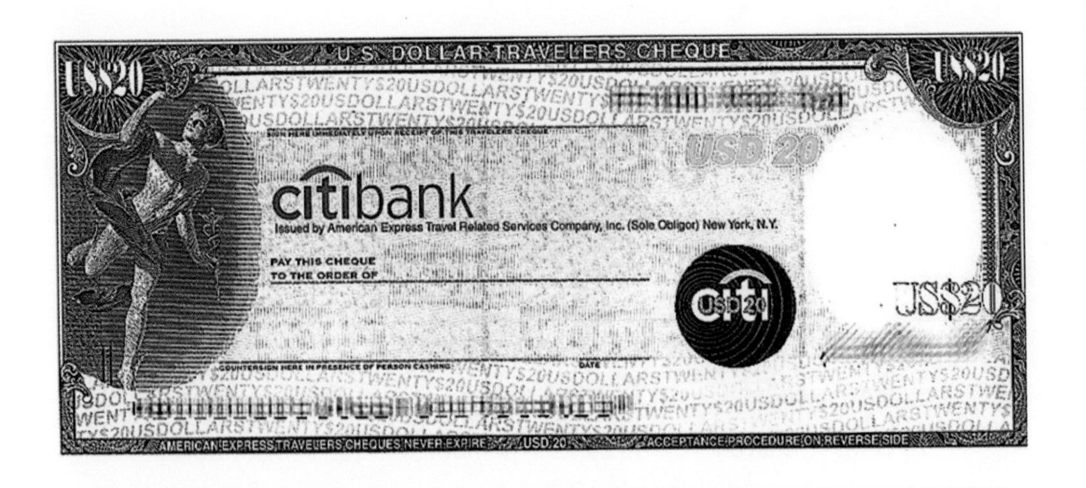

10-2　旅行支票兌換 053

要求將支票兌現	1	I would like to cash some traveler's checks.	我想要把這些旅行支票換成現金。
要求查看護照	2	Can I see your passport, please?	請出示您的護照。
要求簽名	3	Please sign each check.	請在每張支票上簽名

10-3　向旅客服務中心詢問住宿事宜 054

要求提供資料	1	Would you please provide me with some information about accommodations?	請問你們可以提供一些住宿資訊嗎？
可否代訂旅館	2	Could you book a hotel room for me?	請問你們可以幫我代訂旅館房間嗎？
	3	Can you help me find a place to stay in the city?	你們能幫我在這裡找個住的地方嗎？
預算限制	4	What's your budget?	請問您的預算是多少？
	5	Around $30 per night.	一晚大概 30 美元。
	6	I'm hoping to spend no more than $30 for one night.	我希望一晚不要超過 30 美元。

告知一般價格	7	I have no idea about the market price.	我對行情一點概念也沒有。
	8	$30 is the average price for a room in the downtown area.	市區一個晚上的行情是 30 美元。
詢問便宜的旅館	9	Is there anything cheaper?	有便宜一點的嗎？
要求住市中心	10	I prefer staying in the city center.	我比較想住市中心。
要求住車站旁	11	I want to stay near the train station.	我想住火車站附近。
詢問如何到旅館	12	How do I get to the hotel from the airport?	請問從機場怎麼去旅館？
	13	You can take the subway.	您可以搭乘地下鐵。
告知決定旅館	14	I'll take it.	我就住這間飯店吧。
告知手續費	15	Our commission is $5.	我們將收您五美元的手續費。
詢問付費方式	16	Do I need to make the full payment here?	請問要在這裡一次付清嗎？
	17	You can pay half here and the other half at the hotel.	您可以在這裡先付一半，到旅館再付另一半。
告知付費方式	18	You could pay the full fare here.	您可以在這裡一次付清。
	19	I prefer to pay in daily installments.	我想分天付。
	20	I'd like to pay half here first.	我想先在這裡付一半。
提供住宿證明	21	How do I prove that I have booked the room?	請問要怎麼證明我已經有訂房呢？
	22	I will give you a receipt.	我會給您一張訂房收據。

10-4 向旅客服務中心詢問其他資訊 055

廣播服務	1	Please page Mr. Ron Smith for me.	請幫我廣播一位榮恩・史密斯先生。
	2	Your last name, please?	請問您貴姓？
提供旅遊資訊	3	What are the most famous sightseeing places in London?	請問倫敦最出名的觀光景點是什麼？
	4	You can get the information from this tourist map.	您可以參考這份觀光地圖。
地圖服務	5	Do you sell city maps here?	請問有沒有賣市區地圖?

英文姓名 English Name

對華人來說，要搞清楚西方人的名字，實在不是容易的事。其實只要先熟記以下單字，就不會再把西方人的姓名搞混了。

英文姓名主要有三個部份：姓氏、名字跟教名（中間名）。其排列順序是：

名字 + 教名（中間名）+ 姓氏

教名大部分僅以首字母（initial）表示，但教名不是必有的。姓氏、名字和教名的英文用字，美國跟英國略有不同，如下：

範例

- **Jennifer Lawrence** 珍妮佛・勞倫斯
- **Robert Downey Jr.** 小勞勃・道尼
- **Donald J. Trump** 唐納・J・川普

名字	教名	姓氏
given name（美）	**Christian name**	**family name**
first name（英）	**middle name**	**last name**（美）
		surname（英）

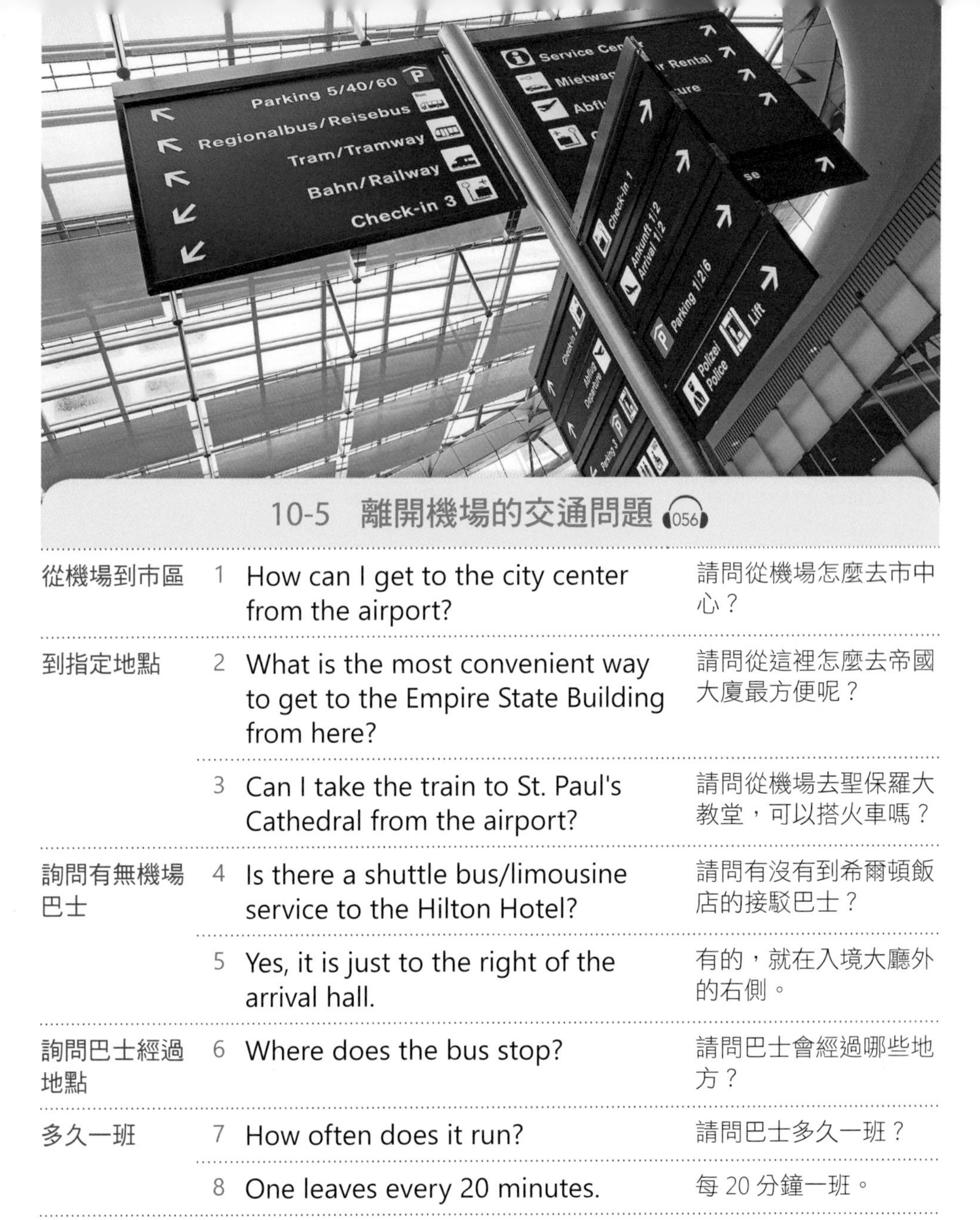

10-5 離開機場的交通問題 056

從機場到市區	1	How can I get to the city center from the airport?	請問從機場怎麼去市中心？
到指定地點	2	What is the most convenient way to get to the Empire State Building from here?	請問從這裡怎麼去帝國大廈最方便呢？
	3	Can I take the train to St. Paul's Cathedral from the airport?	請問從機場去聖保羅大教堂，可以搭火車嗎？
詢問有無機場巴士	4	Is there a shuttle bus/limousine service to the Hilton Hotel?	請問有沒有到希爾頓飯店的接駁巴士？
	5	Yes, it is just to the right of the arrival hall.	有的，就在入境大廳外的右側。
詢問巴士經過地點	6	Where does the bus stop?	請問巴士會經過哪些地方？
多久一班	7	How often does it run?	請問巴士多久一班？
	8	One leaves every 20 minutes.	每 20 分鐘一班。
詢問是否有來回票	9	Do you sell round-trip tickets?	請問有沒有賣來回票？
詢問價錢	10	How much does it cost to get to the city center?	請問去市中心要多少錢?
進出機場多加費用	11	All the taxis from the airport charge an additional $2.	所有從機場出發的計程車，要多加兩美元。

機場服務意見表 Airport Satisfaction Survey

WOULD YOU LIKE TO PRESENT ANY SUGGESTIONS OR IS THERE ANY EXPERIENCE YOU HAD AT OUR AIRPORT YOU WOULD LIKE TO REPORT TO US?

SUGGESTION

What can we do to serve you better in the future?

COMPLAINT

1. Where did it happen?

Departures	Arrivals
☐ Information Counter	☐ Immigration
☐ Check-in Counter	☐ Baggage Claim
☐ Airline Counter	☐ Travel Agency Counter
☐ Travel Agency Counter	☐ Exchange Counter
☐ Shop	☐ Customs
☐ Exchange Counter	☐ Information Counter
☐ Security Checkpoint	☐ Toilet
☐ Immigration	☐ Taxi/Bus Stand Point
☐ Boarding Gate	☐ Bank
☐ Restaurant	☐ Other
☐ Airport Lounge	
☐ Toilet	
☐ Bank	
☐ Other	

2. What happened? (Please provide a brief, factual description of the situation. State names of person(s) who were involved or who witnessed the situation.)

3. When did it happen?

Date: Time: Flight number:

Your Details

Name: ☐ Mr. ☐ Ms.

Address (Please note that we can't send you the results of your report if you don't leave an address.) :

Telephone number :

E-mail address (Optional) :

You are ☐ Airline crew ☐ Passenger ☐ Meeting/Seeing off a passenger ☐ Other

Signature:

Thank you very much for your suggestions and your time.

您願意提供建議給本機場，或針對您在本機場曾遇到的事情提出申訴嗎？	
建議	
您認為本機場可以提供那些更好的服務呢？	
投訴	
1. 發生地點？	
出境大廳	**入境大廳**
☐ 旅客服務處	☐ 移民局出入境檢查
☐ 劃位櫃台	☐ 提領行李處
☐ 航空公司櫃台	☐ 旅行社櫃台
☐ 旅行社櫃台	☐ 外幣兌換櫃台
☐ 商店	☐ 海關
☐ 外幣兌換櫃台	☐ 旅客服務處
☐ 安全檢查局	☐ 洗手間
☐ 移民局出入境檢查	☐ 計程車／巴士招呼站
☐ 登機門	☐ 銀行
☐ 餐廳	☐ 其他
☐ 機場貴賓室	
☐ 洗手間	
☐ 銀行	
☐ 其他	
2. 發生何事？（請簡要具體說明發生經過，列明有關人員或目擊者的姓名。）	
3. 何時發生？	
日期 : 時間 : 班機編號 :	
您的資料	
姓名： ☐ 先生 ☐ 小姐	
地址（請注意若無地址，我們無法告知您此意見書之結果。）：	
電話號碼 ：	
電子郵箱 (可寫可不寫) ：	
您是 ☐ 航空公司員工 ☐ 乘客 ☐ 接／送機人士 ☐ 其他	
簽名： 非常感謝您的意見跟時間。	

Unit 4

Accommodation
養精蓄銳住宿篇

Chapter 11

登記住宿 Checking In

情境式對話 // 旅館內住宿登記 057

F → Front Desk　R → Ronald Dickson

F	Good afternoon. What can I do for you?	午安，請問有什麼可以為您服務的嗎？
R	Hi, my name is Ronald Dickson. I have a reservation. Can I check in now?	你好，我叫羅納德．狄更森。我訂了一間房，現在可以辦住宿登記嗎？
F	Do you mind repeating your last name, please?	可以請您再說一遍您的姓氏嗎？
R	Dickson, D-I-C-K-S-O-N.	狄更森，拼成 D-I-C-K-S-O-N。
F	Let me see. Yes, Mr. Dickson, I have your booking record here. You booked a double room for two nights. Is that correct?	我查查。是，狄更森先生，有您的訂房紀錄。您訂了兩晚的雙人房，是嗎?
R	Right.	對。
F	Could you fill out this form first, please?	請您先填這張表。
R	No problem. (Filling out the form.) Here you are.	好。（填表中）寫好了。
F	Do you have your passport with you? I need to take a look at it.	您有沒有帶護照？我需要查看。

R	Sure. Here it is.	有，在這裡。
F	OK, Mr. Dickson, here are your passport, room key and breakfast vouchers. Your room number is 1266, on the twelfth floor. Breakfast is served every morning from 7 to 10 a.m. The dining hall is on the fourth floor.	好的，狄更森先生，您的護照還給您，這是您的客房鑰匙和早餐券。您的客房在 12 樓，1266 號房。早餐在每天早上 7 點到 10 點供應，餐廳在四樓。
R	Thank you. Oh, I have a meeting tomorrow morning. Can I have a wake-up call?	謝謝你。對了，我明天早上要開會，可以使用晨喚服務嗎？
F	Of course. What time do you want us to get you up?	當然可以。您要我們什麼時候叫醒您？
R	Twenty to seven, please.	請在 6 點 40 分叫醒我。
F	OK. I've set it up for you.	好的，我已經為您設定好了。
R	Thank you.	謝謝你。
F	You're welcome. Enjoy your stay at our hotel.	不客氣。祝您在本飯店住宿愉快。

hotel reception & service bell

receptionist & concierge

旅遊小句 When can I check in?

11-1 預訂房間的住宿登記 058

辦理住宿	1	Hello. I would like to check in.	你好，我要辦住宿。
可辦理住宿時間	2	When can I check in?	請問什麼時候可以辦住宿？
	3	You can check in after 2 p.m.	下午兩點以後都可以辦。
詢問提早入住	4	I took a red-eye to come to the city, and I am extremely tired now. Is it possible that I check in now?	我是搭乘紅眼航班來到這裡的，我現在非常疲憊；請問我可以現在登記入住嗎？
	5	I'm sorry, early check-in is not available for now, since we have no vacancy.	很抱歉，我們目前沒有空房間，無法讓您提早入住。
說明已先預訂	6	I booked the room from Taiwan.	我在臺灣就訂好房間了。
透過旅行社訂房	7	My travel agency booked a room for me.	我的訂房是旅行社幫我訂的。
	8	I reserved a room through my travel agency in Taiwan.	我在臺灣透過旅行社訂房。
說明訂房時間	9	I called last night to book a room.	我昨天晚上打電話訂了房間。
提供訂房確認單	10	Here is the confirmation slip.	這是預訂確認單。
訂房種類	11	What type of room did you reserve?	請問您是訂什麼房型?
	12	A single room.	單人房。

確認住房時間	13	Did you book the room for two days?	請問您是訂兩晚的房間嗎？
	14	No, it should be a week.	不是，是一個禮拜。
	15	I think there's a mistake. I booked a room for one week.	我想這有問題，我訂了一個禮拜的房。
填寫表格	16	Please fill out this registration form.	請您填寫這張住宿登記表。
	17	What is this section for?	請問這欄要填什麼？
需填項目	18	Is this for my home address in Taiwan?	請問這裡是寫我在臺灣的住址嗎？
查閱護照	19	May I see your passport, please?	可以請您出示護照嗎?
	20	Do you need to see my passport?	請問你要看護照嗎？
確認房間樓層	21	Is the room on the fifth floor?	請問房間是在五樓嗎？
鑰匙交管	22	Please return the key to the front desk when you leave the room.	您出門時，請將鑰匙交回櫃檯。
	23	Can I keep the key myself?	我可以自己保管鑰匙嗎?
行李服務	24	We will bring your baggage to your room right away.	我們稍後會幫您把行李送到房間。
	25	Thanks, but I will take care of it myself.	謝謝，但我自己提就可以了。
電梯位置	26	Where is the elevator?	請問電梯怎麼走？
	27	This way, please.	這邊請。

11-2 臨時詢問與辦理住宿 059

詢問是否有空房	1	Do you have any vacancies for tonight?	請問你們今天晚上還有空房嗎？
需要的房間種類	2	What type of room would you like?	請問您要住哪種客房?
	3	A single room for three nights.	單人房住三個晚上。
有空房	4	Yes, we have a vacancy.	沒問題，我們還有空房。
已客滿	5	I am afraid we have no vacancies right now.	很抱歉，目前所有的客房都滿了。
有房間但不符合需求	6	I am sorry, but the only room left is a double room.	很抱歉，只剩一間雙人房了。
	7	OK, I will take it.	好吧，那我就住那間。
請求介紹其他旅館	8	Could you please recommend another hotel nearby?	可以請你介紹附近還有哪家旅館嗎？
	9	You might try the Season Hotel across the street.	您可以試試對街的四季旅館。
僅能提供數天住宿	10	I am sorry, but we can only offer you a room for two nights.	很抱歉，我們只能提供兩個晚上的住房。

hotel key card

中間需換房	11	Would it be possible for me to change to another room later on?	請問晚一點還有房間可以換嗎？
	12	I could arrange for you to stay in a double room on your last night.	我可以在最後一晚幫您換到雙人房。
	13	I think I can find you a double room for the third night.	我想可以在第三晚幫您換到雙人房。
房間價錢	14	How much is it per night?	請問住一晚多少錢？
	15	It's €40 for the single room, and €63 for the double room.	單人房是 40 歐元，雙人房是 63 歐元。
詢問是否可給折扣	16	Is there a discount if I stay for three nights?	住三晚有優惠嗎？
	17	I can give you a 5% discount.	我可以給您打九五折。

11-3 住宿期間的相關事宜 060

詢問退房時間	1	When should I check out?	請問什麼時候要退房？
	2	Please check out before noon.	請在中午 12 點以前退房。
詢問早餐時間	3	When can I have breakfast?	請問我什麼時候可以用早餐？
	4	We serve breakfast from 7 to 10:30 a.m.	早餐在早上 7 點到 10 點半供應。
詢問是否供應報紙	5	Could you deliver a newspaper to my room each day?	可以請你每天都送報紙到我房間嗎？
	6	We have the *Los Angeles Times*, *Washington Post*, and *New York Times*. Which would you like?	我們提供《洛杉磯時報》、《華盛頓郵報》及《紐約時報》，您想看哪一種？
詢問其他服務項目	7	Are there any other services available?	請問飯店還有提供什麼服務？
	8	We also provide dry-cleaning, laundry and wake-up call services.	我們也提供衣物乾洗、水洗及晨喚服務。

詢問旅館提供設備	9	Do you have any other facilities in the hotel?	飯店還有什麼設備？
	10	We have a sauna, an indoor swimming pool, and several conference rooms.	我們提供三溫暖、室內游泳池及數間會議廳。
付款方式	11	How would you like to pay?	請問您要怎麼付款？
刷卡付費	12	Can I pay by credit card?	可以用信用卡嗎？
	13	Yes, but we don't accept American Express.	可以，但是不接受美國運通卡。
以旅行支票付費	14	Do you take traveler's checks?	你們收旅行支票嗎？
	15	Sure, but I'll need to see your passport.	是，但要請您出示護照。

飯店設備 Hotel Facilities

飯店內

fitness center gymnasium
（縮寫 **gym**）健身中心

convention center/conference hall
健身中心

buffet restaurant
自助餐廳

international cuisine restaurant
各國風味餐廳

indoor/outdoor swimming pool
室內／外游泳池

sauna
三溫暖

tennis court
網球場

squash court
壁球場

coffee shop
咖啡廳

golf course
高爾夫球場

aerobics studio
有氧舞蹈中心

nightclub/bar/lounge bar
夜店／酒吧

飯店設備 Hotel Facilities

客房內

- cable TV 有線電視
- pay-per-view 付費頻道
- Wi-Fi access 無線網路
- mini bar 迷你吧臺
- in-room air-conditioning control 室內空調
- voice mail answering service 語音答錄服務
- computer outlets 電腦專用插座

fire extinguisher 滅火器

kettle 熱水壺

hair dryer 吹風機

fax machine 傳真機

personal safety locker 私人保險箱

refrigerator/icebox（美語舊稱）冰箱

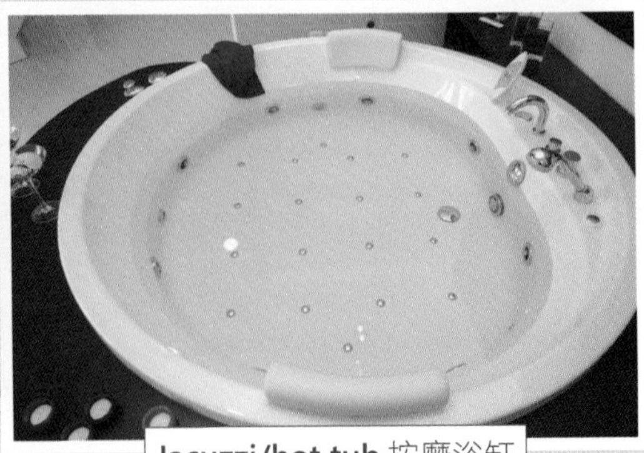

Jacuzzi/hot tub 按摩浴缸

旅館房間 Room Facilities

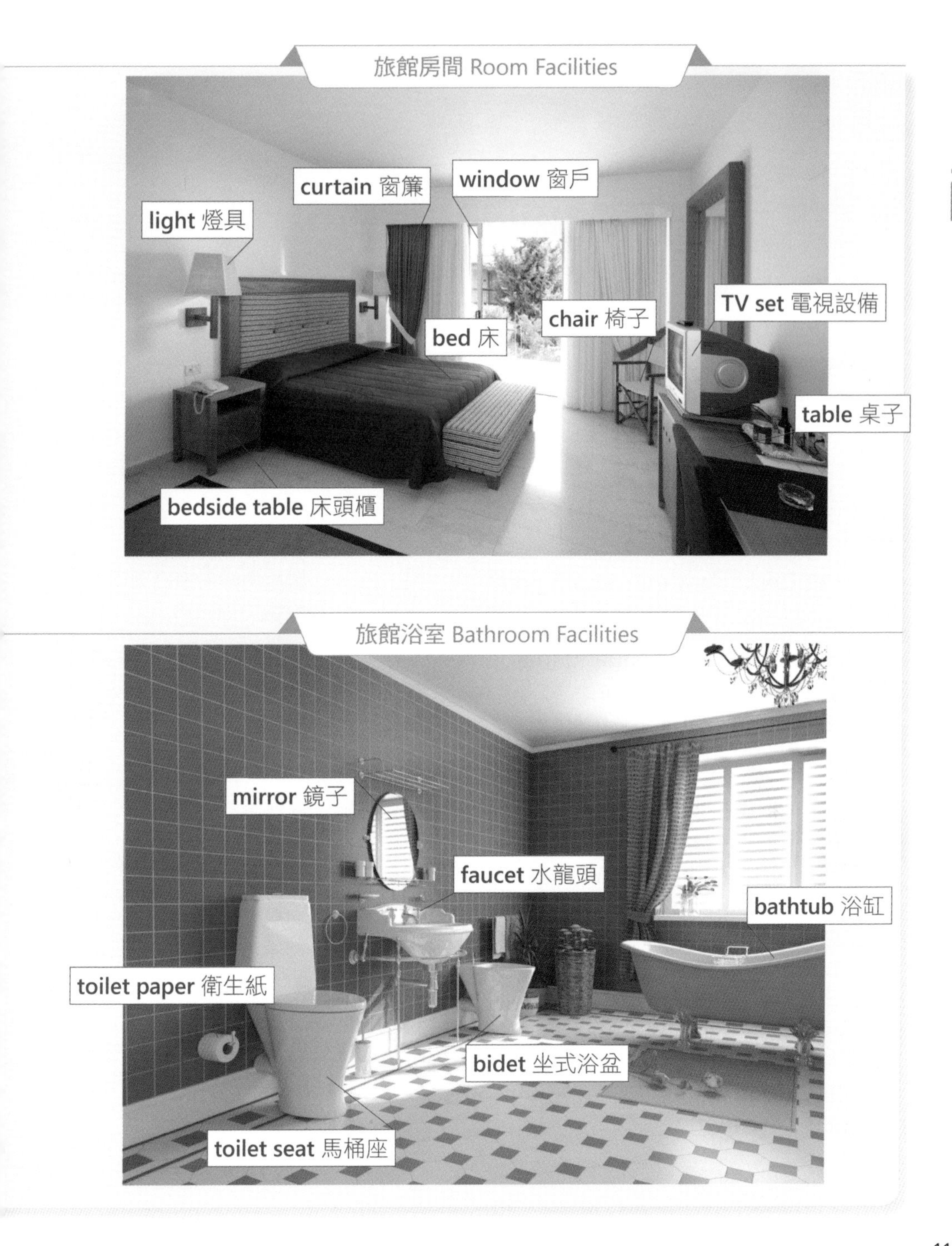

旅館浴室 Bathroom Facilities

Chapter 12

使用旅館服務與設施 Using Hotel Services and Facilities

情境式對話 打電話至櫃檯 061

F → Front Desk　A → Austin Huang

On the phone	電話中
F　Front Desk. How may I help you?	櫃檯您好。很高興能為您服務。
A　Hello, this is Austin Huang in Room 923. My office in Taiwan needs to fax me some information. Can I ask them to fax it to the hotel?	你好，我是 923 房的奧斯汀．黃。我臺灣的公司要傳真給我一些資料，我可以請公司傳真到飯店嗎？
F　That's no problem, Mr. Huang. Our fax number is 323-278-6600. Just ask whoever sends it to write down your name and room number on the top of the fax. When we receive it, we will send it right up to your room.	黃先生，這沒問題。我們的傳真號碼是 323-278-6600。只要請對方在文件的上方，註明您的姓名與房號就可以了。我們收到時，會立即送至您的客房。
A　That's great. By the way, could you please tell me how to use the telephone in my room? I'd like to make a call to Taiwan and several other cities here in the States.	真是太好了。另外，你能告訴我怎麼使用房間內的電話嗎？我想打電話到臺灣還有到美國的其他城市。

F	Sorry, Mr. Huang. I am afraid you can't make international and long distance calls directly from your room. But if you give me the phone number, I can place the call for you.	黃先生，很抱歉，客房裡無法撥打國際與長途電話。但要是您給我們號碼，就可以由我們為您代撥電話。
A	I see. In that case, would you please make a call to L.A. for me now? The number is 310-998-3100. I'd like to speak to James Lee, please.	這樣啊。那麼現在可以幫我打電話到洛杉磯嗎？號碼是 310-998-3100。請找詹姆斯．李。
F	Hold on a second. I will connect you. (A few minutes later.) Mr. Huang, your party is on the line now.	請稍候，我會為您接通。（數分鐘後）黃先生，對方現在已在線上。
A	Thank you very much.	非常謝謝你。

飯店服務介紹 Hotel Services

Laundry 衣物送洗

The hotel offers an excellent service. In the wardrobe you will find a price list and laundry bags.

本旅館提供優良的服務，衣櫃內附有價目表與洗衣袋。

Electricity 電源插座

220 volts. 適用 220 伏特。

Baby Sitting 保母服務

For this service, please call our housekeeper before 4 p.m.

若有需要，請於下午 4 點前聯絡客房管理部。

CHECKOUT 退房

We would like to remind you that checkout is 12 p.m.

提醒您，退房時間為中午 12 點。

Information (dial 4) 櫃檯

Please dial 4 for the front desk to request service.

請撥電話號碼 4，櫃檯將會為您服務。

Doctor 醫生

Please contact concierge.

請聯絡櫃檯人員。

Music 音樂

One radio channel and three genres of music.

音樂頻道有三種音樂可供選擇。

Messages (dial 9) 留言服務

Please dial 9 if you want to check whether there are messages for you.

若您想查看是否有您的留言，請撥電話號碼 9。

Housekeeper (dial 7) 客房清潔人員

Please contact housekeeping for any circumstance related to your room (e.g., lightbulb replacement, repairs, etc.). After midnight, please dial 9 for the operator.

若有任何與房間有關的問題（如更換燈泡、修繕等），請與客房清潔人員聯絡。午夜過後，則請撥 9 由接線生為您服務。

Lost and Found Property 失物招領

Please contact the housekeeper.

請聯絡客房管理部。

旅館的工作人員與職務 Hotel Staff and Their Duties

飯店的工作人員職權劃分清楚，所以要先清楚知道每個人的工作為何。若不清楚可向櫃檯詢問。

receptionist 櫃檯

負責受理登記、鑰匙交接、留言、傳達與房間分配。

porter 行李員

行李託運與保管。

housekeeper
清潔人員

打掃整理房間。

cashier 收銀員

計算住宿費用、貨幣兌換與管理寄物箱。

operator 接線生

早上晨喚服務與電話轉接。

concierge
櫃檯服務人員

預約劇場座位、旅遊行程或寄信。

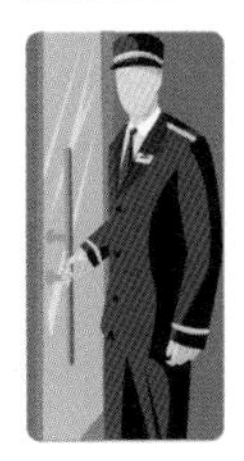

doorman 門房

替客人開／關飯店或計程車門。

給小費的秘訣 Tips

是否要給小費，因不同國家文化而異。

- 若帳單上寫「含服務費」，就不必再給小費。
- gratuity 表示「小費」。
- 非高級飯店不用給小費。
- 請旅館服務生送東西、拿行李、叫計程車或巴士，都應給予小費，飯店清潔人員清理房間時，可將小費放在床頭。

旅遊小句 *May I have a pot of hot water?*

12-1 房內設備的供應與修理 062

索取額外毛巾	1	May I have two more towels, please?	請問可以再給我兩條毛巾嗎？
	2	Sure. We will send them up to you in just a minute.	沒問題。稍後會有服務人員為您送上。
索取額外被子	3	May I have an extra blanket?	請問可以再給我一條毯子嗎？
要求換床單	4	The bedcover/bed sheet is dirty. Please have it changed.	這套床單髒了，請換掉。
要求供應熱開水	5	May I have a pot of hot water?	請問可以給我一壺熱開水嗎？
於開飲機取用熱開水	6	Where can I get some hot water to drink?	請問哪裡有熱開水？
	7	You can get hot water from the drinking fountain at the end of the hallway on each floor.	每層樓走廊走到底都有飲水機，您可以從那裝熱水。
詢問可否生飲水	8	Can I drink the tap water?	請問水龍頭的水可以喝？
	9	I'm afraid you can't drink the tap water.	很抱歉，水龍頭的水不能生飲。
冰箱內有免費飲用水	10	Where can I get some free drinking water?	請問房間裡有免費的飲用水嗎？
	11	There are two complimentary bottles of water in your fridge.	您的冰箱裡有兩瓶免費礦泉水。

使用空調	12	How do I operate the air conditioner?	請問空調怎麼用？
	13	Is this central air conditioning?	請問這是中央空調嗎？
空調壞了	14	The air conditioner is not working. Please have someone fix it.	我房間的空調沒辦法用，麻煩來修一下。
吹風機壞了	15	The hair dryer is not working. Please bring me a new one.	我這裡的吹風機沒辦法用，請幫我換新的。
	16	Can I borrow a hair dryer?	請問可以借吹風機嗎？
電燈壞了	17	The lamp doesn't work.	我房間裡的燈不亮。
保險箱的使用	18	How do I use the safety deposit box?	請問保險箱怎麼用?
請求幫忙打開保險箱	19	I forgot my password for the safety deposit box. Could you please help me?	我忘了保險箱的密碼，可以請你幫忙打開嗎？

12-2 旅館櫃檯服務 063

交付鑰匙	1	I'd like to leave my room key here while I am out.	我要外出，想要把鑰匙留在這裡。
索取鑰匙	2	May I have the key for Room 318?	我要拿 318 房的鑰匙。
忘了帶鑰匙	3	I locked myself out. Could you open the door for me?	我把鑰匙留在房間裡了，可以幫我開門嗎？
詢問是否可代收傳真	4	Can you receive faxes for me?	請問你們可以代收傳真嗎？
	5	Please indicate the name of the receiver and the room number clearly on the fax.	只要請對方在傳真上清楚註明您的姓名與房號就可以了。

詢問是否販售郵票	6	Do you sell stamps for international postcards here?	請問你們有沒有賣國際明信片的郵票？
	7	Sorry, we don't. But you can buy stamps in the post office. It's nearby.	很抱歉，我們沒有，但您可以在附近的郵局買到。
要求代為寄信	8	Can you mail this letter for me?	請問可以幫我寄這封信嗎？
	9	Sure/No problem at all. Just put your letter in the mailbox.	沒問題，請將您的信件投入這個郵筒。
請求寄快遞	10	Could you please send this parcel by express/special delivery?	請問可以幫我把這包裹寄快捷／限時專送嗎？
	11	Yes, and I will record it on your bill.	沒問題，費用會記在您的帳單上。
詢問是否有傳真或郵件	12	Are there any faxes or letters for Room 603?	請問有沒有給 603 房的傳真或信件？
	13	There aren't any letters for you, but there are two faxes.	有兩份傳真，沒有信件。
詢問是否有留言	14	Is there any message for Room 288?	請問有沒有給 288 房的留言？
要求寄物於櫃檯	15	May I leave this here? My friend will come to collect it later.	請問可以把這個留在這裡嗎？我朋友晚點會來拿。
	16	No problem. Please fill out this form.	沒問題。請填寫這份表格。
詢問是否可代沖洗照片	17	Would you please do me a favor and have these rolls of film developed?	請問可以幫我把這些底片送洗嗎？

12-3 使用電話與網路 064

詢問電話如何使用	1	Could you please tell me how to use the phone?	請問怎麼使用房間裡的電話呢？
	2	Please check the "Telephone Directory" in your room.	您的客房裡有「電話指南」可以參考。
打內／外線的方法	3	How do I make internal/external calls?	請問內線／外線怎麼撥？
	4	For internal calls, please dial the room number directly.	內線請直接按房號就可以了。
	5	For external/outside calls, please dial 0 first and then the number you want to call.	外線請先按「0」，再按您要撥的號碼。
撥打長途電話	6	Please make a long-distance (collect) call for me to Phoenix.	麻煩幫我打(對方付費的)長途電話到鳳凰城。
設定晨喚服務	7	I need a wake-up call at 8 a.m. tomorrow.	我要明天早上八點的晨喚服務。
	8	No problem. It's all set.	沒問題，幫您設定好了。
使用網路	9	Can I get online in my room?	請問房間裡可以上網嗎？
	10	You can go to the Entertainment Center on the second floor for Internet service.	您可以到二樓的娛樂中心使用網路。
使用無線網路	11	Do you provide Wi-Fi service?	你們有提供無線網路嗎？
	12	Yes, our Wi-Fi service is available in all rooms.	有的，您在房間即可享用我們的無線網路。
	13	Could you please tell me what the Wi-Fi password is?	可以請你告訴我無線網路的密碼嗎？
	14	Sure. It's on your receipt.	沒問題，它就在您的收據上。

從客房內撥打電話 Phone Calls

常見的幾種電話撥打的英文如下：

① 市內電話：local call
② 長途電話：long-distance call
③ 國際電話：international call
④ 對方付費電話：collect call

通常在飯店房間的電話上或電話旁會有電話的使用說明，以下為一基本範例：

① 市內或長途請先撥 0：For city or long-distance calls, please dial 0 first.
② 內線請直撥房號：Room-to-room calls, dial the room number.
③ 總機請先撥 9：Dial 9 for the operator.
④ 櫃檯請先撥 4：Dial 4 for the front desk.
⑤ 餐廳請先撥 5：Dial 5 for the restaurant.

如果您需要撥打對方付費電話或是國際電話，
請撥 9 轉接總機，總機人員將會為您撥號。

If you want to make a collect call or an international call,
please dial 9 for the operator. The operator will connect you.

12-4 客房用餐 065

客房用餐	1	Front Desk. What can I do for you?	櫃檯您好，很高興為您服務。
	2	I'd like to order room service, please.	我想要叫客房服務，麻煩你。
	3	Hold on a second. Let me put you through to room service.	請稍候，我幫您轉到客房服務部。
客房點餐	4	May I take your order?	請問您要點什麼？
	5	This is Room 506. Could you please send up a continental/European breakfast for us?	這是 506 號房，可以請麻煩送一份的歐式早餐嗎？

12-5 送洗衣物 066

詢問送洗服務	1	Do you have a laundry/dry-cleaning service?	請問你們有衣物水洗／乾洗的服務嗎？
告知送洗需求	2	These items of clothing need to be dry-cleaned.	這些衣服要乾洗。
詢問送洗方式	3	How do I request laundry service?	請問我要怎麼送洗衣服？
	4	Just leave your clothing items in the laundry bag and fill out the accompanying form.	請您將衣服放入洗衣袋裡，然後填寫袋上的表格就可以了。
收取衣物時間	5	When do you collect laundry?	請問什麼時候會收要送洗的衣服？
	6	Every day at 10 a.m.	每天早上 10 點會收。
衣物送回時間	7	When will my clothes be ready?	請問什麼時候可以拿回衣服？
	8	It usually takes two to three days. The laundry is returned at 4 p.m. every day.	通常要兩到三天。我們送回衣物的時間是每天下午 4 點。

詢問是否可以緊急處理	9	This is urgent. I need this suit back by 10 a.m. tomorrow.	這套西裝很急，我明天早上 10 點要穿。
	10	We charge an extra $8 for express service.	急件要加收八美元。
詢問收費方式	11	How much does laundry service cost?	請問送洗費用是多少？
	12	Please refer to the price list.	請參照價目表。

12-6 更改住宿事項 067

延長入住	1	Is it possible for me to extend my stay here for two more nights?	請問我可以再住兩個晚上嗎？
	2	I am afraid there's only one night available.	很抱歉，我們只剩一晚的空房了。
提早退房	3	I am afraid that I have to leave a day earlier because of a change of schedule.	我的行程改了，恐怕要提早一天退房。
	4	No problem. I will make the changes for you.	沒問題，我會幫您更改住房紀錄。
要求加床	5	Can you put an extra bed in my room?	請問我的房間可以多加一張床嗎？
	6	We can provide you with a cot.	我們可以提供您摺疊式的小床。
要求換房	7	My room faces the street, and it's too noisy. May I change to a quieter room?	我的房間面對街道太吵了，可以幫我換安靜一點的房間嗎？
	8	I am afraid we have no vacancies now. I will let you know once we have a room available.	很抱歉，現在沒有空房。一有空房我會立刻告知您。

洗衣清單 Laundry List

① **Please list the quantity of each article, failing which, the hotel count must be accepted as correct.**
請列出每件物品之數目，若未列出，則以飯店收件數目為準。

② **The hotel is not responsible for things left in pockets. The management will not be responsible for any loss or damage to things left in clothing.**
飯店對於口袋內之物品不負保管責任，若衣物內之任何物品遺失或遭到損害，管理部門不負任何責任。

③ **Liability for damage to clothing is limited to no more than ten times the charge for laundering.**
衣物於送洗期間遭到損害，賠償不得超過洗衣費用之十倍。

④ **There is a 25% extra charge for same-day service after 9 a.m.**
每日早上九點後送洗的當日服務，加收 25% 額外費用。

NAME 姓名：
ROOM NUMBER 房號：
DATE 日期：
PLEASE TICK 勾選：
☐ **Return today** 當日還
☐ **Return tomorrow** 隔日還

Special Requests 特殊要求

☐ **Please mend, sew on button, remove stains, etc.**
請修補、縫上鈕子、去除髒污等。
☐ **Other** 其他 ______________

Men's 男性衣物	Number 數量	Price 單價
tie/necktie/cravat 領帶／領結／領巾		4.50
shirt 襯衫		8.50
silk shirt 絲質襯衫		10.00
pants/trousers/slacks 褲子		8.50
raincoat or trench coat 雨衣或風衣		12.00
jacket 外套		12.50
sport jacket 運動外套		12.50
blazer 休閒西裝外套		12.50
overcoat 大衣		16.00
tuxedo（dinner jacket） 燕尾服		12.50
dinner suit 西裝禮服		22.00
two-piece suit 兩件式西裝		22.00
three-piece suit 三件式西裝		23.00
vest/waistcoat 背心		3.00
sweater/pullover/jumper/jersey 毛衣／套頭衫／針織衫／毛線衫		8.50

Women's 女性衣物	Number 數量	Price 單價
gloves 手套		6.00
scarf 圍巾		4.50
shawl 披巾		6.00
blouse 上衣		8.50
silk blouse 絲質上衣		10.00
skirt 裙子		11.50
pleated skirt 百褶裙		18.50
shorts 短褲		11.00
culottes 褲裙		12.00
jeans 牛仔褲		8.00
pants/trousers/slacks 褲子		8.50
jacket 外套		12.50
coat 大衣		16.50
sweater/pullover/jumper/jersey 毛衣／套頭衫／針織衫／毛線衫		8.50
raincoat 雨衣		12.00
dress 洋裝		12.50
evening gown 晚禮服		20.50
lady's suit 女用套裝		23.50
pant suit 褲裝		20.50
underwear/bra 內褲／胸罩		4.50
Total 合計	**Guest's Signature** 簽名	

Chapter

13 退房 Checking Out

情境式對話 在飯店櫃檯辦理退房

068

F → Front Desk　D → Daphne Ai

D	Hi. I want to check out now. My room number is 702. Here is the key.	你好，我要退房，我是 702 房的房客，這是鑰匙。
F	Thank you, Ms. Ai. You have been with us for three nights at CA$78 per night, so your room total is CA$234. You also made one international call to Germany, two long-distance calls to Vancouver, and three local calls. Your telephone bill comes to CA$22.	艾小姐，謝謝您。您在本飯店住了三晚，每晚是 78 加元，所以住房費總共是 234 加元。另外，您曾撥了一通國際電話到德國，兩通長途電話到溫哥華，以及三通本地電話，所以電話費總共是加幣 22 元。
D	Right.	沒錯。
F	Our record shows that you also had one bottle of orange juice and one bottle of beer from the fridge. Is that correct?	我們的紀錄也顯示，您曾從冰箱取用一瓶柳橙汁與一瓶啤酒，沒錯嗎？

D	I am afraid there is a mistake. I didn't drink any juice or beer. All I had was two bottles of mineral water, but as I recall, the water is free.	好像有問題。我沒喝柳橙汁或啤酒，只喝了兩瓶礦泉水，不過我記得礦泉水是免費的。
F	Let me check again. Oh, you are right. I am truly sorry about that. OK, now, let's see. Your total bill is CA$256. How would you like to pay?	我幫您再查查看。噢，您說的沒錯，真的是十分抱歉。好的，可以看到您的帳單總金額是加幣 256 元。請問您要怎麼付款？
D	Credit card, please.	用信用卡，麻煩你。
F	OK. Please sign your name right here.	好的。請在這裡簽名。
D	Here you go.	簽好了。
F	Thank you very much, Ms. Ai. We hope to serve you again in the future.	艾小姐，非常謝謝您。希望將來還有機會再為您服務。

旅遊小句 I want to check out.

13-1 辦理退房 069

退房	1	I would like to check out.	我要辦退房。
提早付款	2	I will leave early tomorrow morning. Can I settle my bill now?	我明天一大早要離開，可以現在付款嗎？
要求晚點退房	3	My plane leaves in the afternoon. Can I check out later?	我是搭下午的飛機，可以晚一點再退房嗎?
	4	We charge an additional fee if you stay more than six hours.	如果您待超過六小時，我們會額外收費。

13-2 搬運及寄放行李 070

要求幫忙搬行李	1	Please send a porter to help me with my baggage.	請問可以派一位行李員來幫我搬行李嗎？
請人於指定時間搬行李	2	I am leaving at 10 a.m. tomorrow. Please have someone come and take my baggage to the lobby at that time.	我明天早上十點要離開，到時候請派人幫我把行李提到大廳。
寄放行李並填表	3	May I leave my baggage here?	請問可以把行李寄放在這裡嗎？
	4	Please fill out this form and attach it on your baggage.	請填寫這張表，貼在您的行李上。
詢問寄放行李時間	5	Could you keep my baggage until this afternoon?	請問可以幫我保管行李到下午嗎？
	6	You can take your luggage to the cloakroom.	您的行李放到行李房就可以了。
欲拿回物品	7	May I have my valuables back, please?	請問我可以拿回我的貴重物品嗎？
遺失行李牌	8	I lost my luggage tag.	我弄丟了行李牌。

13-3 結帳 071

冰箱的食物	1	Did you take anything from the fridge?	請問您拿過冰箱內的任何東西嗎？
	2	Two bottles of beer.	我拿了兩瓶啤酒。
帳單費用	3	Your total bill comes to CA$223.	您的帳單一共是 223 加元。
	4	Pardon me? CA$223?	你是說 223 加元嗎？
費用明細	5	May I have the itemized bill, please?	請問可以給我帳目清單嗎？
告知未使用但取的費用	6	I didn't make any outside calls.	我沒打過外線電話。
	7	I never had room service.	我沒叫過客房服務。
告知帳單有誤	8	There's a mistake with the bill.	這帳單有問題。
	9	I will double check it.	讓我再確認一下。
	10	I apologize for the extra charge.	抱歉，跟您多收費了。
確認費用明細	11	Is this the charge/fee for my international call to Hamburg?	這是我打電話到漢堡的國際電話費嗎？
確認費用	12	Is that everything?	請問帳單上包括所有項目嗎？
合作的信用卡	13	Which credit card gives me a discount?	請問有沒有哪家信用卡可以打折？
	14	You can get a 5% discount if you use an HSBC credit card.	如果您用匯豐銀行信用卡可打九五折。

Unit 5

Transport
四通八達交通篇

Chapter 14 搭乘計程車 Taking a Taxi

情境式對話 // 呼叫計程車服務 (072)

H → Happy Cab Company　M → Miriam Soong

H	Good morning! Happy Cab. What can I do for you?	早安，哈比車行，很高興為您服務。
M	Hello. I need a cab[1] tomorrow morning.	你好。我要叫明天早上的車。
H	Yes, Madam. Where would you like us to pick you up?	好的，女士。請問您希望我們去哪裡接您？
M	I'm staying at City Hotel.	我住在城市旅館。
H	And where do you want to go?	那您要到哪裡？
M	I want to go to the Central Station.	中央車站。
H	No problem. What time would you like to leave?	沒問題。您要幾點搭車？
M	My train leaves at half past ten. So could you be at the hotel at 10 a.m.?	我要坐十點半的火車，所以可以請十點來旅館接我嗎？

H	Sure. May I have your name, please?	好的。請問貴姓大名？
M	This is Miriam Soong.	梅莉安・宋。
H	Ms. Soong, just in case, may I have your hotel room number?	宋小姐，方便提供您的旅館房號嗎？只是以防萬一。
M	I'm in Room 803.	803 號房。
H	OK. Ms. Soong. We will send a cab to the City Hotel tomorrow morning at 10. And you want to go to the Central Station. Is that correct?	好的，宋小姐，我們會在明天早上十點派車到城市旅館接您。您要搭到中央車站。以上正確嗎？
M	Yes. Can you tell me approximately[2] how much the fare will be?	正確。請問可以知道大概要多少錢嗎？
H	It depends on the meter, of course, but in your case, it will probably be around $7, including the pick-up fee.	我們當然是照哩程計費的。不過依您的情況來說，包含接送費大概會是七塊錢左右。
M	I see. Thank you. Good-bye.	我知道了。謝謝，再見。
H	See you tomorrow morning.	明天早上見了。

[1] cab [kæb] (n.) 計程車

[2] approximately [ə,prɑksəmɪtlɪ] (adv.) 大約

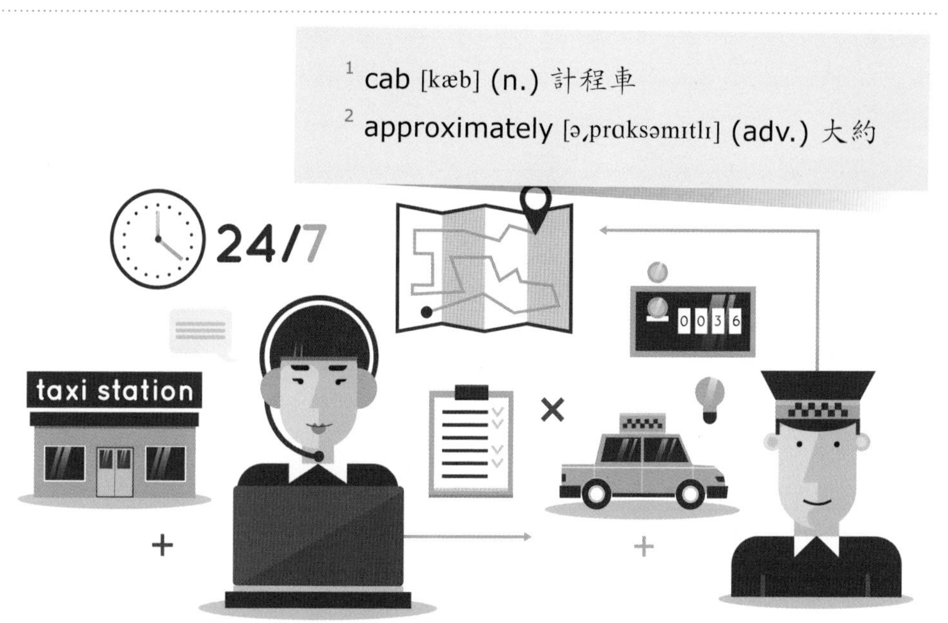

旅遊小句 Is there a taxi stand nearby?

14-1 招攔計程車 073

找尋計程車招呼站	1	Is there a taxi stand nearby?	請問附近有計程車站嗎?
詢問何處可叫車	2	Where can I catch a taxi?	請問哪裡可以叫計程車?
	3	The valet can help you to get a taxi in front of the hotel.	您可在飯店外面請服務人員替您招車。
請人代叫車	4	Please call a taxi for me.	請幫我叫計程車。
詢問是否可於路上叫車	5	Can I hail a taxi on the street?	我可以在路邊攔計程車嗎?
路上攔車	6	Taxi!	計程車！

14-2 電話預約叫車 074

打電話叫車	1	Is this Fast Taxi?	請問是法斯特車行嗎？
請對方馬上派車	2	Please send a cab to the Four Seasons Hotel.	請你們派一輛車來四季大飯店。
	3	The taxi will arrive/be there in ten minutes.	車會在十分鐘後到。
預約時間地點	4	I need to leave at ten tomorrow morning. Please pick me up at the Hilton Hotel.	我明天早上十點要走，麻煩請到希爾頓飯店來接我。
詢問乘客資料	5	May I have your family name, please?	請問您貴姓？
詢問費用	6	How much will the fare be?	請問要多少錢？
	7	It goes by the meter reading.	費用是照計費表來收的。
計費方式	8	The first kilometer is $3, and there is an increase of 20 cents for each additional 100 meters.	前一公里收三元，之後每 100 公尺加收 20 分。

14-3 告知前往地點 (075)

告知地點	1	Universal Studios, please.	請到環球影城。
告知路口	2	The intersection of Third Street and Flower Street, please.	請到第三街和花街的交叉口。
告知地址	3	Liverpool Street, No. 100, please.	請到利物浦街 100 號。
最近的商店	4	Please take me to the nearest supermarket.	請帶我到最近的超市。
給載明地址的紙條	5	To this address, please.	請到這個地址。

14-4 乘坐中提出詢問與要求 (076)

要求開後車箱	1	Could you please open the trunk?	可以麻煩開後車箱嗎？
要求幫忙提行李	2	Would you carry my bags for me, please?	可以麻煩幫我提行李嗎?
冷氣調節	3	Could you please turn up the AC?	可以麻煩把冷氣開強一點嗎？
開／關窗戶	4	May I open/close the window?	請問我可以開／關窗戶嗎?
	5	Could you please lower/raise the window a bit?	可以麻煩把窗戶開大／關小一點嗎？
趕時間	6	I am in a hurry. Can you please go a little faster?	我趕時間，可以麻煩開快一點嗎？
開慢一點	7	Could you please slow down?	可以麻煩開慢一點嗎?
詢問所需時間	8	How long does it take from here to Macy's?	請問到梅西百貨要多久？

14-5 告知下車處 077

前面停車	1	Please stop over there.	請停在那裡就可以了。
停在目標物前（用手指前方）	2	Please stop in front of the post office.	請停在郵局的前面。
過馬路後停車	3	Please stop on the corner after the next intersection.	過了下個路口後在街角停車。
路口下車	4	I want to get off at the next intersection.	我在下個路口下車。
要求等待	5	Do you mind waiting for me for a few minutes?	可以請你在這裡等我一下嗎？
要求告知抵達	6	I want to take a rest. Please let me know when we get there.	我想休息一下，到了請叫我。

taxi in the UK

taxi in Thailand

taxi in Germany

taxi in Hong Kong

14-6 乘坐中提出詢問與要求 078

問費用	1	How much is the fare?	請問多少錢？
	2	It's $4.50.	四塊五。
給小費	3	Here is $5. Keep the change.	五塊給你，不用找了。
要求找錢	4	I'd like my change, please.	麻煩找錢。
確認費用	5	What does the meter say?	請問計費表上是多少錢？
沒小額鈔票	6	I don't have any small bills.	我沒有小額的鈔票。
對費用有疑問	7	The price is different from the meter reading.	怎麼錢跟計費表不一樣？
	8	The extra 50 cents is for a dispatched taxi.	多出的 50 分是叫車費用。
費用加乘	9	There is a ten percent surcharge on night rides.	夜間搭乘要加收一成費用。

指路 Giving Directions

指引路徑的基本片語：

◊ **over there** 在那裡

◊ **next to** 在……旁邊

◊ **in front of** 在……前面

◊ **opposite of** 在……對面

◊ **on your right**
on the right-hand side 在右手邊

◊ **on your left**
on the left-hand side 在左手邊

◊ **behind**
at the back of 在……後面

◊ **at the corner of** 在……轉角處

◊ **go straight on** 直走

◊ **go down/along** 沿著……走

◊ **turn right** 右轉

◊ **turn left** 左轉

◊ **go past** 經過

Chapter 15

搭乘公車 Taking the Bus

情境式對話 詢問如何搭乘公車

079

B → Bus Station Attendant　M → Mike Hou

M	Excuse me, but I am new here. Can you provide me with some information?	請問一下，我是第一次來這裡，可以請你們提供一些資訊嗎？
B	Sure. What would you like to know?	當然可以。您想知道什麼？
M	I want to go to UCLA. Can you tell me which bus I should take, please?	我要去加州大學洛杉磯校區，請問可以坐哪一路公車？
B	Several buses will get you to UCLA from here. You can take any bus from number 180 to number 185.	有好幾路公車可以到，180 到 185 路公車您都可以搭。
M	How long does it take from here to UCLA?	那麼去到那裡要多久？
B	It depends on the traffic. Normally, it takes about 25 to 30 minutes.	要看路況。一般大概要 25 到 30 分鐘。
M	When does the next bus leave? Is there a long wait?	那下一班公車是什麼時候？要等很久嗎？

B	Oh, no need to worry about that. The buses run every five to ten minutes.	不用擔心，每五到十分鐘就會有公車。
M	That's great! By the way, how much is the bus fare[1]?	太好了。對了，搭公車要多少錢？
B	Let me check. The fare to UCLA is $1.25 one-way. It's cheaper if you buy a return ticket, which costs just $2.	我查查看。去加大洛杉磯校區單程要 1.25 美元，買來回票的話比較便宜，只要兩美元。
M	Can I get a ticket here?	我可以在這裡買票嗎？
B	I'm afraid not. You have to buy your ticket from the driver.	很抱歉，不是在這裡買票，要向公車司機買。
M	I see. Thanks a lot for your help. Goodbye.	原來如此。非常謝謝你幫忙，再見。

[1] fare [fer] (n.)（交通）費用

旅遊小句 // *Do I have to transfer?*

15-1 詢問搭車路線及轉車 (080)

索取資訊	1	Please give me a bus route map and timetable.	麻煩給我一張公車路線圖和時刻表。
詢問公車號碼	2	Which bus goes to Dodger Stadium?	請問到道奇隊球場要坐哪路公車？
	3	Bus numbers 20 to 25 all go to the baseball stadium.	20 到 25 路都有到棒球場。
班次時間	4	How often does the number 63 bus run?	請問 63 路公車多久一班？
	5	It runs every ten minutes during peak times and every 20 minutes during off-peak times.	尖峰時段是十分鐘一班，離峰時段二十分一班。
下一班時間	6	When does the next bus leave?	下一班車什麼時候會開？
早晚班次	7	When does the first/last bus leave?	首班／末班車是幾點開？
詢問是否到某處	8	Does this bus go to Sunset Boulevard?	請問這路車到日落大道嗎？
是否需換車	9	Do I have to transfer?	請問要轉車嗎？
何處轉車	10	Where should I transfer?	是在哪裡轉車？
何處候車	11	Where is the bus stop?	請問哪裡有公車站？
搭乘時間	12	How long does it take to get to UC Berkeley by bus?	請問坐公車到加州大學柏克萊校區要多久？
何處下車	13	Where should I get off for the City Library?	請問到市立圖書館是在哪一站下車？

確認路線	14 Which bus goes to Boston?	請問哪一路公車會到波士頓？
	15 Am I on the right bus for Boston?	請問我這是到波士頓的車嗎？
確認上車處	16 Where do I board the bus for San Diego?	請問往聖地牙哥的公車是在哪上車？
詢問有幾站	17 How many stops are there between here and Chicago?	請問從這裡到芝加哥會停幾站？

15-2 車資付費方式 081

詢問費用	1 How much is the bus fare to Central Park?	請問搭公車到中央公園要多少錢？
詢問應何時付費	2 Can I pay on the bus?	是上車投錢嗎？
告知付款方式	3 Can I get change back?	可以找零嗎？
	4 We don't give change on the bus.	車上不找零。
告知票種	5 I would like to buy a weekly pass/ one-day pass.	我要一張週票／一日票。
告知張數及地點	6 Two return tickets to San Francisco, please.	麻煩到舊金山的來回票兩張。
詢問票價	7 How much are the one-way and return tickets?	請問單程和來回票各是多少錢？

15-3 確認並要求告知下車車站 082

確認下車處	1	Should I get off here for Union Station?	請問聯合車站是在這裡下車嗎？
詢問轉車處	2	Should I get off at the next stop to transfer to Beverly Hills?	請問去比佛利山莊是在下一站轉車嗎？
詢問下車方式	3	Should I press the button when I want to get off?	請問我要下車是按那個鈕嗎？
告知要下車	4	Next stop, please.	下一站下車，麻煩你。
要求到站告知	5	Please let me know when we reach Chinatown.	到了中國城請告訴我。

15-4 坐過站或提早下車時 083

搭錯車	1	I took the wrong bus.	我坐錯車了。
坐過頭	2	I missed my stop. Please let me off.	我坐過站了，請讓我下車。
下錯站	3	I got off at the wrong stop and needed to get back on the bus. Here is my ticket.	我剛剛下錯站要再上車，這是我的車票。

15-5 搭乘長途巴士時的相關問題 084

出示證件	1	I have a bus/coach pass.	我有巴士卡。
要求額外保險	2	I would like the insurance, too.	我的車票要加保險。
	3	The insurance costs $3.	那要多付三塊。
置放行李	4	Can I take my bags on the bus with me?	我的行李可以放在車上嗎？
停留時間	5	How long will the bus stop here?	請問這站會停多久？
再開車的時間	6	What time do we leave again?	請問等一下是幾點開車？
詢問車上是否有洗手間	7	Is there a lavatory on the bus?	請問車上有洗手間嗎？

double decker bus

旅遊資訊補充包　巴士 Bus

名稱

在國外旅遊時，巴士依到達距離而有不同的稱呼。在市區行駛或開到鄰近地方的公車稱為 **bus**，若是長途的客運，在美國稱 **long-distance bus**，在英國則稱 **coach**。

種類

以外型區分，可分為單層巴士或雙層巴士（**double decker bus**）；後者為英國的「特產」，許多人到英國時，都會嚐嚐搭乘雙層巴士的滋味。若以功能來分，除了一般的公車外，在倫敦、紐約、雪梨等許多的大城市，都有觀光巴士（**tour bus**）。觀光巴士有時也會與其他大眾運輸工具配合，買了票後，除了可以在規定的效期內自由上下車參觀名勝古蹟、著名觀光景點外，還可以搭乘其他交通工具，非常方便。

付費方式

在美國，市區公車都是投幣式，車上不找零，所以上車前記得先準備一些零錢。若是要轉乘其他巴士，司機會給一張轉乘卡（**transfer card**），這樣下段旅程將可較便宜或是免費。

在英國則相反，上車購票時司機會找零，有時可以在上車時就告知是買來回票，相對會較便宜且方便，回程上車時出示票券即可。至於長途巴士，則大多是先在站內購票後再上車。

long-distance bus (coach)

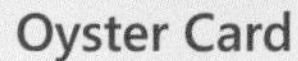

Oyster Card

Metro Card

票種

如果遊覽一個城市時會常搭乘巴士，不妨考慮較為優惠的票種，如一日票、週票等。購票後，只要在使用期限內，都可以不限次數使用。此類資訊通常在各地的公車站都會提供，也可在出發前先上網查詢。

折扣方式

這裡是指長途巴士的折扣方式。有時可先買巴士卡，買了卡後，乘坐所有長途客運皆可打折；另外，以英國為例，購買長途巴士的票，可以極低價（約 2 英鎊）加買乘客意外險，既安全又便利。

現今許多城市都有推出各自的交通卡，如紐約的 **Metro Card**、洛杉磯的 **Tap Card**，和倫敦的 **Oyster Card**，功能就如同臺北的悠遊卡，可供搭乘城市內的大眾運輸工具。交通卡本身有一定的成本價，然而車資必須另外加值，使用這種交通卡搭車大眾運輸工具，價格有機會比一般的票面價划算；再加上這種交通卡通常可供退款，當旅客離開的時候，可以退回未用到的金額，對於遊客而言非常經濟實惠。

Chapter 16 搭乘地下鐵
Taking the Subway

情境式對話 詢問車票折扣與優惠票

085

I → Information Center　T → Tracy Yu

T	Excuse me. I want to go to Chinatown. Can you tell me which tube line I should take and where I should get off, please?	不好意思，我要去中國城，請問我要坐哪條地鐵線，並在哪站下車？
I	No problem. Let me show you this tube map. Here we are now: Victoria Station. From here, take the Victoria Line to Green Park, and then change to the Piccadilly Line. Get off at Leicester Square. Chinatown is a short walk away.	我來為您解説一下這張地鐵路線圖。我們現在是在這裡：維多利亞站。從這裡搭乘維多利亞線到綠公園站，接著換到皮卡迪利線。在萊斯特廣場站下車，走一小段路就可以到中國城了。
T	Thank you. What's the fare?	謝謝。請問車票多少錢?
I	A single ticket to Leicester Square is £4.90. A return ticket is £9.80.	到萊斯特廣場站的單程票是 4 英鎊 90 便士，來回票是 9 英鎊 80 便士。

T	That sounds expensive. I am a student. Can I get a discount?	聽起來滿貴的。我是學生，這樣有優惠嗎？
I	Do you have an International Student Card? If you do, you can get 25% off. Or you can buy a monthly pass. That's quite a bit cheaper.	您有國際學生證嗎？有的話可以打 75 折，或者您也可以買月票，那樣會便宜不少。
T	Well, I'm not staying here that long. I'm only going to be here for about a week.	嗯，我不會在這裡待這麼久，大概只會待一個禮拜。
I	Then you can try a weekly pass. It's only £32.40 for Zone 1 and Zone 2. You can use it as many times as you like.	那麼您可以試試週票。在第一區與第二區之間搭乘只要 32 英磅 40 便士，可以不限次數搭乘。
T	That sounds great. I'll take one.	聽起來很棒，就這個了。
I	You have to go to the ticket counter and get your ticket there.	您要到售票處購買並取票。
T	I see. You've been very helpful. Cheers.	我知道了。你幫了很大的忙，謝謝。

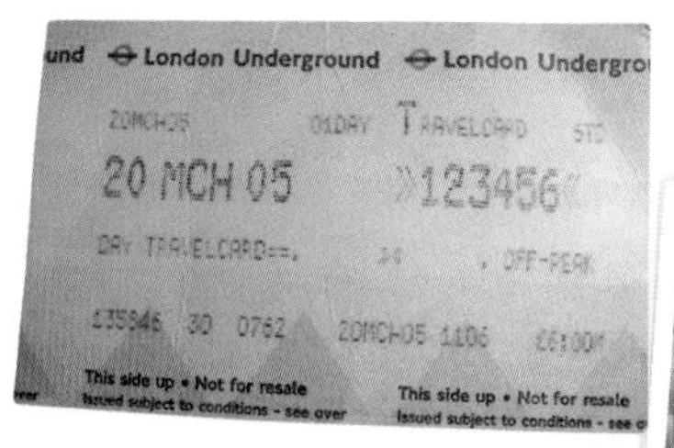

London underground ticket

gate

London underground ticket machine

旅遊小句 Do you have a student discount?

16-1 購買地鐵票 086

詢問買票處	1	Can I get a ticket from the ticket vendor?	請問可以從售票機買票嗎？
	2	Where should I go to buy a ticket?	請問票是在哪裡買？
機器是否找零	3	Can I get change from the ticket vending machine?	請問售票機會找零嗎？
換零錢	4	Where can I get some small change?	請問哪裡可以換零錢？
	5	Where can I change a $10 bill?	請問那裡可以換十元鈔票？
	6	You can go to the ticket counter/ exchange machine to get change.	您可以去售票處／兌幣機換。
詢問票種	7	What kinds of tickets do you sell?	請問有賣什麼票？
	8	We have daily, weekly, and monthly tickets.	我們有一日票、週票及月票。
票價	9	What is the price of a one-day pass?	請問一日票是多少？
辦理週票的資料	10	What do I need to buy a one-week pass?	請問買週票需要什麼資料嗎？
	11	We just need a passport-size photo.	要準備一張護照用的照片。
學生折扣	12	Is there a student discount?	請問有學生優惠嗎？
	13	Show me your international student card/ID, please.	請出示您的國際學生證。

詢問票期	14 When is my ticket valid till?	我的票可以用到什麼時候？
其他可使用的交通工具	15 Can I use my ticket for other means of transportation?	我的票搭乘其他交通工具嗎？
驗票方式	16 Do I need to insert the ticket in the slot?	請問票要插入這個插孔嗎？
	17 Which way should I insert the ticket?	請問票是哪個方向插入？
感應卡	18 This is a sensor ticket. You don't need to insert it.	這種票是靠感應的，不需插入。

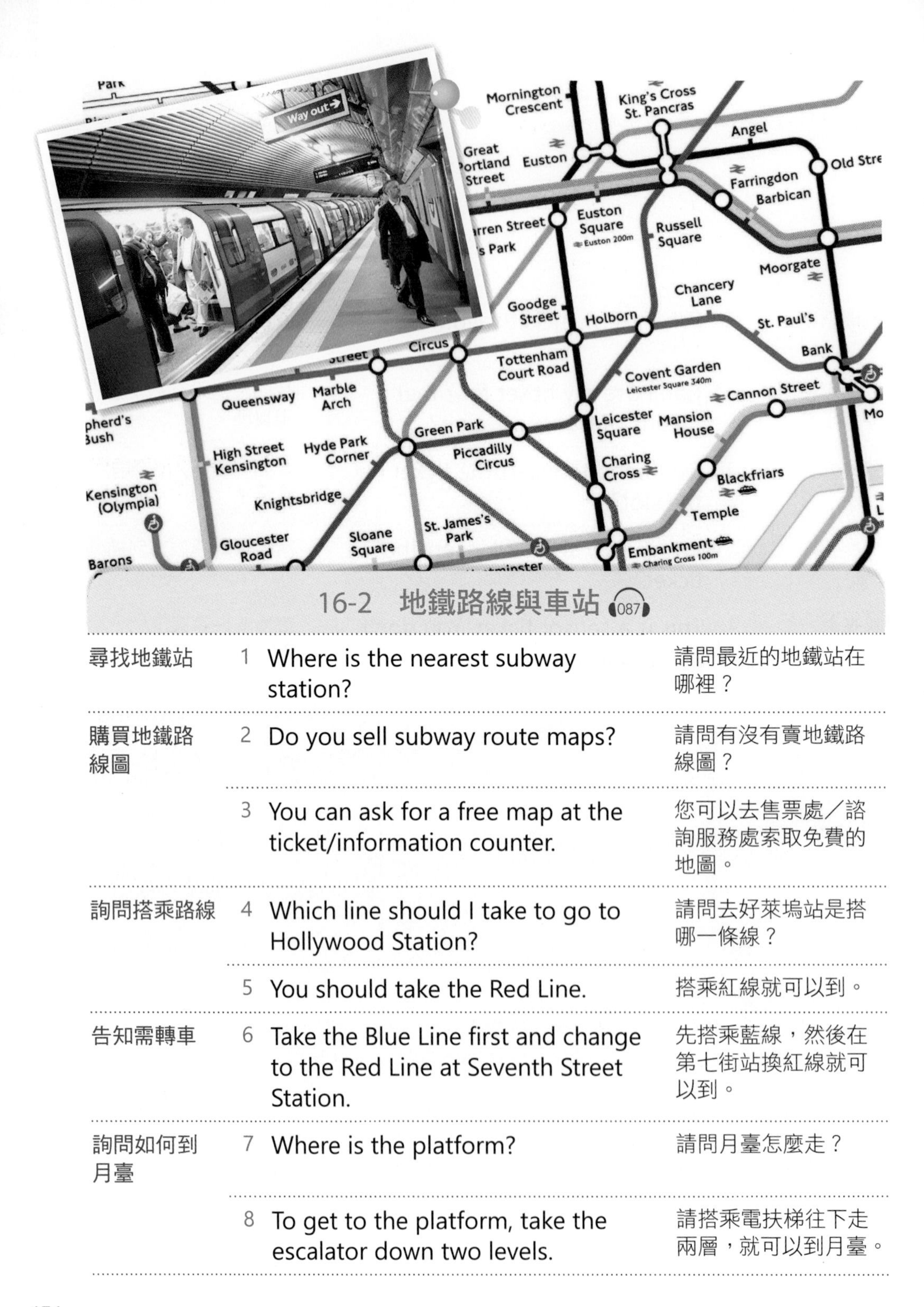

16-2 地鐵路線與車站

尋找地鐵站	1	Where is the nearest subway station?	請問最近的地鐵站在哪裡？
購買地鐵路線圖	2	Do you sell subway route maps?	請問有沒有賣地鐵路線圖？
	3	You can ask for a free map at the ticket/information counter.	您可以去售票處／諮詢服務處索取免費的地圖。
詢問搭乘路線	4	Which line should I take to go to Hollywood Station?	請問去好萊塢站是搭哪一條線？
	5	You should take the Red Line.	搭乘紅線就可以到。
告知需轉車	6	Take the Blue Line first and change to the Red Line at Seventh Street Station.	先搭乘藍線，然後在第七街站換紅線就可以到。
詢問如何到月臺	7	Where is the platform?	請問月臺怎麼走？
	8	To get to the platform, take the escalator down two levels.	請搭乘電扶梯往下走兩層，就可以到月臺。

詢問搭乘月臺	9	Where is the platform for trains going south?	請問哪個月臺是要南下的？
	10	You have to go across to the opposite side. This platform is for trains going north.	南下的要到對面，這個是要北上的。
確認月臺	11	Is this the platform for Brooklyn College?	請問要往布魯克林學院是在這個月臺嗎？
找尋出口	12	Where is the exit/way out for Chinatown?	請問中國城是走哪個出口？
	13	It's Exit Number 3. You will see a sign that says "Chinatown" right before the exit.	3 號出口，那個出口前會有牌子指示「中國城」。

國際學生證 ISIC

1953 年時，國際學生旅遊聯盟（International Student Travel Confederation）推動成立，此非營利組織也在國際發行國際學生證（International Student Identity Card，簡稱 ISIC），為世界各國的學生做學生身分的認證。

年滿 12 歲的學生（請注意，一定要是學生！）即可辦理，此為聯合國教科文組織（UNESCO）唯一背書認可，唯一國際通用的學生證件。

有了這張學生證，出國可以享有多重折扣，如可以購買學生優惠機票、博物館及美術館的優惠門票等；其他觀光景點的門票及火車票、公車票等，也都可以憑學生身分獲得不少優惠。出國旅遊的學子千萬不能少了它。

各國地鐵介紹 Subway Systems of the World

名稱

各國對地鐵的稱呼不一，以下是幾個地區的用法，找地鐵站時，只要找到正確名稱，跟著標示走就可以囉！

國家	用法	備註
① 美國	**Subway**	有些城市（如洛杉磯）稱為 **Metro** 或 **Metro Rail**，或者直接標示標示「**M**」。
② 英國	**Underground** **Tube**	英國的地鐵歷史最古老，因為在地底下如管子一般交錯分部，所以又稱為 **tube**。在英國，**subway** 是指地下道，找地鐵站時可千萬別走錯。
③ 法國	**Metro**	上車時，必須自行拉桿或按鈕，門才會開。
④ 香港	**MTR**	全名為 **Mass Transit Railway**。
⑤ 新加坡	**MRT**	全名為 **Mass Rapid Transport**。
⑥ 日本	**Subway** **Train**	日本許多大城市都有不同的地鐵或是火車，交通方便。

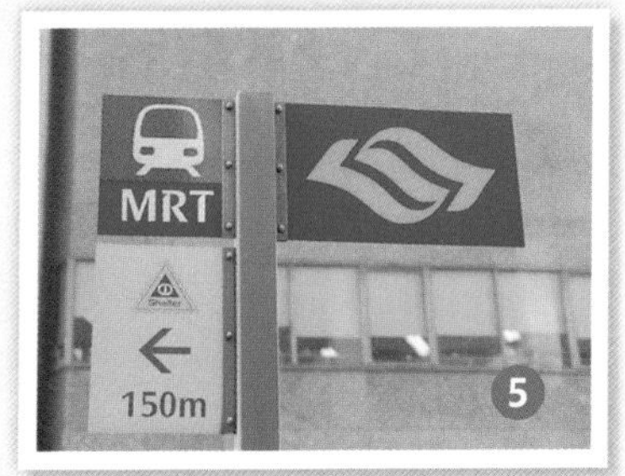

票種

一般車票都會以距離及旅遊時間來區分，因此約有以下幾種票種：

- **單程票（single-journey ticket）**
  如果只到某地，之後不會再搭車，買單程票就是最划算的選擇。

- **來回票（round-trip/return ticket）**
  如果確定回程，建議在買票時就買來回票，通常比兩張單程票便宜，亦可省下再次買票的麻煩。

- **區間票 （limited zone ticket）**
  如果只在某個區域活動，就可買該票種。如搭乘倫敦地鐵遊覽倫敦市中心，就可買 Zone 1 與 Zone 2 兩區的票。

- **一日票（one-day pass/daily pass/one-day travel card）**
  如果想在某地到處觀光，一天內會不斷出入地鐵站，購買此票種方便又划算。

- **週票及月票（weekly pass/monthly ticket）**
  如果待在某地時間較長，就可根據停留時間購買週票或是月票，有的會要求須附一張照片以貼在車票上。

Chapter

17 搭乘火車 Taking the Train

情境式對話 // 購買火車票 088

B → Booking Clerk S → Stacy Shen

S	Good morning. I want to buy a ticket to Seattle.	早安，我要買一張到西雅圖的票。
B	When do you want to leave?	請問您要什麼時候的？
S	Next Monday morning.	下星期一早上。
B	First class or economy class?	您要頭等艙還是經濟艙？
S	Well, coach will be fine.	嗯，經濟艙好了。
B	There are three trains departing for Seattle in the morning. When would you like to leave: 7:30, 9:40 or 11:50?	早上有三班車會開往西雅圖，分別是 7:30，9:40 與 11:50。您要哪一班？
S	The earliest, please.	最早的那一班，麻煩你。
B	OK. One-way or return?	好的，您要買單程票還是來回票？
S	Return. I am planning to come back on next Thursday or Friday night, but I'm not sure which yet. What should I do?	來回票。我預計是下星期四或星期五晚上回來，但時間還不確定。我該怎麼做呢？

B	Well, I can book you a return ticket for next Thursday night. If you decide you don't want to come back then, you can change your ticket at the Seattle's King Street Station. Of course, make sure you do it before the train leaves.	這樣的話，我可以為您訂下星期四晚上的來回票。如果您決定到時候不要回來，可以在西雅圖的國王街站更改車票。當然了，請您務必要在發車前更改。
S	That will be great. Thank you.	太好了，謝謝。
B	No problem. The total price is $45. If you do decide to change your ticket, you'll be charged a $2 change fee.	不用客氣。您的車票一共是 45 元。如果您確定要更改車票，我們會向您收兩元的更改手續費。
S	Is there any way I can get a discount?	請問有什麼優惠方案嗎？
B	Do you have a Railway Discount Card?	您有鐵路折扣卡嗎？
S	No, I don't.	沒有。
B	Sorry, but we only offer discounts to those holding the card.	那麼很抱歉，我們只提供各項優惠給持卡人。
S	I see. Here is $45.	我懂了。這是 45 元給你。
B	And here are your tickets. Thank you, and have a nice trip.	這是您的車票。謝謝，祝旅途愉快。

旅遊小句 Where is seat 29W?

17-1 購買火車票 089

直達車票	1	Are there any nonstop trains to Athens?	請問有沒有直達雅典的火車？
快車票	2	Two express tickets to Atlanta, please.	請給我兩張到亞特蘭大的快車票。
臥鋪票	3	One sleeper to Denver, please.	一張到丹佛的臥鋪票。
上下鋪	4	I prefer the upper berth.	我要上鋪。
	5	We only have lower berths left.	只剩下鋪了。
詢問是否有空位	6	Are there any seats available on the six o'clock train to Rome?	請問六點往羅馬的車還有位子嗎？
強調車種	7	I want to take an express train, not a local train.	我要搭快車，不是慢車。
詢問抵達時間	8	What time does the train reach/ arrive in Edinburgh?	請問這班車是什麼時候到愛丁堡？
詢問下班火車時間	9	When is the next train to Rotterdam?	請問下一班往鹿特丹的車是什麼時候？
使用火車票	10	I would like to use my ten-day pass starting today.	我從今天開始用十日火車票。
要求啟用火車票	11	Please validate my pass.	請啟用我的車票。
買青年票	12	What is the age limit for the youth ticket?	請問青年票是幾歲可以用？
買團體票	13	We have four in our party. Can we get the group rate?	請問我們有四個人，可以買團體票嗎？
買兒童票	14	What is the children's fare?	請問兒童票是多少錢？

17-2 前往火車月臺 (090)

找尋月臺	1	Which platform is for the train to Cambridge?	請問往劍橋是在哪個月臺？
	2	Platform 9A.	9A 月臺。
更改月臺	3	Has the train to Copenhagen been changed to platform 8B?	請問往哥本哈根的車是改到 8B 月臺嗎？
確認是否在某地停靠	4	Does this train go to Vienna?	請問這班車會經過維也納嗎？
找尋座位	5	Where is seat 29W?	請問 29W 的位子是在哪裡？
	6	Row 29, next to the window.	第 29 排靠窗。
找車廂	7	In which carriage can I find seat 29W?	請問 29W 的位子是在哪個車廂？

schedule board

express train

dining car

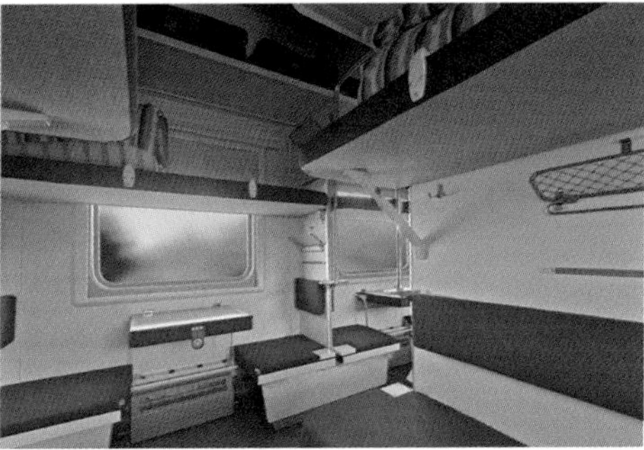
sleeper train

17-3 詢問搭乘火車的相關事宜 091

車上用餐	1	Is there a dining car on this train?	請問車上有餐車嗎？
	2	No, but you can get something to eat in the sixth carriage.	沒有，但您可以在第六車廂買到食物。
詢問是否有零食推車	3	Do you have a food trolley on the train?	請問車上有推車賣食物嗎？
餐廳及販賣部位置	4	The dining car is in the sixth carriage. You can also buy something to eat in both the first and the last carriages.	第六車廂是餐車，你也可以在第一節和最後一節車廂買東西吃。
洗手間位置	5	Where is the lavatory?	請問洗手間在哪裡？
	6	The restroom is located in the next carriage.	在下一節車廂。
驗票	7	Please show me your ticket.	請出示您的車票。
	8	Just a second. It must be here somewhere.	請等一下，它一定就在這裡。
告知坐錯車	9	You are on the wrong train. This train doesn't go to Montreal.	您坐錯車了，這班車不會經過蒙特婁。
	10	I think I'm on the wrong train. Can you help me?	我想我坐錯車了，請問你可以幫我嗎？
告知何處換車	11	You can get off at the next station and change to another train.	您可以在下一站下車換車。
	12	Where can I get help after I get off?	請問下車後可以去哪裡尋求幫助？
詢問還有幾站到目的地	13	How many more stops are there before we get to New York?	請問到紐約還有幾站？
詢問靠站時間	14	How long will the train stop here?	請問車會在這裡停多久？

火車旅遊 Traveling by Train

遊歐之旅

搭火車旅遊是非常方便又容易的事，在歐洲大陸更為便利，其中又分為許多不同的票種，如**歐洲二十八國火車通行證（Eurail Global Pass）**、**北歐四國火車通行證（ScanRail Pass）**、**巴爾幹半島火車通行證（Balkan Flexi Pass）**等，可以在事前向各大旅行社購買。

出國前，可以先確認是在單一國家或是在多國旅遊，有了事先的規畫，確認要去旅遊的國家、預計停留的時間、旅遊的人數等，就可以事先購買歐洲國鐵票，省去許多麻煩。此外，這些票有時也可搭乘一些指定的渡輪、蒸汽船或是觀光巴士，亦可以優惠價參加某些觀光行程等，相當划算。

另外，搭火車遊歐洲不可錯過的另一條路線，為英國倫敦到法國巴黎的**歐洲之星（Eurostar）**，此路線經由海底隧道穿越英吉利海峽（**English Channel**）連接英法兩國。

不論搭乘哪一種火車，最好都能事先確定再訂票，一旦開票後，不論是要退票或是更改時間、地點，都是一筆不算少的費用。

玩遍北美

在北美旅遊時，也有方便的火車系統可搭。如果想同時遊覽美國及加拿大，可以購買 Amtrak 公司出的**美國火車通行證（USA Rail Pass）**，然而此通行證主要通行路線還是在美國本土，無法觸及加拿大的各個城市。若是想以加拿大為主，則可購買 VIA 公司所出的**加拿大火車通行證（Canrail Pass）**。至於須注意的購票與乘車細節，則與歐洲的車票大致雷同。

鐵路時刻表 Railway Timetable

各國火車站通常每月會發行長程巴士、渡輪及火車時刻表

❶ **Table No.** 時刻表編號

❷ 火車路線
（此表為巴黎－慕尼黑－維也納－布達佩斯）

❸ **train type** 車種
EC：Euro-City trains
（歐洲跨國城際快車）
IC： Inter-City trains
（歐洲各國城際快車）

❹ **train number** 班次號碼

❺ **Notes** 註記
針對列車別在欄外加以註明，有無睡鋪或列車的呼叫方式等等。

❻ 停靠站名

❼ **d.**（**departure**）出發時刻

❽ 國境車站

❾ **a.**（**arrival**）到達時刻

❿ 需追加費用

⓫ 車內販售飲料點心的標記

⓬ 餐車

⓭ 列車名

⓮ **1, 2cl.** 頭等、二等車廂有床位

⓯ **2cl.** 二等車廂有簡易床鋪

⓰ 以數字代替星期幾

⓱ 直達

⓲ **v.v.** 反方向也一樣

① Table 32	② PARIS-MÜNCHEN-WIEN-BUDAPEST					
③ train type	EC	EC	IC			EC
④ train number	65	65	792			67
⑤ Notes	🍴 B⚡	🍸 C⚡ ⑩	🍸 ⑪			🍴 D⚡
⑥ Paris Est................ ⑦ d.	0478	0478	|	|	|	1914
Nancy................................d.	1031	1031	|	|	|	2000
Strasbourg ....d.	1154	1154	|	|	|	2014
Kehl ⑧ 🏛 ....d.	1205	1205	|	|	|	2049
Baden Baden .... ⑨ a.	1230	1230	|	|	|	2200
Karlsruhe Hbf ....a.	1248	1248	|	|	|	2238
Stuttgart Hbf ....a.	1343	1343	|	|	|	1914
Ulm Hbf ....a.	1453	1453	|	|	|	2000
Augsburg Hbf ....a.	1534	1534	|	|	|	2014
Munchen Pasing ....a.	1602	1602	|	|	|	2049
Munchen Hbf ....a.	1612	1612	|	|	|	2000
Salzuburg Hbf 🏛 .....a.	1755	1755	1914	|	|	2238
Bischofshofen.............a.	|	1827	2000	|	|	1914
Schwarzach St Veit ...a.	|	|	2014	|	|	2000
Badgastein...................a.	|	|	2049	|	|	2014
Villach Hbf ....a.	|	|	2200	|	|	2049
Klagenfurt Hbf............a.	|	|	2238	|	|	2200
Linz Hbf ....a.	1920	|	|	|	|	2238
Radstadt ....a.	|	|	|	|	|	|
Stainach Irdning.........a.	|	|	|	|	|	|
Selzthal........................a.	|	|	|	|	|	|
Grax Hbf.......................a.	|	|	|	|	|	|
Wien Westbahnhof...a.	2115	2115	|	|	|	|
Hegyeshalm 🏛 ....a.	|	|	|	|	|	|
Györ..............................a.	|	|	|	|	|	|
Budapest keleti..........a.	|	|	|	|	|	|

Notes

⑬ A--**ORIENT EXPRESS**- 🛏 1,2 cl., 🛌 2 cl. And 🚃 Paris-Wien and v.v.; 🛌 2cl. and Paris-Budapest and v.v.; 🚃 and 🍴 Salzburg-Budapest and v.v.; 🚃 and 🍸 Paris- Strasbourg and v.v.

B--MOZART- 🚃 and 🍴 Paris-Wien and v.v.

C-- 🚃 Paris –Graz and v.v. 🍴 Paris and Salzburg and v.v.

D--MAURICE RAVEL-🚃 and 🍴 Paris- Munchen-Budapest and v.v.

E--KALMAN IMRE- 🛏1, 2cl., 🛌 2cl. and ⑰ 🚃 Munchen-Budapest and **v.v.** ⑱

⑭ G-- 🛏**1, 2cl** ., 🛌 2cl. and 🚃 Paris-Munchen-Wien and v.v.

⑮ H-- 🛌 **2cl.** and 🚃 Munchen-Wien and v.v.

J-- BARTOK BELA- and 🍴 Frankfurt (Main) -Stattgart- Wien and v.v.

h--Wien Hutteidorf

n--Arrive 1038 on 2-6 July 23- Sep. 6 (not Aug. 16)

o-- Munchen Ost. ⑯

⑩ ⚡--Supplement payable.

Chapter 18 租車 Renting a Car

情境式對話 // 詢問租車細項 092

C → Car Rental Company　R → Rodney Lu

R	Hi. I'd like to rent a car for three days.	你好，我想租三天的車。
C	Then you've come to the right place. May I see your driver's license, please?	那您來對地方了，請出示您的駕照。
R	Here is my international driving permit.	這是我的國際駕照。
C	OK. What kind of car would you like?	好。請問您要租哪種車？
R	A compact will be fine. May I see your price and car list first?	小型車就好。我可以先看有什麼價位和車款嗎？
C	Sure. We have Honda, Toyota and Volkswagen models. Do you have a preference?	可以。我們有本田、豐田及福斯的車款。請問您有偏好嗎？
R	I think I will take the Honda Accord.	我想就本田 Accord 好了。
C	Great. The price is $50 per day. There is also a $100 deposit[1]. When you return the car, we will give you your deposit back if the car is not damaged or doesn't have any serious problems.	好的。價格是一天 50 元，另外要 100 元的押金。您還車時，如果車子沒有損壞或是其他嚴重的狀況，我們會把押金退還給您。

R	I see. Do you charge for mileage?	了解。請問行駛哩數怎麼收費？
C	No, there is unlimited mileage. Do you want to buy insurance?	那是免費的，沒有限制。您要保險嗎？
R	Of course. Full coverage[2], please.	當然，請保全險。
C	That's an extra $20 a day.	那麼我們一天會向您另收 20 元。
R	I understand. Where should I return the car?	我知道了。請問可以在哪裡還車？
C	You can return it to any of our branches here in the state.	您可以在我們全州的任何一家分店還車。
R	OK. Can I take a look at the car before I rent it?	好。我可以在租車前先看一下那輛車嗎？
C	Sure. This way, please.	沒問題。這邊請。

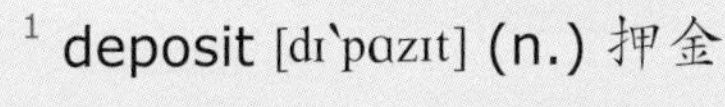

[1] deposit [dɪˋpɑzɪt] (n.) 押金

[2] coverage [ˋkʌvərɪdʒ] (n.) 保險項目

try (it)

international driving permit

旅遊小句 // I would like to rent a car.

18-1 詢問租車資訊 093

租車	1	I would like to rent a car.	我要租車。
租車期間	2	How long would you like to rent it for?	請問您預計要租多久？
	3	One week.	一個禮拜。
大小車型	4	What type of car do you prefer?	您要租哪種車？
	5	A compact car will do.	小型車就好。
車種	6	Manual or automatic?	您要手排車還是自排車？
何種車款	7	Is there a particular make or model you would prefer?	您有偏好哪一種車款嗎？
	8	Do you have a Civic 2000 here?	你這裡有喜美 2000 嗎？
國際駕照	9	Do you have an international driving license?	請問您有國際駕照嗎？
	10	Right here.	這裡。
押金	11	We need a deposit of $200.	您需付 200 塊的押金。
費用	12	How much is the daily rental?	一天的租金是多少？
	13	It costs $100 per day.	一天是 100 塊。
優惠	14	We're offering a special one-week rate of $500, with free insurance.	租一個星期優惠價 500 塊，加送保險。
加油	15	Is there anything I need to do when I check in?	我還車的時候需要做什麼嗎？
	16	The fuel tank is full now. You will need to refill it before returning the car.	油箱現在是滿的，您還車時也要是滿的。

保全險	17	May I have full insurance coverage, please?	可以保全險嗎？
	18	Sure. It's an extra $20 per day.	好的，一天另收您 20 塊。
保意外險	19	I only need the accident insurance.	我只需要保意外險就可以了。
GPS 的提供	20	Do you provide GPS for free?	你們有提供免費的 GPS 嗎？
兒童安全座椅的提供	21	Child safety seats need to be reserved, and the fee is $13 per day.	兒童安全座椅需要預約，費用是每天 13 塊。
限定還車地點	22	Where should I return the car?	請問是在哪裡還車？
	23	You need to return the car here.	車子要開回這裡。
還車地點不限	24	Can I return this car in Houston?	請問可以在休士頓還車嗎？
	25	Sure. Any of our branches in the state of Texas will be fine.	您可以在我們位於德州的任一家分店還車。（休士頓位於德州）
哩程限制	26	Is there a mileage cap?	行駛哩數有限制嗎？
	27	We have no mileage restrictions.	我們沒有哩程限制。
簽約前看車	28	May I see the car first before signing the contract?	簽合約前我可以先看看車嗎？
要求換車	29	I don't think I want this one after all. Can I see another?	我覺得這部車不合適，我可以看別輛嗎？

租車 Renting a Car

到美、加、英、紐澳等國旅遊時，租車也是一種很好的方式，可以隨心所欲到喜歡的景點遊玩。如果要租車，建議在出發前先上網或是打電話訂車，車商就會在約定的時間，將車子送到指定地點或是機場。機場裡的租車櫃檯也可以索取相關資料。最重要的是，在出發前一定要先辦好國際駕照，否則將無法租車。

另外，在英、紐澳等國開車是右座駕駛，不同於國內的左駕，開車時要小心。有些右駕國家可租到左駕的車，但不建議租此類的車，因為與其他車的座位相反，更容易發生危險。

租車前切記先試車，並檢查車子本身是否有刮痕或是受損，須事前與店員說清楚。另外，小到油錢該由哪一方支付，大到若發生意外或事故，該由哪一方承擔責任等情況，都必須先當面談清，以免事後衍生更多的問題，當了冤大頭。

18-2　開車上路 094

詢問方向	1	How do I get to Melbourne?	請問墨爾本怎麼去？
	2	Get on the highway and keep going south.	沿著公路南下就會到了。
迷路	3	I am lost.	我迷路了。
	4	Where can I get on the freeway?	請問高速公路怎麼走？
走錯路	5	I am going the wrong way.	我走錯路了。
轉彎	6	Where can I make a U-turn?	請問哪裡可以迴轉？
	7	Should I turn left at the first intersection?	請問是在第一個路口左轉嗎？
	8	Do you mean I should turn right at the second traffic light?	你是說在第二個紅綠燈右轉嗎？
路標	9	Are there any signs along the way?	請問沿路有什麼路標嗎？
停車	10	Can I park here for a while?	請問我可以在這裡停一下車嗎？
找停車場	11	Is there a parking lot around here?	請問這附近有停車場嗎？
	12	Do they have their own car park?	請問那裡有附設的停車場嗎？
停車費用	13	What does parking cost here per hour?	請問停車每小時多少錢？

道路標示 Road Signs

在美國，highway 指「公路、幹道」；高速公路可稱為 freeway、expressway、thruway 及 superhighway。同一條公路會因地方不同而變成高速公路或一般道路。除了東部某些地方，大部分的路段是免費的，即使要收費也很便宜。

美國公路有州際公路（Interstate）、國道（U.S. Route）及州道（State Route）。東西向的 highway 是偶數號，南北向的 highway 是奇數號，他們的分道點是以 highway 的號碼與方位標示（例如 South、North），而不是用目的地的名稱。

INTERSTATE ROUTE
州際公路

PEDESTRIAN CROSSING
行人穿越道

DO NOT ENTER
禁止進入

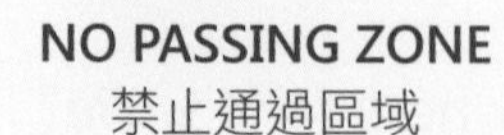

NO PASSING ZONE
禁止通過區域

STOP
停車再開

U.S. ROUTE
國道

RAILROAD CROSSING
鐵路平交道

NO RIGHT TURN
禁止右轉

國際駕照申請辦法

所需資料	費用	申請流程	備註
① 身分證或居留證正本 ② 六個月內的二吋彩色照片二張（不得使用合成照片） ③ 駕照正本（需在有效期內且距效期三年以上） ④ 護照影本（查核英文姓名）	250 元	① 備齊相關證件 ② 到各地監理所 ③ 填寫申請表格 ④ 當場領取國際駕照(處理時限：一小時)	除國內駕照被吊銷或註銷者，不得申請國際駕照外，國內駕照為「輕型機車」或「普通輕型機車」者，亦無法申請國際駕照。

DETOUR
繞道

MINIMUM SPEED 40
最低速限 40 英哩

DO NOT PASS
禁止超車

NO U-TURN
禁止迴轉

SPEED LIMIT 55
最高速限 55 英哩

NO TURN ON RED
紅燈禁止轉彎

NO LEFT TURN
禁止左轉

ONE WAY
單行道

YIELD
讓路

18-3 加油 095

找尋加油站	1	Is there a gas station nearby?	請問附近有加油站嗎？
加油種類	2	Fill it/her up, please.	請加滿。（英語用法中，男性常會以 she/her 稱呼車。）
	3	What kind of gas would you like?	請問要加哪一種油？
	4	Unleaded/Regular/Premium (gas), please.	無鉛／普通／高級汽油。
一公升費用	5	How much is it for one liter/gallon?	請問每公升／加侖多少錢？
何處付費	6	Where do I pay?	請問是在哪裡付錢？
尋求協助	7	How do I use this pump nozzle?	請問要如何使用油槍？
需求加油	8	I'm getting low on gas. I need to make a stop at the gas station.	我快沒油了，我需要去加油站。
	9	My tank is almost empty. Would you fill it for me, please?	我的油箱沒油了，可以請幫我加油嗎？
	10	Could you open your gas cap, please?	可以請你打開加油蓋嗎？
告知需加油量	11	Five gallons of premium, and could you check the oil, please?	要加五加侖的高級汽油，還有可以麻煩檢查一下機油嗎？
	12	Give me five gallons of premium and a quart of oil, please.	請加五加侖的高級汽油和一夸特的機油。
需求打氣	13	Could you pump up the tires, please?	可以請你將輪胎打氣嗎？

gas pump nozzle

汽油的講法 Gasoline

名稱／說法	美式英語	英式英語
石油	gas/gasoline	petrol
加油站	gas station/ filling station	petrol station

gas pump

加油須知 Fuelling up

國外的許多加油站都是自助式的，其中又分為兩種：

① 先繳費並告知服務員要加多少錢的油，繳費後直接將油槍插入油箱，等到計費器達到所繳費用時就會自動停下。

② 先自行加油，加完後再付費。

18-4 故障與意外 096

檢查煞車	1	There is something wrong with my brakes. Please check them for me.	我的煞車有點問題，請幫我檢查一下。
更換水箱	2	Your radiator is not good. You need a new one.	您的散熱器燒壞了，必須換一個。
車子拋錨	3	My car has broken down.	我的車子拋錨了。
車子爆胎	4	I've got a flat tire.	我的車子爆胎了。
檢查輪胎	5	Please check the tire pressure for me.	請幫我檢查胎壓。
找拖車	6	Please send a tow truck to this location.	麻煩派拖車到這個地點。
告知所在地點	7	Where are you now?	請問您現在在哪裡？
	8	I'm just past the 155-kilometer mark on the state highway.	我剛過州際公路 155 公里
	9	I'm just to the north of Exit 79.	我剛好在 79 號出口以北不遠的地方。
出車禍	10	I had an accident.	我出車禍了。
	11	I just got into a fender-bender.	我剛剛發生擦撞。
通知家屬	12	Please inform my emergency contact.	麻煩通知我的緊急聯絡人。
需要證明	13	Please give me an accident report.	麻煩給我一份事故證明書。

18-5 歸還租車 097

還車	1	I want to return this car. Here is the rental agreement.	我要還車，這是租車合約。
確認車況	2	Hold on a second, please. I need to check the car first.	請稍候，我要先檢查一下車子。
	3	Please wait here. I have to go through the return procedure first.	請稍後，我要先照還車程序來辦理。
有刮痕	4	There is a scrape on the door. What happened?	車門上有刮痕，請問是怎麼回事？
	5	I must have dented it when I opened the door. But it's not that bad.	一定是我開車門時不小心撞凹了，可是並不明顯。
	6	It was there when I rented it.	那是我租車時原本就有的。
要求付費賠償	7	Unfortunately, we're going to have to ask you to pay compensation.	我們恐怕要請您支付修理費。
	8	That's completely unfair.	那完全不合理。
要求扣除押金	9	We will use your deposit as compensation.	我們會扣留您的押金做為賠償。
加滿油	10	Is the gas tank full?	請問油箱加滿了嗎？
歸還證件	11	OK, then Mr. Tai. That's it. Here's your license and receipt. Thank you.	邰先生，一切都沒問題了，這是您的駕照和收據，謝謝。
	12	Everything checked out fine. Here's your license and your copy of the agreement. I am going to return your ID and give you the receipt.	一切都沒問題了，這是您的駕照和合約影本。您的身分證件還給您，這是您的收據。

Unit 6

Restaurants
垂涎三尺餐廳篇

Chapter
19 選擇餐廳 Choosing a Restaurant

情境式對話 電話訂位 098

R → Restaurant Reception　H → Hank Norris

R	Hello, Good Taste Restaurant. Good afternoon. How may I help you?	好美味餐廳您好。午安，很高興為您服務。
H	I would like to reserve a table for tonight.	我想要訂今天晚上的位子。
R	For how many people?	有幾位呢？
H	Four, please; at 7 o'clock.	四位，要訂七點。
R	I am afraid that we don't have any tables open at that time. Do you mind waiting until 7:30? There's a table available then.	很抱歉，那個時段已經客滿了。可以等到七點半嗎？那時候才有空位。
H	7:30 will be fine.	那就七點半吧。
R	Terrific. We can only hold the table for you for 15 minutes, so please be sure to arrive before 7:45.	好的。不過我們只能保留 15 分鐘，所以請務必要在 7 點 45 分以前到。
H	I understand. By the way, can we have a table in the non-smoking section next to the window?	我知道了。另外，我們可以選非吸菸區靠窗的位子嗎？

R	No problem.	沒問題。
H	Do you have a dress code?	你們有服裝上的規定嗎？
R	Not really. We're pretty casual. Just don't wear sandals and shorts. Other than that, anything is OK.	沒有，我們都是很輕鬆的，只是請不要穿涼鞋和短褲，除此之外都可以。
H	I see.	了解。
R	Can I have your name and contact number, please?	可以請您留下姓名和聯絡電話嗎？
H	Sure. My name is Norris. The phone number is 1361-666-4640.	我姓諾里斯，電話是1361-666-4640。
R	Thank you, Mr. Norris. We're looking forward to seeing you and your party this evening at 7:30.	諾里斯先生，謝謝您。本餐廳恭候您與您朋友於今晚七點半蒞臨。
H	Thank you.	謝謝你。

旅遊小句 What is the specialty of house?

19-1 推薦與尋找餐廳 099

請人介紹餐廳	1	Do you know any good restaurants around here?	請問你可以介紹這附近不錯的餐廳嗎？
	2	Which restaurant do you prefer?	您想去什麼樣的餐廳？
找特定餐廳	3	Are there any good French restaurants in this area?	請問這裡有不錯的法國餐廳嗎？
找便宜餐廳	4	Where can I find a cheaper restaurant in this neighborhood?	請問這附近有比較便宜的餐廳嗎？
告知餐廳地點	5	You can find many restaurants downtown on Charling Road.	您可以到市區的查令路，那裡有很多餐廳。
詢問餐廳位置	6	Do you know where the Delicious King is?	請問你知道美味王餐廳怎麼走嗎？
	7	Turn right here and then go straight for two blocks.	從這裡右轉，再過兩條街就到了。
詢問餐廳的電話或地址	8	Do you have the telephone number or address of Roster Restaurant?	你有羅思特餐廳的電話或地址嗎？
	9	You could ask directory assistance.	您可以打查號臺問。
請人指出方位	10	Could you please circle the location of the restaurant on this map?	你能幫我在地圖上圈出餐廳的位置嗎？
詢問菜色	11	What is the specialty of the house?	請問這家餐廳有什麼招牌菜？

詢問是否需預約	12	Do I need to make a reservation?	請問要先訂位嗎？
	13	Making a reservation is recommended, as we get very busy on weekends.	我們建議預約，因為週末常會爆滿。
請人幫忙預約	14	Could you please phone the restaurant and reserve a table for me?	請問你可以幫我打電話到那家餐廳訂位嗎？
可否步行	15	Can I walk there?	請問走路去可以到嗎？

19-2 預約訂位 100

詢問可否電話預約	1	Do you take telephone reservations?	請問你們接受電話訂位嗎？
	2	We don't accept reservations over the phone.	我們不接受電話訂位。
訂位	3	We would like to make a reservation for five people for this Saturday at 7 p.m.	我們有五個人，想訂這禮拜六晚上七點的位子。
	4	Sorry, we have no tables available for that time.	很抱歉，那個時段都客滿了。
	5	When will you have a table, then?	那請問幾點會有位？
靠窗的位子	6	Could we have a table next to the window?	有靠窗的位子嗎？
包廂位子	7	We would like to sit in a booth.	我們要訂一間包廂。
非吸煙區位子	8	We want to sit in a non-smoking area.	我們要訂非吸菸區的位子。

靠角落的位子	9	Do you have a corner table for five?	請問有五個人、靠角落的位子嗎？
詢問穿著規定	10	Do you have a dress code?	你們有服裝上的規定嗎？
	11	Please wear formal/casual attire.	請穿正式的服裝／便服就可以了。
詢問是否需穿西裝	12	Do I need to wear a suit and tie?	請問我需要穿西裝打領帶嗎？
座位保留時間	13	How long can you hold the table for me?	位子可以保留多久？
	14	We will reserve your table for 15 minutes.	我們會保留 15 分鐘。
詢問最低消費金額	15	What is the minimum per person?	每個人的最低消費是多少？

19-3 更改或取消訂位 101

告知會遲到	1	I'm going to be there 20 minutes late. Would you please hold my table?	我會晚 20 分鐘到，可以請你們保留位子嗎？
更改時間與日期	2	May I change this evening's reservation to tomorrow at noon?	請問我可以把今晚訂的位子改成明天中午嗎？
取消訂位	3	I want to cancel my reservation for tonight.	我想取消今晚訂的位子。

各國常見料理 Common Foods for Each Country

美國是民族大鎔爐，所以食物也包含了各民族的口味。其中以漢堡（burger）、牛排（steak）、炸雞（fried chicken）、薯條（fries）、熱狗（hot dog）、三明治（sandwich）為常見菜餚。此外，美國人在重要節日或全家團圓時，喜歡吃烤火雞（roast turkey）、烤牛肉（roast beef）等大餐。

United States
美國

hamburger 漢堡

steak 牛排

chicken nugget 雞塊

French fries
薯條

hot dog 熱狗

sandwich 三明治

最知名的要算炸魚和薯條（fish-and-chips）了。chips 其實就是美式英語的薯條（fries）。此外，烤牛肉（roast beef）、牧羊人派（Shepherd's pie）、約克郡布丁（Yorkshire pudding）等，也都是英國常見的食物；哈吉斯（haggis）則是蘇格蘭的傳統佳餚。

United Kingdom
英國

fish-and-chips
炸魚薯條

Shepherd's pie
牧羊人派

roast beef
烤牛肉

haggis
哈吉斯

Yorkshire pudding
約克夏布丁

法國菜因地理位置不同，烹調方法及口味也有差異。常見的有長棍麵包（**baguette**）、田螺（**escargot**）、魚子醬（**caviar**）、鵝肝醬（**foie gras**）、松露（**truffle**）等。

France
法國

baguette
長棍麵包
（法國麵包）

escargot 田螺

caviar 魚子醬

truffle 松露

foie gras 鵝肝醬

大家一定會馬上想到義大利麵（**pasta**）和披薩（**pizza**），其實義大利麵有非常多的種類，人們最熟悉的 **spaghetti**，指的是又細又長的麵；**macaroni** 是指通心麵，**penne** 是兩頭尖尖的斜管麵，**lasagna** 是千層麵，而包了餡的義大利水餃則稱為 **ravioli**。義大利菜常見的甜點有提拉米蘇（**tiramisu**）與義大利冰淇淋（**gelato**）。

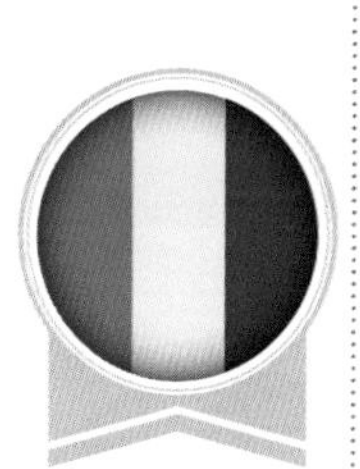

Italy
義大利

pizza 披薩

pasta 義大利麵

tiramisu 提拉米蘇

lasagna 千層麵

ravioli 義大利水餃

gelato 義大利冰淇淋

最有名的就是香腸（bratwurst）、豬腳（pork knuckles）和酸菜（sauerkraut）。德國香腸有超過 1,500 種的不同種類，有些可以直接當開胃菜，有些則需在食用前烹煮。

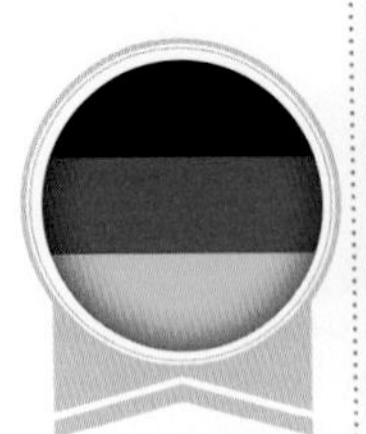
Germany
德國

bratwurst
德國香腸

sauerkraut
德國酸菜

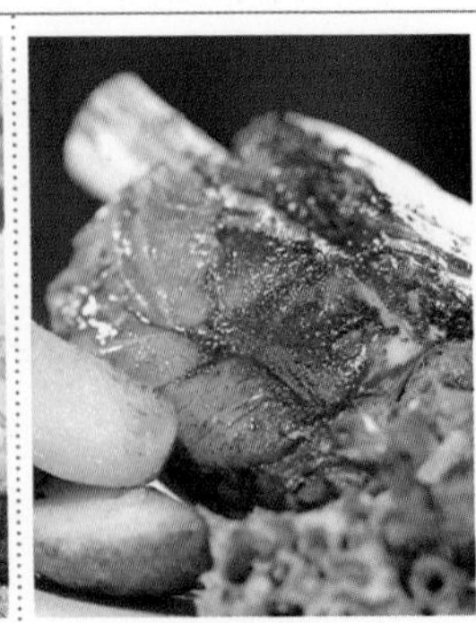
pork knuckles
德國豬腳

最常見的為以下幾種：壽司（sushi）、生魚片（sashimi）、拉麵（ramen）、蓋飯（donburi）、天婦羅（tempura）等；而湯品則以味噌湯（miso soup）最知名。

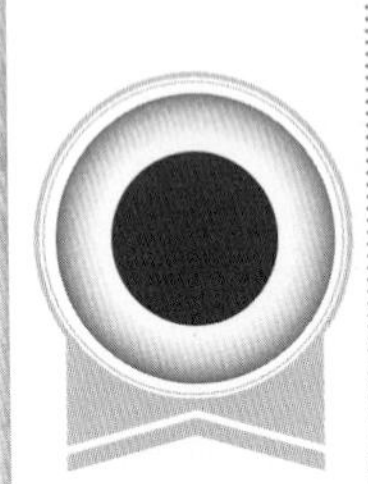
Japan
日本

sushi 壽司

sashimi 生魚片

ramen 拉麵

donburi 蓋飯

tempura 天婦羅

miso soup 味噌湯

泡菜（kimchi）是韓國料理中的重要成員，常與米飯一起食用，種類繁多；韓國菜餚以飯食為主，如石鍋拌飯（bibimbap）、韓式炒年糕（tteokbokki）等，另外還有常見的韓式烤肉（gogigui）、部隊鍋（budae jjigae）、韓式炸雞（Korean fried chicken）。韓式活章魚（sannakji）亦為相當有名的特色料理。

South Korea
南韓

kimchi 泡菜

bibimbap 石鍋拌飯

tteokbokki 韓式炒年糕

gogigui 韓式烤肉

budae jjigae 部隊鍋

sannakji 韓式活章魚

咖哩（curry）和印度烤餅是最有名的。咖哩種類繁多，添加不同的香料（spices）就會有不同的口味；而烤餅的也分有不同的等級與製作程序，其中饢（naan）為常見的一種。飲品類則以酸奶（lassi）與印度奶茶（Masala chai）最為知名。

India
印度

spices 香料

curry 咖哩

naan 饢

lassi 印度酸奶

Masala chai 印度奶茶

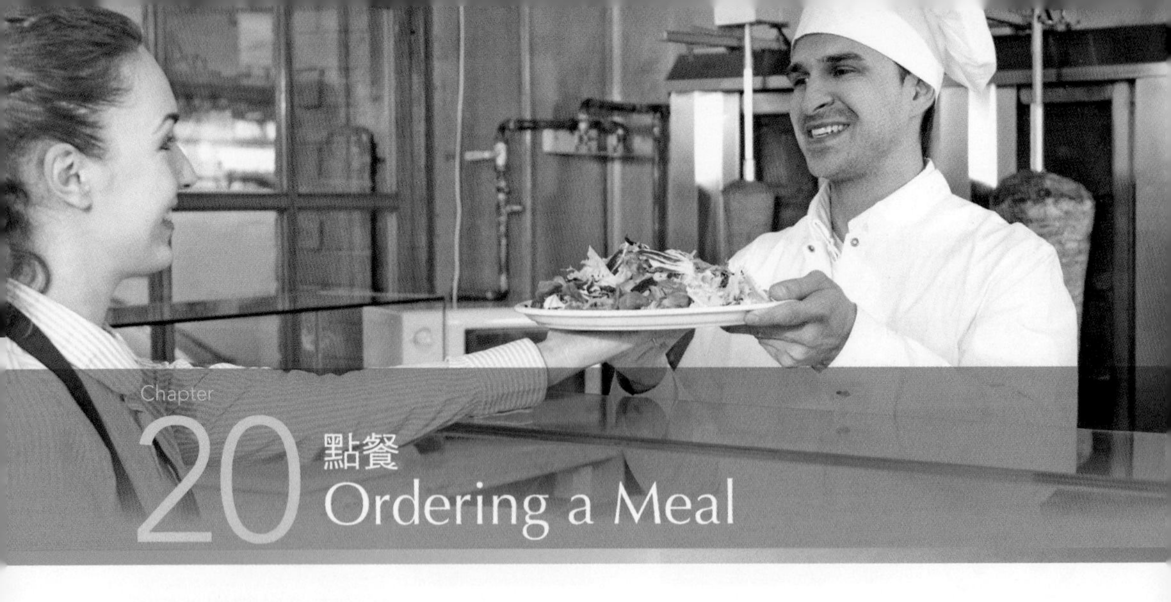

Chapter

20 點餐 Ordering a Meal

情境式對話 // 請求協助點餐 (102)

W → Waitress　C → Calvin Ting

W	Good evening, sir. Here is our menu. Would you like something to drink before you order?	先生，晚安。這是我們的菜單，請問點餐前要喝點什麼嗎？
C	Yes. Sparkling mineral water, please.	好，請給我氣泡礦泉水。
W	No problem. Are you ready to order now, or should I come back later?	好的。您是要現在點餐，或是我稍後再來？
C	This is my first time here. Could you help me to order?	我第一次來，可以請你幫忙我點菜嗎？
W	Sure. Would you like an appetizer?	可以啊。您要開胃菜嗎？
C	What do you recommend?	你有推薦的嗎？
W	Our most popular starters are steamed asparagus and smoked salmon.	我們的招牌開胃菜是清蒸蘆筍與煙燻鮭魚。
C	I will try the smoked salmon, please.	我試試煙燻鮭魚好了，麻煩你。
W	Good. How about a salad or a soup?	好的。那您要來份沙拉或湯品嗎？

C	I am not that hungry, so I think I'll skip the salad. But I would like some mushroom soup, please.	我不是很餓，就不點沙拉了，但是請給我一份蘑菇湯。
W	All right. How about your main dish? Is there anything you don't particularly like?	好。那您要點什麼主餐？您有沒有什麼忌口的食物？
C	I am allergic[1] to crab, and I don't eat lamb. What's your special today?	我對螃蟹過敏，也不吃羊肉。有什麼今日特餐嗎？
W	Iceland codfish[2]. It's very fresh and tender.	今日特餐是冰島鱈魚，這道菜非常鮮嫩。
C	That sounds good. I will take that.	聽起來不錯，就點那個好了。
W	Right. How about some dessert after your meal?	好。您餐後要來份點心嗎？
C	I would like a dish of vanilla ice cream and a pot of Earl Grey tea, please.	我要一份香草冰淇淋，還有一壺伯爵茶，麻煩你。
W	Very good, sir. I will get your order into the kitchen and be right back with your sparkling water.	沒問題，先生。我這就將您點的菜單送入廚房，並為您送來氣泡水。

[1] allergic [əˋlɝdʒɪk] (adj.) 過敏的
[2] codfish [ˋkɑdfɪʃ] (n.) 鱈魚

旅遊小句 A table for four, please.

20-1 預約訂位情況 103

告知已訂位	1	I am William Hong, and I reserved a table for this evening.	我今天晚上訂了位，名字是威廉・洪。
告知訂位時間與人數	2	I reserved a table for two at 8 p.m.	我訂了晚上八點兩個人的位子。
告知沒有訂位	3	We didn't make/don't have a reservation.	我們沒有訂位。
目前無座位	4	A table for four, please.	我們要四人桌。
	5	Sorry, all our tables are full now.	很抱歉，目前都客滿了。
詢問需等候時間	6	How long do we have to wait for a table?	請問我們要等多久才有位？
	7	About 30 minutes. We have quite a long line/queue at the moment.	大約要 30 分鐘。目前還有很多人在排隊。
詢問用餐人數	8	How many people do you have in your party?	請問你們有幾個人？
	9	We have two people now, and two more will come later.	現在是兩個，還有兩個等一下到。
告知所需座位	10	Could we have a table for six?	請問有六個人的位子嗎？
	11	Sorry, we only have a table for four right now. Would you like to take it?	很抱歉，只剩四人的位子，請問要坐嗎？

要求位置已被預訂	12	We'd like to sit by the window. Is that possible?	我們想要坐靠窗的位子，請問可以嗎？
	13	I am sorry. Our window tables are all taken.	抱歉，靠窗的位子都訂走了。
要求坐在非吸菸區	14	Could we sit in the non-smoking area?	請問我們可以坐在非吸菸區嗎？
	15	The non-smoking area is full right now. Do you want to keep waiting or sit in the smoking section?	目前非吸菸區已客滿，請問你們要等，還是要坐在吸菸區？
坐吧臺	16	How about sitting at the bar?	您願意坐在吧臺嗎？
要求有位子時告知	17	Please let me know when a table is ready.	有位子的時候請通知我。
被帶位	18	Your table is ready. Please come with me.	您的桌位已準備好,請跟我來。
	19	Are we sitting in the corner?	請問我們是坐角落的位子嗎?

20-2 詢問菜單內容 104

要求菜單	1	May we have a menu/wine list, please?	請問有菜單／酒單嗎?
	2	Do you have a Chinese menu?	請問有中文菜單嗎？
餐前酒	3	Would you like some wine with your meal?	請問上菜前要喝點酒嗎？
	4	Please give us two glasses of red wine.	請給我們兩杯紅酒。
	5	Can you recommend a nice wine at a reasonable price?	可以請你推薦價格合理又不錯的酒嗎？
要求點餐	6	We would like to order now.	我們現在要點餐。
告知稍後再點餐	7	Are you ready to order?	請問可以點餐了嗎？
	8	Could you give us a moment, please?	可以請再給我們一些時間嗎？
請人介紹餐點	9	I am not familiar with Italian food. Do you have any recommendations?	我對義大利菜不是很熟悉，可以給我一點意見嗎？
	10	I am a vegetarian. What do you recommend?	我吃素，有什麼素菜推薦嗎？
不吃的食物	11	What kind of food can't you eat?	請問有什麼是您不能吃的？
	12	I am allergic to pork.	我對豬肉過敏。

20-3 點餐 105

開胃菜	1	Would you like an appetizer?	請問要開胃菜嗎？
	2	I would like to start off with oysters.	我要來點生蠔開胃。
沙拉	3	I'd like a salad, please.	麻煩給我一份沙拉。
	4	Do you want Thousand Island or Ranch dressing?	請問您的沙拉要加千島醬還是田園醬？
招牌菜	5	What is your house specialty?	你們招牌菜是什麼？
	6	Our roast chicken is very good.	我們的烤雞非常好。
詢問特餐種類	7	What is today's special?	請問今日特餐是什麼?
點特餐	8	We would like to have two of today's special.	我們要兩份今日特餐。
是否提供套餐	9	Do you have any set meals/ courses?	請問有套餐嗎？
詢問附餐	10	What comes with the steak?	牛排的附餐是什麼？
	11	Baked potato or French fries.	有烤馬鈴薯或薯條。
不想久候的餐點選擇	12	I'm in a hurry. What's fastest to prepare?	我趕時間，什麼菜出最快？
	13	I suggest that you order the seafood rice.	我建議您點海鮮飯。
點主菜	14	I would like the lamb chop.	我要一份羊排。
	15	How would you like your lamb chop cooked?	請問您的羊排要幾分熟？

告知食物熟度	16	I would like to have my steak rare/ medium/well-done.	要三分／七分／全熟。
點相同食物	17	What are they having? I would like to order the same thing.	請問他們點的是什麼？我想點一樣的。
	18	That's our sirloin steak.	那是沙朗牛排。
詢問餐點口味	19	Is this dish spicy/sour?	這道菜辣／酸嗎？
蛋的做法	20	How do you like your eggs, scrambled, fried, or boiled?	您要炒蛋、煎蛋或是水煮蛋？
	21	I'd like my eggs hard boiled/sunny-side-up/over-easy, please.	我要全熟的水煮蛋／太陽蛋／雙面煎半生荷包蛋。
醬料種類	22	What sauce goes best with this steak?	這牛排配什麼醬料最好吃？
	23	The cream, mushroom, and black pepper sauces all complement it very well.	配上奶油醬、蘑菇醬和黑胡椒醬都非常好吃。

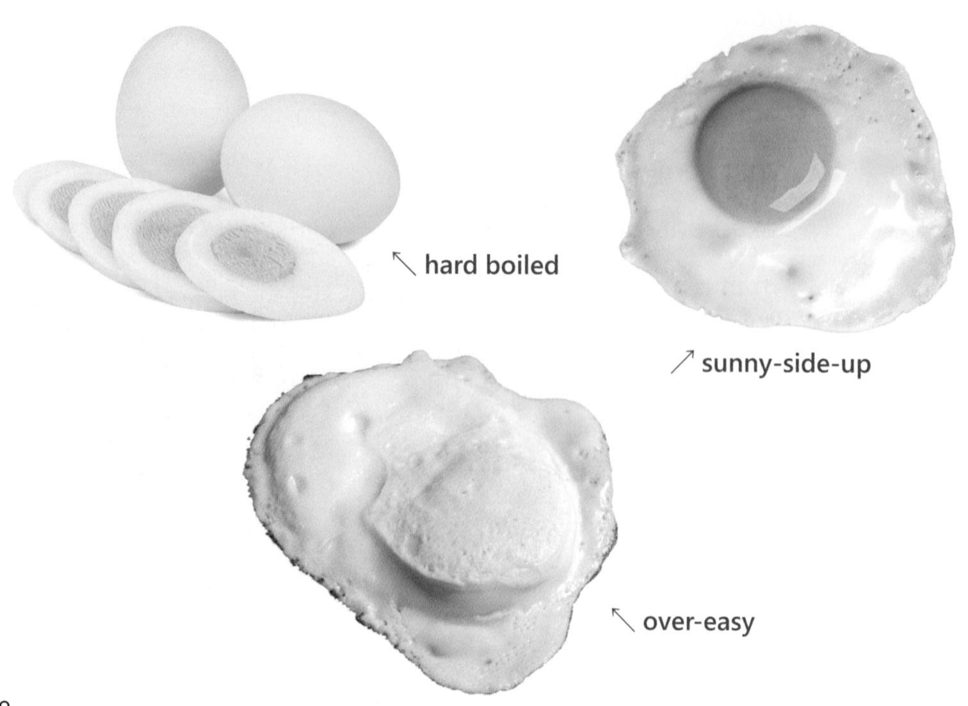

餐後點心	24	What would you like for dessert?	請問您點心要點什麼？
	25	I would like the caramel pudding/ cheesecake.	焦糖布丁／起士蛋糕。
飲料	26	What would you like to drink after your meal?	請問您餐後要喝什麼？
	27	Would you like coffee or tea?	請問您要咖啡或是茶？
	28	Please bring me a cup of espresso/ Earl Grey tea.	請給我一杯濃縮咖啡／伯爵茶。
是否加糖或奶	29	Would you like milk or sugar?	您要加牛奶或糖嗎？
結束點餐	30	I think that's enough.	我想就點這些了。
	31	OK. I'll be right back with your order.	好的，我會馬上為您上菜。

常見菜單品項 Common Menu Items

沙拉 Salad

fruit salad 水果沙拉

Caesar salad 凱薩沙拉

Greek salad 希臘沙拉

garden salad 田園沙拉

chicken salad 雞肉沙拉

開胃菜 Appetizers／前菜 Starters

oysters 生蠔

smoked salmon 煙燻鮭魚

shrimp cocktail 雞尾酒鮮蝦

湯品 Soups

pumpkin soup 南瓜湯

corn chowder 玉米濃湯

minestrone 義式蔬菜湯

borsch
羅宋湯

French onion soup
法式洋蔥湯

gazpacho
西班牙涼菜湯

海鮮 Seafood

lobster 龍蝦

shrimp 蝦子

crab 螃蟹

salmon 鮭魚

octopus 章魚

squid 烏賊

主菜 Main Courses

steak 牛排

fish fillet 魚排

chicken fillet 雞排

pork 豬肉

lamb 羊肉

stuffed eggplant 釀茄子（素）

附餐 Side Dishes

mashed potato 馬鈴薯泥

onion rings 洋蔥圈

baked potato 烤馬鈴薯

French fries（美） / **chips** （英）薯條

mushrooms 蘑菇

義大利麵 Pasta

spaghetti 細麵條

penne 斜管麵

farfalle 蝴蝶麵

conchiglie 貝殼麵

cannelloni 義大利麵捲

tortiglioni 蔥管麵

tagliatelle 鳥巢寬麵

rotini 螺旋麵

lasagna 千層麵

macaroni 通心粉

ravioli 義大利水餃

甜點 Desserts

cheesecake 乳酪蛋糕

Crème brûlée 烤布蕾

apple pie 蘋果派

pudding 布丁

tiramisu 提拉米蘇

chocolate mousse 巧克力慕斯

brownie 布朗尼

sundae 聖代

ice cream 冰淇淋

soufflé 舒芙蕾

lemon tart 檸檬塔

baked Alaska 熱烤阿拉斯加

酒精飲料 Alcoholic Beverages

brandy 白蘭地

Scotch whisky 蘇格蘭威士忌

vodka 伏特加

tequila 龍舌蘭

cocktail 雞尾酒

cider 蘋果酒／西打

beer 啤酒

red/white wine 紅／白葡萄酒

其他飲料 Other Beverages

coffee 咖啡

black tea 紅茶

soda 汽水

hot chocolate 熱可可

lemonade 檸檬水

juice 果汁

Chapter 21

用餐情況 Dining Situations

情境式對話 餐點遲遲未上 106

R → Restaurant Waitress　I → Issac Tang

I	Excuse me, miss.	小姐，不好意思。
R	Yes, sir. How may I help you?	先生，需要什麼服務嗎？
I	We have been waiting for more than 30 minutes, but our order has not come out yet. Why is it taking so long?	我們等點好的菜等了 30 分鐘了，可是菜還沒來。請問怎麼會這麼久？
R	Sorry about that. I thought another server had already brought you your meal. I will check on that for you right away.	很抱歉發生此事。我以為另一位服務生已經上菜了，我立刻去查。
I	A waiter did come by, but he had the wrong order.	一位服務生是來過，但他上錯菜了。
R	I am really sorry. Let me go and ask now.	真的很抱歉，我現在就去問。
I	Thank you. But before you do, could you do me a favor?	謝謝。不過你去問之前，可以請幫我一個忙嗎？
R	Certainly. What is it?	當然，請說。

I	We are pretty hungry, so could you please bring us some more bread? And some more butter and jam, too.	我們很餓，所以可以請你送來一些麵包，還有一些奶油和果醬嗎？
R	That's no problem. What kind of bread do you prefer? Whole wheat or white?	沒問題。你們想要哪種麵包，全麥或是白麵包？
I	I like white, but my friend likes whole wheat. So could you bring us both?	我要白麵包，但我朋友要全麥的，所以可以請兩種都要嗎？
R	Of course. Anything else?	好。還需要什麼嗎？
I	Oh, I think we need more water, as well.	噢，我想我們也需要加水。
R	OK. I will check on your order immediately and be right back with your bread and water.	好的。我會立刻查清楚你們點的菜，並送麵包和水來。
I	Great. Thank you.	好，謝謝。

white bread

wheat bread

rye bread

oatmeal honey bread

旅遊小句 Yummy!

21-1 形容餐點 107

好吃	1	Yummy!	好好吃喔！
嫩	2	This meat is very tender.	這肉很嫩。
香	3	This dish smells good/terrific.	這道菜很香。
酥脆	4	This fried chicken is nice and crispy.	這炸雞酥脆好吃。
多汁	5	This pear is juicy.	這水梨水分很多。
新鮮	6	This bread is wonderful. Really fresh!	這麵包非常好吃。真的很新鮮！

21-2 抱怨餐點 108

餐點未到	1	Why is my order taking so long?	為什麼我點的餐還沒上？
未點餐點	2	I didn't order this.	我沒有點這個。
餐點冷掉	3	My meal is cold.	我的菜是冷的。
髒餐具	4	This plate/spoon looks dirty.	我的盤子／湯匙看起來髒髒的。
煮太久	5	This meat is too tough.	這肉太老了。
有腥味	6	The fish doesn't taste fresh.	這魚是腥的。
生的	7	This meat is still pink in the middle.	這肉中間還是粉紅色。
沒熟	8	This chicken is undercooked.	這隻雞沒有煮熟。
不新鮮	9	This salad doesn’t look fresh.	這沙拉看起來不新鮮。
烤焦了	10	This bread is burnt.	這麵包烤焦了。
餿了	11	This milk is spoiled.	這牛奶酸掉了。
有不明物	12	There is something in my soup.	我的湯裡有東西。
不脆	13	These fries are not crispy at all.	這些薯條一點也不脆。

太辣	14	This soup is too spicy/hot.	這湯太辣了。
太鹹	15	This dish is too salty.	這菜太鹹了。
太油	16	This soup is too oily/greasy.	這湯太油了。
沒味道	17	This dish is practically tasteless.	這菜沒味道。

21-3 用餐中提出要求 109

加麵包	1	Please bring me more bread.	請再給我一些麵包。
加水	2	Could you please bring me some more water?	可以請幫我加水嗎？
要求看菜單	3	May I have another look at the menu, please?	可以請再給我看一下菜單嗎？
要求給餐具	4	I dropped my fork. May I have a new one?	我的叉子掉了，可以請給我一支新的嗎？
要求送調味料	5	May I have some more chili sauce/soy sauce?	我可以再要一些辣椒醬／醬油嗎？
取消部分餐點內容	6	I think I'll skip the coffee/tea. Just bring me my vanilla ice cream.	請直接上香草冰淇淋，我不要咖啡／茶了。
要求打包	7	Please pack/box up the leftovers for me.	請幫我把剩菜打包。
要求清理桌面	8	Please clear away our table.	請幫我們收一下桌子。

Chapter 22 用餐後 After the Meal

情境式對話 用餐後結帳 110

R → Restaurant Waiter D → Delia Tsai

D Would you give me my bill, please?	可以請給我帳單嗎？
R Of course, madam. I have it right here.	好的，女士，帳單給您。
D Let me see. Excuse me, but what is this for?	我看看。不好意思，但這是什麼費用？
R That's the roast beef with baked potato.	那項是烤牛肉佐洋芋。
D We didn't order that. All we had was one roast chicken dinner, and a T-bone steak with fries, and some onion rings.	我們沒有點這道菜。我們點的是一份烤雞大餐、一份丁骨牛排附薯條，還有一些洋蔥圈。
R Oh, there must be some mistake. Sorry about that. I will deduct the roast beef from the total and be right back with you.	噢，一定是哪裡出了差錯。抱歉發生此事。我會將烤牛肉這項從總金額扣除，並立刻回來。
A few minutes later.	數分鐘後。
R Madam, here is your bill.	女士，您的帳單。

D	Is the service charge included in the bill?	請問有包含服務費嗎？
R	Yes, it includes a 10% service charge.	是，含一成的服務費。
D	I see. Do you accept credit cards or traveler's checks?	是這樣啊。可以刷卡或是用旅行支票嗎？
R	We accept credit cards and personal checks, but not traveler's checks, I am afraid.	我們接受刷卡和個人支票，但不接受旅行支票。
D	OK. Here's my VISA card.	好吧。這是我的威士卡。
R	Do you need a receipt?	請問要開收據嗎？
D	Yes, please.	是的，麻煩你。
R	No problem. I will be right back.	好的，我馬上回來。
D	By the way, we can't finish our French fries, roast chicken and onion rings. Can I take the leftovers[1] home with me?	還有，我們吃不完薯條、烤雞和洋蔥圈。可以幫我們打包嗎？
R	Sure. I'll box those up for you in just a moment.	沒問題，我會立刻為你們打包。

[1] leftovers [ˋlɛft͵ovɚs] (n.) 剩菜

旅遊小句 Check, please.

22-1 結帳 111

要求結帳	1	Check, please.	我要結帳。
詢問價錢	2	How much is the total?	總共多少錢？
各付各的	3	Let's go Dutch/fifty-fifty.	我們要分開算。
帳單有誤	4	The bill seems not correct.	錢好像算錯了。
未點項目	5	I didn't order any crab.	我沒有點螃蟹。
詢問費用	6	What is this charge for?	請問這是什麼費用？
找錯錢	7	You gave me the wrong change.	你錢找錯了。
要收據	8	I'd like the receipt.	要開收據。
付費方式	9	Can I pay by credit card?	可以刷卡嗎？
	10	Do you take American Express?	可以刷美國運通卡嗎？
詢問是否已含服務費	11	Is there a service charge?	請問這含服務費嗎？
	12	A 15% service charge is automatically added to the bill.	這已內含一成五的服務費。
不用找零	13	Keep the change.	不用找錢了。

22-2 合影留念 (112)

詢問可否拍照	1	Can I take a photo in the restaurant?	請問餐廳裡可以拍照嗎？
請人拍照	2	Could you take a photo for us?	請問可以幫我們拍張照嗎？
要求與對方合影	3	May we have a photo with you?	請問我們可以跟您合照嗎？
謝絕照相	4	I'm sorry, but photos are not allowed in this restaurant.	很抱歉，本餐廳不允許拍照。

付款方式 Ways to Pay

pay by credit card 信用卡付款

pay by cash 現金支付

pay by mobile phone 手機支付

pay by personal check 個人支票付帳

Chapter 23 速食店與酒吧 Fast-Food Restaurants & Pubs

情境式對話 // 速食店點餐 (113)

R → Restaurant Clerk　S → Sharon Liao

R	Good evening. Can I help you?	晚安，請問要點什麼餐？
S	I would like meal number 3, please.	我要三號餐，麻煩你。
R	One Beefy Burger meal. All right. And what would you like to drink?	一個大牛肉堡餐。好的，請問要什麼飲料？
S	Lemonade, please.	請給我檸檬水。
R	Regular or large?	您要中杯或是大杯？
S	Large, please. I am pretty thirsty.	請給我大杯，我口很渴。
R	Do you want to add 50 cents and get the large fries?	請問您要加 50 分換大薯嗎？
S	I don't think I can eat that much. The regular size will be fine.	我想我吃不了那麼多，中薯就可以了。
R	OK. Is there anything else?	好的。還要點什麼嗎？
S	No, thanks.	沒有了，謝謝。
R	Is this for here or to go?	是內用還是外帶？

S	It's for here, please.	內用。
R	All right. That'll be 2 dollars and 95 cents.	好的，總共是 2 元 95 分。
S	Here is $3.	3 元給你。
R	Thank you. Here's your receipt and your 5 cents change.	謝謝您。您的發票和 5 分。
S	Thanks. May I have some extra ketchup, pepper, and napkins, please?	謝謝。可以請給我多一些番茄醬、胡椒粉和紙巾嗎？
R	Sure. Here you go, and here is your meal. Sorry to have kept you waiting.	可以啊。請取用。這是您點的餐，抱歉讓您久等了。
S	Oh. Where can I get a straw?	對了，哪裡有吸管？
R	You can find the straws in the big box on the counter right over there.	那邊櫃檯上的大盒子裡面有。
S	Good. Thank you.	好，謝謝。
R	You are welcome. Enjoy your meal.	不客氣，祝用餐愉快。

旅遊小句 I would like meal number 5.

23-1 在速食店點餐 114

告知餐點名稱	1	I would like meal number 5.	我要五號餐。
告知點餐內容	2	Chicken nuggets and fries, please.	我要雞塊和薯條。
點飲料	3	I'd like a cup of black iced tea.	我要一杯冰紅茶。
	4	Small, medium, or large?	請問要小杯、中杯、還是大杯？
詢問可否續杯	5	Can I refill my coffee?	請問咖啡可以續杯嗎？
	6	The first refill is free.	可以免費續杯一次。
外帶餐點	7	Two fried chickens and one Fanta to take out, please.	我要外帶兩塊炸雞和一杯芬達汽水。
告知對餐點的要求	8	I would like a chicken breast instead of a leg, please.	我想要雞胸，不要雞腿，麻煩你。
更改餐點	9	I've changed my mind. I don't want the chicken nuggets. Please change that to a chicken burger.	我改變心意了，請把雞塊改成雞肉堡。
需稍作等待	10	The fries will be up in about three minutes. Do you mind waiting?	薯條要等約三分鐘，您介意等候嗎？
詢問用餐方式	11	Will that be for here or to go?	請問是內用還是外帶？
	12	Take out/To go, please.	外帶，麻煩你。
不是所點的餐點	13	I ordered the beef burger, not the fish fillet.	我點的是牛肉堡，不是魚柳。
	14	Sorry. I will change that for you right now.	抱歉，馬上為您換。

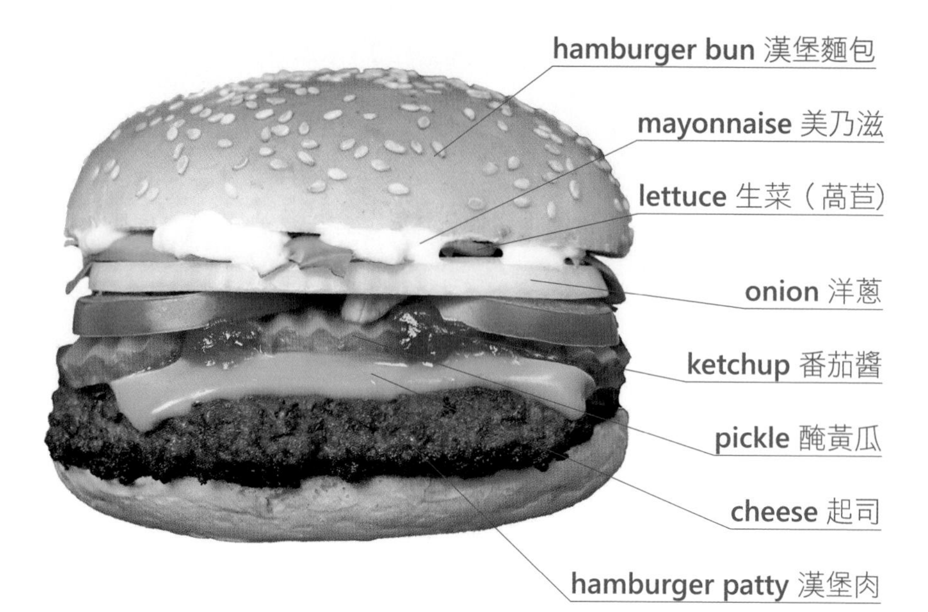

告知不要某些配料	15	Please don't put any pickles or olives on my sandwich.	我的三明治裡不要有醃黃瓜或橄欖。
	16	How about onion?	那要洋蔥嗎？
詢問是否要醬料	17	Do you want mayonnaise or mustard?	要加美乃滋或芥末醬嗎？
	18	Both, please. And put a little extra of each.	都要，麻煩你，要多一點。
索取醬料	19	Please give me some mustard and ketchup.	我要一些芥末醬和番茄醬。
索取餐具	20	I need some napkins and straws.	我要一些紙巾跟吸管。
尋找餐具	21	Where can I get some napkins and straws?	請問哪裡有紙巾和吸管？
	22	Right over there. Please help yourself.	在那裡，請自行取用。
與人共用餐桌	23	Can I sit here?	我可以坐這裡嗎？

23-2 在酒吧享受餐飲 115

點伏特加	1	One vodka and lime on the rocks, please.	請給我一杯伏特加萊姆，要加冰塊。
點相同的酒	2	May I have another, please?	可以請再給我一杯嗎？
詢問下酒菜	3	Do you have any snacks or desserts?	請問有什麼小菜或點心嗎？
乾杯	4	Cheers!	乾杯！
	5	Let's toast to the happy couple!	讓我們為這對神仙眷侶乾杯！
	6	The pub closes in five minutes. Bottoms up, everyone.	酒吧再五分鐘就要打烊了。乾了吧，大家。
詢問啤酒品牌	7	A beer, please.	我要一杯啤酒。
	8	What brand would you like?	請問要什麼牌子的？
告知啤酒種類	9	I would like a draft beer.	我要生啤酒。
	10	A bottle?	瓶裝的嗎？
半品脫酒	11	A half pint will be fine.	半品脫就好。 * 品脫：僅用在口語表示啤酒容量，約為 568 毫升。

酒吧內的菜單 Menu in the Pub

啤酒 Beer

draft beer 生啤酒

ale 愛爾啤酒

pale ale 愛爾淡啤酒

lager 窖藏／拉格啤酒

Lambic 自然發酵酒

stout 司陶特黑啤酒

porter 波特啤酒

Weizen 德式小麥啤酒

fruit beer 水果啤酒

調酒 Cocktails

screwdriver 螺絲起子

vodka lime 伏特加萊姆

cosmopolitan 柯夢波丹

bloody Mary 血腥瑪莉

margarita 瑪格莉特

gin and tonic 琴湯尼

mojito 莫希多

Martini 馬丁尼

Long Island iced tea
長島冰茶

Tequila Sunrise
龍舌蘭日出

blue Hawaii 藍色夏威夷

whiskey coke
威士忌可樂

點心 Snacks

taco 墨西哥炸玉米餅

Nachos 墨西哥烤玉米片

popcorn 爆米花

mixed platter 綜合拼盤

chicken wing 雞翅

cheese stick 起司條

Unit 7

Entertainment
動靜皆宜娛樂篇

Chapter

24 市區觀光 Downtown Sightseeing

情境式對話 // 詢問一日遊 116

I → Information Receptionist　V → Vicky Cheng

V	Hi. Could you please recommend some interesting one-day tours? I would like to join one.	你好，我想參加一日遊。請問你可以介紹一些好玩的一日遊行程嗎？
I	Sure. What kind of places are you interested in? Historical sites? Modern attractions?	沒問題。請問您是對名勝古蹟比較有興趣，還是對現代景觀比較有興趣？
V	I like both. Is there a trip that combines the two themes?	都有。有這兩種都有的行程嗎？
I	How about the Regal One-Day Tour? It includes Westminster Abbey, Buckingham Palace, Tower Bridge of London, and the London Eye.	那包含了遊覽西敏寺、白金漢宮、倫敦塔橋和倫敦眼的皇家一日遊，您覺得如何？
V	Sounds perfect. How much is it?	聽起來很棒。多少錢？
I	4£0 for one person.	一人 40 英鎊。
V	I see. How about lunch? Do you provide it?	了解。那你們會提供午餐嗎？

I	I am afraid not. But you can have lunch at the Tower Bridge. There are lots of restaurants and cafés nearby. We stop there for one hour.	很抱歉不會。不過您可以在倫敦塔橋那裡吃午餐，那附近有很多的餐廳和咖啡廳。我們會在那裡休息一個小時。
V	Right. What's the schedule?	好，那行程是怎麼安排呢?
I	We leave for Westminster Abbey at 8:30 a.m. and get back to the London Eye at four in the afternoon.	我們在早上八點半出發前往西敏寺，下午四點回到倫敦眼。
V	Great. Can you pick me up at my hotel?	好。請問你們可以到我住的飯店接我嗎？
I	Where are you staying?	您住哪裡？
V	At the Holiday Inn on Liverpool Street.	利物浦街上的假日旅舍。
I	That will be no problem. We'll pick you up at 8 a.m. Just be sure to be waiting for us outside the hotel on time.	沒問題。我們會在早上八點去接您，只是請務必準時在飯店外面等我們。
V	OK. Thanks. See you tomorrow morning.	我會的，謝謝你。明天早上見。

Westminster Abbey

London Eye

Buckingham Palace

旅遊小句 // How much is the admission fee?

24-1 前往旅遊服務中心 117

找尋旅客服務中心	1	Where is the (tourist) information center?	旅客服務中心怎麼走?
	2	There's one in the city center next to the city hall.	在市中心市政廳的旁邊有一處。
索取免費地圖	3	Where can I get hold of a free city map?	哪裡可以拿到免費的市區圖?
索取簡介	4	May I have a tourist brochure, please?	可以請給我觀光簡介嗎?
詢問指南是否免費	5	Is the tourist brochure free?	觀光指南是免費的嗎?
詢問旅遊景點	6	Are there any interesting places to see here?	這裡有什麼好玩的地方?
詢問古蹟	7	What is the most famous historical spot in the city?	這個城市最出名的名勝古蹟是哪裡?
	8	York Castle is the best known.	約克古堡最出名。
詢問交通工具	9	What is the most convenient way to get to the Metropolitan Museum?	怎麼去大都會博物館最方便?
門票	10	How much is the admission fee?	門票是多少錢?
今日是否開放	11	Is St. Peter's Cathedral open today?	聖彼得大教堂今天有開放嗎?
詢問一日遊景點	12	Which spots are suitable for a one-day trip?	有什麼地方適合一日遊嗎?
要求在地圖上圈出景點	13	Could you please circle those spots on my map?	請問你可以幫我在地圖上把這些景點圈起來嗎?

24-2 詢問當地旅遊行程資訊 118

行程種類	1	What kind of tours do you have?	你們有什麼樣的行程?
推薦行程	2	What do you recommend?	你可以推薦一些行程嗎？
詢問特定觀光團	3	Is there a tour of UC Berkeley?	有參觀加州大學柏克萊校區的行程嗎？
詢問該團簡介	4	May I have a tour brochure for this trip?	有這個團的簡介嗎？
詢問名額	5	Is there an opening for the Wednesday tour?	星期三的行程還有名額嗎？
旅遊內容	6	What will I see during this tour?	這次的行程有什麼可看之處嗎？
導遊費用	7	How much should I tip the tour guide?	請問導遊小費一天多少？
旅程時間	8	How long is this tour?	請問這個行程有多久？
詢問行程費用內容	9	What fees are included in your Stonehenge tour?	你們的巨石陣行程有包括那些費用？
	10	The admissions to Stonehenge and bus fare are included. In addition, we provide English, Chinese, German, and French guide options.	巨石陣門票與車資都包括在裡面了，我們也有提供導覽，有英文、中文、德文與法文供您選擇。

Stonehenge

24-3 參加當地旅遊行程 (119)

報名參加旅遊團	1	I am interested in joining the Blue Mountain one-day tour.	我想參加藍山一日遊。
預約報名處	2	Could I reserve a place here?	請問可以在這裡報名嗎？
一團人數	3	How many people are there in a tour?	一團有多少人？
是否至飯店接泊	4	Could you please pick me up at my hotel?	請問可以到我住的飯店接我嗎？
詢問集合點	5	Where is the meeting point?	要在哪裡集合？
詢問行程時間的頻率	6	I'm very interested in this tour, but I'm booked today. When will you have it again?	我對這個行程非常有興趣，但我今天沒空，你們什麼時候還會有呢？
	7	This one is available every day except Friday.	除了禮拜五以外，每天都會有這個行程。
出發時間	8	When do you depart?	請問幾點出發？
中文導遊	9	Do you have any Chinese-speaking tour guides?	請問有中文導遊嗎？
回程時間	10	When will we return from the excursion?	請問幾點會回來？
是否包含餐費	11	Does the fee include meals?	費用包含餐費嗎？
是否可自由活動	12	Will I have some free time at Sydney Olympic Stadium?	到了雪梨奧運會場有自由活動的時間嗎？

24-4 市區觀光巴士 120

詢問有無觀光巴士	1	Are there any sightseeing buses?	請問有觀光巴士嗎？
詢問搭乘處	2	Where can I take a sightseeing bus?	請問哪裡可以搭觀光巴士？
詢問費用	3	How much does it cost to take the Blue Route sightseeing bus?	搭藍線觀光巴士要多少錢？
詢問停站處	4	Where will the Purple Route sightseeing bus stop?	紫線觀光巴士在哪停靠？
可否再上車	5	If I get off the bus, can I get back on another one later with the same ticket?	下車後還可以用同一張票再上另一部車嗎？
車票可否聯搭	6	The ticket is valid for all the buses on the Red Route.	這種票可以搭乘所有的紅線巴士。

詢問乘車路線	7	How many routes do you have?	你們有幾種路線呢？
	8	We have only one route, which includes 14 main attractions in London, as you can see on the map. The full loop takes about one hour. You can buy our “hop-on, hop-off” ticket, which is valid for 24 hours to take the bus with unlimited times.	我們只有一條路線，就像您在地圖上看到的，我們會經過 14 個倫敦主要景點。搭乘一趟大約會花費一個小時，您可以購買我們的「隨上隨下」票，供您於 24 小時內不限次數搭乘。
詢問巴士頻率	9	How often does the bus operate?	巴士多久來一班？
	10	It runs every 10 to 15 minutes.	每 10 到 15 分鐘就會來一班。
語音導覽	11	Is there an audio guide on the bus?	車上有語音導覽嗎？
使用導覽的方式	12	How do I use this audio guide?	請問這個語音導覽怎麼用？

免費徒步行程 Free Walking Tour

現在有不少主要城市都有提供免費徒步行程，由專業的導遊帶領旅客認識當地景點，深入探索當地的文化。此種行程有時會有不同語言的選擇，但大多數時候以英語為主；最大的特色在於不強制收取任何費用，而是讓旅客依心情與導覽內容給予導遊「小費」。

如果想嘗試用特別一點的方式觀光市區，也可以參考以下不同的探索行程：

cycling tour

segway tour

helicopter tour

boat tour

carriage tour

rickshaw tour

Chapter 25

博物館與美術館 Museums & Galleries

情境式對話 詢問展覽的注意事項 121

I → Information Receptionist　R → Roxanne Kuan

I	Welcome to the British Museum. How may I help you?	歡迎蒞臨大英博物館。有什麼可以為您服務的嗎？
R	This is the first time I've been to the museum. Could you please give me some pointers about where to start?	我第一次來這裡。你可以介紹一下要從哪裡開始參觀嗎？
I	Sure. As you probably know, we have many great collections and exhibits. I'm not sure what you're interested in, but there is a fascinating mummy exhibit going on right now. It's a great way to learn more about ancient Egyptian culture and history. Maybe you would like to start there.	沒問題。如您大概知道的，本館有大量的館藏與展覽。我不確定您對什麼有興趣，但本館目前有很棒的木乃伊特展，是了解古埃及文化與歷史的絕佳途徑；您或許會想從這項展覽開始。
R	Sounds cool. Is there a Chinese-speaking tour guide?	聽起來很不錯。請問有中文導覽嗎？
I	Sorry, there isn't. Right now, we only have tours conducted in English, French, Spanish and Japanese.	很抱歉沒有。本館目前只有英語、法語、西班牙語及日語的導覽。

R	That's OK. By the way, can I take photos inside?	沒關係。對了，可以在裡面拍照嗎？
I	I am afraid not. All our exhibits must be carefully protected, so photography is not permitted. You will see a souvenir shop at the end of the tour. We have replicas[1] of almost every item in every exhibit. You can also get postcards, guidebooks, key chains and toys there.	很抱歉不能。本館所有的展覽品都是一定要謹慎保護的，所以並不允許拍照。參觀結束後您會見到紀念品販售處，有幾乎所有展出文物的複製品，您能在那裡購買明信片、導覽手冊、鑰匙圈和玩具。
R	OK. Thank you very much. I have a much clearer idea now.	好，非常感謝。我現在比較清楚了。
I	You are welcome. I hope you enjoy our collections.	不客氣。祝您參觀愉快。

[1] replica [ˋrɛplɪkə] (n.) 複製品

旅遊小句 // Do I need to buy a ticket?

25-1 參觀前的相關諮詢 122

詢問館場特色	1	What kind of gallery is it?	請問這是什麼樣的美術館？
	2	This gallery exhibits contemporary art.	這間美術館展示當代的藝術品。
詢問展期	3	How long will this exhibition continue?	這場展覽是到什麼時候？
詢問何時更換作品	4	How often do the exhibits change?	展覽品多久會換一次?
詢問是否需門票	5	Do I need to buy a ticket?	我需要購買門票嗎？
	6	Some parts of the collection are free, but others require tickets.	部分展覽是免費參觀，但特定的展覽要購票。
詢問門票費用	7	I have an international student card. May I have one student ticket, please?	我有國際學生證，請問我可以買一張學生票嗎？
	8	I bought the Paris Museum Pass/Paris Pass at the information center yesterday. Does it mean that I don't have to pay for admission?	我昨天在旅客服務中心買了巴黎博物館通行證／巴黎通行證，這代表我不需要付門票了嗎？
詢問導覽時間	9	When is the next guided tour?	下次導覽是什麼時候?
要求中文導覽	10	Do you provide an audio guide in Chinese?	有中文的語音導覽嗎?
找尋出入口	11	Where is the entrance/exit?	請問入口／出口怎麼走？
詢問想看的內容	12	What are you interested in here?	您對這裡哪方面的展覽有興趣？

要求特定畫作	13	Do you have Renaissance or Impressionist paintings?	有文藝復興時期或印象派的作品嗎？
要求給予建議	14	Is there anything particular that I shouldn't miss?	有什麼特別的展覽是不容錯過的嗎？
寄物	15	Do I need to leave my bags in the locker?	請問包包要放在寄物櫃嗎？
索取導覽圖	16	May I have a floor map of the exhibition, please?	請問有展覽樓層導覽圖嗎？

城市通行證與博物館通行證 City Pass & Museum Pass

旅遊中不可錯過的，就是極具藝術與歷史價值的美術館與歷史建築了。不過這些美術館與旅遊景點的入場費往往不太便宜，如果是前往巴黎、羅馬等歷史悠久的城市，票價則就更加可觀了。

若是想要為旅遊省點錢，旅客不妨考慮許多城市都會推出的博物館通行證（**Museum Pass**），這種通行證可供旅客在效期之內（通常是一天、三天、七天來算）進入大部份的美術館以及一些著名歷史建築，價格比起一張一張購買門票便宜許多。只是必須要注意使用期限是由第一次使用通行證進入旅遊景點的當天開始計算，而且必須要連續使用才行。

旅客也可以考慮城市通行證（**City Pass**），這種通行證除了包括一些博物館通行證沒有的景點與旅遊項目之外，還會提供一次巴士觀光、遊船觀光、腳踏車觀光等搭乘券，有些城市的通行證甚至也結合了交通票券的功能，讓旅客也不用再額外負擔交通費，對於遊客來說也是非常划算的選擇，因此旅遊之前，不妨先查查看當地是否有這些經濟實惠的通行證。

25-2 進入參觀 (123)

詢問真品	1	Is it an original/a copy?	這是真跡／複製品嗎？
詢問畫名	2	What is this painting titled?	這幅畫的名稱是什麼？
詢問作者	3	Who painted it?	這是誰的作品？
詢問年代	4	When was it finished?	作品是什麼時候完成的?
詢問畫法	5	What is this drawing technique called?	這是什麼畫法？
詢問可否錄影／使用閃光燈	6	May I videotape these works?	請問可以錄影嗎？
	7	Are flash photos allowed?	請問可以用閃光燈拍嗎？
詢問其他展場位置	8	Which way is it to the Sculpture Room?	請問雕塑展覽廳怎麼走？

25-3　逛紀念品區 124

找尋明信片	1	Where can I buy postcards of the art display here?	請問哪裡可以買到展覽品的明信片？
找尋中文版	2	Is there a Chinese version of this book?	請問這本書有中文版嗎？
詢問書籍	3	Are there any books about mummies and the history of Egypt?	請問有關於木乃伊和埃及歷史的書嗎？
購買產品	4	Two of Van Gogh's *Sunflowers* posters, please.	我要買兩張梵谷的《向日葵》海報畫。
特殊要求	5	Please put the poster in a protective tube.	海報畫請用紙筒包起來。
要求包裝	6	I'd like to have this sketchbook wrapped as a gift.	素描本請幫我包裝成禮物。

Chapter 26 戲劇、音樂劇與演奏會 Plays, Musicals, & Concerts

情境式對話 // 購買劇院的票 125

B → Booking Clerk　E → Evelyn Shang

E	Hi, I've heard a lot about the musical *Mamma Mia!* Is it a comedy?	你好。我聽過很多有關《媽媽咪呀！》這部音樂劇的事情，這是喜劇嗎？
B	Yes, it is. It's very popular. All the songs are from ABBA, you know, the famous band from Sweden. It's well worth seeing.	是啊，非常受歡迎。劇裡所有的歌曲都是 ABBA 唱的，你知道，瑞典最有名的樂團，很值得一看。
E	You've talked me into it! May I have two tickets for tonight?	說得我都等不及要看了！我可以買兩張晚上的票嗎？
B	Sure. Where would you like to sit?	好的。請問您要坐哪一區？
E	I really have no idea about what seats there are, but I probably can only afford the cheaper tickets.	我還真不知道有什麼樣的位子可以買，但我大概只能買得起便宜一點的票。
B	How about $20 for one person? Does that sound about right?	一人 20 元如何？聽起來不錯吧？

E	That sounds fine. I will take two of those. Where are the seats, by the way?	是很不錯，就買兩張。順便問一下，是哪裡的座位？
B	They are upper circle seats, on the third floor.	是樓上的座位，在三樓。
E	Do you think I can see the whole stage?	你覺得我可以看到整個舞台嗎？
B	Yes, you can. Maybe not very clearly, but there is a telescope right in front of you. It costs $1.	可以的。或許沒有那麼清楚，不過座位前方有一部望遠鏡，使用費一塊錢。
E	I see. When does the musical start?	我了解了。音樂劇什麼時候開始？
B	It starts at 7:30 p.m. It finishes at around 9:50 p.m. There's also a 15-minute interval[1].	七點半開始，大約 9 點 50 分結束，中場休息 15 分鐘。
E	OK. Thank you very much.	好，非常謝謝。
B	Here are your tickets. Enjoy the show!	這是您的票。祝觀賞愉快。

[1] interval [ˋɪntɚvḷ] (n.) 中場休息

旅遊小句 Do you sell opera tickets here?

26-1 諮詢相關資訊 (126)

尋找節目表	1	Where can I get a list of plays being shown currently?	請問哪裡有目前的劇目演出資訊？
找尋娛樂雜誌	2	Do you have an entertainment magazine for this week?	請問你們有這個星期的娛樂雜誌嗎？
詢問特別表演	3	What popular shows are playing this week?	請問這個星期有什麼有名的表演嗎？
詢問特定場地的表演	4	What is on at the Guild Theater tomorrow night?	請問工會戲院明天晚上有什麼表演?
詢問意見	5	Is there an opera I shouldn't miss?	有哪一部歌劇是不容錯過的嗎？
詢問劇場	6	I want to see *Cats*. Which theater is showing it?	我想看《貓》，請問有哪個劇場在演？
詢問表演期間	7	When will *Les Misérables* be playing at the Royal Theater?	請問《悲慘世界》什麼時候會在皇家劇院演出？
詢問購票處	8	Where can I buy a ticket?	請問在哪裡買票？

Cats

Les Misérables

詢問是否賣票	9	Do you sell opera tickets here?	請問這裡有賣歌劇的票嗎?
便宜的票	10	Are tickets for the afternoon show cheaper?	請問下午節目的票有比較便宜嗎?
表演期間	11	How long will the ballet be running?	請問這齣芭蕾舞演期多長?
是否有休息時間	12	Will there be an intermission?	請問有中場休息時間嗎?

26-2 購票及其他入場須知 127

詢問是否販賣特定劇票	1	Do you have a ticket for *The Phantom of the Opera*?	請問你們有《歌劇魅影》的票嗎?
確定場次與位置	2	I'd like two box seats for next Saturday's *Swan Lake*.	我要買下星期六《天鵝湖》的兩張包廂座位票。
詢問價格	3	What are the prices?	請問有哪些票價?
	4	There are four different prices—$30, $50, $80, and $100.	有 30、50、80、100 美元等四種價位。
	5	The only seats left are the $60 seats.	目前只剩 60 美元的座位。

The Phantom of the Opera

Swan Lake

詢問特定位置票價	6	How much is it for seats in the front row?	前排的位子要多少錢？
要求座位	7	Do you still have a seat available in the upper circle?	樓上的座位還有空位嗎？
	8	The play is standing room only. Would you like a ticket?	只剩站位了，請問要買嗎？
購買最便宜的票	9	I'd like two of the cheapest tickets for tonight's show.	我要兩張今天晚上表演最便宜的票。
	10	All of the tickets for tonight are sold out already. Do you want one for tomorrow night's performance?	今晚已經沒有位子了，您願意買明天晚上的嗎？
詢問是否仍有座位	11	Do you still have a seat for this Saturday's symphony?	請問這個星期六的交響樂表演還有位子嗎？
買相連的位置	12	Can I have four seats next to each other?	我可以要四張位子在一起的票嗎？
	13	Which area would you like to sit in?	請問您要哪一區的？
要求看座位圖	14	May I see the seating chart, please?	請問有座位平面圖可以給我看嗎？
使用折價券	15	Can I use this coupon to get a discount?	可以用折價券換折扣嗎？
告知位置	16	Here is your ticket. Your seat is in the fifth row of the dress circle.	這是您的票，座位在二樓第五排。

衣著規定	17 Is there a dress code?	有服裝上的規定嗎？
	18 No sandals, sneakers, or jeans.	不能穿涼鞋、球鞋及牛仔褲。
詢問開演時間	19 What time does the show begin?	幾點開始表演？
	20 The show starts at 7:30. Doors open at 7:00.	七點開始入場，七點半表演。

表演節目 Types of shows

opera 歌劇

ballet 芭蕾

play 戲劇

musical 音樂劇

modern dance 現代舞

pop music concert
流行演唱會

classical music concert
古典音樂會

26-3 準備入場觀賞表演 128

出示票	1	Here is my ticket.	這是我的票。
請求協助	2	I can't find my seat. Could you please show me where it is?	我找不到位子，請問可以告訴我在哪裡嗎?
	3	No problem. Just follow me.	沒問題，請跟我來。
尋找座位	4	How do I get to the upper circle?	請問三樓怎麼去?
	5	Take the stairs right over there.	請往那裡上樓。
	6	Please go upstairs from either side.	請從兩側樓梯上樓。
確認座位	7	Excuse me. Is this row E?	請問這是 E 排嗎？
	8	This is row F. Row E is one row down.	這是 F 排，E 是前一排。

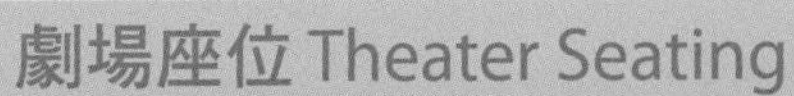

劇場座位 Theater Seating

① STAGE	舞臺。
② STALLS	一樓正廳，最靠近舞臺的座位。
③ DRESS CIRCLE	二樓座位。
④ UPPER CIRCLE	三樓座位，若劇院只有兩層樓，則指二樓後排的座位。
⑤ BALCONY/BOX	舞臺樓上兩側的包廂。
⑥ STANDING SEAT	站立席。

然而有時會因劇場大小不同，座位名稱會有變動（如有些劇場不提供站票），最好是請售票員出示座位平面圖，確定購買的座位。

Chapter

27 秀場餐廳與夜店 Cabarets & Nightclubs

情境式對話 // 安排去秀場餐廳 129

S → Samuel Nelson　E → Erica Wen

S	Erica, since this is your first time in New York, I'm going to take you out to a fabulous place tonight.	艾莉嘉，由於這是你第一次來紐約，我今天晚上要帶你去一個好地方看看。
E	Where are we going?	我們要去哪裡？
S	We're having dinner at a famous cabaret. Have you ever heard of Club Boisterous?	我們要去一家有名的秀場餐廳吃晚餐。你有聽過狂歡俱樂部嗎？
E	No, I never have. Why are we going there in particular?	從沒聽過。為什麼要特別挑那裡？
S	They have great magic shows every night. I was there once, and it was excellent. I think you will love it.	那裡每天晚上都有很棒的魔術表演。我去過一次，超棒的。我想你會喜歡的。
E	Sounds fun. But it's kind of late. Do you think we can get a good table?	聽起來很好玩。可是有點晚了，你認為我們有好位子坐嗎？

S	Don't worry about it. I booked a table three days ago. We have the best seats, right in front of the stage.	放心，我三天前就訂好位了。位子可是最好的，就在舞台正前方。
E	Wow! By the way, what should I wear? Is there a dress code?	好耶！對了，我要穿什麼？那裡有沒有服裝上的規定？
S	Yes, there is. It's pretty formal. Do you have an evening dress and some high-heels?	有，要穿很正式的服裝。你有晚禮服和高跟鞋嗎？
E	Yes, I packed them especially for something like this. Thank you so much for planning all this for me.	有啊。我為了參加這種場合，可是特別打包帶著。謝謝你為我準備這一切。
S	You are welcome! But you'd better hurry. We don't want to miss the show!	不用客氣啦！不過你得快點。我們可不想錯過演出！
E	OK. Let me go get changed.	沒錯。那我換裝去了。

旅遊小句 // What kind of music do they play?

27-1 尋找秀場餐廳與夜店 130

尋找秀場餐廳	1	Is there a cabaret you would recommend?	請問這裡有什麼不錯的秀場餐廳嗎？
詢問推薦原因	2	What is special about it?	那裡有什麼特別的表演嗎？
詢問何處可看表演	3	Where can we see some interesting shows?	請問哪裡有好看的秀?
	4	The Mirage is a good choice. It's famous for its special white tiger show.	可以去海市蜃樓，那裡以特別的白老虎秀聞名。
尋找夜店	5	Which nightclub is the most well-known?	請問哪家夜店最有名?
詢問播放何種音樂	6	What kind of music do they play?	那裡都放什麼樣的音樂？
找爵士樂俱樂部	7	Are there any jazz clubs here?	這裡有爵士俱樂部嗎?
詢問 D J 名氣	8	Which club has the most famous DJ?	請問哪家的 DJ 最有名?

DJ = Disk Jockey

專長於選擇並播放音樂，且在現場以電腦混音，製造出不同於原曲的獨特音樂，來為不同的場合烘托氣氛者。一個 DJ 的表演風格和表演技巧必須隨時視場合情況所變化，以維持現場的氣氛。

27-2 詢問入場相關事宜 131

是否需先訂位	1	Do I need to make a reservation?	我需要先訂位嗎？
確認是否有票	2	Can we still get a ticket?	我們還買得到票嗎？
詢問是否很多人	3	Is it crowded on weekends?	週末會不會有很多人?
年齡限制	4	Is there an age limit?	有年齡限制嗎？
	5	Yes, you are not allowed to enter if you are 18 or under. May I see your passport?	有的，未滿 18 歲不得進入。可以請借我看您的護照嗎？
穿著限制	6	Is formal dress required?	要穿正式服裝嗎？

27-3 購買門票並詢問表演時間 132

要求票種	1	We would like two tickets near the center of the stage, please.	我們要兩張靠近舞臺中央的票。
要求換位	2	Are there any front-row seats available?	請問有前面一點的位子嗎？
門票價位	3	It's $50 per ticket without dinner. If you'd like to include dinner, the ticket will be $75.	門票不含晚餐一張 50 塊，包含晚餐則是 75 塊。
表演開演時間	4	When do the first and second shows start?	第一場和第二場表演是什麼時候開始？
表演時間長短	5	How long is the show?	這場表演是多久?
何時結束	6	When will the show finish?	表演幾點會結束？
詢問打烊時間	7	When does the club close tonight?	今天是幾點會打烊?

27-4 入場後事宜 133

保管外套	1	May I leave my coat with you?	請問可以幫我保管外套嗎？
	2	We charge $5 per garment.	一件衣服要五塊保管費。
有寄物櫃	3	You may leave your things in one of those lockers over there.	您可以將東西放進那裡的寄物櫃。
禁止拍照	4	May I take photos during the show?	請問看秀時可以拍照嗎？
	5	Taking photos is not permitted here.	這裡禁止拍照。
有照片在賣	6	You can buy some excellent performance photos at the entrance.	您可以在入口處買到一些精彩的表演照片。

Chapter 28

遊樂園 Amusement Parks

情境式對話 // 談論遊樂園 134

C → Cynthia Ou　J → Jack Fisher

J	Hey, Cynthia. I am going to Universal Studios with some classmates this coming Sunday. If you're still going to be here, would you like to come with us?	嗨，辛西雅，我這星期天要和幾位同學去環球影城，如果你還會在這裡，要和我們去嗎？
C	I will still be here, and I would love to go with you! But how are we getting there?	我還會在啊，我可是很想跟你們去呢！但要怎麼去？
J	By car. It is not very far from here—only about 30 minutes.	坐車。從這不會很遠，只要大約 30 分鐘而已。
C	What are the park's main attractions?	那遊樂園有什麼好玩的？
J	They have a great roller coaster, and there is a Jurassic Park ride where you can see some dinosaurs. We can also take the E. T. Adventure ride where you ride a bicycle that carries E. T. back to his home planet. And of course, there are many interesting things about moviemaking to see.	那裡有一部非常大的雲霄飛車，還有一輛侏儸紀公園列車，可以坐著看一些恐龍。我們也可以去玩 ET 冒險之旅，就是騎著腳踏車載 ET 回他原來的星球。當然，還可以去看很多拍電影相關的好玩東西。

C	That sounds great!	聽起來太棒了！
J	The best thing is that since I am a California resident, admission is a lot cheaper if you go with me.	最棒的是我是加州居民，如果你跟我去，門票會便宜很多。
C	How nice! What time are you planning to leave?	太好了！你們打算幾點出發？
J	They're open from 8 a.m. to 10 p.m. It's the high season now, so I think we should get there as early as possible.	那裡從早上八點開到晚上十點。現在是旺季，所以我想我們要盡早到那裡。
C	How about picking me up here at 7 in the morning? That will give us a whole day to hang out at the park.	那早上七點來接我怎麼樣啊？那樣就會有一整天的時間可以在遊樂園玩了。
J	Great. I will let the others know. See you Sunday!	好的，我會通知其他人，星期天見囉！

旅遊小句 // Where is the ticket booth?

28-1 遊樂園的營業時間與交通 135

詢問營業日	1	Is Universal Studios open during the Christmas holidays?	請問環球影城會在聖誕節假期間開嗎？
詢問營業時間	2	What time does Disneyland open?	請問迪士尼樂園幾點開門？
詢問距離	3	Is it far from here?	那裡很遠嗎？
詢問交通工具	4	What is the most convenient way to get there?	怎麼去那裡最方便？
確認停車場	5	Can I park my car there?	那裡有地方可以停車嗎？
搭公車	6	Is there a direct bus?	有直達的公車嗎？
搭乘專車	7	There is an express bus that runs directly between the airport and Disneyland. It's perfect for us!	有專車往返於機場和迪士尼樂園之間，這正適合我們！

28-2 購買遊樂園門票 136

尋找售票處	1	Where is the ticket booth?	請問售票亭在哪裡？
買學生票	2	Two student tickets, please.	請給我兩張學生票。
	3	Please show me your student card.	請出示您的學生證。
表示有居民證	4	I am a California resident. Can I get a discount?	我有加州居民證，我可以打折嗎？
詢問票價	5	How much is the admission?	請問一張票多少錢？
告知票種	6	One adult and three student tickets, please.	我要一張全票和三張學生票。

詢問費用包含項目	7	Does the admission include everything?	是一票玩到底嗎？
	8	The ticket allows you to visit every attraction once. However, you'll have to pay for the second time round on some attractions.	所有設施都可以使用一次，而部分設施使用第二次要再付費。
詢問聯票	9	Is it less expensive to buy a combination ticket for the amusement park and the zoo?	如果買遊樂園與動物園的聯票，會比較便宜嗎？
網路購票	10	I bought the ticket online, and here is my printed e-ticket. How shall I use it?	這是我在網路上買的門票的影本，我該如何使用它？
	11	Just present it at the main entrance. You won't have to wait in line to buy a ticket.	在大門口出示它即可。您不需要再排在購票隊伍中。
	12	Excuse me. I purchased my ticket online, but I forgot to bring it.	不好意思，我在網路上買了票，但我沒有帶來。
	13	Don't worry! We can reissue your ticket. I just need to see the credit card you used to purchase your e-ticket, your passport, and the confirmation email.	別擔心！我們可以重新開票給您，我只需要看您購票的信用卡、護照以及購票確認信。

快速通關券	14	What is the difference between the express pass and the express pass unlimited?	快速通關券與無限次快速通關券有什麼不同？
	15	You can use the express pass to skip queues to regular attractions for one time. The express pass unlimited lets you enjoy unlimited priority access to each participating attraction.	快速通關券可以讓您減少一次排隊時間，無限次快速通關券則可讓您無限次數的享有設施的優先入場。

28-3　進入遊樂園之後的詢問事宜 137

詢問最好玩的設備	1	Which attraction is the best?	這裡什麼最好玩？
找特定遊樂設施	2	Where is the roller coaster?	雲霄飛車在哪裡？
找洗手間	3	Where can I find a restroom?	洗手間怎麼走？
詢問現在位置	4	What is this area we are in now?	這裡是哪一區？
找尋出口	5	Where is the nearest exit?	最近的出口怎麼走？
詢問玩法	6	How does this racing car work?	這個賽車怎麼玩？
詢問隊伍的目標	7	Is this the line for the pirate ship?	這個隊伍是要坐海盜船的嗎？
遊行時間	8	When will the Mickey Parade start?	請問米奇遊行什麼時候開始？
煙火秀	9	Is there a fireworks show tonight?	請問今天晚上有煙火秀嗎？
詢問是否開放	10	Is the Haunted House open today?	請問鬼屋今天有沒有開？

詢問限制	11	Are there any rules for this ride?	這項設施有任何的限制嗎？
	12	We have a minimum height requirement. You must be at least 122 cm tall.	我們有身高限制，遊客身高必須至少 122 公分。
	13	Please stow all loose personal articles, including camera and video equipment, in the lockers provided or with a non-rider.	請將所有會鬆落的個人物品，包括相機與攝影裝備都寄在置物櫃內，或是交給非搭乘者的旅客保管。

28-4 請求工作人員協助 138

迷路	1	I am lost.	我迷路了。
尋人	2	Could you please page a friend for me?	請問可以幫我廣播找朋友嗎？
遺失物品	3	I lost my bag in the labyrinth.	我在迷宮掉了背包。
告知物品外觀	4	It is a red Nike bag, about this big.	那是一個紅色的 Nike 包，大概這麼大。
有人受傷	5	My friend is hurt. Please send someone to help him immediately.	我的朋友受傷了，請馬上找人來幫忙。
遺失寄物箱鑰匙	6	I've lost the key to my locker.	我的寄物櫃鑰匙掉了。

旅遊資訊
補充包

遊樂設施 Amusement Park Facilities

roller coaster 雲霄飛車

Ferris wheel 摩天輪

pirate ship 海盜船

carousel 旋轉木馬

free fall 自由落體

haunted house 鬼屋

bumper car 碰碰車

bumper boat 碰碰船

swing ride 旋轉鞦韆

river rapids ride 漂漂船

log flume/ride 水上雲霄飛車

4-D theater 4-D 劇場

Chapter

29 賭場 Casinos

情境式對話 // 談論賭場 139

W → Wilson Tolley M → Maxine Kang

W Maxine, you must be pretty excited about going to the casino tonight, right?	梅可馨，你一定對今天晚上要去賭場很興奮，對吧？
M Yes, very! I have never been to a casino before. Tell me, what should I wear?	是的，非常！我以前從沒去過賭場。告訴我，我該怎麼穿？
W Oh, you can just dress casually. Jeans and a T-shirt will be fine. You should bring your passport with you, though.	噢，穿便服就好了，穿牛仔褲和 T 恤就很好了，不過你要帶護照就是了。
M Why?	為什麼？
W You look quite young. They might want to check your age. You have to be at least 20 to get into the casino.	你看起來很年輕，賭場可能會檢查你的年齡。必須要滿 20 歲才能進賭場。
M I see. Hey, what games can I play there? Is there anything easy?	了解。那我在那裡可以玩什麼遊戲？有什麼簡單的嗎？

W	I recommend that you start with the slot machines or craps. Those are the easiest ones. I play them a lot, too!	我建議你從吃角子老虎或丟雙骰玩起，那些都是最簡單的遊戲，我也很常玩。
M	What exactly are they? Can you explain the rules?	那些到底是什麼遊戲？可以解釋一下規則嗎？
W	With craps, each player or "shooter" rolls two dice[1], and the other players at the table make bets with their chips. As for the slot machine, nothing could be easier. Just put a coin into the machine, then pray for good luck! Last time, I won $500! So today's trip is like free.	丟雙骰嘛，就是其中一個玩家擲兩顆骰子，桌邊的其他玩家則會以籌碼下注。至於吃角子老虎最簡單了。只要把一枚硬幣投進機器，接下來就祈禱好運出現啦！我上次去玩，贏了500 塊！所以今天去跟免費的沒兩樣。
M	No kidding! I hope I'm lucky, too! I will buy you dinner if I win, to thank you for taking me to the casino.	真的假的！希望我也很幸運啊！如果我贏了，會請你吃晚餐，好答謝你帶我去賭場。

[1] dice [daɪs] (n.) 骰子

旅遊小句 Where do I get chips?

29-1 進入賭場前 140

請人推薦	1	Which casino would you suggest I go to?	請問你推薦我去哪家賭場呢？
詢問地點	2	Excuse me, where is the Gold Nugget Casino?	不好意思，請問金塊賭場怎麼走？
營業時間	3	What are the business hours?	請問營業時間是幾點到幾點？
年齡限制	4	Is there a minimum age to enter?	有沒有規定要滿幾歲才能進去？
衣著限制	5	Can I dress casually?	可以穿便服進去嗎？

29-2 兌換錢幣並尋找適合遊戲 141

找兌幣處	1	Where do I get chips?	請問籌碼在哪裡換？
換代幣	2	$200 in chips, please.	我要換 200 塊的籌碼，麻煩你。
	3	What denominations would you like?	請問要換成哪種面額的？
換現金	4	Please cash in your chips.	請將籌碼換成現金。
尋找遊戲	5	What can I play?	有什麼遊戲可以玩？
詢問玩法	6	How do I play this game?	這個遊戲怎麼玩？
玩吃角子老虎	7	I would like to try the slot machine.	我要試試吃角子老虎。
中獎	8	You've hit the jackpot!	您中獎了！

29-3 加入賭局 142

要求加入	1	May I join in?	請問我可以加入嗎？
最低金額	2	What is the minimum bet?	請問最少要下注多少?
下注	3	Place your bet, please.	請下注。
	4	I will bet $10 on this.	我下注十塊。
追加	5	Would you like to hit or stay?	您想要追加或不跟？
	6	I will keep going.	我要追加。
不跟	7	I'll stay.	我不跟了。
再玩一次	8	Once more, please.	再來一次。
退出	9	I quit.	我退出了。

常見賭場遊戲 Typical Casino Games

① 吃角子老虎（SLOT MACHINE）

投硬幣到機器裡，依照螢幕上的圖畫或數字組合，會有不同倍率的獎金。是最多入門者喜愛的遊戲。

② 賭輪盤（ROULETTE）

在數字輪盤上下注，可從不同數字選擇，球停在選擇的數字上就算贏。除了賭數字外，也可賭顏色（紅或黑）、奇數或偶數等。依機率而各有不同的賠率。

③ 百家樂（BACCARAT）

和莊家比賽，誰的牌先接近 9 就算贏。賭金很高，如果沒有很多預算，最好別輕易嘗試。

④ 21 點（BLACKJACK/TWENTY-ONE）

這跟撲克牌的 21 點規則一樣，一個人可以拿兩張以上的牌，看誰的點數最接近 21 卻不超過就贏。

⑤ 擲雙骰（CRAPS）

桌邊每位玩家都有機會下注，每一輪的第一次擲骰稱為 come out role（第一擲），後面的輸贏都與這第一擲有關，玩家須在第一擲前押擲骰結果會不會過關。

3
4
5

Chapter 30 體育比賽 Sporting Events

情境式對話 // 安排去看球賽 143

K → Kimberley Chong　T → Tom Morris

T	Say, Kimberley. There is a baseball game today here in Seattle. Are you interested in going with me?	嘿，金柏莉，今天西雅圖有場棒球賽，有沒有興趣跟我去看啊？
S	What teams are playing?	什麼隊在比？
T	The Seattle Mariners are hosting the Detroit Tigers. I'll bet it's going to be a really exciting game. Both teams are red hot.	地主隊西雅圖水手對上底特律老虎隊。這兩隊都是熱門強隊，我打賭比賽一定會精采萬分。
S	Why not? Can we still get tickets?	那當然去啊。還可以買到票嗎？
T	No problem. The website said that there are still tickets available.	沒問題。網路上寫還可以買到呢。
S	Great. What time does the game start? And how do we get to the stadium? Is it far?	太好了。比賽什麼時候開始啊？另外我們怎麼去球場？很遠嗎？

T	The game starts at 6 p.m. We can take a bus to the stadium. It's about an hour from here to downtown Seattle. But let's go early so we can go to the Seattle Mariners' shop before the game, and you can buy some souvenirs and gifts for your friends. They also have T-shirts and jackets. I always like to wear clothes with the Mariners' logo on them.	球賽晚上六點開始。我們可以坐公車去球場，從這裡到西雅圖市中心大概要一個小時，不過我們早點去好了，這樣可以在比賽前先去西雅圖水手隊的店裡逛逛，你也可以買些紀念品和禮物給朋友。那裡也有 T 恤和外套。我向來喜歡穿有水手隊標誌的衣服。
S	Well, that means that I had better bring some spending money then!	啊，那就是說我最好帶多點錢去！
T	Maybe. But I promise you, it is worth it. You'll have a great time.	或許吧。不過我向你保證，那很值得的。你會玩得很開心。

旅遊小句 // What is the score?

30-1 觀看比賽前詢問 144

詢問賽事	1	What sporting events are being held there this week?	請問這禮拜有什麼體育賽事嗎？
比賽日期	2	When are the Yankees playing?	請問洋基隊什麼時候有比賽？
賽程表	3	Where can I get a program?	請問賽程表在哪裡拿?
找尋球場	4	Where is Dodger Stadium?	請問道奇隊的球場在哪裡？
購買紀念品	5	Do they sell souvenirs at the stadium?	請問球場有販售紀念品嗎？
參賽球隊	6	What teams are playing today?	請問今天是哪兩隊比賽？
球賽結束時間	7	When is the game scheduled to end?	請問比賽大概幾點會結束？

30-2 購買球票與索票 145

何處買票	1	Where can I get tickets for today's match?	請問今天的球賽門票可以去哪裡買？
購買球賽門票	2	May I have two tickets for level one, please, as close to the infield as possible?	我可以要兩張底層的票嗎？愈靠近內野愈好。
網路購票	3	May I book a ticket online?	請問可以在網上訂票嗎？
取預訂票	4	Where should I pick up the tickets that I reserved online earlier?	我已經網路訂票了，請問要去哪裡拿？
	5	You can pick them up at the ticket office. You'll need to show a printout of your receipt to collect your tickets.	您可以在售票處取票，但你需要印出購票證明才能取票。

30-3 觀看各球類比賽 146

詢問先發名單	1	Who are the starting players for today's game?	請問今天的先發球員是誰？
詢問棒球投手	2	Who is the pitcher today?	請問今天的投手是誰?
詢問領先隊伍	3	Who is ahead?	現在誰領先？
詢問比數	4	What is the score?	現在比數是多少？
	5	The Yankees are leading the Red Sox by three.	洋基隊領先紅襪隊三分。
	6	The Yankees are ahead of the Red Sox 4 to 1.	洋基隊以四比一領先紅襪隊。
被判罰球	7	Manchester United just got a penalty.	曼聯隊剛剛得到罰球機會。
全壘打	8	A homerun! How about that?	全壘打！怎麼樣啊？
加油	9	Lakers! Go! Go! Go!	湖人隊加油！
犯規	10	He committed a foul.	那個球員犯規。
灌籃	11	Jeremy Lin just made a slam dunk!	林書豪剛剛灌籃了！
延長賽	12	The game is going into overtime now.	現在要打延長賽了。

旅遊資訊補充包

運動相關術語 Terms About Sports

常見球賽

soccer/football（美／英）足球

tennis 網球

volleyball 排球

ice hockey 冰上曲棍球

(American) football 美式足球；橄欖球

rugby 英式橄欖球

baseball 棒球

basketball 籃球

badminton 羽毛球

table tennis / ping-pong 桌球

golf 高爾夫球

bowling 保齡球

billiards 撞球

squash 壁球

棒球相關術語

選手	coach 教練	pitcher 投手	catcher 捕手
	batter 打擊手	infielder 內野手	outfielder 外野手
	shortstop 游擊手	umpire/official/ referee 裁判	MVP 最有價值球員
場地／設備	baseball field 棒球場	home plate 本壘	first/second/third base 一／二／三壘
	pitcher's mound 投手丘	batter's box 打擊區	dugout （賽場中）球員休息處
	bat 球棒	glove 手套	
技巧	throw 投球	hit 安打	homerun 全壘打
	stolen base 盜壘	safe 安全上壘	
計分	strike 好球	ball 壞球	strikeout 三振出局
	double play 雙殺	error 失誤	hit by pitch 觸身球

籃球相關術語

選手	forward 前鋒	center 中鋒	guard 後衛
場地／設備	basketball court 籃球場	frontcourt 前場	backcourt 後場
	basket/rim 籃框	backboard 籃板	
技巧	pass 傳球	charge 進攻	defend 防守
	dribble/bounce 運球	shoot 投籃	layup 上籃
	reject 蓋火鍋	slam dunk 灌籃	timeout 暫停
計分	three pointer 三分球	bank shot 擦板球	foul 犯規
	traveling/walking 走步	reaching in (foul) 打手	charging 帶球撞人
	penalty shot/foul shot/free throw 罰球		

足球相關術語

選手	lineman 線審	captain/leader 隊長	forward/striker 前鋒
	central attacking midfielder 前腰	central defending midfielder 後腰	center back 中後衛
	left/right back 左／右邊衛	goalkeeper 守門員	
場地／設備	field 足球場	goalpost 球門柱	crossbar 球門楣
	goal 球門	goal line 球門線	penalty area 禁區
	touchline/sideline 邊線	locker room 球員休息室	
技巧	kick-off 開球	pass 傳球	dribble 盤球／帶球
	header 頭球	corner ball 角球	free kick 任意球
	slide tackle 鏟球	shoot 射門	throw-in 擲界外球
計分	offside 越位	fake injury/dive/diving 假摔	body check 阻擋
	yellow card 黃牌（警告）	red card 紅牌（離場）	goal 進球
	stoppage/injury time 傷停補時	penalty kick PK 大戰	draw 平局

美式橄欖球相關術語

選手	center 中鋒	offensive guard 哨鋒	offensive tackle 絆鋒
	quarterback 四分衛	running back 跑衛	tight end 邊鋒
	linebacker 線衛	cornerback 角衛	safety 安全衛
場地／設備	football field 橄欖球場	yard line 分碼線	end zone 達陣區
	goalpost 門柱	helmet 頭盔	
技巧	kick 踢	tackle 擒抱	interception 抄截
計分	touchdown 達陣	holding 阻擋	pass interference 干擾傳球

Unit 8

Shopping
血拼高手購物篇

Chapter 31 購物訊息 Shopping Information

情境式對話 // 詢問購物退稅 147

S → Store Clerk　Y → Yolanda Hsieh

Y	Hi. I am a tourist here. I just bought a leather jacket for $150. Can I get a tax refund?	你好，我是觀光客。我剛剛買了一件 150 美元的皮外套，請問可以退稅嗎？
S	I think so. May I see your passport so I can get your information, please?	我想可以。可以請您出示護照，讓我看您的資料嗎?
Y	Sure. Here you go.	好，護照給你。
S	Thanks, Ms. Hsieh. I will make out a tax refund form for you.	謝小姐，謝謝，我會寫一張退稅單給您。
Y	I'm not sure what to do with the form.	我不清楚這張單子要做什麼。
S	When you leave the country, just take this form and the jacket you just bought to the customs office at the airport. After confirming your information, they will stamp the form and mail it to our office.	您出境時，只要拿著這張單子和您剛買的外套到機場海關，海關會在確認您的資料後，在單子上蓋章，並把單子寄回本店。
Y	Is that all?	那樣就可以了？

S	After we receive the form, we will send your refund to you.	我們收到單子以後，會把您的稅款退給您。
Y	I see. How will I get the refund?	了解。那我要怎麼收到退稅？
S	We can either send you a check or transfer[1] the money to your credit card account.	我們可以寄支票給您，或是把錢轉到您的信用卡帳戶裡。
Y	Well, I prefer transferring the money to my account. That's easier.	那我選擇把錢轉到信用卡帳戶，那樣簡單多了。
S	That's no problem. May I see your credit card for a second?	沒問題。我可以看一下您的信用卡嗎？
Y	Of course.	當然可以。
S	OK, that's all I need. Thanks for shopping with us, and enjoy the rest of your stay!	好的，這樣就可以了。謝謝您至本店消費，祝您後續旅途愉快。
Y	Thank you so much!	非常謝謝你！

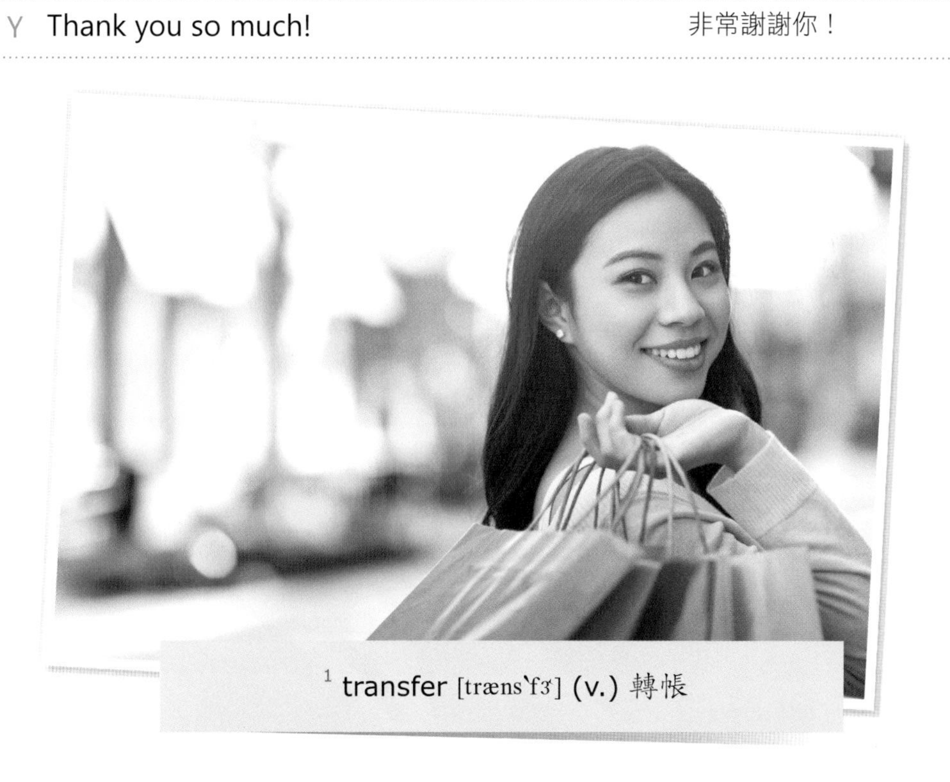

[1] **transfer** [træns`fɝ] (v.) 轉帳

旅遊小句 *Can you make it any cheaper?*

31-1 尋找特定購物地點 148

何處購買電器	1	I would like to buy some electrical appliances. Where should I go?	我想要買一些電器用品，請問哪裡有？
	2	You could try Argos. They have the widest selection.	你可以去愛顧商城，那裡有最多選擇。
尋找購物中心	3	Which shopping center has the best selection?	請問哪家購物中心產品最多？
尋找購物區	4	Is there a shopping outlet around here?	請問這附近有暢貨中心嗎？
尋找市集	5	Where is a flea/antique market?	請問哪裡有跳蚤／古董市場？
市集營業時間	6	On what day is the flea market open?	請問哪一天有跳蚤市場？
詢問城市名產	7	What is this city famous for?	請問這個城市有什麼名產嗎？
尋找設計師店	8	I am looking for the designer clothing shops.	我在找設計師品牌的服飾店。
尋找二手貨店	9	I am looking for some second-hand goods. Where should I go?	我在找二手商品，請問哪裡有？

31-2 詢問商店的營業、交通與折扣 149

詢問週日營業時間	1	Is that store open on Sundays?	請問那家店星期天有沒有開？
詢問一般營業時間	2	What are their business hours?	請問他們的營業時間是？
詢問前往方式	3	Excuse me. How can I get to the Good Buy Shopping Center?	請問一下，真划算購物中心要怎麼去？
可搭乘接駁車	4	There is a shuttle bus leaving for the shopping center every 30 minutes from the train station.	每 30 分鐘都有一班接駁車從火車站開往購物中心。
詢問是否打折	5	Are the department stores holding sales now?	請問百貨公司現在有特價嗎？
詢問折扣期間	6	When will Marks and Spencer have a sale?	請問馬莎百貨什麼時候會有促銷活動？
詢問最低折扣	7	What is the maximum discount?	最低有可能到幾折？
刷卡免手續費	8	Foreign travelers don't have to pay a handling charge if they pay with Master Card at the store.	外國旅客到這家店持萬事達卡消費時，可以刷卡免手續費。

31-3 購物殺價基本用語 150

要求打折	1	Can you give me a discount if I buy more?	如果我買多一點，可以打折嗎？
	2	I can give you ten percent off.	我可以給您打九折。
	3	Can you make it any cheaper?	請問可以便宜一點嗎？
	4	That's our rock-bottom price.	這已經是最低價了。
告知給折扣就買	5	I will take it if you lower the price.	如果便宜一點我就買。
	6	All our prices are fixed.	我們的價錢都是不二價。
要求更低價物品	7	Do you have anything in a lower price range?	請問有沒有便宜一點價位的？
告知能負擔金額	8	My last offer is $50.	我最多只能出 50 塊。

商家常見標語 Common Shop Signs

已售罄

特價中

故障中

打烊

緊急出口

消防集結點

營業中

推／拉

員工專用

31-4 詢問退稅事宜 151

物品是否含稅	1	Does the price include tax?	請問這價錢含稅嗎？
物品可否退稅	2	Can I get a tax refund for this?	請問這個可以退稅嗎？
退稅額度	3	How much do I have to spend to get the tax refund?	要消費至多少錢才可以退稅？
退稅金額	4	How much refund will I get?	會退多少錢？
退款方式	5	Can I get cash back?	會退現金給我嗎？
如何退稅	6	How do I claim a tax refund?	請問怎麼申請退稅？

退稅之準備文件	7	What do I need to get the tax refund?	請問辦理退稅要準備什麼？
	8	You will need your passport, flight ticket, tax refund form, and the items you purchased.	您要備妥護照、機票、退稅申請表及購買的物品。
索取退稅申請表	9	May I have a tax refund form, please?	請問可以給我一張退稅申請表嗎？
何處退稅	10	Where can I apply for the tax refund?	請問我要在哪裡辦理退稅？
	11	You can apply for the tax refund in the airport.	您可以在機場辦理。
退稅條件	12	If you are qualified for a refund, you will get the money immediately.	只要您合乎退稅標準，我們會立即退錢給您。
退款等候時間	13	How long do I have to wait for the refund?	要多久才會收到退稅？
	14	It normally takes about five to six weeks.	通常要五至六個星期。

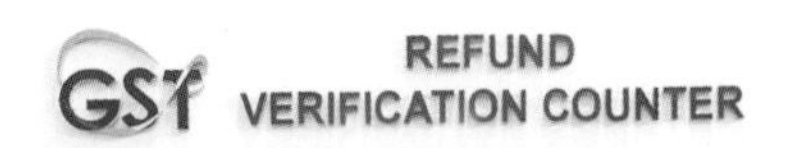

退稅的方法 Tax Refund

出國旅遊消費時，若金額達到該國退稅規定，記得要向店家提出欲申請退稅的要求。通常店家會要求出示護照，並給一張收據與蓋了店章的退稅單。

只要將此兩份文件收妥，在出境機場索取並填寫退稅申請表，連同購買的物品一併辦理，便能申請退稅。接受審查後，將已蓋章的退稅申請表寄回當初購物的店家，即可於一段時間後收到退款（有些國家當場即能退款予旅客。）

退稅方式很多，填寫退稅申請表（VAT Refund Form）時，便可以選擇以現金、支票、或是匯款方式收款。

如果前往旅遊的國家是歐盟國家，且在該國旅行後還要繼續前往其他歐盟國家，則可在行程中的最後一個歐盟國家，統一辦理退稅。

一般說來，欲申請退稅的物品，購買日期須在出國日期起的三個月內，逾期則無法辦理。

Chapter 32 購買服飾與鞋子 Shopping for Clothes & Shoes

情境式對話 購買衣服 152

S → Store Sales　J → Jeffery Sun

S	Good evening. What can I do for you?	晚安，請問有什麼可以為您服務的嗎？
J	Hello. I like this shirt, but I think it's too big for me. Do you have it in a smaller size?	你好。我很喜歡這件襯衫，但我覺得太大了。請問有小一點的嗎？
S	What size do you usually wear?	請問您通常穿幾號？
J	I usually wear a large in Taiwan, but I am not sure what size I am here.	我在臺灣通常穿大號，但我不確定在這裡穿幾號。
S	No problem. Let me measure you. I think a medium will be fine for you.	沒有關係，我幫您量一下。我想您穿中號就可以了。
J	OK. By the way, what other colors does this shirt come in?	好的。另外，請問這件襯衫有哪些顏色？
S	We have six different colors: black, blue, gray, white, green and brown.	我們有六種顏色：黑色、藍色、灰色、白色、綠色以及咖啡色。
J	May I see a blue one?	可以看一下藍色的嗎？

S	Let me see. Oh, I am sorry, but this color is out of stock[1] right now. Would you like to try another color?	我看看喔。很抱歉，這款顏色目前缺貨。您要看別的顏色嗎？
J	Well, in that case, let me see the white one. Oh, if the sleeves are too long, can you alter[2] them for me?	這樣的話，就看看白色的。對了，如果袖子太長，你們可以幫我修改嗎？
S	Yes. We do make alterations[3], but we charge $5 per item.	可以。我們可以幫客戶修改，但每件衣服另收五塊。
J	I see. Can I try it on first?	了解，我可以先試穿嗎？
S	Of course. The fitting rooms are this way, please.	當然可以，試衣間這邊請。

[1] out of stock 無現貨
[2] alter [ˋɔltɚ] (v.) 修改
[3] alteration [ˏɔltɚˋreʃən] (n.) 修改

旅遊小句 Where can I find children's clothing?

32-1 尋找特定部門與產品 153

找尋部門	1	Where can I find children's clothing?	請問童裝部怎麼走？
告知購買對象	2	I am looking for a T-shirt for a teenage boy.	我想找一件青少年男生可以穿的 T 恤。
找尋特定服裝	3	I am looking for some formal wear.	我在找正式的服裝。
買毛衣	4	Do you carry cashmere sweaters here?	請問有沒有喀什米爾羊絨毛衣？
買棉質衣物	5	I am looking for some cotton clothing.	我想找些棉質的衣服。
買高跟鞋	6	I need a pair of pink high-heels. Can you please tell me where I can find them?	我需要一雙粉紅色的高跟鞋，可以請你告訴我哪裡有嗎？
買尖頭靴	7	Do you have any boots with pointed toes?	請問有沒有尖頭的靴子？
買無鞋帶皮鞋	8	I prefer pumps. Do you carry any?	我喜歡不綁鞋帶的高跟鞋，這裡有嗎？

32-2 詢問材質與樣式 154

詢問材質	1	What is this made of?	請問這是什麼料子？
詢問產地	2	Where is this made?	請問這是哪裡製造的？
詢問顏色	3	What other color does this come in?	請問有別的顏色嗎？
	4	We don't have any other colors at the moment.	其他的顏色目前缺貨。
請求調貨	5	Would it be possible to check with one of your other stores?	可以請你幫我確認看看其他分店是否有貨嗎？
	6	I can try to have one transferred, but it'll take three to five days. Is that ok with you?	我會試著幫您調貨，但要等三至五天，請問可以嗎？
詢問花色	7	Is there anything else with a similar pattern or in a similar style?	請問還有類似的花色或樣式嗎？
可否於分店買到	8	Would I be able to buy this at one of your other branches?	請問這個可以在別的分店買到嗎？

32-3 尺寸與試穿 155

可否試穿	1	Can/May I try it on?	請問可以試穿嗎？
詢問尺寸	2	What size is this?	請問這是多大的？
請人量身	3	What is your size?	請問您穿幾號？
	4	Could you please measure me?	可以請你幫我量一下嗎？
其他尺寸	5	Do you have anything larger?	請問有大一點的嗎？
衣服不合身	6	This is too long/short/loose/tight.	這個太長／短／鬆／緊了。
	7	It doesn't fit.	這不合身。
鞋子太緊	8	The shoes are too tight in the front.	這鞋頭太緊了。
尺寸正好	9	This is just my size.	這我穿起來剛好。
詢問他人意見	10	How do I look?	我看起來怎麼樣？
	11	Do I look all right in this?	我穿起來好看嗎？
試穿別件	12	Can I please try on something else?	請問可以試穿別的嗎？
	13	Can I please try a different size?	請問可以試穿別的尺寸嗎？

32-4 要求修改 156

要求幫忙修改	1	Could you please alter the length of this coat?	請問可以幫我改這件外套的長度嗎？
詢問欲改之長短	2	How much would you like it shortened?	請問您要改多短？
	3	Three inches shorter, please.	請改短約三吋。
及膝長度	4	I would like to make it knee-length.	要改到膝蓋的高度。
腰圍縮小	5	I'd like the waist altered to a smaller size.	請把腰圍改小一點。
腰圍放大	6	Please let out the waist by two centimeters.	請把腰圍改大兩公分。
修改時間	7	How long will it take?	請問改好要多久？
要求提早交貨	8	Can you finish it any earlier?	可以早一點改好嗎？
取件時間	9	When can I get it back / pick it up?	請問什麼時候可以來拿？
修改費用	10	How much do you charge for alterations?	修改費用是多少？

32-5 詢問清潔與保存方式 157

能否以洗衣機清洗	1	Is it machine-washable?	請問這可以用洗衣機洗嗎？
是否需乾洗	2	Should it be dry-cleaned?	請問這是要用乾洗的嗎？
	3	No, but don't put it in the washing machine. It needs to be hand-washed.	不用，但請不要放入洗衣機洗，要用手洗。
如何收納	4	How do I store this dress?	請問這件禮服要怎麼收納？
	5	Lay it flat. Do not use a hanger.	要平放，不要吊在衣架上。
是否會縮水	6	Will it shrink?	請問這會縮水嗎？
保存方法	7	Put the paper tubes in the boots when you are not wearing them.	靴子不穿的時候，放紙筒在裡面。
告知清潔方式	8	You can wipe off the shoes with a wet towel.	鞋子髒了的話，可以用濕布擦拭。
使用鞋油	9	What kind of shoe polish should I use?	我該使用哪種鞋油？

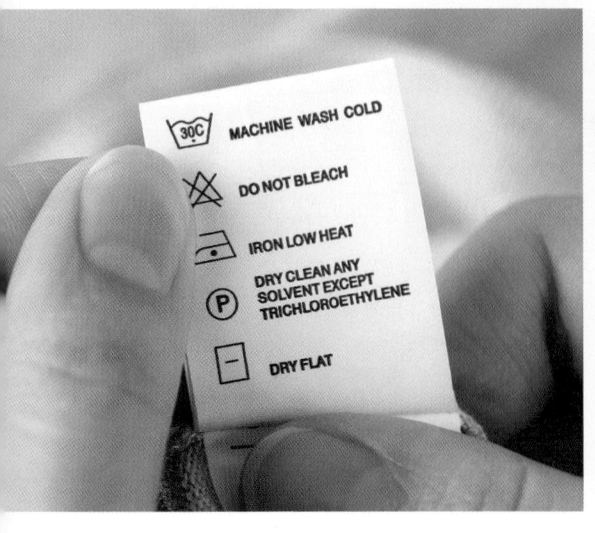

32-6 購買與付帳 (158)

只是看看	1	I am just looking.	我只是看看。
要考慮	2	I want to think about it.	我考慮一下。
不買	3	I think I'd like to pass this time.	這次就先不買了。
決定購買	4	I will take it.	我就買這個。
帳單有誤	5	What I bought is a pair of shoes, not two shirts.	我是買一雙鞋，不是兩件襯衫。
貨品不對	6	This is not what I picked out.	這不是我要的那件。

32-7 購物後抱怨與退貨 (159)

尺碼不對	1	I bought this skirt here last week, but it's too tight. Can I exchange it for a larger one?	我上禮拜買了這條裙子，但太緊了，請問可以換大一點的嗎？
縮水	2	I washed the shirt the way you told me, but it still shrank.	我照你說的方法洗這件襯衫，但還是縮水了。
包裝有誤	3	The shoes I brought home were not the same pair I bought. There must have been a mistake during packing.	我帶回家的鞋，不是當初買的那雙，一定是包裝的時候弄錯了。
要求退貨	4	I would like to get a refund. / I would like to return it.	我要退貨。
要求換貨	5	Can I get a new one?	請問可以換新的嗎？
	6	If you have your receipt, we would be happy to exchange that for you.	如果您有發票，我們很樂意換給您。

旅遊資訊補充包

各式服裝 Clothing

上半身 Tops

coat 大衣

jacket 外套

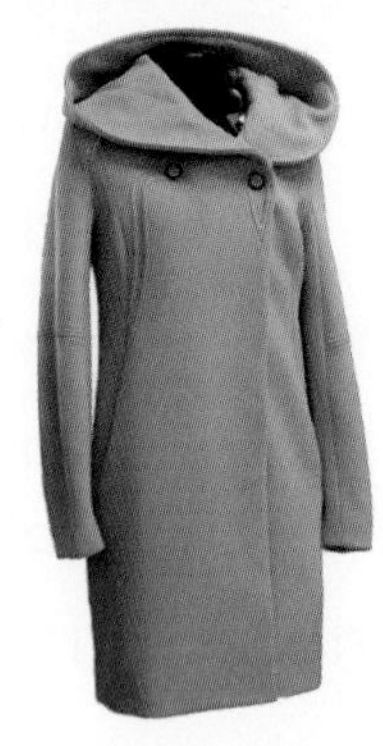
overcoat 長大衣

suit 西裝

shirt 襯衫

sweater 毛衣

blouse 女用上衣

T-shirt T 恤

hoodie 帶帽運動衫

cardigan 開襟羊毛衫

下半身 Bottoms

skirt 裙子

shorts 短褲

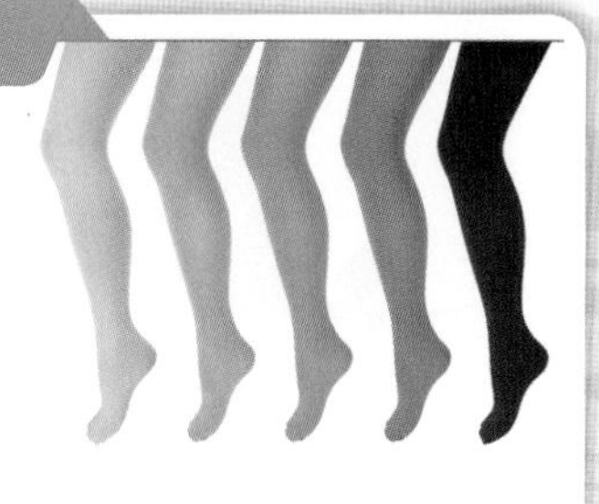
pantyhose/tights
（美／英）褲襪

pants/trousers
（美／英）長褲

jeans 牛仔褲

overalls 吊帶褲

leggings
內搭褲

dress 洋裝

內衣褲與家居服 Underwear & Loungewear

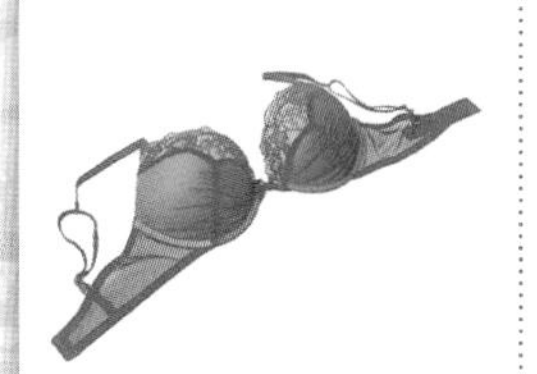
bra 女性內衣

underpants 內褲

boxer (shorts)
男用四角內褲

vest 背心

socks 短襪

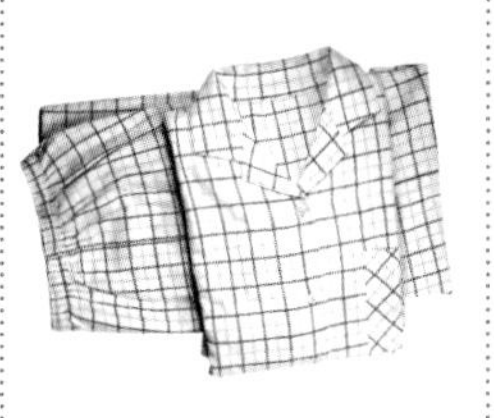
pajamas 睡衣

bathrobe 浴袍

nightgown
睡袍

鞋款 Footwear

sandals 涼鞋

Oxfords 牛津鞋

slippers 拖鞋

high heels 高跟鞋

sneakers 運動鞋

flip-flops 夾腳拖

boots 靴子

loafers 休閒鞋

flats 平底鞋

wellies 雨靴

配件 Accessories

scarf 圍巾

hat 帽子

gloves 手套

belt 皮帶

tie 領帶

sunglasses 太陽眼鏡

尺寸說法 Size

衣飾尺寸

XS (extra small) 特小號

S (small) 小號

M (medium) 中號

L (large) 大號

XL (extra large) 特大號

人體尺寸

head circumference 頭圍

collar measurement 領圍

chest measurement 胸圍

bust measurement 女性胸圍

arm circumference 臂圍

waist circumference 腰圍

hip circumference 臀圍

measurements 三圍

leg length 腿長

各種質料

leather 皮

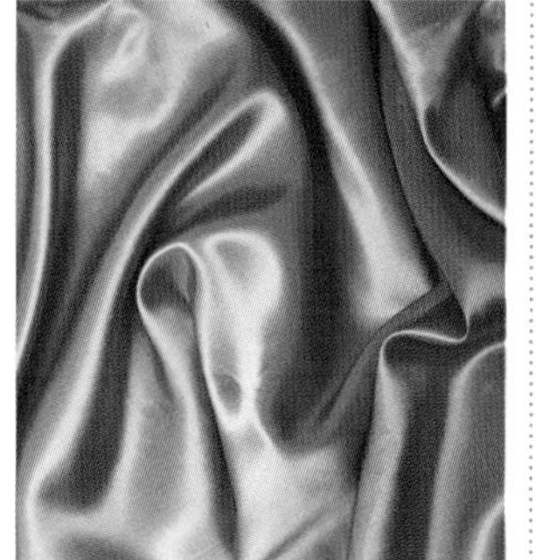

silk 絲

wool 羊毛

artificial leather 人造皮

cashmere 喀什米爾羊絨

cotton 棉

Chapter

33 購買首飾配件 Shopping for Jewelry & Accessories

情境式對話 // 購買胸針 160

S → Shop Salesman V → Veronica Wan

V	Excuse me. Would you please show me that brooch?	請問一下，我可以看一下那支胸針嗎？
S	Sure. Is this the one you want?	可以啊。您是要看這支嗎？
V	No, the one next to it. Thanks. What kind of stone is this?	不是，是旁邊的那支。謝謝。請問這是哪種寶石？
S	It's an emerald. It is from South Africa. Do you want to try it on?	這是祖母綠，產地在南非。您要試戴嗎？
V	Yes, please. How much is it?	好，麻煩你。這支多少錢？
S	It costs £108.	108 英鎊。
V	Wow! That's kind of expensive.	哇！有點貴啊。
S	Actually, it's a very good price, and this is a unique brooch. So you will never need to worry about someone else wearing one just like it.	事實上，這價錢是很划算的，而且這個款式獨一無二，永遠不必擔心別人也會戴類似的胸針。

V	I like it, but it's far beyond my budget right now. Do you have something else in a similar style but at a cheaper price?	我是很喜歡，可是我沒那麼多預算。有類似的樣式但便宜一點的嗎？
S	Well, how about this one? It's made of coral and comes from Hawaii. And it's only a third of the price of the last one. You can have it for just £37.50.	那麼這支如何？這是珊瑚製的，產地是夏威夷，只要剛才那支約三成的價格而已，才 37 英鎊 50 便士。
V	Are you sure it's genuine[1]?	這確定是真品嗎？
S	Of course. Every item here is the real thing.	當然。本店的每樣商品都是真貨。
V	I see. £37.50 is a pretty good price, but £35 is all I can afford. How about it? Can you give it to me for that price?	了解。37 英鎊 50 便士是好價錢沒錯，不過我只能出到 35 英鎊。可以 35 英鎊賣給我嗎？
S	Well, you really seem to like it. So, OK. £35 is fine, just for you.	看來您是真的很喜歡這支胸針。那好吧，就 35 英鎊，這價錢只賣給您。
V	Thank you. That's very nice of you.	謝謝你。你人真好。

[1] genuine [ˋdʒɛnjʊɪn] (adj.) 真正的；非偽造的

旅遊小句 // Are you looking for anything specific?

33-1 購買特定首飾 161

店員提供幫助	1	Are you looking for anything specific?	請問您有特別想看什麼嗎？
買婚戒	2	Do you sell wedding rings?	請問有結婚對戒嗎？
買項鍊	3	I'd like to see some platinum necklaces.	我想要看白金項鍊。
告知預算	4	Do you have earrings or necklaces that cost around $150?	請問有 150 塊上下的耳環或項鍊嗎？
要求看商品	5	May I see the necklace shown in the window?	請問可以看櫥窗裡的那款項鍊嗎？

33-2 詢問尺寸與材質 162

詢問戒圍尺寸	1	What size is this ring?	請問這枚戒指戒圍幾號?
要求量指圍	2	Could you please measure my ring finger?	請問可以幫我量無名指的指圍嗎？
其它樣式	3	Are there any other patterns?	有別的樣式嗎？
詢問寶石種類	4	What is this stone?	這是哪種寶石？
寶石產地	5	Where is the stone from?	這寶石的產地是哪裡？
是否為真品	6	Is it real/genuine?	這是真的寶石嗎？
多少 K 金	7	How many karats is it?	這是多少 K 金的？
	8	It's 18-karat gold.	18K 金。

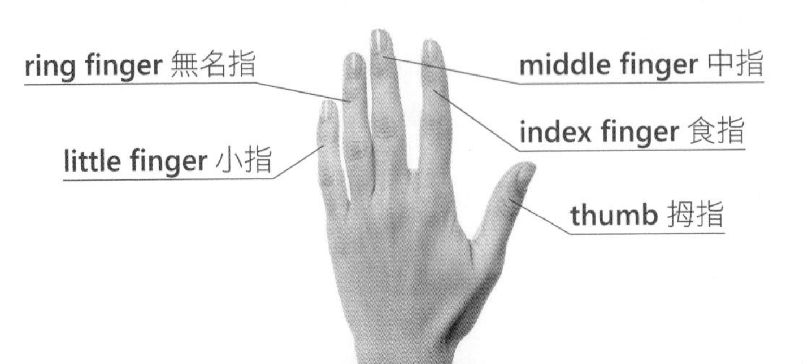

33-3 購買手錶 163

要求看男錶	1	Can I see some men's watches?	請問可以看一些男錶嗎?
買男女對錶	2	Do you carry pair watches?	請問有男女對錶嗎？
詢問手錶功能	3	What functions does this watch have?	請問這手錶有什麼功能?
	4	This is a luminous watch with an alarm function.	這是夜光錶，有鬧鐘功能。
是否有計時功能	5	Does this watch have a timer function?	這隻手錶可以計時嗎?
防水錶	6	I am looking for a waterproof watch.	我要買防水錶。
是否使用電池	7	Does it work with batteries?	這是要用電池的嗎？
可否調整錶帶	8	Can the watchband be adjusted?	這個錶帶可以調整嗎?
詢問價錢	9	How much does a Rolex watch cost?	請問勞力士的手錶多少錢？
有無保證書	10	Do you provide a (worldwide) warranty?	有提供（全球）保固嗎？

鐘錶 Clocks & Watches

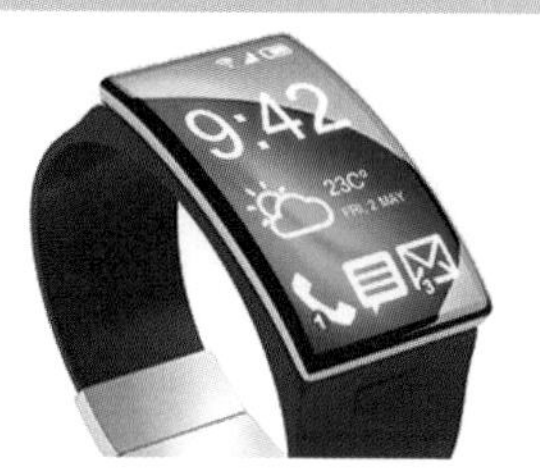

smart watch 智慧手錶

second hand 秒針
watchband (美)
watchstrap (英) 錶帶
hour hand 時針
minute hand 分針

pocket watch 懷錶

alarm clock 鬧鐘

digital watch 電子錶

33-4 眼睛驗光及配眼鏡 164

要求檢查視力	1	Would you please check my vision?	請問可以幫我檢查視力嗎？
詢問視力	2	How is my vision?	請問我的視力如何？
	3	You are slightly shortsighted.	您有輕微近視。
告知眼睛狀況	4	You are shortsighted, with a touch of astigmatism.	您有近視外加一點散光。
買隱形眼鏡	5	I need a pair of contact lenses. Here's the prescription.	我要一副隱形眼鏡，這是處方箋。
詢問何種適合	6	Which contact lenses are better for me, disposable or regular ones?	請問拋棄式或常戴型哪種比較適合我？
買太陽眼鏡	7	I would like a pair of sunglasses.	我要買一副太陽眼鏡。
告知不喜歡之款式	8	I don't like the gold frames.	我不喜歡金邊眼鏡。
要求款式	9	I'd like my glasses with a silver frame and safety lenses.	我要銀色框加安全鏡片的眼鏡。
要求附上眼鏡盒	10	May I have a glasses case?	可以給我一個眼鏡盒嗎？

旅遊資訊補充包　視力 Eyesight

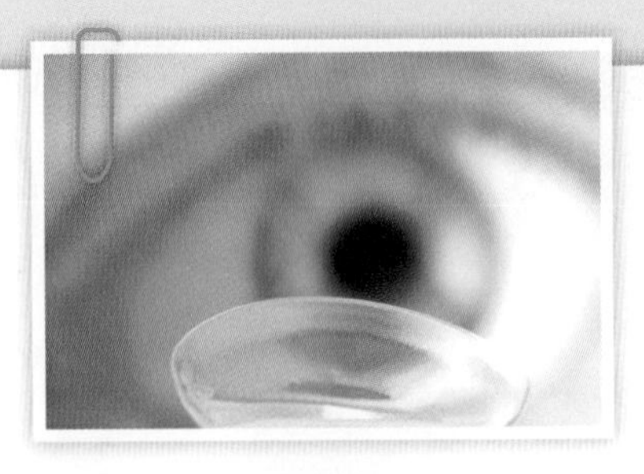

- ◊ **myopia** [maɪˋopɪə] 近視
  nearsightedness (美)
  shortsightedness (英)
- ◊ **hyperopia** [ˏhaɪpəˋropɪə] 遠視
  farsightedness (美)
  longsightedness (英)
- ◊ **astigmatism** [əˋstɪgməˏtɪzəm] 散光
- ◊ **presbyopia** [ˏprɛzbɪˋopɪə] 老花眼
- ◊ **reading glasses** 老花眼鏡
- ◊ **contact lenses** 隱形眼鏡

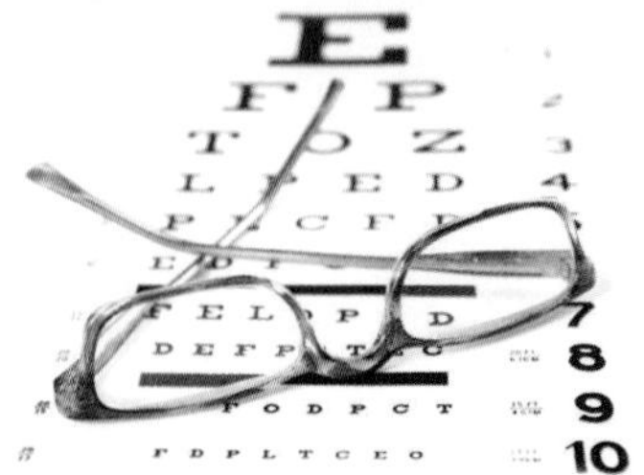

旅遊資訊補充包 首飾與寶石 Jewelry & Gems

首飾 Jewelry

ring 戒指

earrings 耳環

necklace 項鍊

brooch 胸針

bracelet/bangle 手鐲

tiepin 領帶夾

寶石 Gem

diamond 鑽石

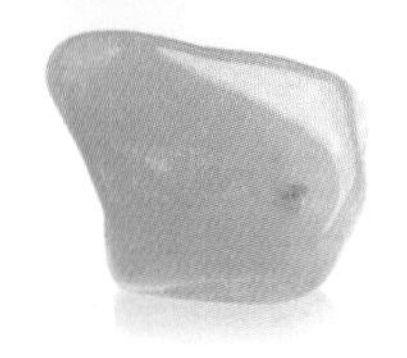
jade 玉

ruby 紅寶石

agate 瑪瑙

sapphire 藍寶石

crystal 水晶

emerald 祖母綠

amethyst 紫水晶

pearl 珍珠

amber 琥珀

Chapter

34 購買化妝保養用品 Shopping for Cosmetics

情境式對話 // 購買化妝品 (165)

S → Store Sales　A → Anrea Tseng

S	May I help you?	請問您需要幫忙嗎？
A	Yes, I am looking for some foundation.	是的，我想找粉底。
S	Do you have a particular brand in mind?	請問您有沒有特別想買哪個品牌？
A	No, but I prefer foundation with some sun protection.	沒有，但我想買可以防曬的粉底。
S	Then I suggest that you try this new product from Bobbi Brown. It's a great foundation, and also protects you from ultraviolet rays[1]. It is our best seller[2] this month, and is on sale just in time for summer.	那我建議您可以試試這款芭比波朗的新產品。這款粉底很不錯，也能抵擋紫外線。這是我們這個月賣得最好的產品，而且只在夏天促銷喔。
A	Sounds good. How much is it?	聽起來不錯。請問多少錢？

S	It's $40. But we are having a big promotion right now: if you spend more than $70 on Bobbi Brown products, you get a complimentary travel pack. Inside the bag, you will find a bottle of shampoo, along with some bath gel, lotion and facial cleanser. Would you like to take a look at some other products as well, so you can take advantage of our special offer?	40 元，不過我們目前有一項大型促銷活動：如果您購買超過 70 元的芭比波朗產品，就可以獲得一組免費的旅行組。裡面有一瓶洗髮精，還有幾瓶沐浴膠、乳液以及洗面乳。您要不要利用這次的優惠，再看看別的產品？
A	Sure. I would like to check out some new perfume.	好啊，我想看看一些新香水。
S	How about this one? It is the latest product, and it has a nice lavender scent, very light and refreshing for summer. Here is the tester. Try it.	這款香水如何？這是新產品，有很好聞的薰衣草香味，清新淡雅，很適合夏天使用；來試試看試用品。
A	It does smell nice. What size bottle is this?	聞起來真的是很不錯。這瓶容量是多少？
S	It contains 100 ml., and it goes for $50.	100 毫升，價格是 50 元。
A	OK. I will take it along with the foundation.	好，我就買這瓶香水還有粉底吧。

[1] ultraviolet ray 紫外線
[2] best seller 暢銷品

旅遊小句 What is your skin type?

34-1 各類彩妝品 166

粉底	1	I would like to buy a foundation with sun protection.	我想找可以防曬的粉底。
遮瑕膏	2	Is there anything that will help cover my freckles?	請問有沒有什麼產品可以蓋住我的雀斑？
	3	I recommend this concealer from Shiseido.	我建議您買資生堂的遮瑕膏。
睫毛膏	4	What's the difference between these two mascaras?	請問這兩款睫毛膏有什麼不同？
	5	This one makes your eyelashes look longer, and the other one creates a bushy effect.	這款可以讓睫毛看起來比較纖長，而另外一款製造濃密效果。
顏色選擇	6	I like bright colors.	我喜歡亮一點的顏色。
指甲油	7	Can I try this nail polish on and see how it looks?	請問可以試用這款指甲油嗎？
口紅	8	Do you have the latest lipstick from Chanel?	請問你們有新出的香奈兒口紅嗎？
	9	What shades do you like?	請問您要什麼顏色？
潤唇口紅	10	Do you have any moisturizing lipstick?	請問你們有沒有潤唇口紅？

34-2 基礎保養品 167

告知膚質	1	What is your skin type?	請問您是那種膚質？
	2	My skin is oily/dry/sensitive/normal.	油性／乾性／敏感性／一般肌膚。
去痘產品	3	Do you have anything that can help me clear up pimples and acne?	請問有沒有可以去除痘痘和拔粉刺的產品？
	4	Yes, this cream has been clinically proven to clear up acne.	有的，這款乳霜經臨床證實可以清除粉刺。
保濕產品	5	Will these keep my face hydrated?	請問這些產品可以讓臉部保濕嗎？
	6	Which one can help my skin lock in moisture?	請問什麼產品可以幫助臉部保濕？
乳液使用	7	How do I apply this lotion?	這種乳液怎麼用？
眼霜使用	8	Do I use this eye cream every day?	這眼霜是每天都要擦嗎？
詢問功效	9	What special effect does this product have?	請問這個產品有什麼特殊功效嗎？

34-3 香水 168

尋找特定香水	1	Do you have the latest Dior perfume?	請問你們有迪奧新出的香水嗎？
何款最受歡迎	2	Which perfume is your best seller?	請問那一款香水最受歡迎？
告知喜好	3	I like light perfumes.	我喜歡淡香水。
詢問味道	4	What are the bottom notes in this perfume?	請問這款香水的後味是什麼？
尋找特定味道香水	5	Which perfume has a jasmine scent?	請問有茉莉花香味的香水嗎？
香水容量	6	How many milliliters are there in this bottle?	請問這瓶香水是多少毫升？
使香味持久	7	How can I get the scent to stay on me longer?	請問怎麼讓香味留久一點？
	8	Spraying the fragrance just behind your earlobes and down along the neck will help.	將香水噴在耳垂後到後頸部位就可以了。

34-4 衛生用品 169

詢問是否販賣	1	Do you carry sanitary napkins/towels/pads or tampons?	請問有衛生棉或棉條嗎？
體香劑	2	Where can I buy deodorant?	請問哪裡可以買到體香劑？
告知所需物品	3	I need to buy some dental floss/flosser.	我要買一些牙線／牙線棒。
詢問最好的廠牌	4	Which brand of mouthwash is the best?	請問哪一牌的漱口水最好？
詢問位置	5	Which aisle can I find the razors in?	請問哪一條走道可以找到刮鬍刀？

旅遊資訊補充包

護理與美妝 Health Care & Beauty

衛生用品與保養品 Hygiene and Skin Care Products

① shampoo 洗髮精
② hair conditioner 護髮乳
③ moisturizing lotion 保濕乳液
④ shower gel 沐浴乳

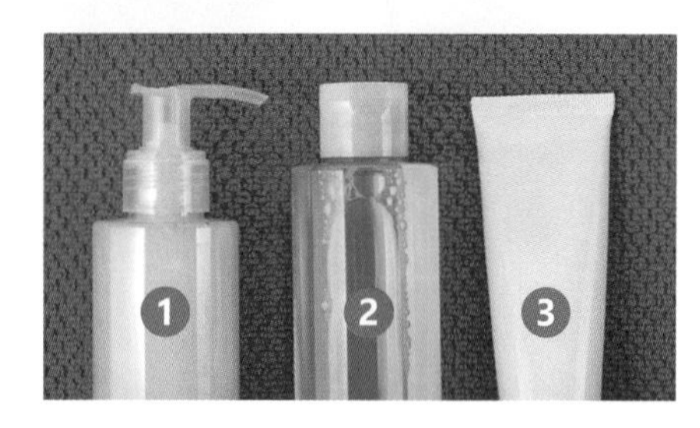

① make-up remover 卸妝水
② toner 緊膚水
③ cleanser 洗面乳

① toothbrush 牙刷
② dental floss 牙線
③ toothpaste 牙膏
④ dental flosser 牙線棒
⑤ shaving cream 刮鬍膏
⑥ razor/shaver 刮鬍刀
⑦ nail clipper 指甲刀
⑧ emery board 指甲銼刀

cream 乳霜

facial mask 面膜

hair gel 髮膠

mouthwash 漱口水

aftershave 鬍後水

deodorant
止汗劑／體香膏

body/face scrub
身體／臉部磨砂膏

sunscreen 防曬乳

化妝品 Cosmetics

① **cosmetic bag** 化妝包
② **brush** 刷具
③ **compact powder** 粉餅
④ **lipstick** 口紅
⑤ **perfume** 香水
⑥ **foundation** 粉底

① **lotion** 化妝水
② **cotton pad** 化妝棉

eye shadow 眼影

powder 蜜粉

BB cream BB 霜

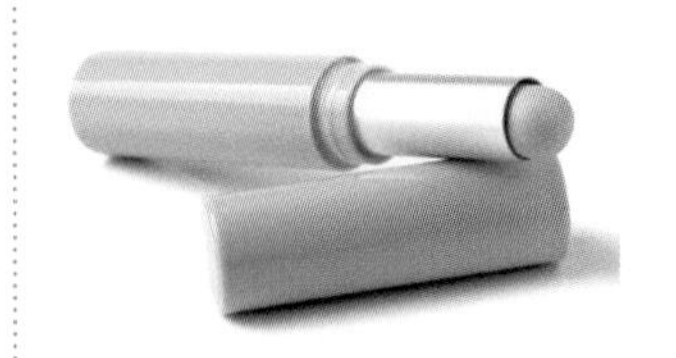

concealer 遮瑕膏

blush 腮紅

lip gloss 唇蜜

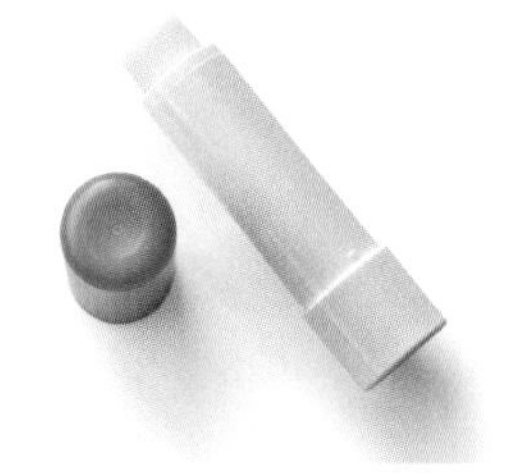

lip balm 護唇膏

eyeliner 眼線筆

eyebrow pencil 眉筆

mascara 睫毛膏

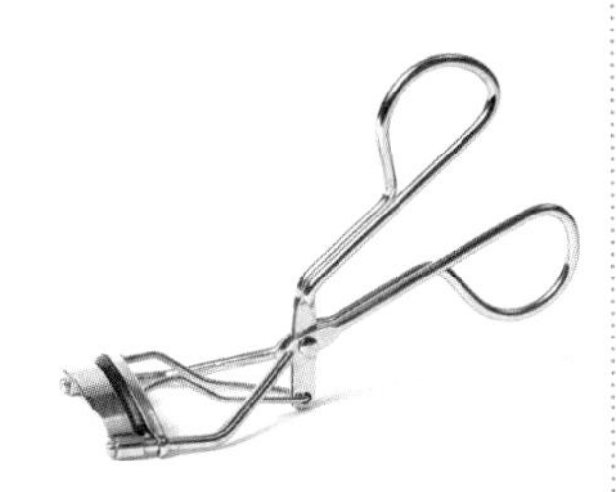

eyelash curler 睫毛夾

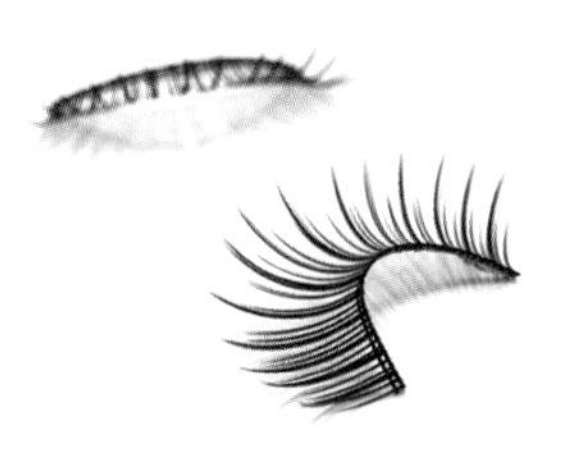

false eyelash 假睫毛

nail polish 指甲油

Chapter

35 購買電子用品 Shopping for Electronics

情境式對話 購買相機 170

S → Store Sales D → Dolores Pan

D	Hi. I am looking for a camera. Is there anything you would recommend?	你好，我想買一臺相機。可以請你介紹嗎？
S	What type of camera would you like?	請問您想買哪一種相機？
D	Well, I don't know much about cameras, so I was thinking to get a digital one.	我不太懂相機，所以我想買一臺數位相機。
S	How about this one? This is our best seller. It has multi-functions[1] and is very user-friendly[2].	您看看這款如何？它是我們最暢銷的機種，具備多功能，非常容易上手。
D	How do I operate it?	這要怎麼操作？
S	First, you insert the memory card into the slot here. Turn the camera on and set the mode to "Photo," so that you can take a picture. Then, all you have to do is aim the camera at what you want to take a picture of, and you'll see the image right here on the screen. When you are ready to shoot, just press the "shutter" button. You see? It's very easy.	先把記憶卡插入這裡的插槽中，接著把電源打開，將模式設定到「拍攝」，這樣才能照相。接下來，您要做的只是把相機對著要拍攝的人或是物體，螢幕上就會出現影像。準備好後，按下「快門」鍵就拍下來了。您看，是不是很容易？

D	It does seem pretty simple, but how do I check the photos I have taken?	看起來的確很簡單，但我要怎麼看拍下來的照片？
S	Just change the mode to "Album," and all the photos will appear one by one on the screen. If you don't like one of them, press this button and select "Delete." The photo will be deleted from the memory card.	只要把模式調到「相簿」，所有的照片就會在螢幕上一張張地顯示出來。如果不喜歡某一張，就按這個按鈕，選「刪除」，就會從記憶卡刪除照片了。
D	I see. It seems easy enough, and is just right for an amateur like me. Do you mind demonstrating some of its other functions?	原來如此。好像很簡單，剛好適合我這個業餘的。你可以介紹一些別的功能嗎？
S	Of course not. Why don't we have a seat inside, and let me get you something to drink?	當然可以。不如我們到裡面坐著談，讓我給您倒點飲料？
D	That will be great. Thanks.	那太好了。謝謝。

1 multi-function [ˌmʌltɪˋfʌŋkʃən] (n.) 多功能
2 user-friendly [ˋjuzɚˋfrɛndlɪ] (adj.) 容易使用的

旅遊小句 Are the lenses changeable?

35-1 購買相機 171

自動對焦	1	Does this camera focus automatically?	請問這臺相機會自動對焦嗎？
伸縮鏡頭	2	Is the lens telescopic?	這個鏡頭有伸縮變焦功能嗎？
詢問畫素	3	How many pixels does this camera have?	這臺相機的畫素是多少？
詢問功能	4	What functions does this model have?	這款相機有什麼功能？
按鈕功用	5	What is this button used for?	這個按鈕是做什麼用的？
詢問機型差異	6	What is the difference between these two models?	這兩款相機有什麼不同？
記憶卡容量	7	How much space does the memory card have?	這記憶卡的容量是多少？
更換鏡頭	8	Are the lenses changeable?	鏡頭是可以換的嗎？
廣角功能	9	Can the lens take wide-angle shots?	這有廣角功能嗎？
介紹功能	10	This camera has full HD video recording and wireless connectivity.	這臺相機可以拍高畫質影片，也有無線連線功能。
	11	This one takes high-resolution photos, and has a wide zoom range.	這臺相機可以拍攝高畫素相片，變焦範圍也很廣。
	12	This camera has various types of camera modes that can be used in different situations, including panoramic photography.	這臺相機供許多用於不同狀況的相機模式，其中包括全景攝影。
是否附贈品	13	Do I get any free gifts if I buy the camera?	我買這臺相機會有贈品嗎？

35-2 購買記憶卡與沖洗相片 172

購買記憶卡	1	I would like to buy a memory card. Which do you recommend?	我想要買記憶卡，你有推薦的嗎？
	2	Well, we have 8/16/32/64-gigabyte cards. It depends on how much capacity you want.	我們有 8/16/32/64 G 的，這取決於您想要多大容量。
沖洗相片	3	Please develop the digital photos in this memory card.	請幫我洗這記憶卡裡面的相片。
	4	I'd like to reprint these photos.	我想要加洗照片。
沖洗尺寸	5	What size prints would you like to have?	請問要洗哪種尺寸？
一般規格	6	I want regular size prints.	一般尺寸。
其他規格	7	I want this picture in size 4 by 6.	要 4 乘 6 大小的。
放大照片	8	Please enlarge these photos to 5 by 7.	這些照片要放大到 5 乘 7。

旅遊資訊補充包

相機 Camera

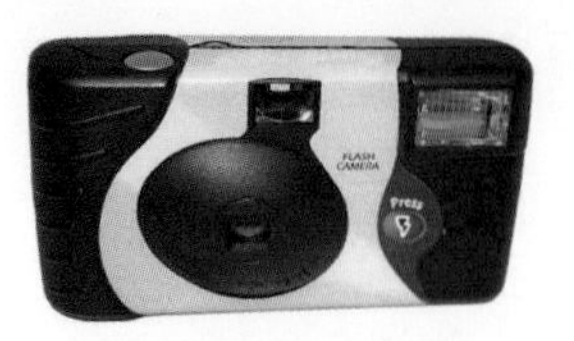

disposable camera / single-use camera 即可拍相機

camcorder 攝影機

tripod 三腳架

action camera 運動相機

digital camera 數位相機

flash/photoflash/flashlight 閃光燈

zoom lens 可變焦鏡頭

digital single lens reflex (DSLR) 數位單眼相機

battery charger 充電器

battery 電池

hood 遮光罩

instant camera 拍立得相機

memory card 記憶卡

selfie stick 自拍棒

35-3 購買電腦及其相關設備 173

買電腦	1	I am looking for a laptop.	我要買一臺筆記型電腦。
螢幕大小	2	I'd like a monitor that is smaller than 13 inches.	我想要小於 13 吋的螢幕。
重量輕	3	Is there anything lighter?	有輕一點的嗎？
外接機器	4	Can I use it with an external DVD rewriter?	這可以外接 DVD 燒錄機嗎？
硬碟容量	5	What's the size/capacity of the hard drive?	硬碟容量有多大？
可否擴充	6	Can I expand the SD RAM?	隨機記憶體可以擴充嗎？
電池續航力	7	How long is the battery life?	電池續航力多久？
詢問電腦系統	8	Which operating system does this PC come with?	請問這臺個人電腦的作業系統是什麼？
	9	This PC comes with Windows 10. But we can upgrade it if you'd like.	這臺個人電腦的作業系統是 Windows 10，但您要的話我們可以幫您升級。
詢問電腦功能	10	How do you input data with this device?	請問要如何將資料輸入進這臺裝置？
	11	Use the on-screen keyboard. Just press here to bring it up.	用螢幕上的鍵盤，按這裡就可以叫出來了。
有無維修點	12	Can I have it repaired in Taiwan?	你們在臺灣有維修點嗎？

電腦配備 Computer Accessories

CPU（**central processing unit**）中央處理器

RAM（**random access memory**）記憶體

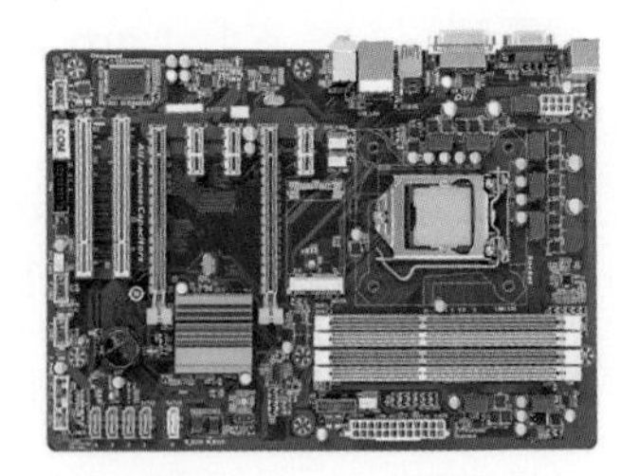

motherboard 主機板

router 路由器

modem 數據機

monitor 螢幕

keyboard 鍵盤

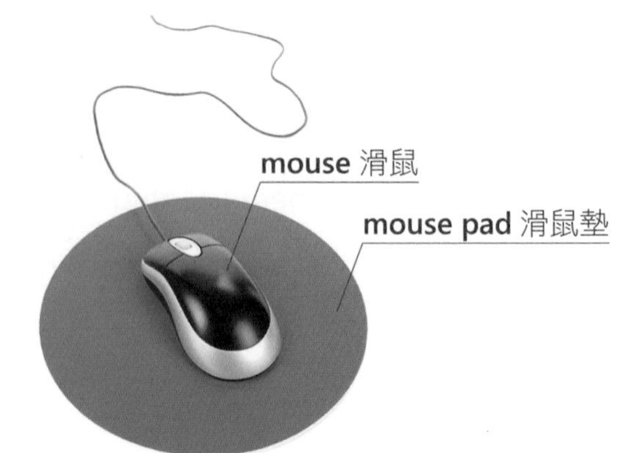

 CD-ROM drive 光碟機	 USB flash drive 隨身碟	 external hard drive 外接硬碟
 USB cable USB 傳輸線	 speaker 喇叭	 headphone 耳機
 webcam 網路攝影機	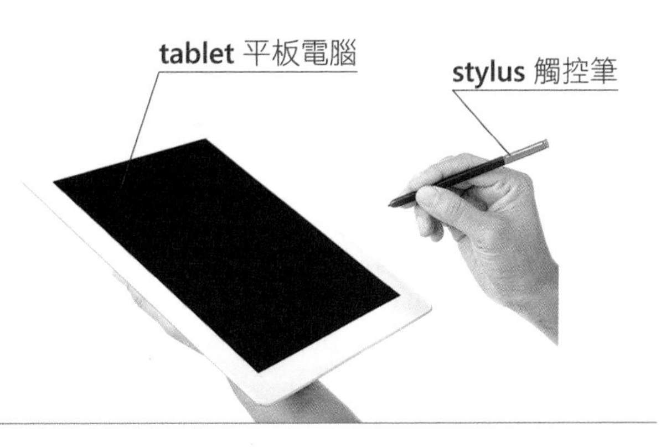	

Chapter 36 購買紀念品 Shopping for Souvenirs

情境式對話 詢問購買紀念品 174

S → Store Sales　D → Della Wang

D	Hello. I am looking for some gifts for my friends. Can you recommend something that would make a good souvenir?	你好。我想買一件禮物送給朋友，可以請你幫我看看有什麼可以當成紀念品的嗎？
S	Sure. We have lots of posters, key chains, T-shirts, mugs, crystal balls, and stuffed toys. They are all suitable souvenirs for friends. Are you looking for anything in particular?	可以啊。本店有很多海報、鑰匙圈、T 恤、馬克杯、水晶球以及填充玩偶，都是很適合送給朋友的紀念品。您有沒有特別想買什麼樣的商品？
D	Well, I think T-shirts are always a good choice. Can you show me one like that on the model?	嗯，我想 T 恤一向是個不錯的選擇。請問可以看跟那個模特兒身上那件類似的衣服嗎？
S	Here you are. This is really popular. It says "My friend went to London and all I got was this T-shirt." You can change "friend" to "daughter," "boyfriend," "sister," "brother," etc. So you can give one to everyone on your list.	就是這件，這件真的賣得很好。它上面寫：「我朋友去了一趟倫敦，而我只得到了一件 T 恤。」您可以把「朋友」改成「女兒」、「男朋友」、「姊妹」、「兄弟」等等，這樣您就可以送給所有想送的人。

D	They're cute! What's the price?	好可愛！請問要多少錢？
S	£15. What sizes would you like?	15 英鎊。您要幾號的？
D	Maybe medium for my girl friends and large for my boy friends. But £15 is a bit expensive. If I buy more, can I get a cheaper price?	送我女性朋友的大概是中號，送我男性朋友的大概是大號。不過 15 英鎊有點貴。多買幾件可以算便宜一點嗎？
S	How many do you want, then?	那您想要幾件？
D	Five.	五件。
S	Well, then I can give them to you at £12 each.	這樣的話，我可以算您每件 12 英鎊。
D	That's great. Then I'll take three mediums and two larges, and I'd like them wrapped separately, if that's possible. Thanks.	太棒了。那我就買三件中號兩件大號，如果可以的話請分開包裝，謝謝。
S	No problem. Just give me a few minutes.	沒問題。請稍待片刻。

旅遊小句 Where can I find a souvenir shop?

36-1 購買紀念品 175

詢問商店	1	Where can I find a souvenir shop?	請問哪裡有紀念品商店?
詢問特定物品	2	Where can I buy high-quality mugs?	請問哪裡可以買到高級的馬克杯？
請人推薦	3	What should I buy for my friends as gifts?	請問可以買什麼禮物送給朋友？
購買預算	4	Is there anything around €14?	請問有沒有 14 歐元左右的商品？
決定購買	5	I want to buy a poster of Paris.	我要一張巴黎的海報。
告知數量	6	I will take three of these, please.	這個要買三份，麻煩你。

36-2 要求包裝及運送 176

禮品包裝	1	Can you gift wrap this for me?	可以請幫我包成禮物嗎?
收納海報	2	Please put the posters in a tube.	請把海報裝在紙筒裡。
特殊包裝	3	Could you please use bubble wrap to protect the vase?	可以請用氣泡布裝來保護這個花瓶嗎？
分開包裝	4	Can I have a separate bag for each item?	可以請幫我把每件商品分開給一個袋子嗎？
包裝材料	5	I don't need the box. A plastic bag will do.	不用盒子裝，用塑膠袋就可以了。
包裝紙顏色	6	May I have blue wrapping paper?	請問有藍色的包裝紙可以包裝嗎？
加上緞帶	7	Please put a ribbon on it.	請綁上一條緞帶。
送至飯店	8	Can I have it sent to my hotel?	請問可以幫我送到我住的飯店嗎？
要求郵寄	9	Please send this furniture to Taiwan by sea.	這件傢俱要請用海運寄到臺灣。
詢問郵寄時間	10	How long does it take to ship this?	寄海運要多久？
貨到付款	11	I will make the rest of the payment when I receive the delivery.	我收到貨就會付清尾款。

Unit 9

Communication
無遠弗屆通訊篇

Chapter
37

打電話

Making Phone Calls

P. 324

Chapter
38

郵寄信件與包裹

Sending Letters & Parcels

P. 332

Chapter 37 打電話 Making Phone Calls

情境式對話 // 打國際電話 177

D → Debbie Nail　L → Lester Hsu

L	Debbie, I would like to call my parents. Do you know where I can find a pay phone around here?	黛比，我想打電話給我爸媽，你知道這附近哪裡有公用電話嗎？
D	There is one just around the corner, if I remember correctly.	我記得沒錯的話，附近就有一臺。
L	Oh, I see it. Thanks.	噢，看到了，謝了。
D	You're making an international call, right?	你要打國際電話，是嗎？
L	Right. Can I call overseas with this phone?	是啊。這電話可以打國外嗎？
D	Yes. Do you have a phone card?	可以啊。你有電話卡嗎？
L	I just bought one, but I don't know how to use it.	我剛買了一張，但不知道怎麼用。

D	Show me your card, and I'll help you. First, do you see the free-call number there? Dial it, and an operator will come on the line to help you.	拿出電話卡，我教你。首先，有沒有看到上面的免付費電話號碼？打那支號碼，接通後就會有接線生幫你了。
L	Is that all?	這樣就可以了?
D	Well, no. This is the PIN number of the card. The operator will ask you to enter the PIN, then tell you how much money you have left on the card. After that, you can dial your parents' number.	還沒。這是這張卡的識別碼，接線生會要你輸入識別碼，並會告訴你這張卡的餘額，然後你就可以撥你父母的電話號碼了。
L	Do I need to dial the international code?	要按國際冠碼嗎？
D	Yes, from the States, you have to dial 011 first. Then you dial your country code and the number you're calling.	要。在美國要先按 011，然後按你的國家代碼和要打的號碼。
L	OK. I'll give it a try now. Thanks!	好，我現在試試看。謝啦！

旅遊小句 Where is a pay phone?

37-1 使用公共電話 178

找尋公共電話	1	Where is a pay phone?	請問哪裡有公用電話？
使用方法	2	How do I use it?	請問這怎麼用？
是否先投幣	3	Should I insert some coins first?	請問我要先投幣嗎？
投入金額	4	How much money should I put in?	要投多少錢？
硬幣種類	5	Which coins can I use?	這是投哪種錢幣？
詢問是否有零錢	6	Do you have any small change?	請問你有零錢嗎？
	7	I don't have any coins.	我沒有任何硬幣。
跟人兌換零錢	8	May I get some change, say $5 worth? I need to make a call.	請問可以跟你換五塊錢的零錢嗎？我需要打電話。
使用電話卡	9	Can I use a telephone card with this phone?	請問這臺電話可以用電話卡嗎？
詢問可否撥打國際電話	10	Can I use this phone to call overseas?	請問這臺公用電話可以打國際電話嗎？
可否直撥	11	Can I dial a number directly?	這可以直撥嗎？
請人回撥公共電話	12	Can I ask someone to call me on this pay phone?	請問別人可以打這支公共電話給我嗎？
	13	Sure, just give him the phone number.	可以，只要告訴他電話號碼就可以了。
詢問公共電話的電話號碼	14	What is the number of this pay phone?	請問你知道這支公用電話的號碼嗎？
	15	You will find the number on the top right. That's it.	電話右邊上方可以找到號碼，就是那個。

37-2 購買國際電話卡與 SIM 卡 179

何處買電話卡	1	Where can I get a phone card?	請問哪裡可以買到電話卡？
電話卡種類	2	May I have an international phone card, please?	可以請給我一張國際電話卡嗎？
	3	What face value would you like? We have three different prepaid phone cards, $5, $10, and $20.	有 5 美元、10 美元和 20 美元三種面額的卡，您要哪一種？
何種卡划算	4	Which one do you recommend?	你推薦哪一種？
	5	You can get an extra $5 for free if you buy the $20 card. It's the best deal.	買 20 美元的卡會多送 5 美元，保證划算。
	6	I suggest that you buy the "Easy Call" card for overseas calls.	打國外的話，我建議您買「輕鬆打」電話卡。
卡片費率	7	Which card has the cheapest rate to Taiwan?	請問用哪種卡打去臺灣費率最低？
	8	Please refer to the table.	請參考這張表。
撥打費用	9	What is the rate?	請問費率怎麼算？
	10	You'll be charged $2 every ten minutes, 24 hours a day.	全天候都是 10 分鐘 2 美元。

何處買 SIM 卡	10	Excuse me. Where can I buy a local SIM card with a prepaid data plan?	不好意思，請問哪裡可以買到當地的預付 SIM 卡？
	11	You can buy one from the vending machines in the airport, and there are different plans you can choose from.	機場裡的自動販賣機有販售，其中有許多不同方案供你選擇。
詢問 SIM 卡方案	12	What can I do with this "Traveler's Plan"?	這個「旅行者方案」有提供什麼？
	13	It costs £20, and it's valid for 30 days. It includes 2 GB of data, 200 minutes of domestic calls, and 50 minutes of international calls. If you'll be traveling elsewhere in Europe afterwards, this plan also provides free roaming in several EU countries.	這要 20 英鎊，在 30 天以內提供您 2G 的上網流量、200 分鐘的國內電話與 50 分鐘的國際電話。如果您接下來要去歐洲其他地方旅行的話，在一些歐盟國家也有提供漫遊服務。

國際電話 International Calls

如何在國外打電話呢？

向國內電信公司開通國際漫遊

臺灣的門號在一般情況下，如果沒有特別要求，國際漫遊功能通常是關閉狀態，若是要確認自己的門號是否能在國外打電話，請致電向電信公司客服詢問。

若是不希望在出國期間自己也不清楚的情況下，多出一些如聽取留言或是不小心按到之類的電話費用，也可以在出國前先致電客服，確認國際漫遊是否關閉，這樣此門號將不能聽也不能打，就不會有額外的費用產生了。

如果僅開通國際漫遊功能，即使門號方案有附網路流量，在國外也無法上網；需要網路服務得向電信公司申請國際漫遊上網服務，此服務需另外付費，通常分為日租型與計量型收費，有此需求的旅客也可向電信公司客服洽詢。

向國內電信公司購買國際電話卡

旅客可以在國內預先購買國際電話預付卡，由臺灣撥至國外、或由國外撥至臺灣、或經由臺灣撥至第三國皆可，非常方便。國際電話卡通常提供不同面額，國際電話費按面額扣除，適合出國旅遊使用。

購買當地電話卡

在各地的報攤或雜貨店，都可買到不同電信公司的電話卡，費率不一，可依各人需求選擇。

電話卡上會有三組號碼，首先需撥打免付費電話，接通後輸入卡號，再輸入卡片上提供的密碼。撥打時，電話公司會告知卡片餘款；電話撥通前，也會告知可通話的時限。

購買當地 SIM 卡

大多數的國家當地的電信商，也會在機場或是機場附近的商店，提供國外旅客購買短期使用 SIM 卡的服務。

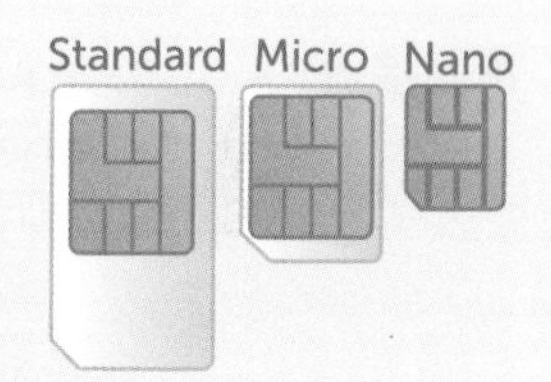

當地電信商的 SIM 卡的方案五花八門，有限定天數以內的、也有計算通話時數可供再加值的；如果想要上網，因為是使用本地電信服務，故沒有數據漫遊的問題，價格也會比數據漫遊便宜，故旅客可以依旅遊天數行程好好規劃。

然而必須注意的是，目前手機的 SIM 卡尺寸有三種：Standard、Micro、Nano，因此必須要注意所提供的 SIM 卡式哪一種尺寸，是否符合手機的規格。

使用通訊軟體

如 Skype、FaceTime 和 Google Hangouts 等服務，均可以讓使用者不管身在何處都可以免費通話，只要能連到無線網路，就能以智慧型手機或電腦與親朋好友聯繫，是不僅便利也相當省錢的選擇。

怎麼打國際電話回國呢？

從國外直撥回國，打對方電話和手機的順序分別如下：

所在國國際冠碼 + 本國國碼 886 + 區域號碼（不含 0） + 市內電話號碼

例：011（美國國際冠碼） + 886 + 2（大臺北、基隆市） + 2365-9739（市內電話號碼）

所在國國際冠碼 + 本國國碼 886 + 手機號碼（不含最前面的 0）

例：011（美國國際冠碼） + 886 + 919-141-549（手機號碼）

37-3 撥打國際電話 (180)

詢問國際代碼	1	What is the international dialing code here?	請問這裡的國際冠碼是多少？
	2	You need to dial 00 to make international calls.	打越洋電話之前必須先撥 00。
請接線生轉接	3	I want to make an overseas collect call to Taiwan. The number is 2365-9739.	我要撥打一通對方付費的國際電話到臺灣，號碼是 2365-9739。
	4	Please give me the country code and the city code first.	請先提供我國際冠碼和城市碼。
電話接通	5	Your party is on the line. Please go ahead.	您的電話接通了，請說。

37-4 向查號臺查詢 (181)

詢問區碼	1	What is the area code for Los Angeles?	請問洛杉磯的區碼是多少？
查詢電話號碼	2	I would like the number for Mr. Tim Smith, please.	麻煩請幫我查提姆·史密斯先生的電話。
	3	Could you please spell the family name for me?	請問姓氏怎麼拼？
確認查詢的人	4	There are three different Tim Smiths. Which one are you looking for?	一共查到三位提姆·史密斯，您要查哪一位？
	5	I am looking for the one who lives on Park Boulevard.	住在公園大道的那位。
告知人名及地址	6	Could you please give me the number of Kevin White on Third Avenue?	可以麻煩查住在第三大街的凱文·懷特的電話嗎？
查無此人	7	There is no record of that name.	查不到這個人。

37-5 電話常用語 182

告知找人	1	May I speak to Daniel Grant, please?	請問丹尼爾·葛蘭在嗎?
請稍待	2	Hold on, please.	請稍等。
接電話用語	3	Speaking.	我就是。
不在	4	He is not here right now.	他目前不在。
忙線	5	She is on another line.	她在講另一支電話。
在忙	6	She is busy right now.	她現在有事。
詢問何人來電	7	May I ask who is calling?	請問哪裡找？
留言	8	Would you like to leave a message?	要不要留言？
要求留話	9	May I leave a message?	請問可以留話嗎？
請對方回電	10	Please ask him to call me back.	請他回電給我。
打錯電話	11	You have the wrong number.	你打錯電話了。
	12	I am sorry for disturbing you.	對不起打擾了。
請求再說一次	13	Come again? Could you repeat that for me?	您說什麼？可以再說一次嗎？
電話問題	14	The line is very bad . . . could you speak up, please?	線路不太穩……可以請您大聲一點嗎？
	15	I think I lost you. Are you still there?	我想電話斷線了，您還在嗎？
	16	I'm afraid I can't hear you.	我聽不到您的聲音。

Chapter

38 郵寄信件與包裹 Sending Letters & Parcels

情境式對話 // 到郵局寄國際信件 183

J → Jonny Ping　P → Post Officer

J	Hello. I would like to send this letter and package to Italy, please.	你好，我要寄這封信和這個包裹到義大利。
P	Sure. How would you like to send them?	好的。請問您的寄送方式是？
J	I would like to send the letter by airmail, please.	這封信請幫我寄航空郵件。
P	Do you want it to be certified?	要掛號嗎？
J	I don't think that will be necessary. But I would like to make it express mail.	我想不用，但要寄快遞。
P	No problem. How about the parcel?	沒問題。那這個包裹呢？
J	How long would it take to go by sea?	寄海運多久會到？
P	About two months. But it is a lot cheaper.	大概要兩個月，不過會比較便宜。

J	Wow, that's a long time. Maybe I'd better send it by air after all.	哇，那真的很久。也許還是寄航空郵件好了。
P	What's inside your parcel?	請問您的包裹裡有什麼？
J	Some clothes, but mostly books for my cousin.	一些衣服，但大部分是給我堂哥的書。
P	In that case, I suggest that you send the package as printed matter. It's cheaper that way, even by air.	那我建議您改寄印刷品，這樣即使是寄航空郵件也會比較便宜。
J	OK, that will be great!	好的，那就太好了！
P	Please fill out this form and indicate the value of the contents.	請填寫這張表，並標明內容物的價值。
J	So how much is the postage?	這樣郵資是多少？
P	The letter costs $3, and the parcel costs $10. So it's $13 in total.	這封信是 3 塊，包裹是 10 塊，一共是 13 塊。
J	OK. Here you are. Thanks a lot.	好的，給你。非常感謝。

旅遊小句 *How would you like to send it?*

38-1 詢問寄信 184

詢問營業時間	1	What are the post office's business hours?	請問郵局是幾點開到幾點？
購買明信片	2	Can I get postcards from the vending machine?	請問可以從販賣機買到明信片嗎？
詢問何者便宜	3	Is it cheaper to send a postcard than a letter?	請問寄明信片比寄信便宜嗎？
寄件方式	4	How would you like to send it?	請問您要怎麼寄？
寄快捷信	5	I would like to send a letter to Taiwan by express mail.	我要寄一封國際快遞去臺灣。
寄掛號信	6	Is it faster to send something by registered mail?	請問寄掛號會比較快嗎？
郵寄時間	7	How long does it take for a letter to get to Taiwan?	請問寄信到臺灣要多久？
首班郵件時間	8	When is the first mail collection?	請問第一班郵件會在什麼時候收？
末班郵件時間	9	Will I be able to catch the last mail collection today?	請問我能趕得上今天的末班郵件收送嗎？

38-2 寄送包裹 185

詢問包裹櫃檯	1	Which counter should I go to to send a parcel?	請問寄包裹要到哪個櫃檯？
寄包裹	2	I would like to send this parcel to Taiwan.	我要寄這個包裹去臺灣。
	3	Please fill out this form.	請填寫這張表。
包裹內容	4	What is inside the parcel?	包裹裡面是什麼？
	5	They are all just personal belongings.	都只是個人物品。
是否為易碎品	6	Are the contents fragile?	裡面是易碎品嗎？
	7	No, they are just books.	不是，只是書。
寄印刷品	8	You can send them as printed materials. It's much cheaper that way.	您可以改寄印刷品，比較便宜。
內容物價值	9	Please indicate/write down the value of the contents.	要聲明／寫下內容物的價值。
是否申報	10	Do I need to fill out a disembarkation form?	請問我需要寫海關申報表嗎？
投保	11	Would you like to buy insurance?	請問您想要保保險嗎？
	12	Yes, please insure it for $20.	好的，請保 20 美元。
要求放在秤上	13	Please put/set the parcel on the scale.	請將包裹置於磅秤上。
	14	Is it overweight/too heavy?	有沒有超重？
告知重量及費用	15	This parcel is five kilograms, so the postage is $10.	這個包裹五公斤，所以郵資十美元。

38-3 郵票 186

何處買郵票	1	Where can I buy stamps?	請問郵票要在哪買？
購買郵票	2	Ten 20-cent stamps, please.	請給我十張 20 分的郵票。
明信片郵票	3	I would like ten stamps for international postcards, please.	請給我十張國際明信片的郵票。
	4	Where would you like to send this?	您想要寄到哪裡呢？
紀念郵票	5	I would like ten commemorative stamps, please.	請給我十張紀念郵票。
操作郵票販賣機	6	How do I use the stamp vending machine?	請問這臺郵票販賣機怎麼使用？
何處有郵票販賣機	7	Do you know if there's a place other than a post office where I can buy stamps?	請問你知道除了郵局以外，我還可以在哪裡買到郵票嗎？
要求其它樣式	8	Do you have any other kinds of stamps?	請問有其他款式的郵票嗎？
	9	We sell first-class and second-class stamps only.	我們只有賣第一類與第二類郵票。

旅遊資訊補充包

郵政字彙 Postal Service Terms

郵務計費
- ◊ 郵票 stamp ❶
- ◊ 郵資 postage ❷

郵務運送
- ◊ 郵筒 mail box ❸
- ◊ 郵差（美）mailman / letter carrier
  （英）postman

郵遞方式
- ◊ 印刷品 printed matter
- ◊ 限時專送 special delivery ❹
- ◊ 掛號郵件 registered mail /（美）certified mail /（英）recorded delivery
- ◊ 快遞 express mail ❺
- ◊ 易碎品 fragile ❻
- ◊ 航空郵件 air mail ❼
- ◊ 海運 by sea

寄／收件
- ◊ 寄件人 sender ❽
- ◊ 寄件地址 return address ❾
- ◊ 收件人 recipient ❿
- ◊ 收件地址 mailing address ⓫
- ◊ 郵戳 postmark ⓬

如何寫地址 Address Writing

從國外寄信回國，寫地址經常是一大難題。其實最簡單的方式是用中文寫，並在最後寫上用英文寫下「**Taiwan, R.O.C.**」或「**Taiwan (R.O.C.)** 」即可。

如果想將中文地址翻成英文，也只要掌握以下字彙即可，而且切記英文地址是**由最小的地方單位寫起，愈大單位的放愈後面**，其順序如下：

① 室 **ROOM (RM)**

② 樓 **FLOOR (FL)**

③ 號 **NUMBER (NO.)**

④ 弄 **ALLEY**

⑤ 巷 **LANE**

⑥ 段 **SECTION (SEC.)**

⑦ 街／路／大道 **STREET (ST.) / ROAD (RD.) / BOULEVARD (BLVD.)**

⑧ 鄉、鎮／市／區 **TOWN / CITY / DISTRICT**

⑨ 州／縣／市 **STATE / COUNTY / CITY**

⑩ 郵遞區號 **ZIP CODE**

另外，也可以先到以下的網站查詢相關地址的中譯英寫法，如中華郵政的網站短網址為「https://goo.gl/nLhxOk」。點選「中文地址英譯查詢」即可查詢，依教育部「中文譯音使用原則」規定，我國中文譯音以漢語拼音為準。

中華郵政網站的 QR code

郵局中文地址英譯查詢，著重在信件能送達為主，不如戶政機關或辦簽證需要詳盡地址資料，故地址如全部輸入如村里鄰，反而會查詢不到。「鄰」英譯為 **neighborhood**。「衖」英譯則為 **sub-alley**。

中文地址英譯參考書寫方式

110 臺北市信義區莊敬路 423 巷 8 弄 12 號 2 樓 2 室

Room(1) 2, 2F(2), No. 12(3), Alley 8(4), Lane 423(5), Zhuangjing Rd.(7), Xinyi District(8), Taipei City(9), 110(10)

437 臺中縣大甲鎮中山路一段 825-5 號

No. 825-5, Sec.(6) 1, Jhongshan Rd., Dajia Township, Taichung County 437

Unit 10

Problem Solving
疑難雜症緊急篇

Chapter 39 遺失物品或遭竊 Dealing With Loss & Theft

情境式對話 尋找失物 187

A → Angela Fei　I → Information Center Receptionist

At the train station	在火車站
A　Excuse me. I am looking for the lost and found office.	請問一下，我在找失物招領處。
I　Just turn right here, and it will be on your left. Do you need any help?	就在這裡右轉，左手邊就是了。您需要協助嗎？
A　Yes, thanks. I think I left my bag in the ladies' room. I went back there, but I couldn't find it.	是的，謝謝。我想我應該是在廁所掉了包包，我回去找過，可是找不到了。
I　What was in your bag?	您的手提袋裡面有什麼？
A　Everything! My purse, camera, passport and a map of Athens.	所有東西！我的錢包、相機、護照，還有一張雅典的地圖。
I　Oh, that's too bad! Did you have a lot of money in your purse?	噢，那實在不妙！您的包包裡有很多錢嗎？

A	No, luckily, there was only €20 or so. But my passport, driver's license, student card, and two credit cards were all in there.	沒有，幸好裡面只有 20 歐元左右。但是我的護照、駕照、學生證，還有兩張信用卡全在裡面。
I	Then I suggest that you report your loss to the police, too.	那我建議您也向警方報案。
A	I see. Is there a police station nearby?	了解。這附近有警察局嗎？
I	There is one on the second floor.	二樓就有一間。
A	OK. What do you think I will need to do there?	好。你認為警察會需要我做什麼嗎？
I	They will probably have you fill out a form and ask you what happened.	警方大概會需要您填寫一張表，問您事情發生的經過。
A	I see.	這樣啊。
I	By the way, don't forget to contact your credit card companies and cancel your cards as soon as possible.	對了，別忘了儘快通知您的信用卡公司辦理掛失。
A	That's right. Thank you for reminding me!	沒錯，感謝你提醒我！

旅遊小句 // *Where should I report a theft?*

39-1 物品遺失 (188)

尋找失物	1	Did you happen to see a mobile phone here? I can't find mine.	請問你有沒有在這裡看到一支手機？我手機掉了。
遺落物品在計程車上	2	I left my bag in the taxi. What can I do?	我把包包掉在計程車上了，怎麼辦？
告知有物品遺忘此處	3	I accidentally left my bag here about half an hour ago.	我約半小時之前在這裡，忘了拿走我的袋子。
請求幫忙找尋	4	Can you help me find it?	請問可以幫我找找看嗎？
找尋失物協尋暨招領處	5	Where is the lost and found?	請問失物招領處在哪？

39-2 失物招領處 (189)

不記得失物處	1	I don't remember where I left it.	我不記得掉在哪裡了。
被問及遺失物品	2	What did you have in the bag?	請問袋子裡有什麼？
	3	Well, I had my digital camera, passport, wallet, and a guidebook.	嗯，有數位相機、護照、錢包和一本旅遊指南。
詢問失物外觀	4	What does the bag look like?	請問袋子長什麼樣子？
要求通知	5	Please contact me at this number if you find it.	如果找到了，請打這支電話號碼給我。
	6	OK. I'll let you know if it turns up.	好的，若有人找到我會通知您。

詢問通知時間	7	When can I expect to hear from you?	請問大概什麼時候可以有消息？
確認失物	8	Is this the bag you lost?	這是您的袋子嗎？
檢查失物	9	Is everything still there?	東西是不是都還在？
	10	Nothing seems to be missing. Thank you so much.	東西都在，非常謝謝你。

39-3 物品遭竊 190

有賊	1	Thief!	小偷！
有扒手	2	Pickpocket! Help!	有扒手！救命！
告知遭搶	3	I have been robbed!	我被搶了！
告知遭竊	4	Someone just stole my wallet!	剛剛有人偷了我的皮夾！
找尋警局	5	Where is the nearest police station?	請問最近的警局在哪裡？
詢問報案處	6	Where should I report a robbery/theft?	請問可以去哪裡申報搶案／竊案？

39-4 警察局報案 (191)

描述案發狀況	1	Someone grabbed my bag and ran away!	有個人抓了我的包包就跑了！
詢問案發地點	2	Where did this happen?	請問在哪裡發生的？
詢問發現時間	3	When did you realize it was lost?	您是什麼時候發現東西不見的？
詢問歹徒外型	4	What did the person look like?	那個人長什麼樣子？
詢問所攜現金	5	How much money were you carrying?	您當時身上有多少錢?
	6	I had $300 in cash, three credit cards, and several traveler's checks.	有 300 美元現金、三張信用卡和幾張旅行支票。
要求填寫表格	7	Please fill out this form.	請填寫這張報案單。
會儘速通知	8	We will contact you immediately if we find anything.	若我們有任何發現，馬上就會通知您。

39-5 辦理補件或掛失 192

詢問辦照處	1	Where can I get a new passport issued?	請問護照可以去哪裡補辦？
尋找臺北駐外代表處	2	How can I get in touch with the Taipei Representative Office here?	請問怎麼樣可以聯絡到臺北駐外代表處？
補照時間	3	How long will it take to get the passport reissued?	請問補發護照要多少天？
補照文件	4	What documents do I need to have in order to request a new passport?	申請補照要準備什麼文件？
	5	You'll need to bring a passport photo, a picture ID, and a copy of your missing passport.	您需要帶一張護照照片、一種有照片的身分證件和遺失護照的影本。
詢問可否補發遺失的旅行支票	6	I lost my traveler's checks. May I have them reissued?	我掉了旅行支票，請問可以申請補發嗎？
	7	Do you remember the ticket number?	請問您記得支票號碼嗎？
購買證明	8	Here is the purchase receipt.	這是我的購買證明。
掛失信用卡	9	I want to report a lost credit card.	我要掛失信用卡。
申請臨時卡	10	Can I get a replacement card for now?	請問可以申請臨時卡嗎？

竊案報告 Stolen Property Report

在國外遺失物品時，要到警察局申報遺失。失竊證明表單大致如以下，切記必須馬上前往警察局報案，以掌握事發當時的細節。

NAME 姓名

LAST NAME 姓 : ....

GIVEN NANE 名 : ....

DATE OF BIRTH 生日 : .... DAY 日／.............. MONTH 月／.............. YEAR 年

NATIONALITY 國籍 : ....

ADDRESS 地址 : ....

....

ADDRESS IN THIS COUNTRY 本國地址 : ....

....

WHEN PROPERTY WAS STOLEN 物品失竊時間

.... DAY 日／.............. MONTH 月／.............. YEAR 年／.............. A.M. 早上／.............. P.M. 下午

HOW PROPERTY WAS STOLEN 竊案手法

☐ PICKPOCKET 扒手　☐ AT KNIFEPOINT 持刀搶劫
☐ PURSE SNATCHER 搶奪　☐ AT GUNPOINT 持槍搶劫

WHERE PROPERTY WAS STOLEN 物品失竊地點

☐ ON THE STREET 路上　☐ AT THE STATION 車站　☐ IN THE SUBWAY 地鐵站
☐ IN THE TRAIN/BUS 火車上／公車上　☐ IN THE TAXI 計程車上
☐ AT THE AIRPORT 機場　☐ AT A RESTAURANT/BAR 餐廳／酒吧
☐ IN A STORE 商店　☐ AT THE HOTEL 飯店　☐ IN THE ROOM 房內
☐ IN THE LOBBY 大廳　☐ OTHER PLACE 其他地方 ....

ITEM(S) MISSING 失物

☐ BAG 包包　☐ HANDBAG 手提包　☐ SUITCASE 行李箱　☐ WALLET 皮夾
☐ WATCH 手錶　☐ CAMERA 相機　☐ VIDEO CAMERA 攝影機　☐ PASSPORT 護照
☐ CREDIT CARD 信用卡　☐ CASH $ .... 現金 .... 元
☐ TRAVELER'S CHECK $ .... 旅行支票 .... 元
JEWELRY 珠寶首飾：☐ NECKLACE 項鍊　☐ EARRINGS 耳環　☐ RING 戒指
MATERIAL 材質：☐ GOLD 黃金　☐ SILVER 銀　☐ PEARL 珍珠　☐ OTHER 其他

TOTAL AMOUNT 總遺失金額 : ....

SIGNATURE 簽名 : ....

物品遺失 Lost Property

在國外旅遊若是物品遭竊或是遺失，都是一件掃興的事。如何將損失降到最低呢？那就是在出國前先影印所有文件，一份留給家人，一份隨身攜帶，但要與正本分開。如此一來，萬一不幸遇到什麼事情，便能將不便減到最低。

遺失護照

先到警察局辦理失竊證明（Report of Theft）或是遺失證明（Report of Loss），這樣就不用擔心有人冒用身分。之後，再憑證明文件至本國駐外大使館或代表處補辦護照。如果出發前已準備好護照影本，就可以省去多項手續。

遺失旅行支票

旅行支票的購票證明最好與正本分開存放，並記下支票號碼。如果有購票證明或支票號碼，到銀行時將可直接申請補發，甚至只需要一通電話即可完成手續，並在短時間內取得補發的支票。

遺失信用卡

為避免信用卡遭盜刷，最好能立即通知發卡銀行，要求停卡或是掛失。某些發卡銀行甚至可以在短時間內補發新卡，並送至你手上。

遺失手機

須儘速向電信業者客服專線掛失 SIM 卡，並辦理停話，以避免話費損失；去警察局報案之餘，也可以利用 IMEI 碼（手機的身分證號，可在手機上輸入「*#06#」來查詢手機本身的 IMEI 序號）或定位 App 尋找手機。多數人的手機都有不少的帳號和密碼記錄，切記要更改密碼並清除隱私資料，防止個資遭竊。

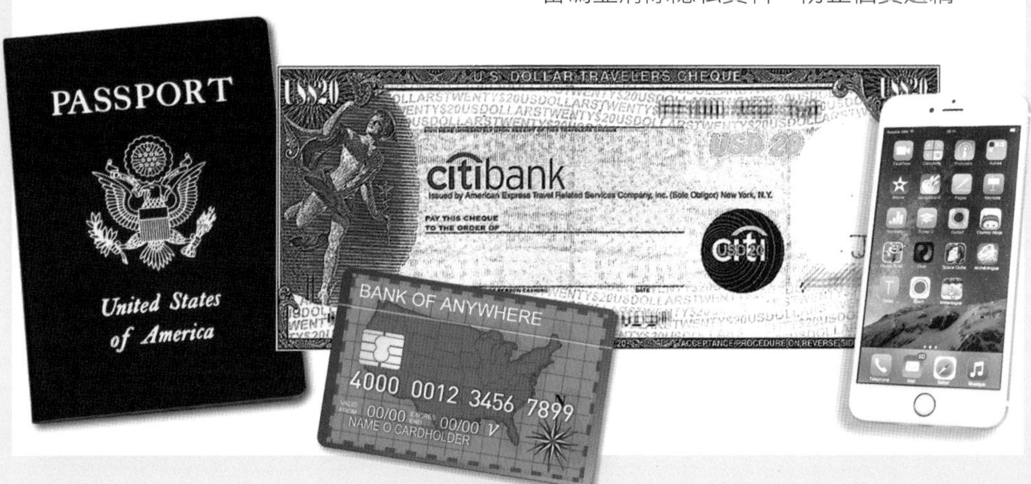

Chapter

40 生病就醫 Dealing With Illness & Medical Care

情境式對話 // 身體不舒服求診 (193)

D → Doctor York V → Victor Liang

D	Good afternoon. What seems to be the problem, Mr. Liang?	午安，請問哪裡不舒服呢，梁先生？
V	Afternoon, doctor. I'm not feeling well at all. I have a headache and sore throat. Besides, I've been coughing a lot.	午安，醫生。我非常不舒服，我頭痛、喉嚨也痛，還一直咳嗽。
D	How long have you had these symptoms[1]?	症狀有多久了？
V	Since last weekend, for about four days already.	上週末就開始了，已經約有四天了。
D	Let me check your temperature. 38.5 degrees Celsius. You have a bit of a fever.	來量一下體溫。38.5 度，你有一點發燒。
V	What do you think is wrong with me?	你認為我得了什麼病？
D	Not sure yet. Do you have a stuffy nose[2]?	還不確定。你會鼻塞嗎？
V	No, but my nose runs a lot.	沒有，可是會一直流鼻涕。
D	I see. It looks like you have the flu. I will write you a prescription[3]. Are you allergic to anything?	了解，這樣看來是得了流行性感冒。我會開一張處方，有沒有對什麼過敏？

V	I don't think so. Does the medicine have any side effects?	應該沒有。請問藥有副作用嗎？
D	You will feel a bit sleepy for a few hours after you take the medicine, which is fine, because what you need now is rest.	服藥之後的幾個小時會有點昏昏欲睡，不過因為你現在需要的就是休息，所以不要緊。
V	OK. How do I take the medicine?	那就好。那服藥方式是？
D	Don't worry. Just take the prescription to the pharmacy. The pharmacist will give you further instructions on that.	別擔心。只要拿著處方箋到藥局，藥劑師會向你進一步說明的。
V	Thanks a lot.	非常感謝。
D	Not at all. Have a good rest for a few days, and drink lots of fluids. I'm sure you'll be feeling a lot better soon.	不會。好好休息幾天，多喝水，你很快就會覺得舒服許多。

[1] symptom [ˋsɪmptəm] (n.) 症狀；徵兆
[2] stuffy nose 鼻塞
[3] prescription [prɪˋskrɪpʃən] (n.) 藥方

旅遊小句 I feel sick.

40-1 預約掛號 194

預約醫生	1	I would like to make an appointment with Dr. Smith for tomorrow morning.	我要預約掛號明天早上的史密斯醫生。
詢問家庭醫生名稱	2	Who is your family doctor?	請問您的家庭醫生是誰？
	3	That would be Dr. Johnson.	是強生醫生。
告知已預約	4	I made an appointment last week.	我上禮拜預約過。
要求會中文的醫生	5	Do you have any Chinese-speaking doctors?	請問有會說中文的醫生嗎？

旅遊資訊補充包 疼痛 Pain

① **sharp pain** 刺痛
② **dull pain** 隱隱作痛
③ **severe pain** 極度疼痛
④ **stinging pain** 刺痛；灼痛
⑤ **throbbing pain** 陣痛；抽痛
⑥ **gripping pain** 絞痛
⑦ **piercing pain** 刺骨的痛
⑧ **splitting pain** 撕裂或割傷的痛
⑨ **continuous pain** 連續不斷的痛
⑩ **sudden pain** 突然痛起來
⑪ **chronic pain** 慢性疼痛
⑫ **acute pain** 急性疼痛

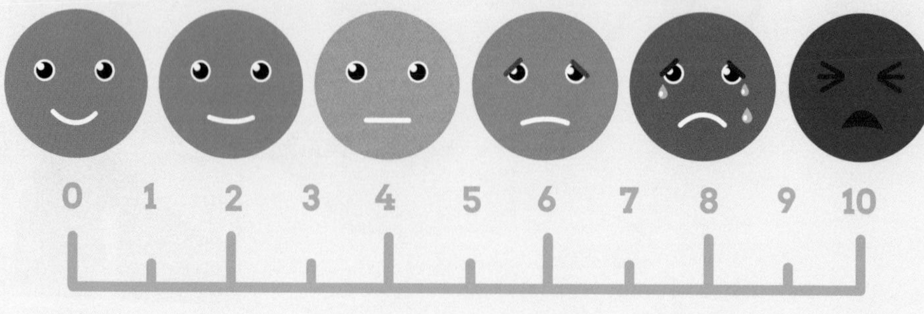

40-2 緊急狀況 195

需要急診	1	I don't have an appointment, but it's an emergency.	我沒有預約，但這是緊急事件。
叫救護車	2	911? Please send an ambulance right away.	是 911 嗎？請馬上派一輛救護車過來。
心臟病發	3	My friend is having a heart attack. What can I do?	我的朋友心臟病發作，我該怎麼辦？
	4	Stay calm. Is there anyone nearby who knows CPR?	保持冷靜，附近有任何人會心肺復甦術嗎？
發生車禍	5	We are on the highway. There has been an accident.	我們在公路上，有車禍發生了。
即將臨盆	6	I'm calling from 13 High Street. Somebody here is in labor!	這裡是高街 13 號，有人要生了！

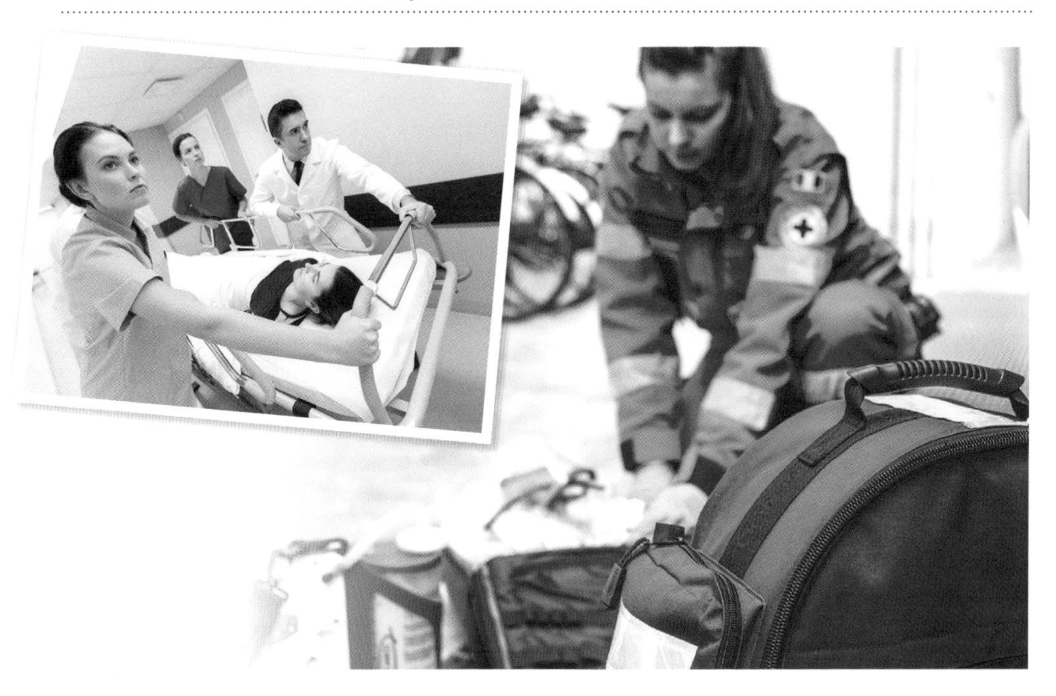

40-3 醫生問診 196

表示不舒服	1	I feel sick.	我不太舒服。
說明症狀	2	I feel dizzy and nauseous.	我頭暈想吐。
病發時間	3	When did the symptoms start?	請問症狀什麼時候開始的？
有無食慾	4	How's your appetite?	胃口怎麼樣？
進食情況	5	Have you eaten anything out of the ordinary lately?	最近有沒有吃什麼不一樣的東西？
會否藥物過敏	6	Are you allergic to any drugs?	有沒有對什麼藥過敏?
	7	I am allergic to aspirin.	我對阿斯匹林過敏。
詢問病情	8	What's wrong with me?	請問是什麼病？
	9	You have the flu.	流行性感冒。
康復時間	10	How long will it take me to recover?	要多久才會好？
應避免的食物	11	Are there any foods I should avoid?	有沒有什麼不可以吃?
告知注意事項	12	Don't stay up late drinking.	不要熬夜喝酒。
是否需回診	13	When do I need to see you again, doctor?	醫生，請問什麼時候要複診？

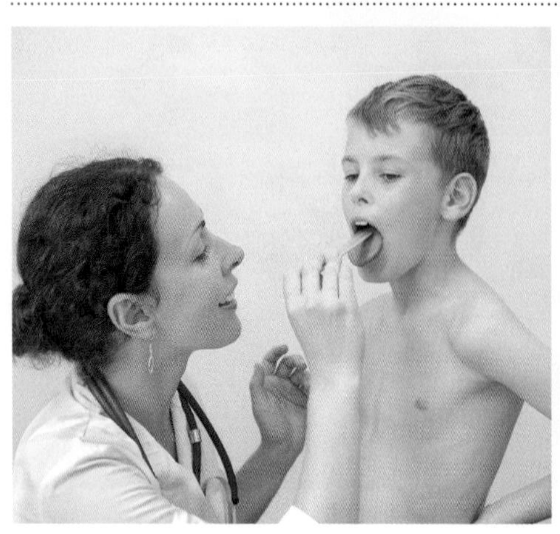

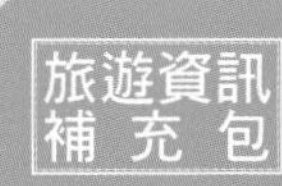

人體各部位名稱 The Human Body

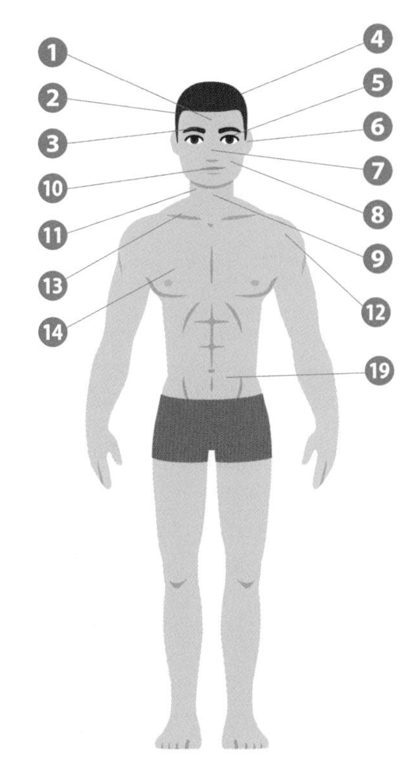

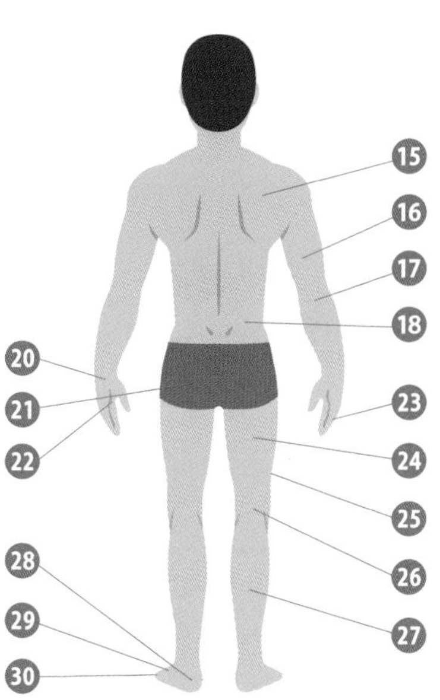

① face 臉
② head 頭
③ eyebrow 眉毛
④ hair 頭髮
⑤ eye 眼睛
⑥ ear 耳朵
⑦ nose 鼻子
⑧ cheek 臉頰
⑨ throat 喉嚨
⑩ mouth 嘴

⑪ neck 脖子
⑫ shoulder 肩膀
⑬ clavicle/collarbone 鎖骨
⑭ chest 胸部
⑮ back 背部
⑯ arm 手臂
⑰ elbow 手肘
⑱ waist 腰部
⑲ abdomen 腹部
⑳ wrist 手腕

㉑ bottom/hip 臀部
㉒ hand 手
㉓ finger 手指
㉔ thigh 大腿
㉕ leg 腿
㉖ knee 膝蓋
㉗ calf 小腿
㉘ heel 腳跟
㉙ foot 腳
㉚ toe 腳趾

40-4 檢驗與治療 197

量體溫血壓	1	I need to take your temperature and blood pressure.	我要量你的體溫和血壓。
排洩物檢驗	2	I will need you to do stool and urine tests.	我需要你做糞便和尿液檢驗。
X 光檢查	3	You need to have a chest X-ray taken.	你需要做胸腔 X 光檢查。
需住院	4	You need to be hospitalized.	你需要住院。
需動手術	5	You need to have an operation.	你需要動手術。
需打針	6	I am going to give you an injection.	我要幫你打一針。

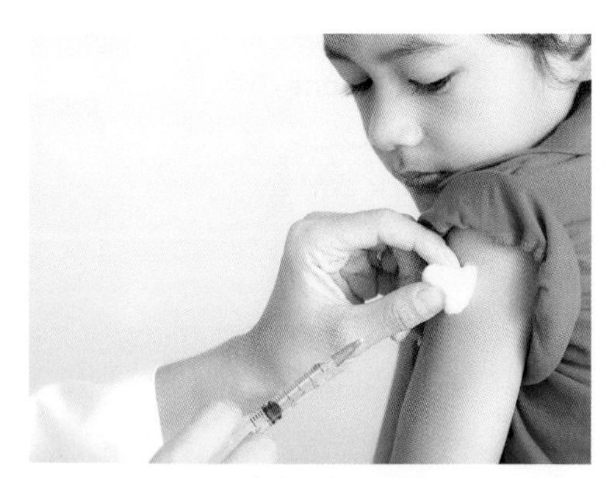
injection

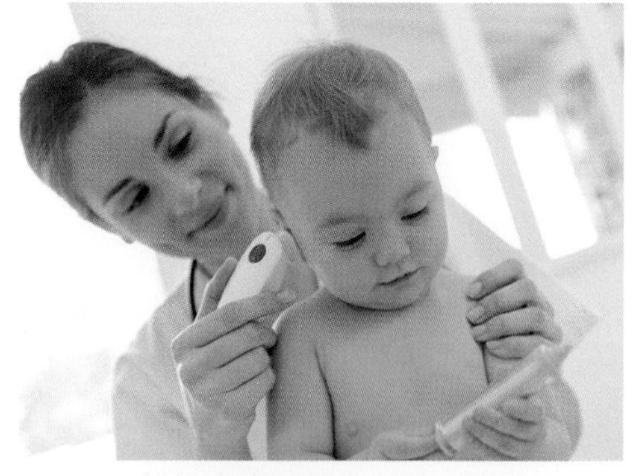
take someone's temperature

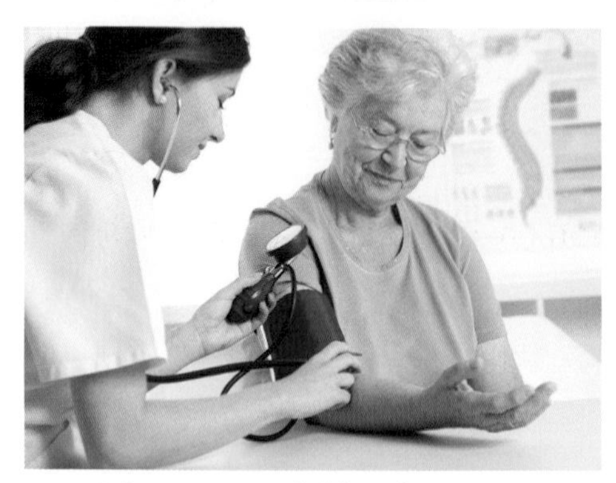
take someone's blood pressure

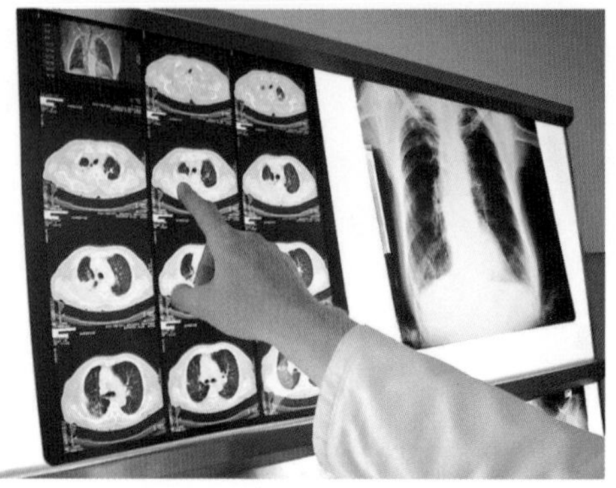
take an MRI and an X-ray

40-5 藥局領藥 198

沒有處方箋	1	Can I get the medicine without a prescription?	請問沒有處方箋可以拿藥嗎？
有處方箋	2	Here is my prescription.	這是我的處方箋。
買止痛藥	3	I would like some painkillers.	我想買一些止痛藥。
買頭痛藥	4	What do you have for a headache?	請問有治頭痛的藥嗎？
止瀉藥	5	Does this medicine work for diarrhea?	請問這藥對腹瀉有效嗎？
便秘藥	6	What do you recommend for constipation?	請問你推薦什麼可以治便祕的藥?
有無副作用	7	Are there any side effects?	這有沒有什麼副作用？
買維他命	8	What kind of multi-vitamins would you recommend?	請問你推薦哪種綜合維他命？
服藥時間	9	When do I take this medicine?	這藥是什麼時候要吃?
	10	Take it after meals and before bed.	於飯後及睡前服用。
飯前服用	11	The medicine should be taken before meals.	藥要在飯前吃。
服藥間隔時間	12	Take two tablets once every six hours.	每六小時吃兩顆藥。
退燒藥	13	Take the antipyretic if you have a severe fever.	如果發高燒就吃這退燒藥。

旅遊資訊補充包

症狀與疾病 Symptoms and Illness

耳鼻喉科 Otorhinolaryngology/ENT (Ears, Nose and Throat)

- **running nose** 流鼻水
- **stuffy nose** 鼻塞
- **nosebleed** 流鼻血
- **sore throat** 喉嚨痛
- **cough** 咳嗽
- **tinnitus** 耳鳴

家醫科 Family Medicine

- **cold** 感冒
- **fever** 發燒
- **influenza/flu** 流行性感冒
- **allergy** 過敏
- **asthma** 氣喘
- **headache** 頭痛
- **bruise** 瘀青
- **burn** 燒傷
- **cut** 割傷
- **contagious disease** 傳染病
- **migraine** 偏頭痛

心臟內科／心臟血管外科 Cardiology/Cardiovascular Surgery

- **heart attack/disease** 心臟病
- **palpitation** 心悸
- **hypertension/low blood pressure** 高／低血壓

running nose

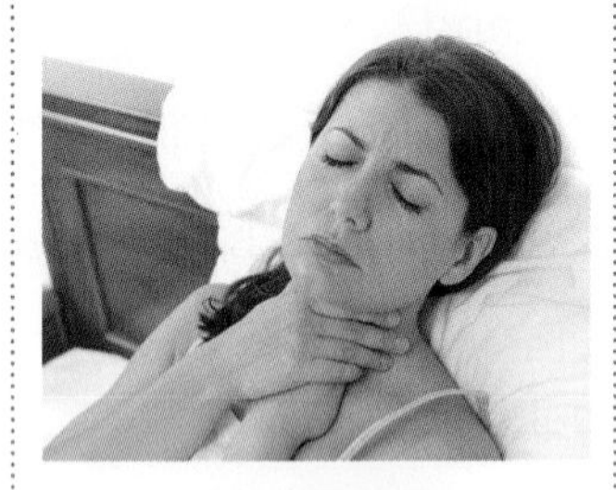

sore throat

cough

headache

asthma

heart attack

骨科 Orthopedics

- **backache** 背痛
- **bone fracture** 骨折
- **sprain** 扭傷

牙科 Dentistry

- **toothache** 牙痛
- **cavity/tooth decay** 蛀牙

肝膽腸胃科／大腸直腸科 Gastroenterology

- **stomachache** 腹痛
- **indigestion** 消化不良
- **food poisoning** 食物中毒
- **constipation** 便秘
- **diarrhea** 腹瀉／拉肚子
- **appendicitis** 盲腸炎

精神科 Psychiatry

- **depression** 憂鬱症
- **panic attack** 恐慌發作
- **anorexia nervosa** 厭食症

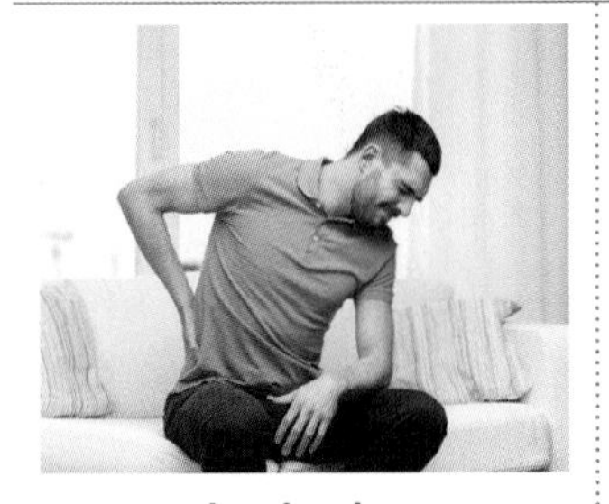
backache

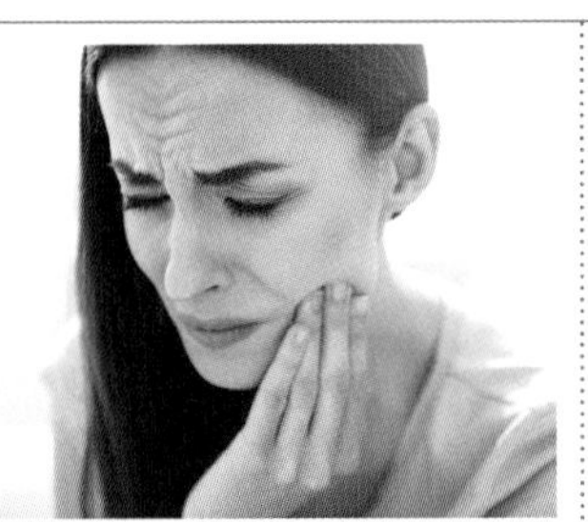
toothache

stomachache

food poisoning

depression

bone fracture

藥物的說法 Medicine Terms

- **medicine/drug** 藥
- **painkiller** 止痛藥
- **aspirin** 阿斯匹林
- **antibiotics** 抗生素
- **steroid** 類固醇
- **laxative** 瀉藥
- **sleeping pill** 安眠藥
- **birth control pill** 避孕藥
- **syrup** 糖漿

↙ **capsule** 膠囊

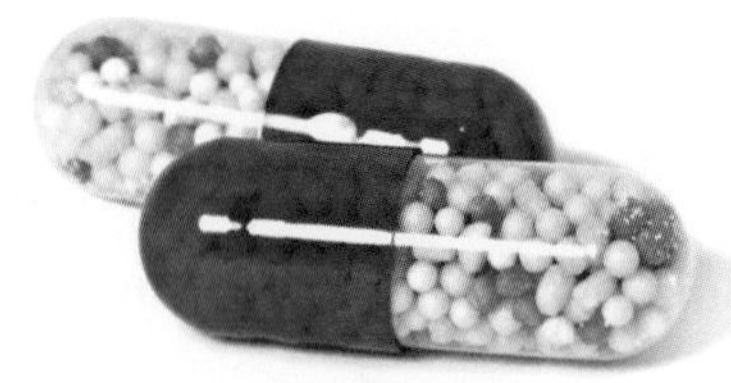

↙ **tablet** 藥片

↙ **liquid medicine** 藥水

↙ **powder** 藥粉

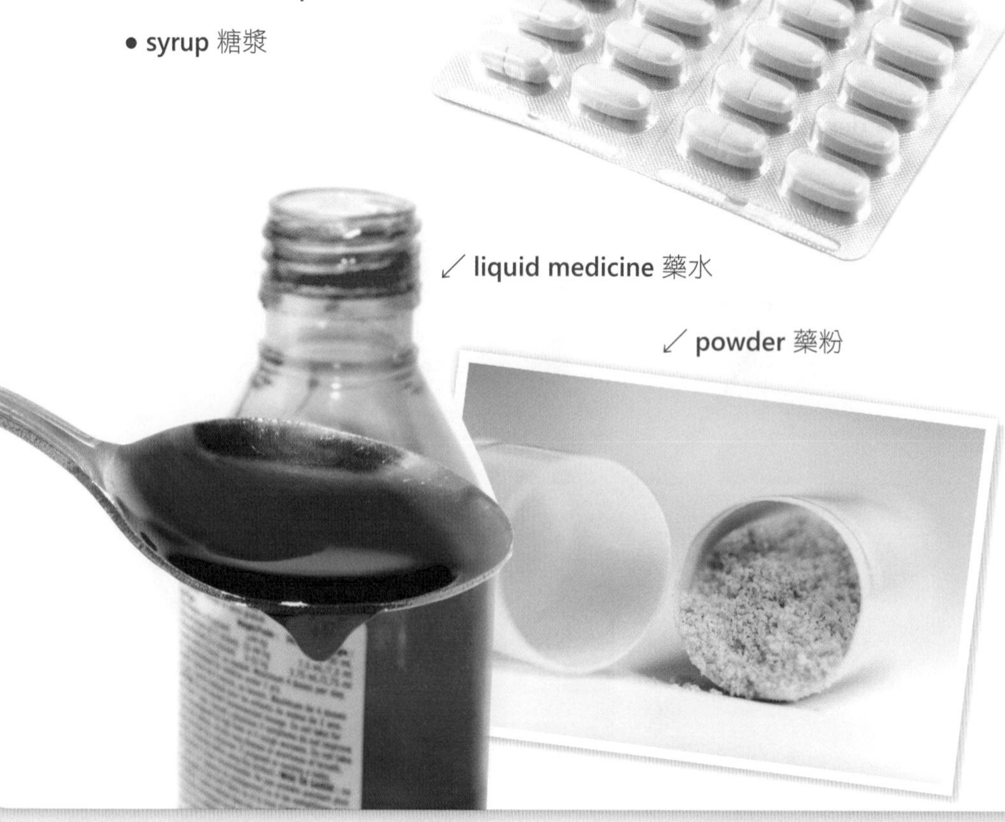

✓ **eye drop** 眼藥水

✓ **pill** 藥丸

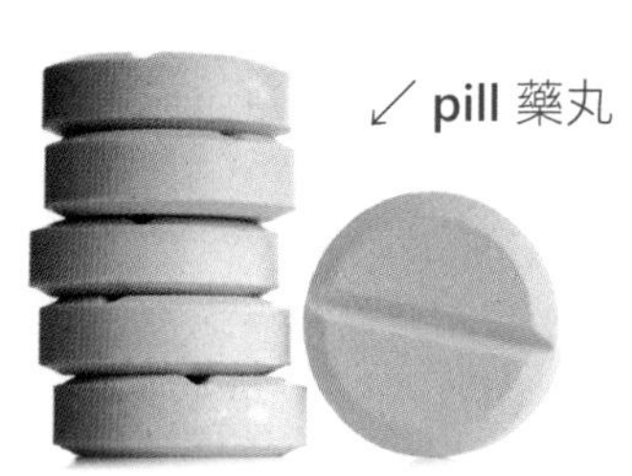

✓ **Band-Aid** OK 繃

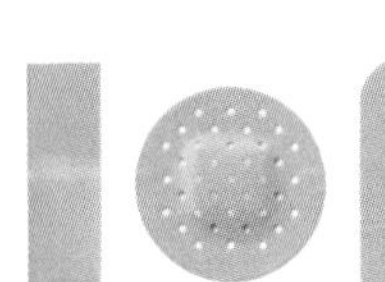

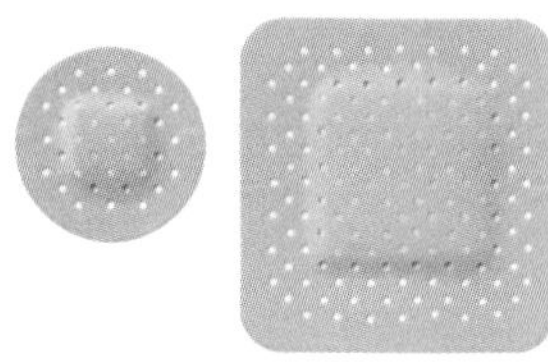

✓ **bandage** 繃帶

✓ **ointment** 軟膏

Appendix 貼心旅遊小幫手

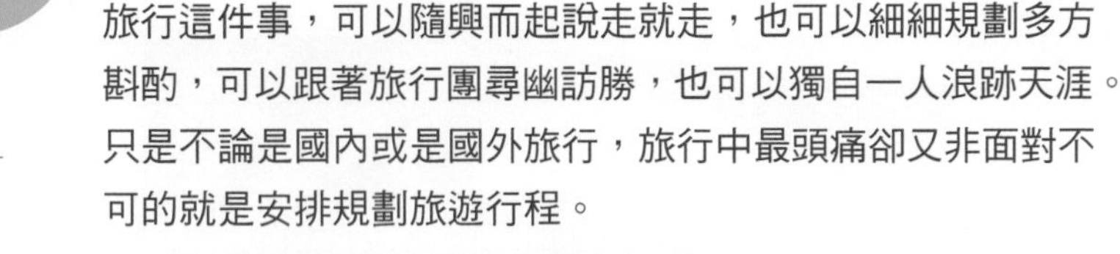

旅行這件事，可以隨興而起說走就走，也可以細細規劃多方斟酌，可以跟著旅行團尋幽訪勝，也可以獨自一人浪跡天涯。只是不論是國內或是國外旅行，旅行中最頭痛卻又非面對不可的就是安排規劃旅遊行程。

旅行的目的就在於放鬆！為了使旅行更加輕鬆愉快，以下推薦必備的實用旅遊 App 與網站，讓旅程不僅玩得開心，更能玩得放心。

代表介紹的功能以 App 為主

簽證

外交部領事事務局

預計前往旅遊的國家是否需要簽證、可以申請什麼種類的簽證、需要的簽證效期為多少、是否可以多次入境等相關問題，最好還是參考我國外交部的公告，以免輕信錯誤或是非最新的資訊。

網址：https://goo.gl/KloAVD

ESTA 官方網站

我國國民凡持晶片護照赴美 90 天以內，可申請電子簽證（ESTA）入境美國。申請費用為 14 元美金，須以信用卡付款，網站可以選擇中文介面，但須以英文填寫。請留意授權許可的作業時間可能需 72 小時。

網址：https://esta.cbp.dhs.gov/esta/

機票

Skyscanner 

幾乎涵蓋全球所有航空的機票搜尋比價引擎，近年也發展飯店與租車的比價服務。不僅提供搜尋當日的價格，亦可比價前後天與當月價格。

網址：https://www.skyscanner.com.tw/

Momondo 

同樣不直接在網站上銷售機票，而是提供機票的搜尋比價。有提供不同點進出的票價搜尋，另也有提供熱門景點的相關旅遊資訊，如天氣、物價等等。

網址：http://www.momondo.tw/

訂房

Booking.com

擁有全球超過百萬間的合作住宿，提供 B&B、商務旅店、青年旅館等豐富多樣的住宿選擇。其最大的特色在於**訂房之後可以不必馬上付款**（但需要先提供信用卡資料），且有些旅店在預定之後一定期間內可以**免費取消**，對於尚未確定行程的旅客而言是一大吸引力。

網址：http://www.booking.com

Agoda

主要業務集中於亞太區，同樣提供多樣的訂房選擇。特色在於其**保證最低價**，與 Booking.com 的差異在於其所提供的延後付款與免費取消較少。Agoda 鼓勵遊客**寫入評價**，住宿完成之後寫下評鑑，即可累積回饋金以供下次訂房使用。

網址：https://www.agoda.com

Hotels.com

同樣都是訂房網站，Hotels.com 與其他網站與眾不同之處在於，其所提供的**諸多優惠**，如集十晚送一晚、加入會員之後的神祕優惠價、其他經常性的優惠活動等等。

網址：https://tw.hotels.com/

Hotelscombined

對於有些人來說，價格與優惠才是最主要的考量。Hotelscombined 作為一個訂房比價網站，並不與其上三者一樣直接銷售訂房，但是若從此連往其他訂房網站，如 Agoda 或 Hotels.com 等，有機會拿到不定的優惠折扣。

網址：https://www.hotelscombined.com.tw/

地圖

Google Maps

除了眾所皆知的定位導航功能，還可以對於景點與餐廳提供消費者評價、營業時段和介紹資訊。也可標記任何位置，紀錄所到訪的地點或預計前往的位置，亦可利用自訂編輯地圖與路線規劃功能事先畫出自己的旅行路線。功能繁多，可謂旅遊不可不備的智慧幫手。

網址：https://www.googlemaps.com

MAPS.ME

與一般地圖 App 一樣提供導航、景點搜尋與標記地點等功能，最重要的是，介面可選擇為中文，又可供**離線使用**。可於有網路的地方預先下載好預計要前往的城市地圖，並且事先標記好想要去的景點、餐廳與旅館，即使到了當地沒有網路也可以輕鬆抵達。

網址：http://maps.me/en/home

旅遊資訊與行程規劃

Tripadvisor 貓途鷹 

提供世界各地景點、飯店、餐廳等旅遊資訊，也提供互動性的旅遊論壇供旅客交流，並針對旅客的評價給予餐廳和景點排名，在國際旅遊評論網站中具指標性地位。Tripadvisor 亦是一個旅遊搜尋引擎，可提供機票與飯店的比價，也兼有地圖導航定位的功能。

網址：https://www.tripadvisor.com.tw/

背包客棧

國內首屈一指旅遊論壇，供旅客交流各式各樣的情報，或是尋找志同道合的旅伴。網站上有整理好的旅行攻略，也有許多旅客所撰寫的文章與旅遊心得，另也提供機票與訂房的搜尋比價引擎。因本來就是中文網站，會員也以臺灣人居多，資訊的交流更加簡單。

網址：http://www.backpackers.com.tw/forum/

Rome2rio 

作為一個**旅遊交通路線方案**的搜尋引擎，整合如航空、火車、公車及渡輪等交通資訊，並計算出估計的費用與時間。只要輸入想去的地點，便可得到成本最小的交通方案，也可查詢多種交通工具互相轉乘接駁資訊。另也提供鄰近的飯店與景點推薦，有簡體中文的介面。

網址：https://www.rome2rio.com/

KKday

販售全球 50 個以上國家的 **local tour（在地體驗行程）、票券、景點門票、Wi-Fi 分享器**等等的體驗旅遊平台。提供行程品質、交易安全、簡易使用等三大保障，為尚未出發的旅客優先挑選推薦當地特色旅遊行程，並提供中文行程說明，且價格也相當具有競爭力。

網址：https://www.kkday.com

Funlidays 

提供規劃行程與安排路徑等功能，只要輸入想要前往的景點，除了告知景點地理位置與營業時間等資訊，最大特色在於**自動針對行程安排最佳的路徑規劃並預估花費時間**，可以地圖呈現。無網路的時候也可以瀏覽行程，並有中文介面。

網址：http://www.funliday.com/

Evernote 

強大的功能性讓 Evernote 除了日常使用的筆記，也能作旅遊準備規劃。它可以擷取網站上的文章資訊，也可設定代辦事項的提醒通知和管理預訂的機票與住宿等資訊。若是有旅伴，亦可以與旅伴共享所有筆記。離線使用的功能，讓預先存好的所有資料都能輕鬆取得。

網址：https://evernote.com

實用工具

Google Translate 

除了常用的文字翻譯功能，讓旅客將中文轉換成該國語言之外，也有**同步語音翻譯**，可以即時辨識兩種語言，不必再另作切換。**即時鏡頭翻譯功能**，只要將鏡頭對準眼前的文字，就可以輕鬆翻譯成熟悉的語言，讓旅客不用再為溝通問題傷透腦筋。

網址：https://translate.google.com

Avast Wi-Fi Finder 

出國在外始終會需要網路，此款 App 可以在離線狀態中使用，只要照著地圖的資訊走，即會引導旅客找到**免費、安全、訊號穩定**的 Wi-Fi。然而值得注意的是：必須要確認是否為最新版本，由於 Wi-Fi 的熱點清單經常變動，最新版本才能減少走冤枉路的機會。

網址：https://www.avast.com/wifi-finder

XE Currency 

在異鄉使用不同的貨幣要如何好好控制預算，自然要了解匯率。不僅有**同步比較多國匯率**的功能，自建的**計算機功能**也方便讓使用者直接在同一畫面計算，另還提供**歷史匯率的走勢圖**。只要每天重新整理至最新匯率之後，即使在離線狀態也可使用。

網址：http://www.xe.com

Uber 優步 

叫車時 GPS 會自動定位旅客所在地點，只要輸入預計前往處，系統即會預估時間與花費。旅客也可透過系統追蹤紀錄行經路線，並以信用卡付款，**免去與司機的溝通成本**，車資也可能較一般計程車費優惠。須注意的是 Uber 在某些地區並未合法，叫車前務必留意。

網址：https://www.uber.com

緊急救助

旅外救助指南 

由我國外交部為提供國人旅外急難救助服務研發，結合適地性服務（Location-Based Service），提供前往國家之基本資訊、旅遊警示、遺失護照處理程序、簽證以及我國駐外館處緊急聯絡電話號碼等資訊，可離線瀏覽。各種急難救助所需要的資訊，儘管不一定用得到，但不妨還是下載下來以備萬一。

網址：https://goo.gl/S3ghi9

* 資訊時代科技日新月異，訊息變動速度快，此處提供指南以編輯當時為主，故請務必留意網址與資訊可能更新。

觀光英語 Let's Go! 三版

HAVE A NICE TRIP: TRAVEL ENGLISH

作　　者　Kiwi Cheng／Cosmos Language Workshop
審　　訂　Helen Yeh／Jim Knudsen
編　　輯　王婷葦
校　　對　申文怡
內文排版　劉秋筑
封面設計　林書玉

製程管理　洪巧玲
製　　作　語言工場
出 版 者　寂天文化事業股份有限公司
電　　話　+886-(0)2-2365-9739
傳　　真　+886-(0)2-2365-9835
網　　址　www.icosmos.com.tw
讀者服務　onlineservice@icosmos.com.tw
出版日期　2016 年 12 月 三版一刷

郵撥帳號 1998620-0 語言工場出版有限公司
劃撥金額 600 元（含）以上者，郵資免費。
訂購金額 600 元以下者，請外加郵資 65 元。
〔若有破損，請寄回更換，謝謝。〕

國家圖書館出版品預行編目 (CIP) 資料

觀光英語 Let's Go! / Kiwi Cheng 著 . -- 三版 . -- [臺北市] : 寂天文化 , 2016.12
面；　公分
ISBN 978-986-318-526-0（平裝附光碟片）

1. 英語 2. 旅遊 3. 會話

805.188　　105021672